To Dia

Carolina Danford Wright

Old School Rules

Carolina Danford Wright

This book is a work of fiction. Many of the names, places, characters, and incidents are products of the author's imagination or are used fictitiously. Any resemblance to actual events or locales or person living or dead is entirely coincidental.

Copyright © 2021 Llourettia Gates Books, LLC
All rights reserved. This book or any portion thereof may not be reproduced or used in any manner whatsoever without the express written permission of the publisher.

Llourettia Gates Books, LLC
P.O. Box #411
Fruitland, Maryland 21826

Hardcover ISBN: 978-1-953082-09-1
Paperback ISBN: 978-1-953082-10-7
eBook ISBN: 978-1-953082-11-4
Library of Congress Control Number: 2021922146

Photography by Andrea López Burns
Cover and interior design by Jamie Tipton, Open Heart Designs

This book is dedicated to all grandmothers—those who are avengers and those who wish they were.

Contents

About The Granny Avengers, vii

Prologue, ix

Chapter 1, 1

Chapter 2, 8

Chapter 3, 18

Chapter 4, 26

Chapter 5, 38

Chapter 6, 51

Chapter 7, 61

Chapter 8, 68

Chapter 9, 80

Chapter 10, 86

Chapter 11, 93

Chapter 12, 99

Chapter 13, 102

Chapter 14, 111

Chapter 15, 120

Chapter 16, 128

Chapter 17, 134

Chapter 18, 141

Chapter 19, 147

Chapter 20, 154

Chapter 21, 161

Chapter 22, 168

Chapter 23, 172

Chapter 24, 185

Chapter 25, 195

Chapter 26, 206

Chapter 27, 212

Chapter 28, 217

Chapter 30, 222

Chapter 29, 233

Chapter 31, 241

Chapter 32, 252

Chapter 33, 260

Chapter 34, 267

Chapter 35, 274

Chapter 36, 282

Chapter 37, 290

Chapter 38, 302

Chapter 39, 311

Chapter 40, 320

Epilogue, 326

Acknowledgments, 331

About the Author, 333

About The Granny Avengers

THE GRANNY AVENGERS is a new series written by Carolina Danford Wright. Old School Rules is the first book in the series. Each of the protagonists in this series is old enough to be a grandmother. Each is brave and on the side of truth and justice. Some of these heroes act on the spur of the moment because it is the right thing to do. Some, because of circumstances, seem to stumble into being avengers. Other Granny Avengers take over when the criminal justice system has failed to do its job. You will enjoy getting to know these feisty women as they struggle to right the wrongs of the world.

Prologue

Mercedes Carrington was old. She was seventy-five. She was also old school. She remembered black telephones that were hardwired into the wall. She remembered when "Tears on My Pillow" was a brand new song. She remembered luncheons where they served sandwich loaf, and she'd tried to avoid the egg salad and tried to get an end piece that had gobs of extra cream cheese on it.

Her politics had evolved and shifted over the years. She had voted for candidates from all parties, and she had written in Margaret Mead for President in 1972 when she couldn't bring herself to vote for either Richard Nixon or George McGovern. She was a staunch supporter of the military and law enforcement. She also was pro-choice but with limitations. She admitted that she was an anachronism, and she had a wonderful sense of humor. She thanked God every day for that. No one could survive in the world as it existed today without an enormous sense of humor.

Chapter 1

She had already decided this was her last plane flight. Flying had become too difficult. The only airline that flew anywhere close to her small town had made the bathrooms on all their planes so small that Mercedes didn't drink any liquids the day she flew. She did not want to be forced to use the miniscule lavatories. Because she suffered from crippling arthritis, she bought a first-class ticket when she flew long distances.

A first-class seat was supposed to give its occupant more room to maneuver. But even first class had turned into a nightmare. The airline, determined to add more rows of seats to all of its planes in order to increase its bottom line, had pushed even the first-class rows closer and closer to each other. And it seemed, the minute the plane reached cruising altitude, the businessman in front of her always tilted his seat back as far as possible and slept for the duration of the flight from Phoenix to Philadelphia. This was certainly his prerogative to recline his seat, but why did he always have to sit in front of her, Mercedes wondered.

Because she had a difficult time getting in and out of her seat anyway, having the pomaded head of the man in her lap for five plus hours, had pushed her over the edge. This was her last time in the air. Enough was enough. Who needed to punish themselves, at age seventy-five, with flying from place to place...even flying from place to place after having spent seventeen hundred dollars on a first-class ticket?

At least the airline still allowed her to board early. She used a wheelchair in the airport because of her arthritis and the long distances one had to walk to reach the gates. It seemed her gate was always the last one on the concourse. When she asked, it was explained to her that this was because she was flying to such far-away places. The wheelchair attendants were almost always kind and helpful, and Mercedes tipped them generously for not ignoring her and for pushing her down the jetway to the plane.

She was tired and ready to be home. She had one more short flight to go and was hoping she'd allowed enough time to travel from Terminal A to Terminal F in Philadelphia so she could make the commuter flight. The airline had cut flights to the point where there were now only two flights a day between Philadelphia and the airport closest to her small town. Timing was everything. If one missed the last flight out of Philly, one had to spend the night sitting up in the airport. This was difficult for anyone, but it was especially difficult for a senior citizen in a wheelchair.

Fingers crossed that the airport staff at her final destination would be able to find the ramp so she could exit the airplane with dignity. She was still angry about the time the stewardess had told her there was no ramp and she would have to get off the plane the best way she could. Mercedes reminded herself that there were no more stewardesses. Now they were flight attendants. Two years earlier, Mercedes had crawled on her hands and knees backwards down the steps of the steep rolling stairs the airline had pushed up to the plane. Ridiculous. But it could happen again and probably would. Maybe it would happen again tonight. Time to give away those frequent flyer miles. Flying was not fun anymore and had not been for a very long time.

She had eaten a turkey sandwich for breakfast at the Phoenix airport, so she turned down the lunch of the plant-based meat enchilada topped with vegan cheese and an organic jalapeno sauce, with a lentil, quinoa, and kale salad on the side. Really!

She didn't sleep on airplanes, especially with the smell of the hairdo goop on the man sitting in the row in front of her, whose head was under her chin, wafting into her nose. She took her Kindle out of her carry-on and tried to concentrate on reading. Mercedes had always possessed excellent radar when it came to figuring out people, and she had lived long enough to develop a sixth sense.

A male passenger in the row behind her had caused her some concern. He appeared to be of Middle Eastern origin. She had grown up next door to a Middle Eastern family, so she was not xenophobic, but something about this man's eyes and his body language had struck her and was continuing to bother her. There had not been any terrorist attacks on airplanes in the United States for several years. But politics always had to get in the way of common sense, and the rules had changed. Something about this man did not seem right.

Mercedes wished she could get into the aisle to check out the suspicious man with the unnerving eyes, but she was a captive in her seat. She was in an aisle seat, of course. But she knew if she tried to stand up to get out of her row, she would have to put her hand on the back of the seat of the man in front of her to get to her feet. This had happened before. The man whose slumber she had interrupted had turned his stinky head of hair around and glared at her. She had apologized, but considering the fact that the man's head had been encroaching on her personal space for several hours, she wasn't really very sorry.

She was thinking about putting a clothespin on her nose and trying to get some rest when shouting and screaming roused her from her reverie. She looked up to see the flight attendant, a slim African American woman, being held at knifepoint by the man with the dead eyes. He was shouting in a foreign language and held his very threatening and very sharp-looking knife at her throat. Mercedes' first thought was to wonder where the air marshal was. Had airlines discontinued using those law enforcement people completely? She knew the man was speaking either Farsi or Arabic, but she had no idea what the man was screaming about.

He pushed the flight attendant forward down the aisle towards the front of the plane. In spite of having a knife at her throat, she was resisting. There was blood flowing down the front of the flight attendant's uniform. The attacker began to scream at her in heavily accented English. It was obvious he was forcing her towards the cockpit. Everyone in first class knew what a bad thing that would be, if he achieved his goal. But where was the air marshal?

Mercedes was already angry about being on the plane with such a small amount of room for which she had paid such a large amount of money. This behavior by a dangerous passenger made her even angrier. She was not going to go down this way. She still had one more grandchild for whom she had not yet written a book. Richard was going to get his book. Mercedes was determined.

She grabbed her blue and white plastic cane from under the seat in front of her and stuck it out in the aisle. Her aisle seat gave her the perfect spot from which to bring down the hijacker. Mercedes really had not taken time to think about what she was going to do, but she had had enough with Sharia Law and the destruction of the Constitution and the bad boys who wanted to do her country harm.

She hooked the handle of her cane around the ankle of the offending passenger and pulled hard. He stumbled, and she pulled harder. He finally went down. Mercedes struggled painfully to get out of her seat. She grabbed the back of the seat in front of her, and the heck with whether or not she'd awakened Mr. Pomade Hair. She climbed out of her row and stepped up onto the back of the man who was lying prone in the aisle. She grabbed hold of the end of her cane and, using the curved handle end as her bludgeon, she began to bash the head of the man who had by now let go of the flight attendant. The flight attendant was also on the ground, crawling toward the lavatory. She was bleeding.

Mercedes kept bashing and bashing and bashing. He dropped his weapon. At this point, she paused her attack and used her cane like a golf club to sweep the vicious-looking long knife into the plane's kitchenette, far away from the hijacker's hands. She was furious now and was not going to give up. Blood was pouring out of the head of the man who seconds earlier had been shouting Allahu Akbar or something like that. Mercedes was in another world. She was determined that she would not stop until she had beaten this bad man into a bloody pulp.

Finally someone stopped her. A retired policeman from the first row in coach and an active duty air force colonel on leave, who had been seated in the last row of first class, had appeared and were holding the attacker down. Someone put their arms around Mercedes, and someone else tried to take her weapon from her hands. She stopped bashing but refused to give up the cane until she saw that the knife-wielding hijacker had white plastic ties around his wrists and ankles. The military man and the law enforcement guy dragged the hijacker off someplace. There was turmoil and confusion. People were rallying around the flight attendant whose neck was bleeding.

Mercedes collapsed into her aisle seat and watched it all unfold. She had exerted herself way beyond her normal energy limits. Her adrenalin had kicked in to enable her to go on the attack. Now she was paying the price for having done what she had not been able to keep herself from doing. No one came to ask about her. That was fine with Mercedes. She needed time to gather her wits and her few remaining resources.

At some point the captain came out of the cockpit. All of the flight attendants had congregated at the front of the plane, and the injured young woman was being taken care of. The captain came out and spoke with someone who Mercedes thought might be an airline official or another pilot who was hitching a ride. He was not in uniform, but he seemed to know what was going on.

Someone got on the public address system and made an announcement. He said he was the pilot. He said there had been an incident in the first-class section that was now under control. There was no longer any danger to the passengers or to the plane. There was going to be an unscheduled landing because of the incident, and passengers were urged to return to their seats and fasten their seat belts for the upcoming descent into Little Rock, Arkansas. Blah, blah, blah. It was the usual stuff, reassuring the passengers that everything was fine. Coach passengers were instructed to exit the plane and go to a designated area near the gate for questioning. Another plane would be arranged to get them to Philadelphia as soon as authorities had their questions answered.

First-class passengers were told to stay on board after they'd landed. Law enforcement would be arriving on the plane as soon as it was at the gate and would take a statement from each of the twelve people who had been seated in first class. That would take a while. Mercedes listened to all of the announcements. She knew she was going to miss her connection in Philadelphia, but she was even more worried that delays would force her to use the tiny bathroom on the plane. This would not be a good thing. She was worn out and thirsty. Her adrenalin had spiked and then plummeted. She wanted to be home in her own bed, but she knew it would be many hours or even days before that would be possible.

Chapter 2

*M*ercedes was glad no one was making a fuss over her. She was fine. A stretcher arrived to take the injured flight attendant to the hospital. Four men with holstered firearms arrived to escort "the wannabe" hijacker off the plane. Mercedes sighed with relief when she saw that troublemaker being taken away. After he was safely in the burly arms of the authorities, she was able to doze off and get a few minutes of sleep. A nice looking young woman tapped her on the shoulder and woke her up. It was Mercedes' turn to give her statement. The woman introduced herself as FBI Special Agent Arabella Barnes. Mercedes realized there were only three people still on the plane. They had left her until the last.

Mercedes told her story exactly as she remembered it had happened. She had an almost perfect visual memory which had not deserted her in her later years, so she was able to give exact details about what she had seen and heard and done. The special agent seemed surprised.

"You have recounted the event in such specific detail. This is unusual. Your account is more complete than any of the other accounts of people who have told us what happened."

"It happened to me. Of course I know exactly what happened. I was the one who made the decision to use my cane to bring down this terrorist. Of course I am going to remember it with clarity and in detail. I don't think that is surprising at all. Everyone else was just watching what happened...until those two men got control of the hijacker and somebody grabbed my arms to keep me from beating the guy to death with my cane."

"Would you have killed him if somebody hadn't stopped you?"

"Of course I would have. I had no intentions of stopping until I was sure he was no longer a threat. I was standing on top of him. I couldn't let him try to stand up. I was in it to win it. All the way."

"It looks like your bravery probably saved a great many lives today."

"Don't start with that. I was the only person on the plane who had a weapon. At least it seemed as if that was the case. The air marshals never revealed themselves. Somebody had to take that creep down, and I guess I decided it had to be me. I had the opportunity and the means to do it. So I did it. Anyone else who'd had a cane would have done the same thing. I was not going to let him crash this plane. I still have a book to write for my youngest grandchild. I was determined that I was not going to die before I finished writing his book."

The young FBI agent was evaluating Mercedes' account with some curiosity. "Weren't you afraid to engage such a dangerous man, a man with a knife. He was so much bigger than you are."

"I am seventy-five years old. What do I have to be afraid of? And I will bet you anything that I considerably outweigh that skinny little sand flea."

The agent's eyes widened as she listened to Mercedes continue to explain why she had risked her life to take down a man more than forty years younger than she was.

"Once I was standing on top of him, I knew he would never be able to get out from under me. I was just afraid I would fall, and he would get away. That's why I kept bashing him in the head. If I was able to knock him unconscious, he wouldn't be able to escape."

"Because you know more about all of this than any of the other passengers, we are going to want to talk to you again. We are going to ask you to agree to go to a hotel tonight and speak with some other FBI agents tomorrow."

"I've already missed my connection in Philadelphia. My daughter is supposed to pick me up at the airport tonight. She's going to be very worried about me when I don't get off the plane. I need to call her and tell her I won't be on the commuter flight. She tracks my plane flights on her phone, so she knows that for some reason the plane from Phoenix to Philadelphia is stopped in Little Rock. She just doesn't know why. I'm sure she's figured out by now that I can't make my connection, but I need to call her and confirm that so she doesn't go to the airport to pick me up." Spending the night at a hotel in Little Rock was going to be infinitely better than spending the night sitting up in the Philadelphia airport.

"The problem with your calling her is that we are trying to keep news of this attempted hijacking away from the press. Of course, we know that is going to be impossible in the long run. With everybody recording everything on their cell phones, videos of your taking down this guy are going to be all over YouTube and Facebook and everywhere else on the internet. They probably already are. We collected cell phones and tried to erase as many of those videos as we could, but something always slips through. I watched a couple of them, and I have to tell you, I was very impressed with how fast and how efficiently you had that guy on the ground. It was most extraordinary. I don't think a trained special agent or an air marshal could have done it any better."

Mercedes looked closely at the FBI agent to see if she was trying to flatter or manipulate her. She decided the young woman really was impressed with her cane attack. "Don't be too impressed. I just made do with what I had available to me. I don't get around easily these days."

"That makes what you did ever so much more impressive, Ms. Carrington." She paused to listen to something that was being said to her through her earpiece. "Damnation. I was hoping we could get her out of here before they showed up. I don't want anybody to see her. I don't want anybody to know how disabled she really is. You don't really get that from the videos. How can we get her off the plane so the news people can't get a shot at her?"

That phrase caught Mercedes' attention, but she right away realized that it was news people wanting to shoot her with a camera, not with a gun.

"She will be the main witness if this thing ever goes to a trial." Special Agent Arabella Barnes again listened to whoever was speaking to her through her earpiece. "Well, we just don't know that yet, do we? And until we do know for sure, we have to protect her. If he was acting alone, there isn't any problem. He won't get bail. If he was part of a group, we have a problem. So run him through the databases and find out what we are dealing with."

Mercedes listened to the side of the conversation she could hear and was concerned. She tapped Agent Barnes on the shoulder. "My daughter needs to know I am okay and that I won't be on the commuter flight tonight. It's important. She has to drive almost an hour from her house to pick me up at the airport. I don't want her to go to the airport and find that I am not on the plane. She will be very worried when I don't get off the flight. She will have made that drive for nothing. Please, may I send her a text or call her or something?"

Agent Barnes spoke to the person who was on the other end of her earpiece. "We need to let her daughter know that Ms. Carrington won't be arriving on the commuter flight tonight. We don't want the daughter to be alarmed when her mother doesn't get off the plane. We don't want her to report her as a missing person or call the authorities. You have to do something now, before the daughter leaves to pick her mother up at the airport." Barnes listened. "Okay, I will have her text her daughter that she has been delayed because of this incident. If it is going to be all over the news, she can tell her daughter what's happened."

Mercedes was busy composing a text to her daughter. Agent Barnes wanted to read it before she sent it. That was fine with Mercedes. She just did not want to alarm her daughter or have her make an unnecessary trip to the airport. It didn't take long to agree on the wording of the text:

> I am fine on the ground in Little Rock. You know I was on that plane that's in the news. FBI is taking detailed statements about what happened. I will be at a hotel in LR tonight. It's chaos here. I don't know when I will able to get home. I'll keep you posted. Don't try to call. I think they are taking my phone away. Don't worry. Everybody is being nice to this old lady. I love you, Mom

Most people who send texts these days use incomplete sentences and abbreviations to communicate. Mercedes was old-fashioned and still wrote mostly in sentences with correct punctuation, even when she sent a text. She had added the part to her text about 'being nice to this old lady' as a not very subtle hint to Agent Barnes that she had to live up to that comment. She thought Agent Barnes would want to be nice to her anyway.

"I'm very tired. I know this debriefing is going to continue into tomorrow. Can we call it a night, and can you take me to the hotel? Just so you know, I need a bathroom that has a roll-in shower, and I will be ordering from room service. I haven't eaten anything since this morning before I boarded the plane in Phoenix. I can't walk very far on my own, and whenever I am in an airport, I have to use a wheelchair. So to get me out of the airport, you will have to have the airline bring a wheelchair to the door of the plane. I can get from my seat to the wheelchair and from the wheelchair to the car. I will also need a wheelchair when I get to the hotel. Does the FBI have wheelchairs? I am just letting you know what my limitations are ahead of time so there are no misunderstandings."

"We will do our best to take care of you, Ms. Carrington. I appreciate your letting me know what you need and what you can and can't do." Agent Barnes was amazed that a woman who couldn't walk through an airport had been able to take down a terrorist armed with a knife. After hearing how limited this woman's mobility really was, Barnes looked at her with new eyes and even more respect. "You did a very amazing thing on the airplane, you know. There are lots of people who owe you their lives tonight."

Mercedes didn't want to dwell on any of that. "After you have found me a wheelchair, somebody needs to take me to the ladies' room in the airport. The bathrooms in the plane are so small, and they don't smell very good."

"I will be pushing your wheelchair, Ma'am, and I promise we will make a stop at the ladies' restroom on the way to the car. You will be staying at the Capital Hotel in downtown Little Rock. You will have a handicap accessible shower and a shower bench. The hotel is close to the airport and not that far from our offices. Once we leave the airport we will be at the hotel in a few minutes. There will be someone outside your room all night. You are our prime witness, and we plan to take good care of you."

"Do you think all of that is really necessary? To have someone guarding my room? Isn't the guy I took down and bashed in the head in custody? He won't be making bail, will he?"

"No bail for that guy. Don't worry. We just don't know yet if he was operating alone or if he is associated with a group. If he's part of a group, they might try to come after you."

"How will they even know who I am?" As soon as she had said this, Mercedes realized that in these times when everybody had a cell phone, everybody also had a video camera. She realized there would probably be numerous photos and videos of her standing on the back of the would-be hijacker, beating him up with her cane. She knew someone, and more likely several someones, would have given or sold their cell phone footage to one of the cable TV networks. She would be on the 24-hour news cycle. Her daughters would see her. Her grandchildren would all see her trying to beat a man to death. The press had her face. All she could hope for was that they didn't have her name. "I know there are cell phone videos of me and all of that, but they don't know my name, do they? You are the only person who knows my name. The airline wouldn't give them my name, would they? Come to think of it, how do you happen to know my name?"

"I got your name from the passenger list. The airline has strict orders not to give out your name, but who knows. It isn't difficult to hack into airline passenger lists. We have taken steps to block the names of all the passengers who had anything to do with subduing this guy, but everybody is an internet sleuth these days. We will do our best."

Agent Barnes continued. "I have to warn you that there will be people from the press who will want to talk to you when we get off the plane. We've kept you until the last, hoping they will give up and go home. We had to take your cane as evidence. I'm sure you realize that, but someone will be bringing another cane. It won't be as colorful as yours, and it may not be the right height for you. But we'll work it out. It won't be blue and white flowers. Your replacement cane will be just plain black, but that will throw off the press, too. They are already talking on the news about the blue-and-white flowered cane that helped keep this plane in the air."

Mercedes continued to pay attention to Agent Barnes' instructions. "I'm going to ask you to put up the hood of your coat when you get into the wheelchair. We think your being in a wheelchair will be another way to keep the press confused. They won't be looking for a woman in a wheelchair as the hero who saved the day. Nobody on the flight, except the flight attendants, actually know that you use a wheelchair. You were the first person to board the plane in Phoenix, so you were already seated when the others began to board. Keep your head down and your hood up. We will stop to let you go to the bathroom. Then we are taking the employees-only elevator down to the ground level where we will meet an FBI car. There will be someone to help you get in and out of the car." Agent Barnes handed Mercedes a black cane which had miraculously appeared from out of nowhere.

"I'm ready. Hand me my carry-on bag, please. I will keep my head down. Believe me, nobody wants to remain anonymous any more than I do. I hope no one will take a video of me in the wheelchair."

"All the other passengers have gone. We have cleared the press and the curious nosey pokers from the gate. We will be moving fast through the airport, so hang on to your seat."

Mercedes made her way to the door of the plane. She grabbed hold of the backs of the seats and anything else she could find to hang onto. She was hugely relieved when she saw the wheelchair waiting for her in the jetway. Agent Barnes was behind her, and Mercedes collapsed into the wheelchair. They were on their way. When they arrived at the gate, there were a few people hanging around, but no one paid much attention to Mercedes. She felt safe. As promised, they stopped at the first bathroom. The black cane was too tall for Mercedes who was only a few inches over five feet in height, but it was adequate to get her in and out of the restroom. When she was again securely in the wheelchair, she realized how terribly thirsty she was. She might have asked for Agent Barnes to stop so she could buy a bottle of cold water, but she decided she could wait on that. Barnes had a plan in mind for getting her out of the airport with minimal fanfare, and Mercedes was happy to let that be the priority.

She had her head down, so she wasn't able to really see where they were going. They arrived at a curb where there was a dark, official-looking sedan waiting for them. It took only seconds for Mercedes to grab her replacement cane and get herself into the back seat of the sedan. Agent Barnes had her carry-on and climbed into the back seat beside her.

"Your luggage will be delivered to your hotel room. It was complicated getting all the luggage sorted out so the airline could put the rest of the passengers on other flights. Your bags almost went to Cincinnati. That would not have been good."

Mercedes had completely forgotten about her checked luggage. Because she was returning from spending several months at her Arizona home, there were important things in those suitcases. She'd shipped several boxes ahead, but there were still favorite clothes and other things she'd packed that she did not want to lose. She had counted on being back home on the East Coast by the end of today. "Thank you Agent Barnes, for arranging to have my luggage rescued and delivered to the hotel. My luggage would not have been useful to anyone in Cincinnati."

"Do you need anything? I realize you were counting on being at home when you went to sleep tonight."

"I have everything I need, and I'll be fine. The hotel furnishes shampoo and soap. I always carry all my medications, a toothbrush, and a change of underwear in my carry-on...just in case of an emergency. I have plenty of clean clothes in my checked luggage. Depending on how long I have to stay in Little Rock, I may have to have to have you buy a few things for me."

"We hope to be able to get you on your way to being settled by tomorrow night, or by Thursday night at the latest. We will know more about this bad guy by then and can make better decisions about how much danger we think you might be in."

Mercedes had not really thought about the fact that she would be in danger. Danger sounded like such a dramatic word. What had she done when she'd made the decision to hook that guy's ankle with her cane? There really had not been any choice about the action she had taken. She'd done what she had done on instinct. But she began to wonder to what extent her decision might have, in those few seconds of acting on her instincts, changed her life going forward.

Chapter 3

The hotel room was a suite, and it had a roll-in shower. Mercedes didn't need a suite, but it was nice. She wondered who was paying for the suite. She could afford to pay for it, but figured the FBI was paying. Agent Barnes was going to stay in the adjoining room. A door connected the living room of Mercedes' suite with another bedroom and bath next door. The connecting bedroom was probably why they'd given her a suite. There was also someone sitting on a chair outside the door to her room. Yikes! This was serious stuff.

"You may not want to turn on the television, Ms. Carrington. You are all over the news. Pictures of you standing on top of our terrorist and hitting him repeatedly with your cane are the top story of the night. It's okay with me if you want to watch it, but you may not want to relive that over and over again."

"Maybe later." She had to admit she was curious about what the world, and especially her kids and grandkids, were seeing about her on the news. "Right now I am very hungry. It's now almost nine o'clock Central Time, and I need to eat. Low blood sugar makes me grumpy. Please call me Mercedes. Ms. Carrington makes me sound like an old maid school teacher. Where's the room service menu? I have stayed at this hotel before, but it was many years ago. They used to have a five-star chef who was the big feature of their main dining room, but that probably isn't the case anymore. He wouldn't do room service anyway, even if he was still the chef here. I don't have to have anything big. A burger or a sandwich will be fine."

Mercedes ordered a bowl of soup and a club sandwich with French fries. It all tasted good to her. She wished she'd ordered two bowls of soup. Soup was comforting. The fries were skinny and crispy and hot. The kitchen had even sent two little glass bottles of catsup for the fries and a small gravy boat of Russian dressing for the club sandwich, just as she had requested. She drank a Coke. Agent Barnes sat with her while she ate. Arabella Barnes had asked a few questions, but for the most part she allowed Mercedes to enjoy her meal. The bellman had put her suitcases on luggage racks and hung up her coat.

After she had eaten, all Mercedes could think about was taking a shower and going to bed. Agent Barnes could see she was completely exhausted. Anyone would be whipped after what she'd been through today, but being old contributed to fatigue. Mercedes wasn't a spring chicken any more. It had been a very big day for this older lady. She turned on the television set and watched CNN for a few minutes. Agent Barnes was right. She was not ready to relive those few minutes when she had tripped the hijacker and stood on his back. She turned off the TV.

Everything takes longer to do when you get old. Part of this time is spent going slowly and trying to be extra careful so you don't fall. Another part of it is that your body is not as agile and quick to accomplish things as it once was. This was okay most of the time. Mercedes usually had plenty of time. Because of her fatigue, tonight she was moving even more slowly than usual. Being careful was the main goal, but navigating the unknown roll-in shower and trying to keep the water from running out onto the bathroom floor required special surveillance and care. She finally accomplished her mission. Her hair, as well as her entire self, had finally been washed. She remembered exactly where in her suitcases she had packed clean nightgowns. She had a bottle of water and her medications ready for the next morning laid out on the desk that served as a bedside table.

Agent Barnes had insisted she fill out the room service breakfast menu and had hung it on her door. They had to be ready to leave for the FBI offices at 9:45 the next morning. Mercedes wondered if she would be able to function in the morning and be ready to leave her room by then. It took her extra time to get dressed, and she was so worn out tonight, she wondered if she would even be able to get out of bed the next day. Her muscles were beginning to hurt, complaining about the extra activity from the day as Mercedes had yanked on her cane and used it as a weapon to beat up a terrorist. She didn't usually do any of these things, and she never used those yanking and beating muscles. She took some Ibuprophen and hoped she would not be completely stiff and unable to move the next morning.

Breakfast arrived promptly at nine. The well-done omelet had been prepared exactly as she had specified, and the bacon and hash browns were hot and tasted good. It was more breakfast than Mercedes was used to eating, but the stress as well as the unaccustomed physical activity of the day before had left her with an unusually hearty appetite. She ate every bite of food that arrived on the breakfast tray.

What she was not prepared for was Agent Barnes' insisting that she put on an ugly brown wig before they left the hotel room. Mercedes hated wigs. She'd worn wigs for photoshoots for the covers of her books. After the photos had been taken, she'd promised herself she would never put one on her head again. They were hot and uncomfortable. Wigs itched. They made her head sweat and made her hair feel sticky. The hair from the wig always seemed to be able to find its way into her mouth, and she thought she looked very weird when she saw herself in the mirror.

However, it was true that her own white hair was quite distinctive. In the videos she had seen of herself on television the night before, her hair had taken on an almost iridescent quality as the light reflected off her head. Because of the way her hair had shone and glowed and stood out from her head, she'd looked like some kind of elderly avenging angel. She'd thought to herself that she kind of looked like what she imagined the Angel Gabriel might look like standing at the Pearly Gates blowing his horn. Agent Barnes pointed out to Mercedes how striking her white hair was and how it was almost a signature for identifying her. Mercedes knew she was supposed to be maintaining a low profile. She grumbled about it but agreed to wear the wig. It had peculiar, tight, little-old-lady curls, the kind a really bad home permanent puts in your hair. Ugh! No one would ever mistake the terrible brown curly hairstyle for something Mercedes would choose on purpose.

A different wheelchair, a new coat with a hood that had suddenly made an appearance, a wool cap, and a ratty hand-knitted pea green scarf with holes in it had also arrived as part of her disguise. Mercedes sniffed the offending items that made up her new look, grumbled some more, and put on the frumpy articles of clothing. Mercedes did not consider herself to be much of a clothes horse or a fashion plate, but she was not going to put on anyone else's unwashed hat or scarf.

"I will wear these things today and play the part of a homeless woman when I am out in public. I understand the need for me to disguise myself right now. But I will not do this indefinitely, Agent Barnes. It is very uncomfortable, and even though I am elderly, I do have some vanity left about the way I look. Nobody else cares about my pride, but I do. Right now, I look and feel like a dowdy version of my cleaning lady, and I don't like it."

"The most important thing right now is to keep you safe. I don't think any people from the press followed us here to the hotel last night, but they might be staking out the FBI building. We will, of course be taking a circuitous route and entering the building through an underground parking garage, but these media people are very sneaky and very inventive. They always seem to be able to find a way to outsmart us."

Agent Barnes paused. She realized that Mercedes Carrington had no idea about the extent of the firestorm of interest she'd created around herself. The FBI agent knew by now that Mercedes had reacted on instinct. She'd managed to be able to do the right thing in spite of her diminished physical abilities. Agent Barnes knew Mercedes did not seek and did not want any fame or notoriety. But in spite of having acted with the best of intentions, she'd made herself into an icon—an icon for women, for the elderly, for the handicapped, for the weak, for patriots, for America. In a few brief seconds, she had become a hero to all. She would have to learn to live with that.

"You have to realize that you are part of a very big story. Let me rephrase that. You are not just a part of a very big story. You *are* the very big story. You did a very unusual and remarkable thing when you took down that potential hijacker. This incident would have been a big story if an air marshal had saved the day or if a young male passenger or group of passengers had subdued a terrorist. But for an elderly woman who is disabled and uses a cane to singlehandedly bring a hijacker to the ground...well, that is a unique and fascinating event. It is almost unbelievable. The press loves it. The public loves it. Everyone loves this story, this thing you did. I love it. You may not like the consequences of what you've done, but the fact is, you have become famous and heroic. Everybody wants to see you and talk to you and find out what made you do this and what makes you tick. You are big news right now. And now you have completely and inexplicably disappeared. That always adds even more mystery and drama to any story."

Mercedes sighed in resignation and rolled her eyes. "I know. I watched a few minutes of it on CNN last night. Ugh!" Mercedes looked depressed. Finally the accidental hero spoke again. "All right. Let's get this over with. I don't know what more I can say about what happened yesterday. I've told you several times everything I did and everything I was thinking and everything I know. I am happy to cooperate with the FBI. I want to see that little hijacking scoundrel go to prison. That's the bottom line for me. I don't want him to get off. I don't want some slick lawyer to take his case and start crying xenophobia. That is why I am willing to go to FBI headquarters with you today, dressed up like a refugee from the Goodwill store."

Agent Barnes was somewhat disheartened that she had not yet been able to impress upon Mercedes what a remarkable thing she had done and how it was going to change her life. Mercedes didn't think she had really done anything very unusual. She'd done what she had to do to keep the hijacker from reaching the cockpit. It was that simple from Mercedes' point of view. But the fallout from her amazing act of courage was going to be anything but simple.

The wig was just as itchy as Mercedes had imagined it would be. It was a cheap plastic wig, the same kind she bought on Amazon to wear in the photoshoots for her author's photos. Mercedes loved one wig she'd bought on Amazon. It was outrageously long and a wild and fabulous shade of red. Today's wig was a mousy brown color. With its silly curls and waves, Mercedes thought it made her look old. In the 1950s, one of her great aunts had kept a weekly beauty shop appointment to purposely have her own real hair made to look just like this wig. But today, no real person would ever intentionally choose to wear either their real hair or a wig like this. Mercedes thought she was allergic to something in the plastic hair, probably the coloring. No matter what color they were, they all smelled funny. And they tickled.

Mercedes was a writer. She wrote three different kinds of mysteries under three different pseudonyms. She'd started writing youth books and had written one for each of her four grandchildren. She had one more to go. Her youngest and fifth grandchild did not yet have his book. Because she still had his book to write was one of the factors that had motivated Mercedes to stop the hijacking the day before. She'd refused to die in a plane crash before she had written a book for her youngest grandson, Richard.

Mercedes also wrote historical novels, spy thrillers that were set before and during World War II. As a "War Baby" she'd always been fascinated with this period in history and the rise and fall of the Nazis. Her third series of books were humorous mysteries about a group of elderly friends who got together for a yearly reunion at various fancy resorts around the United States. Every year this cast of characters got themselves into and then out of a lot of trouble. Mercedes loved to write. It was her passion and made her endorphins flow.

She thought it was fun to write and publish her books under different pen names. She was crazy about the way she looked in the cheap Amazon wigs, especially the bright red one. The disguises she wore for the photos on the covers of her novels made her chuckle, but she despised the way they felt when she had wigs on her head. She put up with the discomfort for the photoshoots, but those wigs came off the minute the photographs were taken. Today it seemed she was going to have to wear the darn thing for several hours.

Chapter 4

*A*gent Barnes pushed the wheelchair down the hall and onto the elevator of the Capital Hotel. The elevator was enormous. Legend had it that in 1880 President Ulysses S. Grant had stayed at the hotel and insisted that his horse accompany him to his suite on an upper floor. The story was that the elevator was modified to accommodate the horse. No one knew if that story was true or exactly why the hotel's elevator was so large. There were many anecdotes about things that had happened on the famous and infamous elevator.

It was mid-morning, so Agent Barnes and Mercedes had the huge elevator to themselves. The government sedan was waiting at the curb by the side door of the hotel, and Mercedes was able to extricate herself from the wheelchair and get into the car with minimal difficulty. No one took any notice of the old woman in dingy clothes climbing into the back of a navy blue Buick.

The office building where the Little Rock FBI had its headquarters was a fifteen minute drive from the hotel. They pulled into the underground parking garage and stopped beside the elevator. Just as Mercedes exited the car and settled herself into the wheelchair, a man with a video camera jumped out from behind a pylon and began to photograph Mercedes and Agent Barnes. A reporter appeared next and began shouting questions at Mercedes. Security forces instantly arrived and swarmed to surround the two aggressive members of the press.

"Is it true you are a famous writer? What is your real name? Are you really disabled? Where do you live? How old are you?" The questions didn't stop long enough for her to even begin to give any answers.

Mercedes was furious. She shouted back at the reporter and swatted at the video camera with her cane. Her blue and white cane had been confiscated as evidence, so she was now using a plain black one. She shrieked at these two in a voice very unlike her own soft tones. "I don't know why you're asking me these questions. My real name has always been Agnes MacGillicutty. I live in a cardboard box under the Verrazzano-Narrows Bridge, and I am older than dirt. Now get out of my way." She shook her cane at the two young men as Agent Barnes rushed the wheelchair onto the elevator. Security guards seized the video camera and the two reporters.

Agent Barnes was almost laughing. "Why the Verrazzano-Narrows Bridge? How did you come up with that?"

Mercedes snorted. "I really like that bridge. I always have. If I were going to live under a bridge, that's the one I would live under." She smiled to herself. "I see what you mean about the media. They really are tiresome, aren't they? And unrelenting. What a pain in the patootie! I hope they have to spend a lot of time tracking down Agnes MacGillicutty. They'll never find her under that bridge or any other bridge." Mercedes chuckled and seemed pleased with herself for having shouted down the two reporters.

"We can't use this same disguise again, you know. That's the only problem. They have video footage of you in that wig and in those clothes. We've taken possession of the video camera, and we also will seize any cell phones those two might have been using. If we don't, that video will be all over the news tonight. We will have to do something different the next time we take you out."

"Maybe my kids and grandkids won't recognize me. They will be amused and confused by the name and the part about the cardboard box. But they know I love the Verrazzano-Narrows Bridge so they'll know it's me. Ha!"

When they reached the FBI offices, Mercedes told her story again and answered what seemed to be hundreds of questions. They wanted an official deposition, so she was sworn to tell the truth and all of that. There were lights and cameras, and it was all recorded. She wondered if they were afraid she would croak before the case came to trial. They wanted to get her deposition about exactly what had happened, and they wanted to get it now. In case something happened to her, they would have the video of her sworn testimony to present in court. Several different people questioned her. She answered everything clearly and completely. The FBI people seemed pleased with her performance. It wasn't hard for Mercedes. She was just telling the truth. She'd always told the truth...even when people didn't want to hear it.

Someone brought sandwiches and drinks to the room where Mercedes was giving her testimony. She was tired but had questions of her own she wanted answered. She'd answered all of theirs and figured it was her turn to ask a few.

"What have you found out about the man on the plane? Does he belong to a group, or was he acting alone?" Mercedes knew the answer to this question would be important in determining how long she had to stay under the radar.

An uncomfortable silence in the room followed her question. No one wanted to answer her. She knew this meant they probably had not yet been able to find out anything about the hijacker. Agent Barnes spoke up. She felt Mercedes deserved an answer to her question, even if it was not the answer anyone wanted to give her. "Come on guys. Tell her what you know. Or tell her what you don't know. She deserves that."

The senior man in the room, who had silver gray hair and seemed to be in charge of everything, took the responsibility of giving Mercedes the news. What he had to say was not good news for her, and it was not good news for the FBI. "Our hijacker is refusing to cooperate. He used a false name and a fake ID when he purchased his airline ticket and boarded the plane. We don't know his real name. We have run his fingerprints and are working on his DNA. We ran his face through our facial recognition software." The agent paused and took a deep breath. "So far, we have nothing. There were no matches to anybody. We think he is from the Middle East somewhere, but that's all we know. We don't know where he lives. He won't tell us anything."

At least the agent had been honest with her that they had so far been unsuccessful at identifying their suspect in custody. "We might know something about his nationality by tonight...from his DNA. We are looking at the security cameras now and trying to trace his movements back in Phoenix, from before he boarded the plane. We will find out something. I wish we had more to tell you. I wish we had better news for you."

Mercedes was clearly disappointed. She had hoped she would be able to resume her normal life sooner rather than later. This was a blow. She wanted to go home. She wanted to sleep in her own bed. The hotel in Little Rock was very nice, luxurious even, but she had things to do. Any day, she was expecting a shipment of her latest book. The books were being sent to her house in Lewes, Delaware. These were the complimentary books she sent to friends and family, before the books went on sale to the public. She signed each one and wrote personal notes which she included with the newly-printed books. Mercedes looked forward to this part of having her books published. Sending the books and the notes gave her a chance to stay in touch with friends from the various stages of her life. She was anxious to get to work.

"What you're telling me is that I have to stay incognito for a while longer, until you know more?"

The senior agent spoke again. He'd not given her his name so Mercedes had begun to think of him as The Silver Fox. "Yes, I'm afraid that is what we are telling you."

"I hope you realize there is a big fat hole in your attempting to keep me and all of this under wraps. It's my children and grandchildren. I sent a text to my daughter yesterday to let her know I was all right. By now all three of my daughters know I was on that plane, and they know I was the person who appeared all over the news last night. I sent a text to my daughter who lives in Delaware right away so she wouldn't drive to the airport in Maryland to pick me up. By now, they all know and have probably blabbered what they know to their friends and neighbors far and wide and to everybody else."

"We know they haven't done that." The senior man, The Silver Fox, spoke again.

"How do you know they haven't done that? My grandkids text everything they even think of thinking about. They put pictures of their food on Instagram or Snapchat or something like that. They send tweets and do all of that other stuff that kids and politicians and other infantile people do these days.

Blah, blah, blah. TMI as far as I'm concerned. This would be big news for them...about their own grandmother. Do you think they would not put every word of that out on their electronic social media accounts?"

"We sent agents to all three of your daughters' houses last night to talk to them."

"Last night? What? Why? What did you say to them?"

"We told them they would be putting your life in danger if they said anything to anybody about knowing who the person was who appeared on the news reports. Agents spoke to everyone in each household. We assured them that you were fine and were being kept undercover for a while. We explained to them exactly why that is necessary. They all get it. You've got some smart grandkids, you know."

"How did they react to your asking them to keep all of this confidential?" Mercedes knew her daughters and knew they did not like being told what to do.

"What do you think they would say? They love you and want you to be safe. They don't want to do anything that would put you in danger. We blocked their phones, and an agent arrived at each of their houses before they had a chance to send any texts or put anything out on social media. It's all okay. Your granddaughter in Colorado cried with relief when she heard you were all right. When the FBI showed up at the house, she was very afraid that something bad had happened to you. We could have handled that better. I'm sorry if we alarmed them initially. But it was important to be sure they didn't reveal that their mother and grandmother was the woman who had been a hero on the airplane yesterday."

"I know kids and their social media. I don't think my grandkids would do anything intentionally to let the cat out of the bag, but they have phones and they have friends. They might want to share this excitement with their friends who would not be as invested as they are in keeping my identity out of the public domain."

"This is not our first rodeo, Ms. Carrington, with trying to keep information from the public. We had one of our social media experts go to each of the houses and speak specifically with the children about this issue. We walked them through a couple of scenarios that might tempt them. For example, Madison might want to share this exciting news about her grandmother with her best friend Zoe. So she swears Zoe to secrecy. Zoe finds the story so amazing that she can't resist sharing it with her cousin Aiden. So she swears Aiden to secrecy. But Aiden doesn't know you and is not as bought into protecting your identity. He isn't as careful about honoring his vow of secrecy as his cousin Zoe is. Your grandkids readily grasped how telling just one person, how making even one mention to one person, could be deadly to you. They got it. Your grandkids are smart, and they are old enough and responsible enough to understand that actions have consequences."

"Are they safe? Is my family in any danger from what I did?"

"As long as nobody, and I do mean absolutely nobody, knows who you are, they are perfectly safe. We made this point with your kids and grandkids, too. As long as you are unidentified and in hiding, none of them will have to go into witness protection. They all know what witness protection is, and they know if they have to go into that program, they will have to leave their current lives behind. None of them wants that, of course, and the threat of witness protection served as even greater motivation for them to keep all of this secret. We are monitoring their cell phones to insure compliance. We got permission for this from their parents. They realize that kids are kids. We will block any tweets, texts, or other social media posts that have anything to do with you."

"If someone recognizes me and asks someone in my family about whether or not that person on the news was me, what will they say?"

"We talked to them about that possibility. They will say that they agree the person in the news looks a lot like you, but they know it isn't you. They might say it is your doppelganger and make a joke out of it. They might say that they know you are a demon with your cane, but you were not on a plane yesterday. You have not yet left Arizona, and that is a fact. We gave them plenty of ways to deflect and successfully answer all those questions."

"What about my friends? They would have recognized me when they saw the news. There are other relatives who will recognize me, like my cousins in Ohio and Texas and South Carolina."

"We appealed to the major networks and used a little Photoshop creativity with their videos of the take down. There are no doubt some individual videos still out there on people's cell phones, but if they try to sell what's on their phones to the networks or to the newspapers or put it up on YouTube, we will be able to fix the face of the woman who saved the day."

Mercedes was amazed at the great lengths to which the FBI had gone to keep her identity a secret. She was also impressed that they had been able to disguise her face that appeared in the videos with Photoshop-style trickery. She'd seen herself on TV last night, but she hadn't looked closely at the face. She was distracted by the hair. Now she was curious and anxious to watch more of the news footage to see if she could recognize herself.

"Agent Barnes may have already mentioned this to you, but I also wanted to tell you that we immediately removed your name from the passenger list of the plane flight. We substituted the name of another real person who is close to your age and has some characteristics in common with you. She is deceased, don't worry. We have invented a history for this person, and she has a backstory that will have both the media and the bad guys going around in circles for weeks and months. Our stand-in hero is seventy-three and uses a cane. She really did have a home on the Main Line in Philadelphia, in Ardmore, Pennsylvania. We have also given her a home in Sedona, Arizona. She flew out of Phoenix on your flight. She sat in your first-class seat. She will be the person the media will try to track down to find out more about the Hero with the White Hair. As far as anybody knows, Mercedes Carrington is still at her house in Scottsdale. You have not yet left Arizona. You had nothing whatsoever to do with what happened on the American Airlines flight yesterday. We have a woman who looks vaguely like you, who is using a cane just like your blue and white one and is staying at your Arizona house. She will go in and out from time to time, like you do. She is maintaining a low profile there in Scottsdale, as you can imagine."

Mercedes interrupted. "My friends and neighbors will realize it isn't me…the woman there at the house. My next door neighbor knew I was scheduled to leave yesterday to fly back to the East Coast. She will know I am not really still at my house."

"We are going to have you send her a text or an email about that. I am telling you all of this because I want you to understand that we are doing everything possible to keep your name and your face away from the media and away from any possible colleagues of our hijacker." The silver-haired FBI agent who was in charge looked Mercedes directly in the eyes for a while and did not say anything.

"Okay. I get it. And I am grateful. I understand why I need to wear wigs and shaggy clothes and stay at the hotel. I'm sorry I complained about these things. I promise to be more compliant and cooperative in the future. You are doing this for my own good." Mercedes was resigned to the situation. She seemed to fully grasp what was at stake. "But you have my deposition. You don't really need me anymore. If something happens to me now, you still have my sworn testimony."

"We don't want anything to happen to you. If we let anything happen to the woman who is the most revered person in the country right now, we could never live it down. We would never be forgiven. And, your in-person testimony and description of what happened on that plane and what you did will convince any jury that our man in custody is guilty. Once they get a look at you and hear your story, no one will pay any attention to the accusations of xenophobia and the usual BS claims of racism and discrimination. With you on the witness stand, all the fancy pants lawyers the ACLU can find are not going to be able to convince anyone of anything but the truth. We are determined to keep you alive and kicking."

"I promise I will not argue with whatever you ask me to do. Above all, I want to protect my family. If wearing a plastic wig is what's required, I will sleep in the damn thing. Just so you know."

"I think we understand each other. We are making every effort to wrap this up quickly. What we need now is some luck. You must be exhausted with everything that we've put you through today. I know I am. Let's all go home and have a drink and a nice dinner and a good night's rest. We will talk again tomorrow. We will come to the hotel to see you. After the incident in the parking garage this morning, we don't want you coming here again. It was necessary for you to be here today because of the official statement we had to take. We needed the electronics and all of this equipment to do that. From now on, we don't want to put you at risk by transporting you around to any public places, especially to FBI headquarters. It had to be done today. We didn't have any choice. But you saw what happened with those kids who tried to videotape you. There's always some jerk from the press lurking nearby. I'm sorry all that had to happen, but you really did save the day, once again, with your quick thinking."

The Silver Fox continued as he chuckled. "I must say, Mercedes, from all reports, you really fixed those two reporters. Congratulations. I would never have been able to come up with MacGillicutty or with the Verrazzano-Narrows Bridge that fast. We have confiscated the video footage. We have their cell phones and are holding the two overnight in the local jail. We have a plausible story to tell them to throw them way off the scent. Don't worry about them. They will go away quietly."

Mercedes had almost forgotten about the rude encounter with the two aggressive media kids from earlier that day. She hoped that obnoxious disruption had all been put to rest. She was very tired. She wanted to go to sleep in her own bed. She wanted to go home, to her house in Delaware. She admitted to herself that it was probably going to be a very long time before she would be allowed to go back there.

Mercedes was quiet as Agent Barnes pushed her wheelchair onto the elevator. They reached the building's parking garage level, and a car had pulled up very close to the door of the elevator. Mercedes stepped directly from the wheelchair into the back seat of the car. Security was taking no chances this time. She felt like a prisoner, or maybe a queen. Was this what it was like to be a famous person? Maybe this was what celebrities always had to do to avoid the paparazzi. Mercedes had never wanted to be famous. She had written her books under pen names and had avoided book signings when she could. Now that everyone ordered their books over the internet and bookstores were falling like flies, there were no more book signings. Mercedes had never sought the limelight. Now she was famous, according to the news media. This was something she had never wanted to have happen to her. But it had happened, and she hated it.

✖ ✖ ✖ ✖

"You failed. Did you select the wrong man to be a martyr? Nothing should have gone wrong. We hit them unexpectedly. There was not even an air marshal on that flight. It should have happened exactly as we'd planned. How could this have turned into such a disaster? Not only did your man fail to take down the plane, he has been made a laughing stock in the American press. He looks like a stupid fool on television, and maybe he is that. News reports say that an old woman with a cane beat him into submission. That cannot possibly be true. Who is this old woman? You will not be paid. You will be punished for this failure."

Chapter 5

The day with the FBI had worn Mercedes down more than she realized, even more than the day before with all the action on the airplane. When they arrived back at the hotel, they entered the lobby again by the less conspicuous side door, and Agent Barnes quickly pushed Mercedes onto the elevator. Back in her room, all she wanted was to find a big pitcher of water with lots of ice in it and go straight to bed. Agent Barnes insisted that she eat something, and sure enough the food from room service raised her blood sugar. She felt better after eating, and she had recovered enough energy to take a shower. After wearing the sticky wig all day, it was heavenly to be able to wash her hair. Then she collapsed into bed. She fell asleep so quickly she didn't have time to feel sorry for herself or lament her unusual predicament.

She slept late the next morning. Although Mercedes was not a big fan of television, Agent Barnes wanted her to watch the cable network news. She wanted Mercedes to realize what a big story she had become. Agent Barnes also wanted Mercedes to see that the videos of her taking down the hijacker had been doctored to the extent that no one would be able to recognize her. Mercedes was subdued if not depressed that morning, wondering what had happened to her life. But she grudgingly acknowledged that no one would be able to identify her by watching the videos on the news. She also accepted that her actions aboard American Airlines Flight #66 from Phoenix had been heroic and had captured the imagination of the world. She just wanted to go home, and all of this news made it even clearer to her that it was unlikely she would be able to do that any time soon.

Agent Barnes was trying to take good care of Mercedes and made sure she had some coffee and toast that morning. The senior FBI agent on her case, the one Mercedes had named "The Silver Fox," would be arriving at noon with two other agents to discuss what was going to happen going forward. Mercedes dreaded what they would have to say to her about her immediate future and her long-range future. At age seventy-five, Mercedes figured that her short-term future and her long-term future were pretty much the same.

"What are they going to say to me today, Agent Barnes? I don't want to spend any of my time in the witness protection program. Of course, I realize nobody really wants to do that. I just want to get back to my life. I have books to write. I have kids and grandkids I want to spend time with. I have friends. I know my wishes must be secondary to the greater good, but I'm selfish and want to spend the remainder of my life the way I want to spend it."

"We understand these things, and that is why Agent Wilton is coming to talk to you today. That's the name of the older man who is in charge of the investigation, Special Agent Ridley Wilton. He's a good guy. Smart, and he has a heart. He will listen to what you have to say. Mostly he is focused on keeping you safe. If it were up to the FBI alone, we would stash you somewhere outside the country. We'd put you in a safe house in Ireland or Australia or Canada, someplace where no one would ever find you. He wants to talk these things over with you today. Of course he knows all about your extended family and your writing. He respects all of these things about you. You are his top priority right now. He will work with you to decide what is going to happen next."

"If they could figure out who this bad guy is and round up his compadres, we could get this over and done with and move on. I understand it is easier to have something like this resolved quickly on a television program than it is to have that happen in real life. I will try to cooperate, but I am feeling very down about my prospects right now."

"You can't go back to your house in Delaware. I will tell you that right now. I know that's what you want to do, but you can't even consider doing that. The Delaware property is in your own name. We are doing everything we can to prevent the terrorists from finding out what your real name is, but if they should find it out, the house in Lewes will be the first place they would go to find you. You might as well begin to get used to the fact that you can't go back there until this case has been wrapped up."

"I'm sure you already know about my house in Arizona, since you seem to know everything else about me and my houses and my family. I just finished packing up my stuff there so I could put the house on the market. Since my husband died, I've decided that the Scottsdale house is too much to take care of. It's too big for me to live there by myself. I need a smaller place. I've already purchased a one-bedroom condominium in the same development. I've had a house in that development in Scottsdale for more than thirty years. I have good friends there. I want to have a smaller place with less to take care of, but I still want to be close to my friends. None of us are getting any younger, and we want to enjoy ourselves and each other. I am very close to my next door neighbor, and it was a big decision for me to put my house on the market. I really should have done it a couple of years ago."

"Yes, we know about your putting the Scottsdale house on the market. I know you want to sell some of the furniture with the house and plan to take some of it to your new condominium. We know your condominium is still under construction, and it will be a while before you're able to move into it. But it's a good thing you were able to pack up your things and get the big house ready to sell. Your house is scheduled to go on the market next week, but we may ask you to delay that for a while. That reminds me. You need to send your neighbor Rose Lutzy a text and tell her that you are still there—at the house in Scottsdale. I've written up a text for you to send to her. You need to tell her that you didn't take the plane on Tuesday. You have to explain to her why you are still in Arizona and what your plans are for the next few days."

"I have to text her something that isn't true? Is that what I have to do?" Mercedes face fell. She squirmed in her chair. Lying to her dear friend, the woman who had been her next-door-neighbor for three decades, was not something she was prepared to do.

Agent Barnes went into her adjoining hotel room and brought back a new cell phone and a piece of paper. She handed the new phone to Mercedes. "This cell phone is exactly the same model as the cell phone you are currently using, but it is different. The chip, the SIM card in this new phone can be programmed to disguise where you actually are when you make a phone call or send a text or an email. Your old phone has been deactivated. That is, you can't send any communications from it. No phone calls, no texts, no emails, no internet searches.

I know you have lots of notes and files on your old phone, and you can still use it to access all of those things. But from now on you must use this new phone to communicate with anyone and to use the internet. Right now it's programmed to indicate that the phone is in Scottsdale, at your house there. We want everyone to believe you are still there at your house in Camelback Creek, at least for the next several days."

Mercedes picked up the new phone. It looked exactly like her old phone. "I will carry both of these phones in my purse, but only the one with the heart on the back can actually communicate with anyone. I understand. I have to keep both of these phones charged. Ain't technology grand? If anybody cares, this phone will tell them that I am in a place where I really am not. Is that right?"

Agent Barnes ignored the sarcasm in Mercedes' voice and picked up the piece of paper she'd brought with the phone. "Here's what we came up with to explain it all to your neighbors in Arizona. The text is written out on this piece of paper."

> "Had to cancel my flight on Tuesday. Came down with a bad bug. I've been sleeping for two days. Don't come over. Don't want you to catch it. I will recover. Rescheduled my flight for next Wednesday. Pretend I am not at the house. I told Ginger not to put her FOR SALE sign up until after I leave. You may see me drive to the pharmacy. Ignore me. You don't want to catch what I've got. I miss you lots. Love, M.

Mercedes sighed and picked up the new cell phone to begin texting her friend Rose. "I see how this cleverly explains to my friends why there is someone who looks kind of like me moving around inside and outside my house and driving my car. It establishes that I am still in Scottsdale and could not possibly have been on American Airlines Flight #66 from Phoenix to Philadelphia the day before yesterday. I should have sent this to Rose yesterday. She may have already gone over to the house to see why I am still there."

"She hasn't gone over to your house."

"I figured you would know that. But please don't tell me how you know it. It would probably make me angry. Rose will text me back eventually. But she is not glued to her phone like some people are. She may not see the text until tomorrow or the next day."

"She will see it and read it today."

"Don't tell me how you know that."

"This is all for your protection, you know."

"I know that. I am really still in Scottsdale. I never got on the plane in Phoenix. I was never on Flight #66. Whatever happened on that plane has nothing whatsoever to do with me." Mercedes knew it was all for the best, but knowing that did not lift her spirits.

There was a knock on the door, and Agent Barnes went to answer it. The Silver Fox, FBI Special Agent Ridley Wilton, walked into the living room of Mercedes' suite. He was accompanied by two younger agents, one male and one female. The young male carried a large shopping bag of food. He began to set the food out on the table in the middle of the room. Special Agent Ridley Wilton carried a letter-size manila envelope which he dropped on the table.

The Silver Fox explained about the food. "This is lunch from my favorite deli. I always take an opportunity, whenever I possibly can, to have a working lunch from Uncle Max's Delicatessen. His corned beef sandwiches and his turkey sandwiches are the best anywhere. Better than anything I ever had in New York. And his homemade dill pickles. They are to die for. Who would have imagined that Little Rock, Arkansas would be able to outdo New York City in anything as proprietary as their deli sandwiches?"

Agent Barnes handed out drinks, paper plates, and paper napkins. There were containers of potato salad and small bags of chips. There was a large container of dill pickles. In spite of being grumpy and sad, Mercedes admitted that the food looked great. She helped herself to half a corned beef on rye and half a freshly roasted sliced turkey sandwich on sourdough. The pickles were fabulous as advertised.

"I should have introduced myself properly yesterday at FBI headquarters. I was so intent on the business at hand, I was rude. Those kids from the press really ticked me off. I apologize for my bad manners, Mercedes. I am Special Agent Ridley Wilton. These two youngsters are Agent Stephanie Abramowitz and Agent Bobby O'Connor. We are here to try to figure out the best way to protect you for the next few months. We would really like to hide you someplace very obscure and far away, but we will be reasonable. We realize you have a life, and we are going to try to accommodate your wishes as much as we can. We will arrange for you to be able to spend some time with your family members. I suspect you do not want to leave the country, but maybe we can talk you into taking a nice vacation in Canada for the spring and summer."

Mercedes liked The Silver Fox, but she almost burst into tears when he began talking about hiding her away for the next few *months*. The corned beef and the turkey became a lump in her stomach. She realized she was completely at the mercy of whatever the FBI wanted to do with her. Because she wanted so badly to protect her kids and grandkids, she swallowed the words she really wanted to say to Agent Wilton and the others and just nodded her head. "Canada will be all right. As long as I can see my family and have a place to write, I will be fine."

"We considered a lot of different places but have decided to try to talk you into staying in Nova Scotia temporarily. One reason we picked Nova Scotia is because we know you've expressed some interest in renting or buying a place in Maine."

"How could you possibly know that?" Mercedes was miffed.

"You went on the internet and looked at quite a few properties in the Bar Harbor area. You actually talked on the phone to one real estate agent in Northeast Harbor. We did not do anything illegal or secretive to find out that you've been interested in properties in Maine. All real estate websites keep the email addresses of everyone who makes an inquiry. We know what kinds of houses you looked at – locations, price ranges, square footage, styles of cottages, and everything else. We might even be able to help you find something suitable in Maine. But all of that is down the road. For right now, we need to get you out of this hotel and settled in someplace more comfortable and less public."

"What did you tell my kids about all of this?"

"We told them they might not see you for a while. We told them we were doing everything we could to be certain no one, and I mean no one, knew you were involved in the incident on Flight #66. We told them you would not be able to return to your house in Lewes for some time but that we would find you a nice place to live and would take very good care of you. We told them we would arrange for visits once you are settled and we are sure you're safe."

"Do I have a choice in any of this?"

"Of course you do. If you don't want to go to Nova Scotia, we can try to find another place for you to live temporarily. With spring and summer coming up, we figured you'd want to be someplace cooler rather than warmer. Florida or Mexico wouldn't be my choice for a place to spend the summer. Look at the photos of the property and the house in Nova Scotia." Agent Wilton pointed to the envelope he'd put down on the table. "This house and location fulfill all of our criteria for security. You will have a housekeeper who comes in every day for a few hours. She will clean and cook for you and do your laundry. She will do your shopping and bring your mail from the post office. She will run errands for you. Once the weather improves, you will be able to get outside and move around some. Your housekeeper can push you in the wheelchair as long as you don't leave the property. The cottage is very nice. You will like it. It has been recently updated and has a great new kitchen. It has a roll-in shower with a bench and one of those walk-in tubs in the bathroom. The location is pretty isolated, but that's part of the security. You won't be able to get to know your neighbors. We're hoping you will be able to find that place in Maine you've been looking for and can move there by the end of the summer. If you don't find a place, you can always stay in Nova Scotia as long as you like."

Mercedes had never been to Nova Scotia. She'd always wanted to visit there, but she'd been busy with other things and traveling to other places. She opened the envelope that lay on the table and looked through the photographs of the house the FBI had found for her and hoped she would like. The views of the water were spectacular. The house itself was an antique Victorian cottage that shouted charm. The house was small, but the interiors were pleasing. Walls had been taken down to open up and modernize the space. It looked comfortable. The kitchen was all new, and the bathroom was indeed custom-made for a handicapped person. The sunroom that overlooked the water was a room that called to Mercedes. This was the place where she could push the antique table up against the wall of windows and use the table as a desk to write. There was a fireplace in the room and a couple of comfortable upholstered chairs. There was not a lot of furniture, but all the necessities were there. It would be fine.

Mercedes suddenly felt a huge pang of loneliness and longing for her house on the Lewes-Rehoboth Canal in Delaware. She scolded herself and told herself to suck it up and be brave. The Nova Scotia house was in a beautiful location. The small cottage was ideal for her needs. Things could be much worse. She should feel lucky.

She realized all the FBI agents were watching her face closely as she shuffled through the photographs. They wanted her to like the house enough to agree to stay there. She tried to put herself in their shoes. Of course they had to keep her safe. This place they'd found in Nova Scotia, near Halifax, fulfilled their requirements. It seemed as if it could fulfill Mercedes' requirements as well.

She would look on the relocation as an adventure. She'd always wanted to see Nova Scotia, and now she finally would. Different scenery had potential as a setting for new mysteries. She was worried about the food. Food was important to her. She had many food allergies. But there would be lobster. She could live on that. She thought halibut also came from Nova Scotia, and she loved halibut. She thought she remembered something about there not being any more halibut on the East Coast. Lobster would be fine. It would work out. She looked up from the photos and smiled.

"I like it. It is beautiful there in Nova Scotia. Somebody has taken a great deal of care renovating this lovely house. It almost seems made to order for me. The views of the water are amazing. I will be able to write there. But I'm going to need my computer and my printer and a great many other things from my house in Lewes. If we can make that happen, I can live with this. I will look forward to it."

The four FBI agents sitting around the table had been holding their breath, waiting for Mercedes to say yea or nay. Their collective sigh of relief was almost audible. It was obvious she really did like the place and was not just saying she did. She was being gracious and trying to cooperate, but she also was being honest about looking forward to relocating to Nova Scotia. Of all the agents, The Silver Fox seemed especially glad that she genuinely liked the house and the views. He realized it was difficult for someone as old as Mercedes to make a huge transition like the one they were asking her to make, and he was empathetic. But who could not love the views? It was a go. "You are a good sport, Mercedes. We will make sure you have everything you need to continue your writing."

The Silver Fox left, and Agents Stephanie Abramowitz and Bobby O'Connor spent the rest of the afternoon with Mercedes going over what she was going to need in terms of her clothes and medications, her research materials and electronics, and all the other things that would have to be sent from Lewes to the house in Canada. They made countless lists. There was a shipment of the books that Mercedes had recently written that was scheduled to arrive at the Lewes house in a few days. That order could be intercepted, redirected, and sent to a different address in care of a different name. It would delay the order by a few days, but the FBI could manage the changes and make sure that Mercedes eventually and surreptitiously received her book shipment in Nova Scotia.

Mercedes had an almost photographic memory so she knew exactly where all of her important possessions were located. Keeping up with multiple houses over the years had trained her to keep inventories in her head. She had to know where critical items were at all times. She refused to spend time searching for something that was in a different house all the way across the country, thousands of miles away. Her memory and her organizational skills were a great help to these FBI agents who were in charge of relocating Mercedes and her stuff so she could live comfortably and continue to write in her new location.

"So when do I leave for this lovely house in Nova Scotia?"

Agent Bobby O'Connor seemed to be in charge of transportation. "After dinner tonight. You and Agent Barnes will have dinner in the room this evening, and she will help you pack. You have two large suitcases and a small carry-on bag. Right? Someone will come for your two larger pieces of luggage and take them to the plane. After midnight, Agent Barnes will wheel you down to the lobby and out the side door. You will be driven to the airport and board a private jet. Only you and Agent Barnes will be on the plane, besides the pilots, of course. You can sleep all the way to Nova Scotia, if you want. Tomorrow morning early you will arrive at your new temporary home. Agent Abramowitz and I will be going to Delaware to retrieve the things you want from your house in Lewes. How does that sound?"

"How can you get it all organized so fast? Is the house really ready for me?"

"It will be by tomorrow morning. Your boxes from Arizona and Delaware won't arrive for a few days, but within a week, you should have everything you've asked for. You will be able to settle in and enjoy the beautiful scenery. It's early March, so Nova Scotia is still pretty cold. There will be a few more snow storms, but with a new heating system and three fireplaces in your cottage, you will be warm and dry. Most importantly, you will be safe. Meanwhile, we will be doing everything we can to discover the identity of the hijacker."

As if on cue, Bobby's cell phone rang. He answered, listened, and hung up. "That was Agent Wilton. He called to tell me that the DNA results came back on our terrorist. According to his DNA, he has a high percentage of Persian DNA and other DNA we find in people who are of Iranian decent. We are making a very educated guess that he's Iranian. That would probably put him squarely in the Shia camp with Hamas and Hezbollah. This is a big step forward for us. Agent Wilton also says that video footage of our man entering the airport has been located. He arrived by taxi. We are tracking that taxi now. It is almost impossible to avoid detection in today's world. We hope. I will keep you posted on our progress. I realize you want to know what is happening. I don't blame you. We will tell you whatever we can."

Chapter 6

Both Agent Barnes and Mercedes ordered steak dinners from room service that night. It was more than Mercedes usually ate, but she'd also ordered a shrimp cocktail, a Caesar salad, and an order of French fries. Agent Barnes was surprised at the amount of food Mercedes had ordered. "I've heard they have food in Nova Scotia. And I happen to know your housekeeper is quite a good cook. You ordered from room service as if you are afraid that this might be your last meal on earth."

"I'm nervous. I eat when I'm nervous. I like the food here at this hotel. It's much better than the food at most hotels. I am venturing out into the completely unknown. I need to be fortified with comfort food. Shrimp cocktail and sirloin steak and French fries are my comfort food. I am also going to order a glass of red wine to go with my comfort food."

Agent Barnes laughed and also ordered a glass of red wine. "Someone is coming to pick up your two large suitcases before you and I leave for the airport. Your luggage will be taken to the plane before we leave. The reason for this is that we don't want to take the time to load luggage into the trunk of the car when it is sitting at the curb outside the hotel. When I receive the word, we will go down on the elevator and out the side door as usual. The car will pull up, and you will get out of the wheelchair as quickly as you can and get into the back seat. I will be in charge of your carry-on bag. All you have to do is concentrate on getting yourself into the car. We want you outside on the sidewalk for less than 30 seconds. We will leave the wheelchair on the sidewalk, and someone will come and take it away. Now that we know the hijacker is Iranian and probably associated with either Hamas or Hezbollah, the stakes are much higher. If he was some lowlife trouble maker from Somalia, he would probably have been working alone. The Somalis are pretty disorganized and not very good at carrying out any kind of complicated operations. I was betting he was a Somali because he didn't seem that competent."

"Because he was able to be taken down by a disabled old woman who uses a cane?"

"I am not in any way denigrating your performance. You were amazing. The fact that you defeated a guy who is probably associated with one of the most sophisticated and well-organized terrorist groups in the world only increases my admiration for what you did."

"He might be from Iran, but does that necessarily mean he was working with a group rather than acting alone?" Mercedes would have preferred that the hijacker acted alone. She wished he'd turned out to be one of the not-very-smart shmucks from Somalia rather than a member of a well-known terrorist group from Iran.

"We still don't know much about the guy. We don't know his name. But the fact that he is Iranian is significant. The level of precautions we have to take...well, all of that will have to be increased considerably. If we'd known what we know now, we would have put you in the Marriott or some other place with an underground parking garage. We would never have allowed you to be exposed on a public sidewalk anywhere."

"How well did that underground parking garage thing work out for you the other day when we went to FBI headquarters? I like the idea of the public sidewalk. I could be anybody, any old grandma getting into a car. I could be going to visit my grandkids or on my way back to the assisted living facility. I think hiding my arrival in an underground garage made me more obvious and drew unnecessary attention to me."

"The situation remains that we are here at the Capital Hotel now, and we have to get you to the airport safely. So, that's the reason for the thirty-second time limit for you to be out there on the street." Agent Barnes realized all of these extraordinary security precautions were mostly lost on Mercedes. "Please, bear with us just a little longer. Once you are on that plane, you will be truly safe, and Ridley Wilton will relax a little bit. Once you are at the safe house, he will be able to turn his attention to other things. He is protecting you in a way I've never seen him do before. He really wants to put this guy in prison. Terrorists usually blow themselves to bits along with a bunch of other people. We don't often have the chance to question one or take one to court. You are important to Wilton. You are important to the FBI. In fact, whether you like it or not, you are important to the whole country."

Mercedes sighed and her shoulders slumped. It was obvious she hated her hero status and everything that had come with it. "I would not have done anything differently than I did. Except maybe I would have made my plane reservations for a different day."

"Then you would not have been in the right place at the right time to trip the hijacker and stand on his back and try to beat him into submission."

"Right. Somebody else would have had to do that."

"Nobody else had a weapon. Your cane was the only weapon allowed on the plane."

"Where was the air marshal?"

"As of yesterday morning, almost every plane flight in the U.S. is scheduled to have an air marshal back on board. Just so you know."

"Too little too late." Mercedes was out of sorts and taking it out on Agent Barnes. She realized how negative she was being and tried to make herself be nicer. "Arabella, you have been so kind. You have taken wonderful care of me. You have put up with my unhappiness and my whining. I want you to know that I realize I have not been the easiest person to have to watch over. I am very grateful to you…for everything."

"Do you realize this is the first time you have called me by my first name, Arabella, rather than referring to me as Agent Barnes. I wondered if you'd forgotten my name."

"I guess I was trying to be professional. Or more likely I was trying to pretend that all of this wasn't really happening to me. I'm sorry if I lashed out at you or if I was unkind. You have been wonderful."

"You have been one of the easiest witnesses I have ever had to deal with. Anger and frustration are to be expected in situations like this. You've never been unkind. Don't worry about it. You've been a dream compared to most of the people I've had to babysit."

Mercedes felt better after she had cleared the air with Agent Arabella Barnes. "I think I will lie down and rest for a while before we leave. I don't usually sleep very well on airplanes. I know the flight will take about four hours. That puts us into

Nova Scotia very early in the morning. As you know I'm not a very good morning person. Once we arrive in Nova Scotia, do you know how long it will take to drive to the house from the airport?"

"It's less than an hour. But I think there is a snow storm or an ice storm expected in Halifax. That won't affect the plane's ability to land, but it might affect our ground transportation. I think it's a good idea for you to try to take a nap now. The past few days have taken a toll on you, and you need all the rest you can get. I will wake you when it's time to leave. You have had a shower, and you are dressed and ready to go. All you have to do is put on your coat with the hood and get into the wheelchair. I'll take care of the rest."

"What will I do without you, Arabella? You have waited on me hand and foot for the past three days. I'm going to miss you."

"After I deliver you to Nova Scotia, I have to come back to work here at my office headquarters, but you will be seeing me from time to time. Agent Wilton is keeping a close eye on everything about this high profile case. When he comes to Nova Scotia, he will probably bring me with him."

Agent Barnes woke Mercedes at 11:45 that evening. She had the coat with the hood in her hands. "I've checked the room. You've got everything. Time to say goodbye to the Capital Hotel and get on with your life. I think you have an email from your neighbor Rose Lutzy. You can check it on the plane. I suggest one more trip to the bathroom before we leave. There's a toilet on the plane but I know you don't like those." Agent Barnes smiled at Mercedes.

Mercedes laughed. "I guess I made that pretty clear, didn't I? I've never been in a bathroom on a private plane. Maybe I will like it better. But I will bet it is still pretty small." Mercedes took a deep breath and hoped she was ready. She felt as if this was all happening to somebody else, and she was watching it happen. Dissociating was a reaction to stress and trauma. She knew she was stressed. She put on the coat, pulled up the hood, and sat in the wheelchair. Arabella handed her the black cane.

"We will get you an adjustable cane when you arrive in Canada. I know this one has not been easy to use. You've not complained about it."

"I've complained about everything else. The cane is fine for now. How will I get onto the plane? I know we are leaving the wheelchair behind here on the sidewalk in Little Rock. You know I don't do steps."

"You will have to climb up the ramp on your own to get onto the plane. The plane is not that huge, so the ramp will be easy enough for you to negotiate. You can do it. I've seen you get around the hotel room with the cane. You will be fine."

Mercedes was glad Agent Barnes had so much confidence in her. When one is disabled, the unknown always provokes a degree of anxiety and is sometimes frightening. Everything going forward for the foreseeable future was unknown for Mercedes. She reminded herself that she had decided to face these challenges with the attitude that it was going to be an adventure, which in fact it was.

They left the hotel room. Agent Barnes put the strap of Mercedes' carry-on bag over her shoulder. They rode the elevator down. The side corridor of the lobby was dark. Arabella spoke into her phone. They were outside on the street in a few seconds, just as the car pulled up to the curb. A man jumped out of the passenger seat and helped Mercedes into the back of the car. By the time the door closed, Agent Barnes was already in the back seat beside her holding Mercedes' carry-on bag in her lap. The agent who had helped her out of the wheelchair was back in the passenger seat. They pulled away from the sidewalk and were on their way down South Louisiana Street.

"Twenty-seven seconds. Good job. From the time we stopped the car until we pulled away from the curb. You guys did great. I never saw you move that fast, Arabella."

"Ha! Ha!" Arabella was the sprinter in the Little Rock FBI field office. She had been a track and field champion and had won the state's gold medal for the hundred meter dash three years in a row when she was at college in Missouri. Her fellow agents liked to tease her about how fast she was, but they were in admiration of her abilities.

The three mile drive took a little over ten minutes. The government sedan wended its way to a hangar in a remote part of the Little Rock airport. The door of the hangar swung open, and the car drove inside. The sedan pulled up next to a small jet, and the hangar door closed behind them. A ramp had been pushed to the door of the jet. Mercedes got out of the car and easily made her way up the ramp. Ramps were easy. Steps were hard. Agent Barnes followed closely behind her. There was a man standing inside the door of the plane who offered his arm to Mercedes. She smiled, thanked him, and opted to use her cane. "Do you want me in any particular seat?" Mercedes had never been on board a private plane before, and she was curious about the configuration of the seating. She could choose to sit frontwards or backwards or sideways.

"You will probably want to lie down and try to get some sleep. I suggest one of these long bench-type seats. They are pretty comfortable for sleeping. Can I get you something to drink? I'm not making the flight with you, but I want to be sure you have everything you need before I leave. Agent Barnes knows the plane well. She knows what's in the refrigerator and how to work the coffee machine. You are in good hands."

Arabella put Mercedes' carry-on down on the bench beside her and went to confer with someone in the cockpit. Mercedes had taken the bench seat closest to the bathroom. She fastened her seatbelt. This private plane thing looked pretty sweet to her. She had a couple of friends who owned their own planes, but she'd never actually ridden on one of them. This was a really nice way to travel. Mercedes began to wonder what she might do if she ever won the lottery. Maybe she could have one of these convenient aircraft in her future. She laughed out loud at the unlikelihood that it would happen.

The seats were all leather and smelled nice. It was much cleaner than a commercial airliner. The plane looked as if it could hold about eight passengers. There was a large television screen. Two of the seats had desks. It was all very efficient and compact. Mercedes wasn't going to need to use a desk or watch any television. She intended to sleep if she could.

It was only a few minutes more until Agent Barnes joined her and sat down on the bench seat across from hers. She fastened her seatbelt. The man who had welcomed them on board brought four bottles of cold water and four blankets. Mercedes put one of the blankets over her knees. She smiled and thanked the man who'd brought the water and the blankets. He said goodbye and left the aircraft. The door closed, and the plane slowly made its way out of the hangar.

Because she was used to flying on commercial flights which took forever to board, forever to check everything, forever to taxi to a distant runway, and forever to wait a turn to take off in a long line of other planes, she was shocked at how little time passed after the door of the plane was shut until they were racing down the runway and in the air. It was the middle of the night, so no other planes were waiting to take off, but still. Flying private was definitely the way to go. This would probably be the one and only time Mercedes would ever be able to take a ride like this, and she was going to enjoy it.

The FASTEN SEAT BELTS sign had been turned off. Arabella moved toward the plane's tiny kitchen. "I'm going to make myself a cup of coffee and have a sandwich. Being on an airplane always makes me hungry. They put drinks and sandwiches and chips on these longer flights. There will be ham and cheese on rye, tuna on wheat, and roast beef with cheese on a roll. It's pretty good. The caterer in Little Rock makes the sandwiches fresh for each flight. Not every place does that. Sometimes the sandwiches taste like cardboard. The catering in the south is usually better than it is in other places in the country. We're lucky. Can I get you some hot tea or a soda?"

"I'll take the roast beef and a ginger ale if you have it. I want to sleep, and the tea might keep me awake." Mercedes pulled her phone from her carry-on and read her email from Rose Lutzy.

> "So glad to hear from you. Hope you are better. Thought I saw someone in your house. But no lights at night. I decided it was Maria there on the wrong day. Saw your car drive away. Almost called the cops. Then your car came back. Let me know if I can bring soup or food or if you need anything. Love you, too. Rose"

Mercedes adored her neighbor Rose, and they'd had many fun times together. She wondered when she would see Rose again. Rose would worry if Mercedes did not return to Camelback Creek in the fall.

■ ■ ■ ■

"You need to eliminate him as soon as possible. We had no idea this would turn into such a disaster. I don't care how you do it, but you have to be sure he doesn't talk. His English isn't any good, but our tech guy says the FBI knows now that he's an Iranian. They probably already have a Farsi speaker

in that jail cell. He won't be able to hold out for very long. You have to take care of this. He was supposed to be dead by now, and he was supposed to have taken a plane load of Americans down with him."

◾ ◾ ◾ ◾

"I also hate it that we are going to have to involve someone else, but it's the only way. We have to get someone into the facility to assassinate the idiot Iranian. The FBI knows he took a taxi to the airport, and they are going after the taxi driver. There are not as many security cameras on the streets in the U.S. as there are in Great Britain, but there are enough. You can't get away with things like you could before 9/11. It's a whole new world. We have to end this now."

Chapter 7

Mercedes didn't usually sleep on airplanes, but she'd never before been able to lie down completely with two blankets over her. She was sound asleep when Agent Barnes gently shook her to wake her from her slumber. "We are almost ready to land in Halifax. You had a great night's sleep, and so did I. They must have put something in those sandwiches."

Mercedes tried to rouse herself. "I didn't even brush my teeth last night. I always brush my teeth." She found her toothbrush and toothpaste and a bottle of water and made her way carefully to the bathroom. She quickly brushed her teeth and washed her face with warm water and paper towels from the dispenser. She still felt gritty and told herself she was too old for this kind of slapdash hygiene. She longed to go back to sleep, but she gave herself a little pep talk. Her adventure was scarcely underway. She could not lose heart yet. Her new life was about to begin. When she told herself that, she almost broke down and cried. She wanted her old life back. She didn't want this new life at all. She wondered how her children and grandchildren were. She missed her friend and neighbor Rose Lutzy. She wished she were anywhere but in a plane circling over the city of Halifax in Canada. She was desperate to keep herself from collapsing into self-pity and depression. Coffee would help. That's what she needed.

It was as if Agent Barnes had read her mind. There was a container of hot coffee with cream and sugar in the cup holder next to where Mercedes had been sleeping. She put her toothbrush and toothpaste away in her carry-on bag. She sat down, fastened her seat belt, and began to get some much-needed warmth and caffeine into her veins. She had decided to try a new approach with her attitude. She was going to try to place herself as a character in one of her mystery novels. She would play the part of the character she was building for the story. She would say out loud the lines her character would be expected to speak. This new strategy might help her get through the next hours and days.

The FASTEN SEAT BELTS sign came on, and within a few minutes they had landed and were taxiing to a hangar. Inside the hangar, there was a car waiting for them. By the time Mercedes had made her way down the ramp to the car, someone had stowed her suitcases in the trunk. Agent Barnes was holding her carry-on bag, and in a couple of minutes they were out of the airport and on a highway heading who knows where. It was still dark outside, but the sun was threatening to come up as they drove south from Halifax toward the FBI safe house that would be Mercedes' new temporary home. She shivered although the heat in the car was blasting. The driver of the car had not turned around or spoken a word to her or to Agent Barnes. Mercedes felt as if she wasn't really there. She felt as if she wasn't really anywhere. Maybe she had died in her sleep on the plane? Maybe this was not really happening to her? She lapsed back into her book character and tried to pull herself out of her funk. She wondered if she would feel better when the sun came up.

It was difficult to tell exactly when the sun came up, if in fact it had come up at all. The sky seemed to be lighter, but she still could not see anything out of the windows of the car. The windows were tinted for security purposes. Mercedes understood that. All she could see outside the windows was fog. "Is it always this foggy in Nova Scotia? I can't see anything."

"March is not the best time of year here, I'm told. I've only been here a couple of times before. Once was in the summer, and it was lovely then. There's a lot of rain and fog this time of year. We're traveling on a pretty desolate road in a pretty desolate part of the country. I promise you, the view will improve once you get to the house. The weather might not improve, but when the sun comes out, you will be wowed by the views of the water."

The photographs Mercedes had seen of the house where she would be living indicated that the house was on the water. It was difficult to tell from the photos, exactly how far away the house was from the shore, but she was living for that view from the sunroom of the cottage. If there was a fireplace and a comfortable chair in the room, as the pictures showed there was, she would be able to write at that table.

Writing was her drug, her passion. Writing made her happy. If she could throw herself into her writing, she would be all right. She could get through this difficult transition in her life. She could recover from the trauma of this change and begin to look forward to the future. In her writing, she could find herself again. She finally dozed off and slept until the car stopped.

The house looked exactly as it had in the photographs. Arabella told her that the house had a name. It was called Baird House. The wide, white clapboards were accented with black shutters and a black door. Its charming twin gables made it seem tall. It was sixteen hundred square feet on the first floor. There were supposedly old bedrooms and old bathrooms and lots of storage space on the second and third floors. The owner had not yet had a chance to renovate anything other than the first floor. That was fine with Mercedes. She didn't do second floors of houses any more anyway, let alone even think about ascending to a third floor. The stairway to the second and third floors was closed off behind a door, so she wouldn't have to worry about them.

It was still foggy, so she couldn't see anything beyond the house. There were two steps up to the front door, and there was a railing. Mercedes could do two steps with a railing. The car had stopped right in front of the steps, and she made it to the front door without difficulty. Before she could raise her hand to knock on the door, it was opened by a middle-aged woman in a white apron. She was tall and very thin. Mercedes assumed this was her new housekeeper and cook. She wondered how anyone as thin as this woman was could possibly know anything about food. Mercedes sighed. Somehow they would find a way. Mercedes knew that no one would allow her to starve to death. She knew that lobster abounded in the area. She could order out. If worst came to worst, lobster could be delivered a couple of times a day.

The woman looked cranky and stern until she smiled. Her smile transformed her face and her entire persona. "I was beginning to get worried about you. Hello, Arabella. It's been a long time. I've made your favorite crepes with lingonberries. This must be my new boss." The woman in the apron made this pronouncement clearly, with tongue in cheek, but not in an unfriendly way. Mercedes put out her hand to meet her new housekeeper. "Mercedes Carrington. The crepes sound amazing. When do we eat?"

"Oh, I like you already. You like to eat. I'm Scheherazade MacDougall. Everybody calls me Mac. Ignore the first name. My father was reading *One Thousand and One Nights* when my mother went into labor with me, and he insisted on the name. My mother threatened to kill him when she woke up from the anesthesia and heard what he had decided to call me. Everybody wonders about it, so I tell them everything and get it all out of the way right from the beginning. Do you eat meat? Please tell me you eat meat. You look like you eat meat. Some of the people they bring me these days don't eat anything but tofu. What is it with people? I'd never even heard of a vegan until a few years ago. Vegan cheese isn't cheese. It is something strange and foreign and unhealthy. The term vegan cheese is an oxymoron. I have even been forced to make meals using vegan cheese, and I am hoping and praying you do not eat vegan cheese."

Mercedes was laughing out loud. Agent Barnes was laughing, too. "We are going to get along just fine. We have exactly the same philosophy about vegan cheese. This could be the beginning of a beautiful friendship." Mercedes was greatly relieved. In spite of her extremely thin physique, this woman, Mac, who was to be her new cook and housekeeper, was fabulous. Life was looking up for Mercedes. "Oh, yes ma'am I do like to eat. I'm sure you can tell that from looking at me."

As the luggage was being brought in and Arabella and Mac were catching up, Mercedes looked around her new place. To the left of the front door was the living area with a large living room and fireplace, a dining table with six chairs, and a beautiful, shiny, white and stainless steel kitchen. The appliances were obviously new and top-of-the-line, and the room gleamed. On the other side of the front door was a small study. The study opened into the sunroom with windows on three sides that looked out on the water. A welcoming fire burned in the sunroom fireplace. Further down the hall was a large bedroom with yet another fireplace, the handicap accessible bathroom, and a walk-in closet. Mercedes liked the layout and looked forward to having a real tour of Baird House.

"Come and sit down. I squeezed oranges for fresh orange juice just before you arrived. I am going to make the crepes now while you drink your juice. And guess what, we are having Canadian bacon. Yes, we really do eat Canadian bacon here in Canada." Mac laughed at her little joke. Someone had no doubt challenged her at some time about the Canadian bacon, and she was heading off any remarks about it. "And the so-called Vermont maple syrup that's so famous in the states. Well ten to one, it comes from Nova Scotia or from this part of Canada. It is in fact Canadian maple syrup. That Vermont name is just to convince you Yanks to buy it. So we are having, for your first meal in Nova Scotia, Canadian bacon and Canadian maple syrup." Mac paused and added, "And Swedish pancakes."

They sat down to a grand feast. Mercedes loved the crepes and the bacon and the syrup. She indulged in seconds on everything. Mac was funny and talkative and efficient. She obviously knew her way around the kitchen. She told Mercedes to put her dirty clothes in the laundry hamper in the bathroom. If there were any special instructions about how to wash her clothes, Mac wanted to know about it.

Arabella had to leave to go back to the plane to return to Little Rock. The driver of their car had dropped them off and driven away. Arabella called him to return to pick her up. She said goodbye to Mac and to Mercedes. She was in a rush. She squeezed Mercedes' hand. "I will be calling you and emailing you with updates about what's happening, and I will be back with Agent Wilton one of these days. See you soon. Stay away from town." Arabella smiled and rushed out the door.

"You could probably sleep for a week. Let me show you around and get you settled." Mac had already unpacked Mercedes' suitcases. She'd left the carry-on for Mercedes to unpack. She showed Mercedes where the towels were and where other important things were kept. "I'm going to leave you now. You'll want a shower and a nap. Your boxes are scheduled to arrive day after tomorrow. You won't want any lunch after that huge breakfast, so I will wake you up in time for dinner. On weekdays I stay until after I've cleaned up from dinner. But I will tell you all about my schedule later." The hot water heater is new, and it's the on-demand type. It may take a couple of minutes to get hot, but once it gets going, you'll never run out. I don't care for most new-fangled things, but I love this one."

Mercedes put her dirty clothes in the laundry hamper as directed, turned on the hot water, and stepped into the enormous shower with the perfectly placed built-in bench. She washed her hair. She found her nightgowns in exactly the spot where she would have put them, if she'd put her clothes away herself. Her anxiety had melted away almost completely. Who could be anxious with all those Swedish crepes in their stomach? She fell into the clean sheets on the queen-size bed. Life was looking up, really looking up.

Chapter 8

"*She's an actress, and she's a very good one. We have used her before. She knows the stakes, and she is being paid quite generously.* She loves the money, of course, but I also happen to know she loves the challenge and the risk of playing these roles. She will be perfect. You don't have anybody else in mind, do you?"

"Of course I don't have anybody else in mind. You know that. I just worry she may not have what it takes to carry this off. It's critical that she is able to imitate the voice. And her face is not perfect."

"No, her face is not perfect. It is not as round as Carrington's face, but we are going to have her use cheek implants when she's in public. We have an excellent make-up person who can work miracles, as you know. And we have the wigs. With all that white hair as a magnificent distraction, no one is going to look too closely at her face anyway. Of course, we are not going to put her out in public very often, if at all. We want everyone, and I mean everyone—the press, the enemy, the American public, and the rest of the people in the FBI—to believe we are keeping her very much under wraps. That's what we are doing with the real Mercedes Carrington, and that's what we are going to do with the decoy."

Ridley Wilton was running several parallel operations. One was known only to a handful of his closest and most trusted agents, the agents in Little Rock. The other operation involved handling and hiding a decoy as if she were in fact the true hero, the woman who had stopped the hijacking on Flight #66. Because there were inevitably so many leaks in a huge organization such as the FBI, it was essential that the location of the real Mercedes Carrington be known to almost no one. The FBI as a whole knew that they were hiding the elderly woman who had saved so many lives. Only a few of those outside Wilton's very small inner circle were even privy to what was going on with the seclusion of the stand-in hero. Ridley Wilton was going to do everything he could to run both operations and make this work. It would not be easy.

The press and the public were hungry for information about the older woman who had taken down the hijacker with her cane. Who could not be fascinated with the story? It was a once-in-a-lifetime phenomenon. It was unbelievable. It was uplifting. But it had to be handled with the utmost care and discretion.

Now that the real Mercedes Carrington was safely ensconced outside the country, Ridley Wilton could turn his full attention to the protection of his pretend Mercedes Carrington and to figuring out who had inspired, recruited, and paid the Iranian hijacker. Everyone believed, according to the twenty-four hour cable news channels, that the woman who had taken down the hijacker was still in Little Rock, laying low and recovering from her heroic effort. She was old and she had performed a prodigious feat. Everyone could understand that she would need a few days to recover from what she had done.

Rumors had been spread around that she was in seclusion, that she had been taken to the University of Arkansas Medical Center with a heart attack, that she'd suffered a stroke as a result of the excitement on the plane, that she was staying with friends who lived in Little Rock, that she had gone to stay with one of her children who lived in New Mexico, that she had died, that she had been handed over to the U.S. Marshals and entered the Federal Witness Protection Program. Some of these stories had been put out intentionally to add to the confusion and to give the news channels something to speculate about and discuss. Other rumors had sprung up on their own. Nothing could be confirmed for sure, and no one had been able to find the woman to interview her.

And no one was certain what the woman's real name was. The passenger manifest from Flight #66 listed her as Edwina Carroll from Ardmore, Pennsylvania. She had been on a flight from Phoenix headed for Philadelphia, so it made sense that she lived in the Philadelphia area. A woman named Edwina Carroll had lived in Ardmore for many years, but she had sold her house and moved into an assisted living facility. Neighbors said she had been reclusive. She had dementia, one neighbor said, and no one knew anything about where her assisted living facility was located. No one was able to find her or the assisted living facility, anywhere, in any state in the United States. Edwina Carroll supposedly owned a home in Sedona, Arizona, but no one could find any record of that either. Edwina had disappeared. Or maybe Edwina was not really her name? The mystery surrounding the woman was compounded.

In spite of the fact that Edwina was said to live in Philadelphia, one story which came out about the woman who had become a national hero was that she had an airline ticket with a connection in Philadelphia. This ticket supposedly confirmed that she intended to continue her trip on a commuter flight to Salisbury, Maryland. No Edwina Carroll could be found in Salisbury, Maryland either. Most concluded, therefore, that it made sense to ignore the rumor that the woman had intended to continue her trip on to Maryland.

To add to the confusion over her name, a video taken in the underground parking garage at FBI headquarters in Little Rock claimed that the woman in the cell-phone video was the heroic woman who had taken down the hijacker on Flight #66. The woman in the video that had been photographed in the FBI's parking garage looked nothing like the woman on the news reports, but she did look a lot like a homeless person. The video taken at FBI headquarters showed a shrieking woman in a wheelchair. She was wrapped in a dirty scarf and wore an ugly knit cap on her head. She had odd curly brown hair that stuck out from underneath the knit cap in wisps. She appeared to be a bit mad. She screamed at the photographer that her name was Agnes MacGillicutty. She said she lived in a cardboard box under a bridge in New York City. The cell phone video showed a bizarre encounter with a bizarre individual.

The FBI claimed MacGillicutty had been brought to their attention and transported to their headquarters on a matter that was entirely unrelated to the hijacked airplane. It was a confusing mess. No one knew anything for sure. Speculation ran wild. The stories multiplied upon themselves in the absence of any real information.

The FBI kept making pronouncements that they could not make any comments about an on-going investigation. Their first priority was to protect the identity and the privacy of their primary witness against the hijacker. They did not know if her life was in danger, but they were doing everything possible to keep her safe. They repeatedly made these same obtuse statements about why they could not give out any real information. It was chaos. This was exactly how Agent Ridley Wilton hoped it would remain for as long as possible. For now, the less the press and the public knew about anything, the better.

Someone leaked to the press that the hijacker had been identified as being from Iran. Supposedly, his DNA had shown him to be almost one hundred percent Iranian, and this had led law enforcement to examine his possible ties to Hamas and Hezbollah. The FBI once again trotted out its slogan "If you see something, say something." Of course what this really meant was that you could not say anything about anybody that was politically incorrect or might be interpreted as being xenophobic, so it was basically the "hot air slogan."

There were denunciations about racism. One talking head called for the country to just get over assuming that all terrorists were of Arab descent. Of course, as another pundit pointed out, that was clearly not the case here. He reminded the television audience of what most people already knew, that people from Iran were Persians and were not Arabs at all. It was amazing what people could think of to say when faced with a vacuum.

AGENT ARABELLA BARNES REPORTED BACK to her boss. The trip to Nova Scotia had gone well. Mac and Mercedes were going to get along fine. Mercedes was definitely depressed, but she seemed to like the house.

"Of course, the trip you took to Nova Scotia never occurred. I have fixed the logs so no one knows the plane was ever out of the hangar. I know the pilots, and they never made the trip. They were not FBI. I called in a favor. They never flew that little jet, and neither they nor the plane have been to Nova Scotia in months. My computer people don't know why they've had to wipe the flight plans, but they did it. You were here in Little Rock babysitting Edwina Carroll, whose name we are not disclosing. You have not been out of the country for almost a year."

"All true, sir. Charles met me and did a quick clean-up of the interior of the plane. He replenished the drinks and the coffee. I brought the leftover sandwiches with me. As long as you can make those air miles disappear, there will be no evidence that any flight to anywhere ever took place. Have Bobby and Stephanie taken care of their end?"

"They were in Delaware last night and worked with infrared goggles. No lights were turned on in the house. It took several hours, but they said they found almost everything Mercedes wanted. She is amazing. She knows exactly where everything is, and I do mean exactly. Her instructions were quite precise. I mean, what kind of person knows where every one of their sweaters is kept? I am pretty organized, but I can't hold a candle to this woman. She remembers it all. I've made fun of her in my own mind for being so meticulous, but it made the job at the house in Lewes much easier. They found almost everything. There were two things they couldn't find, but nothing important. These were things the housekeeper could have moved. They boxed it all up. A phony electric company meter reader's utility van arrived very early this morning and parked behind the house. They were able to load the boxes into the van before the sun came up. One of Mercedes' neighbors doesn't live there in the winter, anyway, and only comes for the spring and summer. So there wasn't anyone at home in the house on one side. They think they accomplished their part of the mission without anyone suspecting anything. Let's hope that's true." Ridley had been concerned about sending his people into the house in Lewes and bringing out a bunch of packed boxes. It had gone well, and he was relieved.

"Won't the housekeeper notice that stuff is gone from the house?" Arabella asked.

"We had the daughter call her and tell her she was coming by the house to pick up a few things to send to her mother. Most of the things they packed up were from dresser drawers and desk drawers and filing cabinets. A few things were in the closets, but I have a feeling that housekeeper is not going to notice much. If she notices something is missing, she will assume the daughter took it." Ridley had tried to cover all the bases. There were many moving pieces in this operation and many people who had to be fooled about what was going on.

Arabella summed up what Mercedes' friends in Delaware and Arizona were supposed to think. "So Mercedes' Arizona friends and neighbors will think, as of next Wednesday, that she has returned to her house in Delaware. And her friends and neighbors in Delaware believe she's decided to stay longer in Arizona to organize and oversee packing up her furniture and household belongings to get her house ready to sell. They know she planned to put the Scottsdale house on the market and has purchased a new condominium. So for now the Delaware people believe she is in Arizona."

"We think and hope they believe it, but they won't buy that story forever. They know she won't stay in Scottsdale during the summer. We can get away with saying she's there until it gets really hot. Then we have to have her be someplace else. So, that's the plan. We will put out the word with her Delaware people that her house in Scottsdale has sold. The story will be that she is staying there to supervise moving the rest of her furniture out of the house. That will give us more time."

"You know, Ridley, that sale is, sooner or later, going to happen for real. And my guess is it will happen sooner. The real estate market in Arizona is on fire right now. Mercedes has a wonderful house in a much-sought-after development in Scottsdale. Camelback Creek is an older development. It has a famous golf course. The houses and the lots are large and beautiful. The homes are very well-built, and most of them have been wonderfully maintained. Her house won't be on the market very long. What are we going to do when the house really does sell, and she has to move her furniture out? She isn't going to fly to Scottsdale to take care of that, and her neighbors, especially Rose Lutzy, are not going to believe she would allow someone else to clean the house out for her."

Ridley had an answer for her question. "We think we have that covered. Her daughter who lives in Colorado has agreed to put in an appearance for us at the Arizona house. She's not going to do much actual decision-making about the furniture. We will have our people sort things out...armed, of course, with careful instructions and multiple detailed lists from Mercedes. You can count on that for sure. The house has been staged, so there is minimal furniture remaining there anyway. And there's no 'stuff' left. She gave away a couple of truckloads of things to the Goodwill. The boxes she packed up before she left went to two places. Several boxes were sent to Delaware. Quite a few pieces of furniture and a lot of boxes were put in storage in Arizona. Those will go to her new condo in Scottsdale when it has been completed. Some of the furniture may stay with the house, depending on who buys it. Mercedes has told us exactly what to do with everything. Of course she has!"

Agent Wilton cringed a bit. He had grown fond of Mercedes Carrington, but she was very exacting about her possessions. She knew precisely where she wanted every piece of furniture and every box to go. She had inventories on her computer about the contents of every cardboard box and plastic container she had packed. The boxes were numbered. Wilton was amazed that she was so organized. It bordered on OCD in his opinion. But he had decided that because she knew exactly where every article of clothing and every one of her pots and pans was located, her compulsive organizing had ended up saving his people time and effort. He was thankful for her OCD and the countless lists of what was to go where. He didn't know how she could possibly keep it all straight, but he was willing to go along with her playbook.

Arabella was thinking ahead about what would happen after the house was sold. "I am assuming the Colorado daughter knows Rose. Rose will want to visit with the daughter and find out everything about how Mercedes is doing. We don't want the daughter to have to spend too much time with Rose or have to tell Rose too many lies."

"We've taken care of that. The daughter will fly in to meet with the movers, who will actually be our people. She will drop by Rose's house to say hello and tell Rose she's only in Arizona for one day to be sure the movers get everything going to the right places. She will be polite but won't stay around to chat. Rose will get it that Mercedes does not want to take another long plane flight out to Phoenix to oversee what's left of the furniture in the house. But Rose is very outgoing and very social, and she will want the daughter to come for lunch or for dinner. She also knows that all three of Mercedes' daughters have high-powered jobs they can't easily get away from. She will understand that the Colorado daughter has to accomplish her task and get back to work. I'm not worried about that piece of our puzzle. That may be the only piece I'm not worried about."

"So what are you worried about?" Arabella didn't think Ridley Wilton ever seriously worried about anything. He seemed to have everything under control at all times.

"I've already touched on this big problem. I am concerned that her Delaware friends will think it's odd that Mercedes isn't coming back to Lewes for the summer. Those East Coast people know she wouldn't stay in Arizona for all that unbearably hot weather. To try to cover that contingency we are thinking of planning an imaginary trip to the Oregon Coast for Mercedes for the summer months. The Arizona crowd thinks she is in Delaware for the summer. That makes sense. But will the Delaware people buy the story that she is spending the summer in Oregon? She's never done that before, so why in the world would she decide to do it now? We have to come up with something better than that, something more believable."

"Doesn't Mercedes have some kind of housekeeper or help in Delaware that comes in several days a week? What has the housekeeper been told about why Mercedes hasn't come back to Lewes?"

"Mercedes pays this woman a full salary even during the winter when she's in Arizona. She doesn't want to lose her housekeeper, so she pays her for basically doing nothing for several months. The woman comes in and checks on things. She will forward the mail, and she scolds and pays the landscaping people. She's supposed to change the batteries in the smoke detectors when they go bad which I guess she doesn't really know how to do. Whatever. She makes sure none of the toilets have overflowed and none of the pipes have burst...things like that. It's an old house.

"Mercedes also pays her cleaning people to come in and clean when she isn't there. They come in and clean, even when there's nothing to clean. Maybe they keep the dust down. She doesn't want to lose them either. I guess it's difficult to find good help, so if you have someone you like, you do whatever it takes to hang on to them. You are happy to pay them to do nothing. Mercedes told her housekeeper, before she left for Scottsdale last fall, that she was going to put her Arizona house on the market. She said she would probably have to stay out west longer this year to pack up everything and get the house ready. Because Mercedes told them ahead of time that all of this was going to happen, the housekeeper and the cleaning people didn't expect Mercedes to be back by the end of March as she usually is."

"I'd have thought Mercedes would have let her housekeeper in Lewes know when she was coming home. She would have wanted the house clean and everything ready for her return. Didn't she communicate with the woman before she got on Flight #66? I'm surprised the housekeeper didn't panic when Mercedes failed to show up."

"We have the daughter in Delaware to thank for avoiding that drama. When she heard from her mother that she was staying at a hotel in Little Rock, Emma, the daughter who lives in Delaware, immediately let the housekeeper know that her mother would not be home that night as expected. The plans had changed. It is everyone's good fortune that the daughter didn't mention why her mother was delayed. Emma told Penny, the housekeeper, not to expect Mercedes. Later the daughter called Penny and explained more fully that, at the last minute, her mother thought she had a contract on her house in Scottsdale. Emma told her that Mercedes had decided to extend her stay in Arizona to take care of business there. So Penny is not expecting Mercedes for a while. However, the problem now is how to explain to everyone in Lewes why Mercedes will not be there for the summer. That's my current conundrum."

"We could have her break her hip." Agent Barnes was joking, but Ridley Wilton's eyes lit up. "That is not a bad idea at all. Let me think about that. We don't have to come up with an excuse for several weeks yet. But I like the way you think."

■ ■ ■ ■

"The cost to pay someone to kill him is not an issue. Whatever you have to pay someone to snuff this incompetent joker, pay it. He has to be taken out before he starts talking. It should have been done yesterday or the day before. Whatever he says can only lead the FBI back so far, even if he tells them everything he knows. They will peel away at the layers until they have figured it out. With this one, they will put forth the effort to do that. We did not accomplish what we'd intended to do, but we have succeeded in raising the level of fear in the country. The American public believes that the Islamic threat has returned, not that they ever really believed it had gone away. We have more incidents planned, but we are going to let this one play out and stoke as much anger and resentment as possible. Even in failure, we have been able to get the Americans stirred up about Islamic terrorists again." He laughed.

Chapter 9

"Yeah, those Feebs thought there were only the two of you watching them in the underground garage. They never knew I was hiding behind the cars. They never knew I was there. They didn't know I recorded the whole thing with that MacGillicutty woman in her wheelchair. I feel bad for you two guys, but this was the way we planned it. They must have been shocked, after they'd confiscated the video camera and both of your cell phones, when that video of Agnes showed up on TV. I wonder if they realized even then that there had been a third person in on it. Anyway, we got a lot of money for that little cell phone video. It was everywhere."

"Easy for you to say, Josh. You didn't spend two nights in jail like Gary and I did. And you don't have an arrest on your record. I mean, it is a kind of badge of honor for a journalist to be arrested. Look at that woman, Judith Miller. She went to jail rather than give up a source." Rocco was trying to find something positive to say about his having been arrested. "And, that's a very honorable thing for a journalist... to be jailed because you are sticking by your principles. But we were jailed for trespassing, disorderly conduct, resisting arrest, loitering, disturbing the peace, and a bunch of other stupid, dippy reasons. There was nothing honorable about that, nothing. Just jackass BS charges made up and exaggerated because they were pissed that we were there. It was a public parking garage after all. There was no trespassing. Spending two nights in jail is no picnic either, let me tell you."

"You got your share of the money, didn't you?"

"My parents made me use the money to pay my lawyer to get me out of jail and get a PBJ sentence in court. I don't have anything left from that money now."

"Well, I think we should stick with this story. I know Gary has bailed, but you don't want to drop it, do you?"

"Talk me into not dropping it." Rocco challenged Josh.

"Okay. I think that woman, Agnes MacGillicutty, the one in the wheelchair, is the woman who took down the hijacker. I don't think she is just a homeless person the FBI happened to be taking up to their offices."

"All right, Mr. Smarty, why do you think the woman in the wheelchair was the mysterious Flight #66 hero and not the woman who said she lives under the Verrazzano-Narrows Bridge?"

"If she lived under that bridge, she'd have been taken to FBI headquarters in New York City. She would never have been brought here, no matter what she'd done. Little Rock, Arkansas is a long way for a homeless person to travel from New York, even if it is compliments of the FBI. The FBI would never have transported her all the way from New York City to Little Rock. Homeless people stay on their own turf. You know that. The second reason is the timing. We were in the underground parking garage the morning after the incident on the plane. If I were the FBI, I would have put the woman up in a hotel for the night, fed her, given her medical care if she needed it, kept an agent with her, and brought her in to FBI headquarters the next morning to give recorded testimony, a deposition, something official. The woman is old. She did something extraordinary on that plane, something most men wouldn't have attempted. She could have a heart attack or a stroke as a result of all that unaccustomed physical activity. Something bad could happen to her, something completely unrelated to the plane flight, just because she's old. The FBI are probably afraid she'll kick the bucket before they can get her into court." Josh looked at his fellow investigative journalist to see if he was paying attention. He was.

"I'd have taken her down to FBI headquarters first thing the next day and have her give a sworn deposition, and I would have videotaped her statement. Think about it. They put her in a disguise, but they couldn't hide the fact that she can't walk very well. We know she uses a cane. Everybody in the world knows that. She probably has to use a wheelchair, too, sometimes. My granny used a cane around the house, but when she went out someplace, she used a wheelchair. That's what happens when people get old. They use a cane for short distances, but they have to have that wheelchair for long distances and going to unfamiliar places. That's what my granny used to say anyway. It makes sense."

Josh continued. "Then there is the security thing. Do you think the FBI would have had all those security people around if they'd just been transporting a homeless nobody up to their offices? No way would they have had all those agents standing guard if they'd just brought in some I-am-not-the-hero homeless woman. The woman we photographed was somebody important, and who else would she be but our Flight #66 hero? Are you with me?"

"Okay, so what if she is the woman who took down the hijacker? She's disappeared now. You didn't stick around and wait until she left FBI headquarters. If one of us had been there, we might have followed the car that took her back to her hotel. Then we would have known what hotel she was staying in. We could have staked out the hotel. But, because two of us were arrested and taken to jail, we didn't have anybody else there to do that. So it's another dead end." Rocco always took a negative view of the situation.

"It is not a dead end. Even though we weren't able to follow her, I will bet she was staying in a hotel either close to FBI headquarters or close to the airport. If you were the FBI and you knew you were going to bring the woman in the next morning to question her or take a deposition, wouldn't you put her up at a hotel close to the FBI offices?" Josh was sure he'd figured it all out.

Josh continued. "I used to date a girl who worked the desk at the Marriott which is across the street from the Capital Hotel. Federal Marshals stayed at the Marriott when they didn't have a witness they were protecting. But when they had a witness with them, they stayed with the witness at the Capital Hotel. I know this to be a fact. Everybody who works at the Marriott and at the Capitol Hotel knows this is how they do things. The Marriott is a zoo with a million people in the lobby all the time and bus tours coming and going constantly. The Capital is much less crazy. It is smaller and quieter. It has that side door near the elevator, a perfect place for entering and exiting without having to traipse through the main lobby. I will bet you anything they had her staying at the Capital. The food is good there. They have nice rooms, and lots of the rooms are suites. It's a classy place. She might have had to have a room for a handicapped person. My granny had to have a special handicap shower when she got old. Then she stopped traveling. I will bet, if we hacked into the Capital Hotel's reservations database, we would find that on the Tuesday night in question, someone was staying in their most expensive available handicap-accessible suite. The FBI gets a special room rate. Don't kid yourself. They aren't paying full fare. She probably stayed two or three nights, depending on what kind of condition she was in. Two nights only if they were smart. They would have had to let her rest. Old people get tired easily. She'd had two long days, and she would have been real tired. She would have needed some time to rest. She might even have been hurt. She might have sprained something or hurt her hands beating on that guy. They could have brought a doctor in to see about her injuries. But the longer she stayed at the hotel, the greater the chance somebody would find out she was there. So, they would have wanted to get her out of town, and preferably out of the country, and into hiding as soon as possible. That's the way they do things."

"How do you know so much about all of this? I know you know about old people because your granny lived with you for a long time. But how do you know so much about the FBI and how they operate?"

"I read thrillers. I read books about the FBI and the CIA and the NSA. I like to educate myself. I learn stuff that way. You ought to try it sometime."

"All right. So the woman is probably staying at the Capital Hotel. We don't know anything about what happened to her after she left there, if she's left."

"You have to put yourself in the shoes of the FBI. You have to think like they think. They would want to get her out of Little Rock and someplace far away, a place where no one would think to look for her, someplace remote. Or at least, that's what I would have done if I was in charge of it. The airport is only a short drive from the Capital Hotel. They would have driven her to the airport and put her on a private jet, a plane owned by the federal government, and flown her someplace very obscure. I think they would have liked to get her out of the country, but maybe she wouldn't go along with that. She looked and sounded pretty feisty to me in the parking garage. I will bet she has a mind of her own and would argue with the FBI about where they wanted to stash her. She wouldn't willingly go anyplace she didn't want to go. And she's this big hero, so they have to be nice to her and pay attention to what she wants and what she doesn't want."

"So they flew her someplace obscure. What good does that do us?" Rocco liked to challenge the always-confident Josh.

"We have to figure out how long she was at the hotel and when she would have flown out of town on the government plane. You need to get hacking into the hotel reservations database, and I need to get out to the airport and see if I can poke around there and find out anything. Since the almost-hijacking, they've tightened security at the airport. This is probably true for all the airports in the country. I may have to get some kind of a job there and get a security clearance in order to even be on the grounds, let alone ask any questions. I'll have to look into it."

Chapter 10

"The open house yesterday was a huge success. Of course, as you know, real estate in sunny Arizona is experiencing an enormous boom right now. I could sell a doghouse for a million bucks if it had a pool and a pantry." Ginger, the real estate lady, was full of jokes, but she loved the money she made selling houses in Paradise Valley and in Scottsdale for much more than they were worth.

"How many people came to the open house? More importantly, did we get any offers?" Now that she had finally put her house on the market, Mercedes was anxious to have it sold.

"There were sixteen different groups who showed up to look, mostly couples. A few people brought their kids. I hate that. But they all loved your house. I had to extend the hours of the open house so everyone had a chance to go through." Ginger was relishing the over-the-top interest that Mercedes' home was attracting. "Your staging was very good, and everyone commented on how much they loved the pool. They wanted to know what company had put it in. I told them you'd designed it. They said it was very old school, a real classic, and everybody oohed and aahed. It was a very big hit. Who knew? But one of the real draws, from the comments of the potential buyers, was the fact that you enlarged the walk-in closet in the main bedroom. It's huge, and the women especially were wild about that, of course. Who doesn't love built-ins? Plenty of room for shoes. The other thing everybody fell in love with was the storage in the front hall, those wall panels that are really cabinet doors that hide the yards of shelving for dishes and everything else. They wanted me to open and close the panels again and again. I was afraid I might break them or wear them out. It's a feature no other house in the area has and one which I don't think most of these people have ever seen before. I'd never seen anything quite like it either. It's brilliant. I know you had that made custom when you built the house. All buyers love storage. You can never have too much storage, but what they love even more is hidden storage that's disguised as something else." The excitement in Ginger's voice was apparent, even over the phone.

She continued. "You got two full-price offers at the open house, but I don't think you should accept either one. Your house is already extremely popular, and I think we will be looking at a major bidding war. I'm putting a new, larger ad in the newspaper and in the company flyers today. I've already raised the price to $1.6 million. I have four calls waiting for me at my office, and I am guessing those phone calls are people from the open house wanting to put in offers. Before I called those people back, I wanted to fill you in on what happened yesterday. If we play our cards right, your house could go for a great deal more than you're asking." Ginger was almost salivating at the prospect of a bidding war. Mercedes knew her real estate agent was a very manipulative extrovert and an incredibly aggressive salesperson. Mercedes had hired the woman because of these qualities. Ginger definitely knew what she was doing. Every year Ginger was one of the most successful real estate sales people in the Phoenix area. She would get top dollar for Mercedes and a top-dollar commission for herself.

"I trust you to do whatever will get me the best price."

"I don't think the house will be on the market for even a week. It's going to go fast, even if we hold out for a much higher price. I know you were thinking about buying another property with the proceeds from this sale. I think you said you were looking in Maine. This wouldn't be the best time to be looking at property in such a cold place, but you need to get moving on finding something. I'll keep you posted." Ginger ended the call.

It seemed that anywhere but southern Arizona or points south was "a cold place" for Ginger. Mercedes had just begun to settle into the Nova Scotia house. She didn't want to think about her Arizona house or looking for a house in Maine. She was crazy about the views at Baird House and the wild and constantly changing March weather of the Canadian province. She spent most of her waking hours in the sunroom that overlooked the Atlantic Ocean. She did her writing by those windows and ate her meals at a small table in front of the fireplace in that room. Mac kept a fire going there. Mercedes' writing was inspired by the new setting.

The waves rolled in and the weather rolled in. The fog was always there...at least for a while every day. There were some sunny hours and a few sunny days, but even when it was raining or snowing, it was incredibly beautiful. Mercedes had fallen in love. She had to have this view, or a similar one. She could never live permanently in Canada, but she knew if she ever bought another house, it would have to overlook the Atlantic Ocean. She decided it was time to get serious about looking at properties in Maine. If things worked out with the sale of her Arizona house, she might be able to afford an ocean front place somewhere in the Pine Tree State.

Mercedes and Mac were getting along famously. Mac came at nine in the morning five days a week. She made Mercedes a nice breakfast and got all of the laundry and housework done before noon. She left Mercedes soup, or a sandwich, or a salad for lunch. She went to another job and came back to Mercedes at 4:30 to fix her dinner. On the weekends she came for two hours on Saturday and Sunday mornings. It was a schedule that worked well for both of them. Mercedes had the house to herself for several hours in the afternoons. This was when she did her best writing. The scenery of southern Nova Scotia and the location on the Atlantic Coast, near the fishing village of Terence Bay, provided the perfect ambiance to inspire the mystery novels Mercedes wrote.

Mercedes had learned to love the rain and fog that were frequent visitors to this part of the Atlantic in March and April. She watched the ocean and its constantly changing colors and shapes from her windows in the cottage sunroom. She listened to the rain pound against the roof and the walls and the window panes. She watched the seagulls. She loved the brave and busy little sandpipers as they pecked and hunted for food on the cold beach. She keep her eyes on the dunes and the tides. She occasionally saw a ship in the distance or a reckless smaller boat riding the waves.

She was inside. She was warm. She felt safe with a fire in the fireplace. She was free to write whatever came into her head. Someone was taking care of her. Mac was making her meals. Mercedes' main responsibility right now was just to stay alive. There was comfort in the simplicity of being required to do only that. She almost never left the sunroom except to sleep. It had become her safe haven, her refuge.

Now she was going to have to think about coming out of her cozy cocoon of warmth and wonderful food and writing. She would have to begin to think about the future. She'd only been in Nova Scotia for a few weeks, but she felt as if she'd lived there forever. Even though this house was not her own, she was comfortable in this place. Sometimes she completely forgot that she was in danger; she forgot that someone out there was looking for her and probably wanted to kill her.

She'd known that one day she was going to have to leave the safety of her seclusion at Baird House and testify in a courtroom. She would have to relive it all and retell the story about what had occurred at 35,000 feet when she'd decided she didn't want to die that day. She'd been able to push this to the back of her mind. She hadn't thought she'd have to face the future quite so soon. But now she was under pressure from her real estate agent. It was a good kind of pressure, she told herself, because her house was going to sell for much more money than she'd ever dreamed it would.

But Mercedes had wanted to retreat from the real world for longer than a few weeks. She didn't want to face the future yet. She needed more of a respite. Hiding at the house in Canada had become that respite for her. She hadn't realized, when she had been told she would have to hide, that being in seclusion would turn out to be a good thing for her. But she had found contentment in getting away from it all. She was enjoying her solitude. She felt as if she was suspended in time at Baird House. No one, or hardly anyone, knew she was here. She liked it that she was someplace nobody knew about, that no one could demand anything of her, that she did not exist anywhere real. She slept late and sometimes wrote long into the night. Looking ahead and having to do something about what would happen next in her life threatened the sphere of psychological protection she had created around herself. She had withdrawn from the world, and she liked the feeling of security her detachment had granted her.

She wondered if it was old age, the recent excitement on the airplane, or moving out of all of her usual comfort zones that caused her sharp pangs of melancholia. She missed her family and her friends, although she heard regularly from all of them. Her children and grandchildren Zoomed and sent emails and texts back and forth with her. They'd sent tin boxes of homemade iced sugar cookies. She really wasn't missing very much of their lives.

She would miss her oldest grandson's baseball season this spring and summer. That had hit her hard and made her very sad. She realized she could kind of follow his games on a phone app called Game Changer. It wasn't the same as being at the ball field, but it was a pretty good substitute. Sometimes her grandson's games were even livestreamed. She loved watching those on her computer. She missed Rose and her other friends from Scottsdale and from Lewes, but they emailed each other almost every day.

Part of her discontent was the thought of having to leave Nova Scotia. As disconcerting as the relocation had been at first, she now loved Baird House and its sunroom and the atmosphere in this unexpected part of the world. She was content in this place. She dreaded the thought of having to move again, of going through another relocation to anywhere. Maybe it really was old age. Maybe her sense of adventure had abandoned her. She didn't want to turn into an old fuddy duddy, but the thought of searching for and buying and moving into a new place overwhelmed and depressed her. Maybe when she began looking at houses in Maine, she would cheer up. Meanwhile, she would enjoy the sunroom and the fireplace and the wingchair where she always sat to eat her meals.

The weather so far had not been conducive to taking walks outside. Mac mentioned every once in a while that she was looking forward to pushing Mercedes in the wheelchair along the paths down by the ocean. It remained to be seen if the wheelchair would be able to make it down those paths. Mercedes knew she couldn't go into town and could not leave the property. Terence Bay was the closest town. It was a tiny fishing village with very few inhabitants. Although not too far from Halifax by car, it seemed a million miles away in ambiance and quality of life.

Mercedes often wondered who had purchased this adorable house and had obviously spent so much effort and money on its loving renovation. It was clearly a vacation house or a retirement house or both for an older person. Who else would put in the enormous shower with a bench in just the right spot or the walk-in bathtub? This is what old people did to make houses comfortable for themselves as they were aging. She'd wondered briefly if she could buy this place and stay here. But she loved her country and wanted to live out the rest of her life and die in the United States of America. She told herself she could wait until she knew exactly how much money she was going to get for her property in Arizona before she began looking at places in Maine.

Chapter 11

The computer Mercedes used for writing had arrived with her boxes from Lewes. She kept a laptop at her house in Arizona and a laptop at her house in Delaware. She transported her book manuscripts from Delaware to Arizona and back on thumb drives. This was so much easier than carrying a computer on the airplane. Mercedes' east coast computer was old, but she was used to it. Her arthritic fingers flew across the keyboard, trying to keep up with the words and ideas that flowed from her imagination.

For years, she had used this computer to write as well as to do research on the internet. During the COVID-19 pandemic of 2020, she'd used it to Zoom with her kids and grandkids and with the members of her Ohio high school's graduating class from 1962. They lived all over the country now, but they'd had a wonderful time reuniting on Zoom during the long days of quarantining.

Now Mercedes had two computers on the East Coast. Because of her current status as a person in hiding, she could no longer use her old standby computer to access the internet. She was still allowed to use the computer she had always used to write her manuscripts. But Stephanie Abramowitz or Bobby O'Connor had fixed that computer so she could not use it to access the internet or for Zoom calls or emails or for anything but writing.

Mercedes had bought a second computer that the FBI had chosen. The FBI had programmed the new computer just as they had programmed her new phone. She could use her new computer to access the internet and send emails and all of that, but no one would be able to tell where she really was when she used the special computer. The computer was clever. It pretended it was in Delaware when emailing or Zooming with certain people. It pretended it was in Arizona when it emailed or Zoomed with others. The FBI hoped no one was monitoring anything at all about what Mercedes Carrington was doing because they hoped that no one had any idea who she was. But in an abundance of caution, and just in case, she could use only her "magical computer" when interacting with the rest of the world.

Using her new computer that pretended she was someplace where she really was not, Mercedes began to search the internet again for real estate in and around Bar Harbor, Maine. She had vacationed in Bar Harbor a number of times, so she knew the area pretty well. She'd vacationed in other parts of Maine, and one of her cousins had lived in Brunswick for many years. The parents of her daughter's ex-husband had owned a house in Ogunquit, and Mercedes had spent some time in that area. She'd shopped several times in Freeport. Mercedes also had a very useful large-scale map of the counties of Maine and could find even the smallest places.

Mercedes knew that any place south of Kennebunkport was a traffic nightmare in the summer months. She loved the entire coast of Maine, but if she wanted any solitude or peace and quiet, she would have to be pretty far north. She figured her buddies at the FBI would not want her to live in a traffic-congested tourist area. There were enough tourists and enough traffic in Bar Harbor, especially since large cruise ships had added stops in that charming town to their itineraries. It was great for businesses within walking distance of the harbor, but most home owners in the area did not like the cruise ship invasion.

Ginger was certain Mercedes would sell her Arizona house for at least $1.6 million dollars. Subtracting Ginger's commission and the other taxes and fees she would have to pay at settlement, it appeared as if Mercedes would clear more than a million dollars from the sale of her Scottsdale house.

She searched for ocean front houses in the one million dollar range. There were not many to choose from. Property was ridiculously expensive in the Bar Harbor area. It was a fancy place. Ocean front properties did not come on the market very often. Most of the houses Mercedes found were too expensive and way too big. She did not want a house with six bedrooms, or even four bedrooms. Many ocean front homes were enormous. She wanted a home like Baird House, a smallish, manageable cottage that had the main bedroom on the first floor. She knew that whatever house she bought, she would probably have to renovate the bathroom to make it handicap accessible. She had the money to do that. It didn't matter if there was a second story. She could deal with that. She would use it for storage. She would ignore it or paint it and forget it.

The houses were either too large or too small. They were either too run down and crummy or they were much too expensive. She had looked at everything that was available in her price range. She didn't want to have to build a house. That would take too long. She decided she was going to have to hire a buyer's agent to help her search. Mercedes wondered what name she ought to give when she hired a real estate agent. She emailed Agent Arabella Barnes to ask her.

Agent Barnes emailed her back that the FBI worked with a particular real estate person in the Bar Harbor area. His name was Sam Stevenson. He had helped several witness protection people buy and sell properties in that part of Maine. Mercedes would be able to use her real name when she transacted business with Sam, and she could buy her cottage, when and if she found it, in the name of the limited family partnership that owned her Arizona properties. This answered several questions for Mercedes, and she hoped Sam Stevenson would be able to find her something suitable. Having spent time living in Baird House and enjoying the waterfront views, she was determined to find a similar location in Maine. It would cost a great deal more in Bar Harbor, but Mercedes was not going to settle for something she didn't love. It was too late in her life for mediocrity.

Ginger was keeping her informed about the bidding war for her Scottsdale house. The battle was ramping up. Apparently, there were two buyers who were willing to go to the mat to buy her house. They both seemed to have unlimited funds and were duking it out through their own real estate agents. Ginger was loving every minute of the fight, but her blow by blow description of what was happening was wearing on Mercedes.

Finally, one of the two buyers jumped the price they were offering up to three million dollars. This buyer also offered to pay, on top of the cash she was paying for the house, Ginger's percentage and all of the closing costs.

Mercedes said she didn't think the house was worth three million dollars. Ginger told her the house was worth whatever someone was willing to pay for it. This particular buyer had decided she had to have the hidden storage shelves behind the secret wall panels in the front hall of the house. She was determined to have the house and was willing to pay whatever it took to get it. Mercedes told Ginger to accept the three million dollar offer. She'd had enough. Ginger thought she could squeeze out a few hundred thousand dollars more from the desperation of the buyers, but Mercedes told her to stop.

The deal was done. Settlement would be in sixty days. With the way her housing budget had escalated, Mercedes was less discouraged about the search for her dream cottage in Maine. She might now have the money to buy the perfect place.

More unexpected good news about all the real estate shenanigans came from Mercedes' friend and neighbor, Rose Lutzy. Rose had somehow been privy to the ongoing bidding war over Mercedes' Camelback Creek house. Mercedes was not surprised that Rose had been in the know about the sale and the drama that the sale had generated. Rose was a friend to everyone. She had one of those winning personalities that made everybody love her and want to be her friend. She was also an extraordinary baker. Mercedes was sure that Ginger had succumbed to either Rose's charm or her homemade cookies. She was also sure that Ginger, when she'd talked to Rose, had smelled another listing that might be coming her way. And Rose would not have disabused the real estate lady of that possibility.

When the offers on Mercedes' home had entered the stratosphere, Rose decided to put her own house on the market. It was the right moment to take advantage of the overheated real estate situation in Scottsdale. Rose had always thought she would stay in her house until they carried her out. Her husband had died five years earlier, and Rose had never thought she'd want to leave the home where she and Dennis had lived for more than thirty years.

Then Mercedes had purchased one of the new condos in the Camelback Creek development, and Rose began to look at the modern, smaller, more convenient spaces with fresh eyes. Rose had started to think she might like to sell the big house and move into one of the luxurious condominiums. By that time and even though they were still under construction, they'd all been sold. There was not a single one to be had.

Then the contract to buy the condominium next to Mercedes had fallen through, and the one-bedroom unit came back on the market. Rose didn't know or really care why the contract hadn't worked out, but she jumped on the opportunity. She was ready, and her bid on the brand new condo under construction was accepted. At the same time, she listed her hacienda nestled on its secluded desert acres. The couple who had lost out on purchasing Mercedes' house offered Rose what seemed to her to be a ridiculously large amount of money for her property. Rose accepted the offer. Ironically, the two buyers who had been at loggerheads and had fought it out in what had become a pretty high-stakes and acrimonious battle for Mercedes' house were now going to be next door neighbors. The best part was that Mercedes and Rose were going to be next door neighbors again in their new digs. Someone was watching out for these two old ladies.

Chapter 12

Mercedes' husband of more than half a century had died three years earlier. He had been vigorous up until the end and had died in his sleep at the age of eighty-two. He'd always loved the Kenny Rogers song about knowing when to hold 'em and knowing when to fold 'em. It had of course been a shock and a terrible loss for Mercedes and her children and grandchildren, but they were thankful that their husband and father and grandfather had not had to endure a long and debilitating illness. The best that you can hope for was what had happened to Lincoln Van Fossen Ford. Everyone had called him Ford.

Mercedes and Ford had met each other because of their names. They'd been at a cocktail party, and a mutual friend had introduced them. "Ford," the friend had said, "this lady is a Mercedes. She is classy and beautiful and expensive. She is also smart. Mercedes, this man is both a Lincoln and a Ford. He is elegant, but he is also very dependable. I've always wanted to introduce you two to each other, and today is the day." By the time they married, they'd heard every car joke there was to hear. They made fun of their names, too, and had their own jokes. Ford always deferred to his high-end wife, and he liked to tease that the upkeep on his Mercedes was bankrupting him. Ford frequently mentioned that he was proud to be one-hundred percent made in America.

Ford was an attorney, and their lives had gone from rags to riches as Ford became more and more successful in his legal career. When Ford retired from his position as a federal judge, they sold the house where they'd raised their children and lived and loved and laughed and entertained their many friends during the prime years of their lives. They had always loved Lewes, Delaware and had rented summer houses there during the years when their children were living at home. The couple retired to a wonderful historic house on the Rehoboth and Lewes Canal near downtown Lewes.

They'd enjoyed traveling the world. They spent the winters at their home in Arizona. When Mercedes had been afflicted with debilitating osteoarthritis, they didn't travel as much. They spent more time in warm, dry southern Arizona where Mercedes could spend her afternoons doing laps in their heated swimming pool. Mercedes had embraced a new career as a writer, and Ford had also caught the writer's bug. He'd written a historical biography about one of his relatives who had been an itinerant Presbyterian minister and Civil War hero.

They'd had a good life. Now that Ford was gone, Mercedes found that her house in Scottsdale and her house in Lewes, Delaware were both too large for one person. She loved the houses and her neighborhoods and her neighbors, so letting go was difficult. She had great memories of times with Ford in both these places. Well-fixed financially, Mercedes was an independent woman. She had always been extraordinarily self-sufficient, so the overwhelming loneliness she'd experienced after her husband's death had been unexpected. Rose Lutzy had lost her husband just two years before Ford died, and the two women had begun to spend even more time together.

It was especially galling to Mercedes to have to lie to Rose about what was happening in her life and where she was living and why. Mercedes' children knew what was going on, but in many ways Mercedes was just as close to her friend Rose as she was to people in her family.

Rose would have been thrilled to learn that the mystery woman who had saved the day on the flight from Phoenix to Philadelphia was her good friend and next door neighbor, Mercedes Carrington. The two would have had such a grand time talking about it together and going over and over the whole story. Mercedes would have given Rose a detailed description of the man in the seat in front of her on the airplane. Rose would have laughed out loud at Mercedes' critique on the choices he had made about the scent of his hair gel. Mercedes hated to deprive Rose of the fun of knowing what had happened. Rose would have loved it. Mercedes hoped one day she would be able to share with her dear friend every detail about what had occurred on the plane that day. When you are in your mid-seventies, you never know how many future opportunities for sharing there will be.

Chapter 13

"You know, I'm enjoying the job here at the airport. They figured out right away I was overqualified to be a baggage handler, so they put me in charge of scheduling and overseeing the cleaning and maintenance of the various hangars. I don't actually do any of the cleaning or repairs myself, but I make sure there are people lined up to do it and that they do it on a regular schedule. It took me a few weeks to get up to speed, but now that I've got the hang of it, it's kind of fun. I do it all on my computer and with emails and texts. Once in a while, I have to send somebody to HR because they aren't showing up on time or aren't doing their job. HR does the hiring and the firing." Josh was enjoying his new job and wanted to tell Rocco about it.

"Are you getting anywhere in terms of finding out about Agnes MacGillicutty? That's why you got a job at the airport in the first place. You wanted me to stay with you on this story, and now you've fallen in love with your new job. Where are the big bucks you said we'd make by finding her?" Rocco wanted Josh to focus on the main objective and to hurry up and get the money they were hoping for.

"I haven't forgotten about her. It takes time to build a convincing cover. I am in the process of building trust and getting to know people. I've only been here four weeks. And, my scheduling job takes time. I spend quite a few hours every day actually doing the job I was hired to do. Imagine that? I am getting paid to do this, and I was lucky to get the job. They don't have any idea that I'm a journalist. They saw I had a degree in business, and I am good with computers and databases."

"Because I was in jail, I can't get a good job now." Rocco was pouting.

"Don't put this on me, Rocco. You can't get a good job because you dropped out of college. You partied too much, didn't go to class, and didn't finish your degree. If you want a good job, you ought to go back to school and learn to actually do something."

"I'm a really good photographer, but everybody is a photographer these days. Everybody has a cell phone, and nobody wants to pay anybody else to take photographs for them." Rocco always had an excuse for his lack of employment.

"Stop your whining and go back to school or get a job at McDonald's. I have a really good plan about how to find out if and when Agnes MacGillicutty flew out of Little Rock. But I need access to certain records. I'm working on it. I've been making friends with the woman who takes care of all the paperwork and computer logs for who buys fuel and how much they buy. I need access to the woman's office and to her computer. This is the best way to find out when and how Agnes was spirited away. I'm going to ask the woman who works at the airport to have dinner with me this weekend. Just try to keep your panties from getting in a twist. I'm working on it. These things take time, but once we find the old gal, the payoff will be huge."

Josh had a plan, but he was having second thoughts about keeping Rocco in the loop. He needed a partner, but Rocco was lazy and just wanted the big payoff and the instant gratification. Rocco didn't have any understanding of the long game. Josh was a strategist.

Josh had only been on the job for a few weeks, but he had already identified all the private planes that used hangars at the airport. He knew what companies and government agencies owned these planes and where each of them was kept. He had also identified all the individuals who owned private planes and kept them at the airport. He knew the FBI had a private plane at the airport, and he knew exactly where it stayed all of the time when it was not in the air.

Because Bill and Hillary Clinton had once called Little Rock home and because The Clinton Presidential Library was in Little Rock, the FBI presence in the city was larger than the population of a city its size might normally require. When Clinton was president, the FBI had several planes on call in Little Rock. Now it had one. It was used occasionally. Josh had hacked into the logs. The flight logs indicated that the FBI plane had not left the hangar or the Little Rock airport for eighteen days after the incident on American Airlines Flight #66.

At first Josh was stumped by this. He knew the FBI would have wanted to stash Agnes someplace very far away from Little Rock, and he could not imagine that the FBI had driven the old lady someplace to hide her. They would never have subjected her to a long trip in a car. They had to have flown her someplace, and they would not have allowed her to fly anywhere on a commercial airliner.

Josh knew flight logs could be tampered with and altered to hide things. Entire trips of several thousand miles could be wiped from the computer. Even though the records showed that the FBI's private jet had never left its hangar during the pertinent time frame, Josh did not necessarily believe it. He suspected that the records about the flight he was looking for had been erased. He had a hunch that the FBI plane had actually flown Agnes MacGillicutty out of Little Rock within a few days of her heroic act.

Although he'd only worked at the airport for a short period of time, Josh had figured out there was one database that could not be corrupted and could not be altered. Because somebody had to pay for the fuel to fly every private plane somewhere, Josh wanted to look at the records for who had bought and paid for fuel during the few days that were of interest to him. Because these records involved money, they were more secure from hacking than flight logs, passenger lists, and other kinds of airport data. People paid for their airplane fuel with credit cards or debit cards. It made sense that these computer files were harder to get into.

Josh had a plan. He was trying to make friends with the woman who entered the data about who bought fuel for their planes. He didn't want to be too obvious or come on to strong or too fast with her. She was very professional and strictly business. She would be a tough nut to crack. She wasn't the friendliest person in the world. Josh knew he would have to turn on all of his considerable charm and act really smart.

He had looked at the woman's Facebook page and her Twitter account before he'd struck up his first conversation with her. He knew she liked to cook and liked to read and had two Cavalier King Charles Spaniels as pets. Josh read up everything he could find on the internet about this particular breed of dog. He was hopeless in the kitchen, but he thought he might also have figured out a way to make that work for him. He found a picture of a Cavalier King Charles Spaniel on the internet. He made the internet dog the background wallpaper on his cell phone and adopted the dog as his own.

He named her Elizabeth and decided to call his virtual dog Lizzy. It was no coincidence that the woman he was hoping to romance was named Elizabeth Lacey.

Josh was a journalist. He knew how to sling the bull. He knew how to ask questions. He knew how to get people to talk to him. Elizabeth Lacey would be a challenge, but Josh was determined to do everything he could to get access to her computer. He believed that if he could get into the fueling database, he could find out if anyone had purchased airplane fuel on one of the nights he was guessing the FBI had flown Agnes MacGillicutty out of Little Rock. He already knew how much fuel the FBI's plane used per mile. It wasn't a perfect formula, but he thought he might get some idea how much fuel the plane used and based on that, how far the plane had flown.

As it turned out, Josh's break came from another source entirely. The woman he'd tried to romance, with the phony wallpaper picture of Lizzy, his virtual Cavalier King Charles Spaniel, wasn't biting. He'd not been able to make any headway with her. She'd rebuffed his invitations to lunch and dinner, but he hadn't given up. He was working all the angles.

Josh had been spending considerable time in and around the hangar where the FBI's private jet was warehoused. He'd chatted multiple times with the people who did maintenance on the plane and who worked in the hangar. The FBI had its own mechanics, and no one except those with a special security clearance were allowed to even touch the FBI plane. No one except vetted government employees were allowed to service the jet. But Josh had zeroed in on the man who worked in the area around the FBI jet. This guy's job was to make sure the FBI hangar was clear and clean and ready for the jet to leave at a moment's notice. He made sure the doors to the hangar were always operational and in good shape.

He kept snoopers away from the hangar. He was a long-time airport employee.

Mason Haggarty, who was getting ready to retire at the end of the following year, had been working in the FBI hangar since before the Clinton administration. He had lots of stories about the Clintons and their comings and goings. He had stories of the days when there had been several FBI jets in airport hangars. He knew all about Bill's girlfriends and Hillary's bad temper. During those years, Air Force One was frequently at the Little Rock Airport, but when Bill wanted to slip away for a few hours, he might use one of the smaller jets. The press was always watching the Presidential plane, but few were watching the smaller planes that were kept in more obscure hangars.

Mason loved to talk about those golden days, and Josh was a good listener. If he'd not been focused specifically on the Agnes MacGillicutty story, he would have latched onto the secrets his new friend Mason was telling him. There were quite a few juicy stories in Mason's repertoire. At first Josh listened, and then he began to ask a few questions. He asked Mason how many small FBI jets had been kept at the airport during the Clinton years. He asked Mason if anyone ever used the one FBI jet that was still here, given that the Clintons no longer came to Little Rock. He asked Mason where the FBI plane flew... if it flew anywhere at all these days. He asked Mason when was the last time the FBI jet had gone anywhere.

Mason rambled when he talked. He tried to stay on the subject but got sidetracked by stories that popped into his mind. He talked about the different people who had been the head agents at the FBI in Little Rock in the past 30 years. He talked about where they liked to take the plane. Josh was mostly interested in where the plane had been in the past few months and weeks, but he listened to all of it. That's what a good journalist does.

He finally got Mason to talk about the FBI's current head honcho in Little Rock. It seemed the man liked to fly to Canada. Most of the previous top agents didn't fly the plane out of the country, but this top FBI guy flew to YHZ several times a year. Because Mason was an airport person, he frequently referred to other airports by their airport codes. YHZ was Halifax Stanfield International Airport in Goffs, Nova Scotia.

As he was telling his story to Josh, he got off onto the subject of the codes for various airports. He said that LIT made perfect sense as the airport code for Little Rock. The Canadians, for some odd reason Mason had never been able to figure out, used a "Y" as the first letter for all their country's airport codes. He talked about how YHZ made no sense at all. YHZ was for Halifax in Nova Scotia. He'd always thought it would be better if it was called YHX, not YHZ. Nobody, unless you already knew what YHZ meant, could figure it out. YHX made much more sense. Josh had to agree with Mason on that one.

"Why would the plane be flying there anyway? I didn't think the FBI operated outside the United States. Didn't you say the FBI jet flies there several times a year? When was the last time the jet flew to YHZ?"

"I think they fly witnesses and people like that up to YHZ. I don't know anything for sure, of course, but that's my opinion. This top agent must have a secret place like a safe house or something up there, to make so many trips every year. I have no idea why he goes there so often. The top guy in Little Rock before him liked to fly to Idaho. The jet went to COE quite a bit back then. COE is Coeur D'Alene. It's a very remote place in northern Idaho, close to Canada. Maybe all these FBI guys like to stash their secret witnesses in Canada."

"So, when was the last time the plane was out of the hangar? It seems like kind of a waste to have a plane parked here if no one ever uses it."

"Well, they use it more than they want to admit. I know that for a fact. They fly places and then they erase the flight logs, when they don't want anybody to know they've made a flight. Big secret stuff. Not every flight is a big secret, but more of them than you'd think get erased from the books. Sometimes the FBI uses the government plane but doesn't use the FBI pilots. I've not figured out why they do that, and I don't really think it's because they are using the plane for personal travel. This latest top guy in Little Rock is a real straight shooter. He's strict about expense accounts and not doing personal stuff on FBI time. Some are stricter than others."

"So if he's using the plane, it's always for official reasons?"

"Yep, pretty much. Except I heard that a few weeks ago the plane left on a trip in the middle of the night. And it wasn't flown out by the regular FBI pilots. I don't know if that really happened. I was off the next day, but when I got back the day after, I thought the plane was in a slightly different position than it had been when I was there two days earlier. I notice stuff like that—like exactly how the plane is positioned in the hangar."

"So you think the jet might have made a secret flight the night before you had your day off? I wonder where it snuck off to?" Josh was trying to joke around with Mason a little bit, even though he was dying to cut to the chase.

"Probably YHZ, if I were a betting man. That's what I'd bet."

"When was this? When the plane was in a different position after you got back from your day off?"

"You sure have a lot of questions for a young guy. Are you really interested in all this stuff?"

"Yeah, I'm really interested in it."

"I remember it was right around the time the old woman on the American Airlines flight took down that Muslim terrorist with her cane. I don't usually watch much TV, other than sports, but I watched that day. Of course it was a local story as well as a national story and got a lot of coverage on the local news channels. Also, I couldn't really believe the story they were telling about her. It just seemed so fantastic, way too far out to be true. It was raining that day, and I couldn't play golf like I usually do on my days off. March is pretty iffy golf weather anyway. It doesn't usually get down below freezing in March here in Little Rock, even at night, but once I remember it snowed in early March. I was out on the golf course, already freezing my butt off, and it started to snow on me."

"So the last time you think the plane left on a secret mission was around the time of that flight that was almost taken down?"

"Yep. It was right around then."

"And you think it went to YHZ?"

"Yep, that's what I think…wherever the heck YHZ is. Ha Ha!"

Chapter 14

*T*he man was obviously nervous as he checked in for his flight to Dallas. As he waited in line to put his carry-on and shoes in a bin on the conveyor belt, his demeanor caught the attention of the security people at the Seattle airport. The observers at Sea-Tac had been trained to notice which passengers fidget unnecessarily, which ones seem to sweat more than one might normally be expected to sweat, and which ones won't look you in the eyes. There was a long list of suspicious characteristics and behaviors they'd been trained to be aware of.

This man exhibited all the earmarks of suspicion. He even looked Middle Eastern. It was not all right to take a traveler aside and question him or her on the basis of his or her ethnicity or physical appearance. But it was definitely the job of the security personnel to identify those whose behavior was out of the ordinary. After the incident in the air above Little Rock, Arkansas a few weeks earlier, security had been heightened and tightened in airports around the country. Air marshals were back on planes. The man and woman who kept watch for potential terrorists at the Seattle Tacoma International Airport made a decision to remove the man from the security line and question him.

The protocol for fingering possible troublemakers had proven to be right on target in this case. A horrible tragedy had been avoided. Almost as important as having prevented a hijacking was the fact that no publicity had surrounded either the questioning or the arrest of this potential hijacker. The public knew nothing of the incident. If there were no leaks from inside the FBI, there would be no extravaganza on CNN about this man or what he had planned to do when he was aboard United Flight #837. No elderly white-haired woman hero would be called upon to bring him down in the aisle of the first-class cabin. There would be no weeks-long media speculation about who he was or what his motives were or anything about him. No one would ever know his name or have to try to guess where he'd come from or wonder what in the world had happened to him when he disappeared.

When Ridley Wilton heard, via the FBI grapevine, about this second potential hijacking that had been averted, he contacted the head of the FBI in Seattle. Ridley gave him the "Dutch uncle" lowdown about keeping the terrorist hidden and all information about him away from the public and the press. Ridley had even offered to take the hijacker off the hands of the Seattle FBI office and assume responsibility for securing the terrorist. But Seattle's top agent was also very well-aware of the leaks that are inevitable in an organization as large as the FBI. He understood completely what Ridley was warning him about. The Seattle office had also been screwed by leakers and the press in previous cases.

It was almost always FBI headquarters in Washington, D.C. that generated the leaks. The Seattle office thought they could keep any and all real information to themselves and not allow the giant sieve in D.C. to know what was really going on. Ridley suggested the Seattle office use a decoy terrorist to keep the location of the real perpetrator a secret from everyone until they could question him. The public and the press did not know anything about this hijacker, so the use of a decoy would be to keep the wider FBI organization in the dark about the whereabouts of the real criminal. The head agent in Seattle said he might consider doing this. If he did, he said he would share with the people in D.C. only information about the whereabouts of the decoy. The top guy in Seattle was convinced that the Little Rock case and the Seattle case were linked. The two offices would work together.

The agent in charge in Seattle promised he would be able to secure the man he had in custody. He promised there would be no leaks from his office. There would be no information put out to anyone that an arrest had ever been made. It had never happened. The terrorist was finished and locked up forever in a secret cell. Only a very few people in the FBI even knew he existed. He was a phantom.

The terrorist claimed to have had a knee replacement and presented a letter from an orthopedist to that effect. The doctor's letter was to explain why the airport's metal detector would go off when he walked through it. When the security people decided to question him, they took him to a back room. They demanded that he take off his pants and show them the scar from his knee-replacement surgery. He refused to do this and tried to run. He'd had to be restrained. When his pants were finally removed, he did not have a surgical scar on his knee.

What he did have was a very sharp, very long knife taped to the inside of his thigh. After a few hours of questioning, he cracked and confessed that he had hoped to become a martyr for Allah. He was from Yemen, a member of the Houthi sect, he said. This placed him squarely among the Shia forces which seemed to be behind the previous recent hijacking. He was proud to have been chosen for this great sacrifice that would have guaranteed him, he believed, an important place in paradise. He was not intending to fly the plane into any buildings. His mission was strictly to slit the throat of the flight attendant and the throats of the pilots in the cockpit and crash the plane into the ground in order to kill everyone aboard, himself included. He had no flight training. He did not know anything about how to fly a plane. He did know how to kill.

RIDLEY WILTON HAD SPENT SIX years in the U.S. military before he'd joined the FBI. He had been a member of a little-known special unit of the United States Marine Corps. He had formed unbreakable bonds with the men in his unit, and he had maintained his friendships with them over the years. They communicated frequently and did favors for one another. He trusted them with his life. Because of these connections, Ridley had resources he could call on when he had a special situation. He didn't impose on his former special forces buddies very often, but whenever he needed them, they were always there for him.

The Iranian who had tried to take down American Airlines Flight #66 had been secreted away where he would never be found. Ridley Wilton had arranged for a decoy terrorist who closely resembled the real hijacker in physical appearance to be held and questioned in a less obscure location. This switch was his effort to prevent even those within his own organization from leaking anything to the press. As far as the rest of the FBI knew, the decoy was the real man who had attempted to hijack American Flight #66. Agent Wilton did everything he could to keep the decoy safe, but he feared that it was just a matter of time until the information was leaked by somebody in Washington, D.C., and the decoy would be "taken care of."

It wasn't just leakers in the FBI, although the blatantly open and unsecured texting back and forth between rogue agents had become a public scandal in the late 2010s. In addition to FBI agents who were lovers and openly chatted with each other on their unsecured cell phones, hackers from the outside constantly and unrelentingly broke into FBI computer files searching for classified information. There were no more secrets... for many reasons.

Unfortunately, the computer hackers were everywhere, seeking information about everyone and everything. One or more of these hackers, unknown to the FBI, had identified Wilton's decoy as the Iranian hijacker and pinpointed his prison location. This information was valuable, and Agent Wilton was certain the decoy's location had been sold for a great deal of money to someone who had hired a hit man. It had been critical for the hijacker to be silenced. Wilton had to wonder what the man he had in custody knew that was so important.

Ridley Wilton had not intended for anything to happen to his decoy prisoner. Setting up the pretend hijacker to divert attention from the real hijacker had been meant primarily to throw off the media and the leakers inside the FBI. Wilton did not know how his decoy had been found, but he suspected that someone had hacked into the FBI computer system and found the hijacker that was not really a hijacker. Ridley had tried to make sure there was nothing at all about the real hijacker, the Iranian, recorded anywhere on a computer. If there was any information on a computer anywhere, everybody would eventually know all about it.

The dead man was in fact a real prisoner who had been incarcerated for other reasons. It was with great regret when he was found hanging in his high-security prison cell in Kansas. Nobody believed for an instant that the man had hung himself. It was a Jeffrey Epstein hanging. Besides being furious at the failure to secure the information about the man's whereabouts and the failure to physically protect him, even inside a very well-guarded military installation, Ridley Wilton became even more motivated to find out what the real hijacker knew. It had cost someone a great deal of money to locate the decoy. People had been paid off, and huge risks had been taken to assassinate the pretend hijacker inside a prison. Wilton could only speculate about why somebody believed the man was so important.

The real Iranian hijacker, who was not being kept in a prison but was being held at a top-secret facility where no one could ever get to him, was still refusing to tell them anything. He was enraged that he had not been allowed to sacrifice himself and the rest of the people on the plane so he could attain his place in paradise with all the promised virgins.

After watching many hours of video camera footage and interviewing cab drivers and neighbors, the FBI had been able to find the Iranian's apartment in Tucson, Arizona. It had taken weeks, but once they found out where he lived, they were able to find the name he was using. Whether or not Parviz Kadivar was his real name was of little importance. It was the name he had adopted as his own while he prepared himself to hijack the American Airlines flight. He had of course used a different name when he had purchased his airline ticket. The FBI would be able to trace his movements through the name he used when he lived in Tucson.

Parviz had not thought up this mission all on his own. Someone had recruited him. Money had been paid for this to happen. The man must have a family somewhere, a family that had been intended to profit from Parviz's willingness to martyr himself. Perhaps he had a family in Iran. If those who had sponsored him were in Iran, it would be almost impossible to find them. But Ridley Wilton thought the planning and the financing behind the Flight #66 plot were more likely to be found in the United States. He would almost bet his career on it.

More and more, however, Wilton had the feeling he was missing something important. He wondered why the man on the airplane had acted alone. The 9/11 hijackers had been Sunnis. This man was Shia. Hamas and Hezbollah had hijacked some planes in the 1970s and 1980s. But these Lebanese and Iranian based groups were more into explosives and blowing up things, like the United States Marine barracks in Lebanon in 1983, than they were into hijacking airplanes. And why now? Why were these terrorists targeting airliners again after having been out of that business for so many years?

There had been earthshaking changes on the political scene in the United States, but could those changes have prompted a resurrection of the terrorist hijacker? Something did not smell quite right to Wilton. But he had no clue, yet, about what it was that did not ring true about this crime.

When the Houthi terrorist from Yemen, also a Shia, had been arrested, he had also been sequestered far from the media, far from the FBI's D.C. bureaucracy, and far from those who might want to silence him. Very few people knew about this man's attempts to smuggle a dangerous knife onto a commercial airline flight in order to bring it down. But the incident in Seattle added to Wilton's discomfort about why these terrorist attacks against the airlines had begun again.

■ ■ ■ ■

"We don't have any idea what's happened to him. He was on his way to the airport, and we know he arrived and

went through security. Then he disappeared. We didn't have anybody watching him while he was in the security line at the airport. We had somebody at the gate to be sure he got on the plane. We thought that would be sufficient, but obviously it wasn't. So, somewhere between standing in the line to go through security and the departure gate, he vanished. I might have assumed that the knife was discovered and that he was arrested. But we would have heard something about that. From the beginning, I felt the knife was much too long for the mission, but he was adamant. He insisted that he had to have it to be successful. He is so religious. He claimed the knife had some kind of spiritual meaning or magical powers or something like that. It meant something special to him for some reason. The letter he had about his knees was sketchy, too, I thought. But we've used that same letter before, and it worked fine.

"Our hacker is trying to get into the FBI system. They are always putting up new firewalls that he has to figure out how to get around. We finally took care of the Iranian. We don't think he talked before he died, but we don't know that for sure. The feds somehow managed to find out what his name was and where he was living in Tucson. One problem is that they have some footage of both those hijackers at a Middle Eastern restaurant on Kolb Road in Tucson. The Iranian and the guy from Yemen had dinner there together last year. We don't know for sure how they found out about each other. We are assuming they knew each other from meeting at the mosque. How and why did they make contact? We assume they must have been friends or acquaintances before we hired them.

"Did they know they were both going to be martyrs in our operation? We don't know. Leading up to the operation, we had instructed them specifically many times not to *have any contact with others from their mosque. What were they thinking?*

"There's a sizeable Middle Eastern community in Tucson. Most of these people are hardworking, patriotic, and very loyal American citizens. But there is at least one cell that operates under the radar in that city. Hani Hanjour, the Saudi who flew the American Airlines plane into the Pentagon on 9/11, lived in Tucson for a while. He briefly attended the University of Arizona and took some flying lessons in Pima County. Given that it is kind of a hot spot for religious zealots, it is not entirely surprising that two of our guys were able to meet and have a meal together. In fact, they had dinner in the same restaurant where Hani Hanjour and Mohamed Atta had dinner together a few months before 9/11. Back then, nobody was watching what happened, but now everybody is watching. Did they think nobody was going to notice them? We didn't have any idea they knew each other until the FBI found the footage of them having dinner together. So what's wrong with these two? The idiots!"

Chapter 15

"Since neither of these martyrs is doing any talking, we're not making as much progress as I'd like to be making." Ridley Wilton was frustrated with where his investigation wasn't going. He still had the feeling he was missing something.

Neither Ridley nor Arabella wanted to believe the FBI would put a bug in the office of their top man in Little Rock, but who knew what the NSA or the DIA might hope to find out? Ridley had turned on the noise machine, just in case someone other than Arabella happened to be listening. The noise machine would block any listening devices that might be in his office. If something was confidential, when they were inside the building, Ridley and his agents either used the noise machine or they spoke in a kind of code that only they understood. He hated to think his conversations were being listened in on, but he never hesitated to use the machine.

"We have that footage of the two of them going into and leaving the restaurant in Tucson. Can we use that to get them to talk?" Agent Barnes had taken the lead in the case. She liked Mercedes Carrington and was sympathetic to the woman who had been brave and saved so many lives and then had been forced to go into hiding. Barnes knew how difficult the inevitable isolation that had resulted had been on the older woman.

Arabella was certain about the connection between the hijackers in her own mind. "The two plane hijacking plans have to be linked. We have these two guys using the same MO. There is definitely some kind of a conspiracy. This is not just one individual guy deciding to do something on his own. The two similar hijackings were attempted very close in time. Even if we didn't have that video of them together, there's too much of a coincidence with the two events. They are both working from the same playbook and probably for the same group. And then, of course, there is the clincher, the two of them having dinner together a few weeks before they got on the planes. Well, one of them got on a plane. The other one was stopped before he could, thank goodness."

"My thoughts exactly. These two jokers are martyrs. They are not that smart, and they did not plan any of this themselves. The 9/11 hijackers were all pretty intelligent, or at least the ones who flew the planes were. Even so, someone else planned that tragedy. I'm convinced our two guys took their orders from somebody else. They were told what to do by somebody who organized both events. The question remains, how do we find out who that is?" Ridley had many balls in the air.

The real first hijacker was still safe, but the decoy had been murdered in prison. The second hijacker was safe and was being protected and questioned by the Seattle FBI office. Ridley and the head of the Seattle office were in touch every few days. The hijacker who had never made it onto a plane wasn't talking either. The good news was that, as yet, only a few people in Little Rock and a few people in Seattle knew anything about the second hijacker. The decoy actress, who was pretending to be Mercedes Carrington, was hiding out and was still alive. She had not been discovered.

"We need to find out what they did and where they went in Tucson. Where did they meet? How did they know each other? How did they know each other well enough to make a date to get together for dinner? We know the Iranian lived in Tucson, but we don't know anything about the Seattle hijacker. Did he also live in Tucson? Why was he there having dinner with the Iranian? What about the Imam there at the Shia mosque in Tucson? Did these two martyrs attend the same mosque? That's often where these guys are recruited and where they might have met each other."

Ridley was happy to report that they did have something on this. "We have some of those answers. They did attend the same mosque. I just got some footage this morning of them entering and leaving the building. They didn't attend services together. They always went in and left alone, but who knows what happened once they got inside. The Imam, the one who was there at the time this footage was recorded, had been there for quite a few years. He retired just around the time of the attempted hijackings. How convenient! Another coincidence? I don't think so. The new Imam won't know anything at all about our two hijackers. I doubt that he's ever met either one of them. Again, how convenient. I'm trying to find out where the former Imam is now, but of course he has completely disappeared. Getting information from these people is worse than pulling teeth."

"You will never find him." Arabella didn't know what had happened to the Imam, but she had tried to find these religious people for other cases. When they were gone, they became completely invisible, never to be seen again. Maybe the Imam had been sent back to Iran or maybe he was dead. She knew she would never know what had happened to him, and she knew absolutely that the Imam had vanished so he couldn't talk. "The very fact that he disappeared at this particular time confirms in my mind that he's one of the links in the chain. He is the connection, and he has been forever removed as a possible source of information. I will bet he was gone before the first hijacking plan went active. Even if we'd been able to find him and bring him in for questioning, we were never going to get anything out of him. Actually, the fact that he is so conveniently gone, right on schedule, is all the proof we need that he was in on the plot."

Arabella Barnes had hoped in vain that there was not any organization behind the hijackings. Although she knew there was very little chance that the Iranian and the Yemeni had acted independently, she wished it had been that simple. If it had been just a couple of nut jobs acting on their own, Mercedes Carrington could have gone back to her regular life. She could have testified in court, but there would have been no co-conspirators lurking in the background who might come after her. Because the FBI now knew that multiple people were involved, Mercedes would continue to be at risk until these people were identified and rounded up. She would not be safe until the FBI got to the bottom of who had been behind the planning of these hijackings. She would have to stay in hiding.

Arabella continued. "So, where do we go from here? Let's say we know that the Imam was the person who recruited our two wannabe hijackers. Let's say he even gave them their instructions and prepared them for martyrdom. An Imam is not usually the master planner. He is a religious leader to be sure, but when it comes to terrorist attacks, he is primarily a facilitator. He supports the martyrs and keeps them strong.

He helps them with the practical parts of their plan and with the religious devotion and spiritual parts of their sacrifice. But he doesn't think up the plan. That blind sheikh in Jersey City got a lot of credit for his part in the 1993 World Trade Center bombing, but in the end it turned out he was just another minor player, even a diversion." Ridley agreed that the idea for the hijackings had not originated with the Imam or with the two religious crazies who were in custody.

Ridley was thinking out loud. "So, let's go back and study the heck out of this disappearing Imam. Let's find out everything we can about him. Who met with him and told him what the plan was going to be? I want to know everybody he met with in the months before and after Tweedledee and Tweedledum started going to the mosque. We won't ever know what went on inside the mosque, but we can watch every person who goes in there. There will be somebody who doesn't fit the usual comings and goings. There will be somebody who will set off alarm bells. Once we figure out who that person is, and there may be more than one person involved, we follow them. That's where we will find the money." Ridley felt technology could be a big help in giving them a lead.

"Thank goodness for surveillance cameras and for somebody realizing the importance of keeping these digital videos for more than twenty-four hours." Arabella had been frustrated in the past with the old-fashioned videotapes that were recorded over every twenty-four hours.

Agent Wilton was shaking his head. Arabella had seen him do this several times when they'd discussed this case. "So tell me what isn't sitting right with you. You always shake your head like that when we talk about Mercedes Carrington."

"This whole hijacking thing, coming right at this particular time, has never made sense to me. There is something about it that is out of whack. These two are not like other hijackings, but I can't for the life of me put my finger on exactly what makes them different. Our two guys are not that bright, but does that make the entire plan suspect?" Agent Wilton shook his head again. "I just don't know, really. But something about this just doesn't fit."

"When do you want me to go and visit our white-haired friend again?" Agent Barnes knew Mercedes Carrington was having a hard time because her whole life had been disrupted.

"I don't want anybody to become suspicious of anything we do. The last thing we want is to lead anyone to her. When is your next vacation? I am thinking you could take a few extra days and tack a trip on to the end of your time off. I don't want anybody flying out of Little Rock again to see her. We took a big risk when we flew her there in the first place. We can't take the chance that anybody will see a pattern. We have successfully hidden her, and I don't want to do anything that might give away her location."

ARABELLA WANTED TO LET RIDLEY know what her vacation plans were. "I've scheduled my vacation, and at the end of my week, I'm flying to New Orleans to sit in on those interviews you wanted me to do. Here's a copy of my itinerary. You can let me know what you want me to cover."

Ridley glanced at the itinerary and put it through the shredder. He had memorized the destinations and the flight numbers. He knew she was not going to New Orleans but to New Scotland. He made sure his noise machine was on. "I've had two techs going through the footage of who goes in and out of the mosque in Tucson. We have two good cameras on the mosque, and we've had them there for years. One is across the parking lot at the CVS drugstore. That one is pointed at the front door of the mosque. The other camera is in a tree and keeps an eye on the back door of the mosque. The Imam has living quarters that are connected to the mosque by a breezeway at the rear. The camera in the tree keeps an eye on who comes to see him, too."

"Have they turned up anything out of the ordinary?" Arabella was thankful she hadn't been assigned to watch surveillance videos hour after hour.

"I think they are bored out of their minds. Pretty much the same people go in and out of the mosque all the time. We know all the regulars by now. We ran facial recognition software on a few people we suspected were important, and sure enough they were. But they were the usual suspects we always keep our eyes on anyway. None of the ones they've found so far have rung any new bells for us. There has to be somebody. These people use cell phones, but important business is conducted in person."

"I had hoped you'd found something by now. I wanted to be able to tell Mercedes that the court case was pending and she might be able to go home soon." Arabella so wanted to bring Mercedes some good news.

"No such luck." Ridley also sounded discouraged. "But I think she has settled in pretty well with Mac. She loves that sunroom and spends all of her time in there. Mac says she thinks Mercedes is less depressed. They enjoy each other's company. Mercedes writes all the time. She never turns on the television. She listens to classical music quite a bit, and once in a while she Zooms with her kids and grandkids. Before she goes to sleep at night, she reads. Guess what she reads? Mystery novels. Ha! I can tell Mac really likes Mercedes. She says Mercedes is not at all demanding like some of the other witnesses we've had her take care of. She said we've spoiled her by bringing her a nice little old lady who is polite and thoughtful. She said not to bring her any more of those crude mafia goons. She says they are grumpy and leave the house a mess. She says they act like babies and are always complaining. She says she's too old to put up with that baloney any more. Mercedes loves Mac's food. That goes a long way with Mac."

"I'm looking forward to seeing her. I wish I had something good to tell her."

"We may never have anything very good to tell her. She saves a bunch of peoples' lives, and this is the reward she gets for doing that. Doesn't seem fair does it?" Ridley felt bad for Mercedes, too.

"Life's not fair. We all know that. Mercedes knows that, too. She is smart and she is wise."

Chapter 16

"Just calling to check in on my way to New Orleans. I'm calling from a pay phone. I'm looking forward to a Ramos Gin Fizz." Arabella had been in Middlebury, Vermont for a week and was leaving the next morning to drive to Montreal. She would never be anywhere close to New Orleans or a Ramos Gin Fizz. She would spend the night in Montreal and fly out the next morning to YHZ. It was about a 90-minute plane flight from Montreal to Halifax.

"Oh, good. I'm glad you called. I didn't want to call you on your cell phone, but I have something interesting to tell you. It isn't anything you can share with your Aunt Matilda, but call me at noon tomorrow at the outside number. I'll be waiting for your call." Ridley didn't trust talking about confidential things over his cell phone. He didn't trust Arabella's phone either. With the very close members of his team, he had a special arrangement for them to call him on the pay phone in the Capital Hotel lobby. There weren't many pay phones left anywhere in the world, but the Capital

Hotel still had one. Arabella would call her boss from a pay phone the next day, and he would update her on the latest in the hijacking case. Ridley Wilton would discuss important Bureau business over the hotel's pay phone with Arabella, and then he would treat himself to a delicious lunch in the Capital Hotel bar.

AGENT WILTON WAS ANXIOUS TO share his news with Arabella Barnes the next day when she called the hotel's pay phone. "We finally found something in the videos of the mosque that didn't make sense. It was partly luck and partly one of the techs paying close attention and having a really great visual memory. It's an interesting find, and I want to run it by you to see what you think. There are two people who show up at the mosque together every few days, and one of them is blind. Yes, blind. Can you believe it? But it's not the sheikh! Ha! The other guy always drives the blind man to the mosque in his car. Of course he does! He helps him get out of the car, guides him into the mosque, brings him out of the mosque a couple of hours later, and puts him back into the car. The blind guy uses one of those white canes, you know, like blind people used to use to find their way across the street. The blind don't use those white canes so much anymore, but this guy still uses one." Ridley's voice was animated in a way Arabella hadn't heard since the hijacking case had begun in March.

"The techs have watched these two go in and out of the mosque so many times, they'd really kind of stopped looking at them. They'd become part of the crowd, part of the background. But a couple of days ago, they stumbled on some video footage from another CVS camera that somehow had been thrown in by mistake with the footage from the camera we have set up to watch the front door of the mosque. We record all of the camera footage on thumb drives. A thumb drive with camera footage that was pointed at a CVS door was mistakenly put in with our thumb drives. The CVS has a side door that you can only get into if somebody lets you in. It's kind of like an emergency exit. Because that door is near the pharmacy, there's a camera on it, too. I'm assuming the camera is there to catch people taking drugs out of the CVS. Employees mostly use that door. We're not interested in that footage because of course we only want to see who goes in and out of the mosque." Ridley was on a roll.

"The tech was about to toss the thumb drive with the footage taken of the side door of the CVS when he saw somebody that looked familiar to him leave the drug store through that side exit. Turns out it's the blind guy from the mosque. But he doesn't have his keeper with him this time, and he doesn't have his Middle Eastern clothes or his white cane. And, of course, he isn't really blind. He steps out of the CVS emergency exit door and walks across the parking lot, just as big as you please. He gets into his car and drives away. Definitely not blind. We got the color, the make and model of the car, and the license plate. We have somebody watching his house as of yesterday afternoon." Ridley Wilton finally had something to sink his teeth into in terms of his investigation, and the delight was obvious in his voice.

Arabella was easily caught up in Ridley's enthusiasm. It had been a long investigation without a break. "That's a huge red flag for sure. Why in the world would this guy pretend to be blind and go to a mosque on a regular basis? It's definitely suspicious and worth looking into. "I wondered if all those hours watching the mosques all over the country all these years would ever pay off. I guess in an odd sort of way, this one did. Keep me posted."

Ridley had more to tell her. "The important thing I almost forgot to tell you is that the not-really-blind guy and his friend stopped coming to the mosque a couple of days before the first attempted hijacking took place. The footage the techs have been spending all this time looking at is from months ago. We lucked out because our fake blind man still owns the same car that he was driving when he was pretending to be blind. He still lives in Tucson."

■ ■ ■ ■

"Even though the Iranian is dead, they are making some progress finding out about him and who gave him his orders. They won't accept that he might have been a solo jihadi operating on his own. Of course, we know he wasn't, but we'd hoped the Americans would think he was a loner. A random killer is always more frightening to the public. The FBI searched his apartment but didn't find much. They are going over every inch of every video they can find of the area around his building. They are beginning to interview the people who rang his doorbell or knocked on his door. They are following him, via video cameras around his residence and on the nearby streets. I mean everywhere he went...on foot or in a taxi or on a bus, as well as anybody who picked him up in a car. It's just a matter of time until they've rounded up all these people and talked to them."

"There aren't any videos of inside the mosque, but they will figure it out and will want to put the Imam through the wringer. Of course, we have already taken care of that problem. The Imam left the mosque and left Arizona before the first operation began. Nobody will ever be able to find him. He won't be able to tell anybody anything. He never knew much to begin with, but the Americans are not going to give up on this."

■ ■ ■ ■

"He wants to make a push to find the woman who took our man down on the plane. Even though the Iranian is dead and even though we can't locate the Yemeni, you know they are going to trot her out there for the world to see. They will try the Iranian in absentia or post-mortem or whatever and try to link him to the Yemeni. She's already a hero in the press and in the country. No matter what jury they come up with, they will believe every word that comes out of her mouth. We need to get rid of her. If we can get her out of the picture, their case will have much less impact."

■ ■ ■ ■

"Yes, I also heard she died. But then, I've heard everything there is to imagine about that old lady. One thing I've heard several times is that she's left the country. I've heard she uses a wheelchair. We know she uses a cane. We've tried to hack into the airport's security camera system to get a glimpse of her before she boarded the plane, but we haven't had any luck with that. Nobody can find her on any videos. Nobody knows her real name.

"According to the passenger list on the plane, her name is Edwina Carroll, but my guess is that's a fake name. There was an Edwina Carroll who lived in Ardmore, Pennsylvania, but nobody can find her either. Of course, we're sure that either the FBI or the U.S. Marshals have her stashed someplace under another name. The press has looked everywhere. They are dying to find her and interview her. Can you imagine what a coup that would be? The FBI is hiding her somewhere, or maybe she's kicked the bucket. I mean she's really elderly, and beating up the Iranian had to take a lot out of her.

"Are we ready to go with the third plane? This one has to work. We didn't get any mileage at all out of the Yemeni. He was a total bust, and we can't find hide nor hair of him now. What a waste that was. He can't have disappeared into thin air. Somebody will talk sooner or later...either about the Yemeni or about the old lady. We need to take care of both of them."

Chapter 17

The man who had been a regular attendee at the Tucson mosque, the man who had called himself Ahmed Abdul Kassab when he was pretending to be blind and pretending to be a devout Muslim, was in fact Billy Bob Vickers. His real name was William Robert Vickers, but he had been known as Billy Bob since he'd drawn his first breath in the world. He was kind of an actor and kind of a con man. He specialized in playing parts that lasted for weeks or months, long-term roles. He made a living doing this because he could really "get into" his parts and sustain them over an extended period of time. He also liked disguises. He had the ability to almost become another person. He had lived and worked in Las Vegas doing cons of various kinds until he'd become too well-known there and had to leave town. Since moving to Tucson, he'd worn disguises so he wouldn't be so easily recognized.

His con with the Tucson mosque had lasted for months. He wore a gray wig; a scraggly gray and white Taliban beard;

cheap, baggy foreign-looking clothes; and dark glasses. He not only pretended to be blind but he also pretended to be twenty years older than he really was. He always met the man who drove him to the mosque at the corner of East Speedway and Sycamore. There's a Middle Eastern food market near that intersection. It's not a residential area, and Ahmed, of course, walks everywhere. We assume he told his driver and mosque friend that he rented a room above a business in the area. A lot of those businesses rent the upstairs rooms out, or they live up there themselves. Ahmed waited on the street corner two afternoons a week for his ride to take him to the mosque.

With traffic cameras, the FBI was able to track the car that provided Ahmed with transportation to the mosque. They identified the car in the parking lot of the mosque and followed it backwards with traffic cameras through the streets of Tucson until they found the street corner where the car picked Ahmed up and dropped him off. It wasn't easy, but once they'd found the meeting place, they gathered all the past video surveillance of that corner.

There was Ahmed, regular as clockwork, waiting on the sidewalk twice a week for his ride. After visiting the mosque, Ahmed's driver always delivered him back to the same corner. Ahmed wandered around and sometimes made his way to the food market. When he was certain his Muslim friend and driver had left the area and he was sure no one was watching him, he slipped behind a parked car. took off the gray wig and the beard, collapsed the white cane, and anonymously walked to his vehicle. Billy Bob parked his truck around the corner near a car dealership on Speedway.

Billy Bob didn't have much of a paperwork trail. Apparently he was paid in cash on the down low for whatever jobs he'd had. He hadn't filed any income taxes in a decade. But Billy Bob had a brother with a much higher profile. His older brother was born James Jonathan Vickers and was known as Jimmy John. Jimmy John was a man who loved to protest. He loved to cause trouble. He had done two stints at the Nevada State Prison in Carson City. He didn't seem to have any particular political or religious convictions, so he marched and looted and burned things down with everybody. He had associated and protested with both right-wing and left-wing causes. It didn't seem to matter to him as long as he could be in the center of whatever group was stirring things up and causing chaos.

The FBI had Jimmy John on many videos for the last decade at high-profile protests around the country. They suspected he was a paid protestor. He seemed to have more money to spend than his spotty work history indicated he should. He was employed at low-paying jobs in landscaping, fast food, and other unskilled work. His most lucrative career choice appeared to have been as a bartender at the Owl and the Pussy Pat, a place that featured pole dancers and other kinds of strippers. He'd been fired from that position for stealing money from the till.

Ridley Wilton groaned when he read the reports on the Vickers brothers. He wondered what in the heavens above could possibly have put these two low-life jokers together with the Imam and the hijackers? Billy Bob and Jimmy John were at the opposite ends of the lifestyle spectrum from ultra-religious people who didn't drink alcohol. This was a contradiction that would require serious looking into.

The only clue they might have to follow was that Jimmy John and Billy Bob had both recently bought houses. This was definitely another red flag. Neither brother had any money. They didn't pay their bills or their taxes, and they certainly didn't have the funds to purchase homes. Jimmy John's house was in Las Vegas, and Billy Bob's was in Tucson. The houses they'd bought weren't large or luxurious, but even so, neither one of these two had the money to buy anything. They'd suddenly come into money. Somebody was bankrolling them.

Interestingly, neither house was actually owned by either one of the Vickers brothers. Both houses were owned by an entity called New Vistas Properties, LLC. Ridley knew trying to track down the real owners of the LLC would be pointless. There would be layers of holding companies and fake names. He'd had his people spend some time trying to track the ownership anyway. New Vistas Properties, LLC owned houses in Las Vegas, in Tucson, and all over the Southwest. Ridley Wilton was betting they owned quite a few properties all around the country. The fact that a very obscure LLC with ghost owners had bought houses for the Vickers was another red flag. If there wasn't something nefarious going on, why would anyone go to this much trouble to hide who had bought the houses? Neither Billy Bob nor Jimmy John would know an LLC if it bit them on the behind.

The only reason Ridley Wilton could think of for anybody to buy the houses for these two was to launder money. Purchasing real estate was a favorite way for money launderers to clean their money. This happened in a number of different ways. Ridley had dealt with quite a few money laundering enterprises over the years. But money laundering was more U.S. Mafia and Russian Mafia-style enterprise than it was the style of either Islamic terrorists or the style of the low-level protesters and scammers like the Vickers Brothers. The combining of these hijacking attempts with money laundering did not make any sense. Ridley was still missing something. This crime was all over the map. What was going on?

Ridley felt as if he'd been pushed back to square one. He would never know who really owned New Vistas Properties, LLC. He didn't have enough manpower to keep an eye on Billy

Bob around the clock. Ridley's dilemma was whether or not to bring Billy Bob Vickers in for questioning immediately. Ridley thought he knew pretty much everything that had happened inside that mosque, but he would love to hear it from Billy Bob's own mouth. Should he bring Billy Bob in and grill him now? Or, should he watch Billy Bob and try to figure out who came to see him and who called him? Ridley decided to wait and watch the guy a while longer.

Billy Bob hardly ever left his house, but when they had a window of opportunity, FBI Agent Stephanie Abramowitz was going to load the house up with surveillance technology. They would install cameras and listening devices and put a tracker on Billy Bob's car and on his cell phone. He wasn't likely to skip town now that he had a free house to live in. He seemed to be pretty flush with cash. His gig as the blind guy had probably paid very well. Ridley Wilton's team wanted to know who Billy Bob came in contact with. Because he seemed to be set for money right now, it might be a while before he took on another job.

✖ ✖ ✖ ✖

"They are both loose cannons. We had to use them, but what are we going to do about them now? We can't get rid of them both at the same time. That would certainly draw attention to them, and we don't want that. The younger brother is not as much of a lunatic as the older brother. That Jimmy John is real trouble. He's been in the slammer a couple of times and would sing his head off if he were threatened with going back to Carson City. He's the one to take out. The younger brother Billy Bob is totally clueless. He loves his acting thing, and he's more controllable. He will do whatever the person who is paying him tells him to do. He did a good job for us. He was able to talk the Imam into recruiting our

three martyrs and training them for their mission. Of course, we told him exactly what to say and what to do, but he was the one who did it. Of course those big donations to the mosque helped, too. It was all funded, and not a cent for any of the operations came out of the Imam's budget. And he made a pretty penny on top of it all. Spreading money around never hurts. But I am actually kind of surprised Billy Bob was able to pull it off with the Imam. He actually has some talent."

"The older brother thinks he's getting paid by the Russian mob, and he is. The younger brother has no idea who is paying for the houses, the hijackers, the Imam, and all the rest of it. He thinks all of this largesse comes from his older brother, and it does. Billy Bob knows nothing beyond what Jimmy John gives him and tells him to do. With Jimmy John gone, Billy Bob will have no idea who has been funding all of this. Even if he's taken in for questioning, he has nothing to tell. Billy Bob interacted with the Imam, but that's really all he did. I don't think Jimmy John shared much with his younger brother that he didn't need to know. Jimmy John interacted with us, so we have to take him out. Of course, we ultimately need to get rid of both of them.

"I know he's not happy with the way things turned out. We set up this whole elaborate chain of command to obscure who was really funding this and who was behind it, but all that money and all that planning didn't get us much. It did get us an old lady who embarrassed the heck out of one of Allah's warriors.

"I know he wants her found and killed. But that's turned out to be much more difficult than we had any idea it would be. Nobody has the slightest idea where she is, but we are continuing to work on it. We are watching that FBI jet in the hangar at the Little Rock airport. Sonner or later, the feds are going to have to use that jet to get to her. And we will be right on their tail.

"There's a reporter, a freelance journalist, who is also trying very hard to find our old woman. He's even gone so far as to get a real job at the airport. He's made friends with the guy who keeps the hangar ready, the hangar where the FBI keeps their jet. That journalist has also figured out that the jet is the key to finding the woman.

"I think he just wants to write about her. He wants a scoop. He wants to tell the world about her. He's Josh somebody. I don't think he's in the business of killing people. He wants to talk to her. He's a kid who investigates stuff. But we are keeping an eye on him, too. He's pretty smart and seems to have a knack for finding what he's looking for. We will continue to follow what he does and where he goes. He may be able to lead us to her."

Chapter 18

Arabella drove across the Canadian border to Montreal. She'd talked to her boss about the progress of their case. The next day she flew from Montreal to Halifax. She was almost one hundred percent certain no one was watching her or following her, but she didn't want to take any chances. She had an alternate identity to use in situations like this, and she used that identity to rent the car she had driven to Montreal and to purchase her ticket to fly to Halifax. In Halifax she picked up another rental car and drove to Terence Bay. She would be staying at a hotel in Halifax, but she would check in there later in the day. She wanted to get to Baird House before lunchtime. Mac was going to be at Baird House all day today, and she was serving her famous lobster salad for lunch. Arabella didn't want to miss the lobster salad.

Mercedes and Mac were delighted to see Arabella. Mercedes was anxious to hear all the details about the case. Arabella had been sending her emails and texts to keep her apprised of what was happening, but having the FBI agent with her in person would give Mercedes more of a chance to ask questions. Arabella couldn't wait to sit down to Mac's fabulous lunch.

Mac fixed special bread that accompanied the lobster salad. It was a way of incorporating the tastes of a lobster roll in her own unique presentation. Mac took the classic hot dog-style rolls that restaurants and seafood shacks used to make lobster rolls and cut the bread into squares. She toasted them and buttered them. Eating one of these crunchy rolls with a bite of lobster salad was equal to or better than the lobster roll experience. Mac always served the lunch with blueberry salad, a fruit salad that was composed of blueberries and peaches dressed with balsamic vinegar and fresh basil. It was the perfect accompaniment to the lobster salad. The blueberry salad was mostly a summertime thing, but Mac managed to find blueberries whenever Arabella was coming to visit, no matter the season.

Arabella gave Mercedes a quick rundown on what Ridley Wilton's small team had discovered. She didn't go into details about how any of the information had been uncovered, but she felt Mercedes deserved some kind of report about what had been going on with the investigation. Arabella was disappointed to have to tell Mercedes they had absolutely determined that the hijackers had not been acting alone. Arabella had alluded in an email to a second foiled hijacking that they'd uncovered. She was happy to report that the potential hijacker had been found out before he'd ever stepped onto a plane. Arabella told Mercedes honestly that the FBI believed some kind of organization had recruited these two and had supported their attempts to bring down the airliners.

Mercedes had known there was a second hijacker who'd been caught, but speaking with Arabella about the extent of the organization that had been behind the hijacking was discouraging. Mercedes had so hoped there were no more people who had to be hunted down and brought to justice before it was safe for her to come out of hiding.

Mercedes and Arabella enjoyed the delicious lunch Mac had made for them. Mercedes enjoyed Mac's company tremendously but was delighted to have a visitor from the outside world. An introvert who loved people, Mercedes drew some of her characters from people she observed in real life—in restaurants, on the street, at Little League baseball games, and pretty much everywhere there were people. She missed the people watching that kept her stories fresh with interesting personalities. She didn't want Arabella to leave. Zoom was great, but real human interaction was definitely a cut above.

Arabella was going to check into her hotel, but she would be back in time for dinner. Mac was making her favorite curried chicken, broccoli, and cheddar cheese casserole, a classic from the 1960s. Arabella didn't have time to cook and didn't really like to cook, but she remembered this dish from when her grandmother used to make it. As far as Arabella knew, Mac was the only person who still made this casserole from the old days, and her interpretation of the family favorite was even better than Arabella's grandmother's version had been.

Arabella would switch out her rental car at the airport. It would not do for the same car to be parked at Baird House for any length of time, let alone parked there twice in one day. A car parked briefly could be making a delivery or could be an Uber picking up a fare. A car that returned for the second time in one day might attract attention.

The FBI did not think anybody had identified Baird House in Terence Bay as anything other than a vacation rental, and they were certain nobody had guessed what very special guest was staying there. But Arabella was determined to follow all the procedures and protocols to keep Mercedes unknown to everyone. The goal was to attract as little attention as possible. The FBI would have preferred that no one, including the neighbors next door, know anyone was staying at Baird House. The neighbors were used to seeing Mac coming and going, so her presence was no longer of interest to anybody. But seeing rental cars in the driveway and strangers going in and out might arouse the neighbors' curiosity.

The weather was improving and turning warmer. Soon Mac was going to want to get Mercedes outside in her wheelchair for a trip around the grounds. Baird House was on several acres that separated it from its neighbors. One side of the property bordered a bird sanctuary. Nobody visited the bird sanctuary during the cold, wet, and dreary winter months, but when spring arrived, a few bird watchers with binoculars came early in the mornings, usually at dawn. Not many birders were still watching later in the day. Mac would rearrange her schedule so she could take Mercedes for outings in the early afternoon when the twitcher population was absent from the sanctuary.

Mercedes was going to miss having a fire in the fireplace every day. Mac had promised to light a fire in the late afternoon, even in the spring. It was cool enough in Eastern Canada to have a fire going late in the day, even into the summer months. Mercedes thought she was going to miss the fog and the rainy days, but as she watched from her sunroom, she realized more birds and more ships were outside her windows as the summer approached. She found the sunshine that peeked through the fog cheered her. The dark ocean took on an entirely different character when the sun came out. The salt water sparkled in the sunlight.

Arabella arrived back at Baird House for an early dinner. She had called Ridley Wilton at the Capital Hotel's pay phone to give him a report on Mercedes and to get the latest updates on the investigation. She had news for Mercedes.

Ridley Wilton's team had identified someone they thought could lead them to the person who had funded the hijacking attempts. They were making an arrest in Las Vegas that night. Arabella told Mercedes they felt this guy was an important piece of the puzzle. If they could get him to talk and reveal who had provided him with the money for his role in the operation...and who had bought him a house ..., they thought they would be close to cracking the case. Mercedes might be able to come out of hiding sooner rather than later. Arabella promised more details when she had them.

Mac had gone all out to make this special dinner for the two of them. She'd set the small drop-leaf table in front of the fire in the sunroom. Mac had many seafood chowders and soups in her repertoire, but for tonight she'd made her special lobster Cioppino with vegetables as a first course. She called it lobster vegetable soup, but it was so much more than that. It was a lot of work because Mac cooked the lobster carcasses down to make an extra-flavorful lobster broth. The lobster soup was clear with just a touch of tomato, crisp vegetables of all kinds, and lots of chunks of lobster meat. Mac added a generous spoonful of homemade pesto to the Cioppino. It was a summertime lobster stew. It was really a meal in itself, but Mac was serving it as a first course tonight.

Mac's curried chicken with cheese and broccoli pretty much followed the traditional recipe, but she put in twice the amount of curry seasoning and made double the amount of the yummy sauce. She served the breadcrumb-topped casserole dish with a side that combined homemade egg noodles and homemade fresh spinach pasta. The noodles were lightly buttered and were the perfect accompaniment for the curry. Mac had bought the homemade pasta in Halifax. Mercedes and Arabella were both groaning after the wonderful meal, and each could just manage a dish of chocolate gelato that had come from a special ice cream store in Terence Bay. Mac boxed up some of the soup and some of the casserole for Arabella to take with her. Mercedes was sad to see the FBI agent leave. Arabella was fun, and Mercedes liked her.

Arabella was just getting into her rental car to return to the hotel when she got a special text alert on her phone. The text was from Ridley Wilton, and he asked Arabella to phone him at the Capitol Hotel's pay phone immediately. It was an emergency. Arabella stopped at the first pay phone she found which was outside a convenience store connected to a service station. The pay phone had been vandalized, and the receiver had been torn off the phone. Arabella moved on, and after another failed attempt to locate a functional pay phone, she finally found one that worked near a school playground.

Chapter 19

*R*idley's news was bad. A team from the Las Vegas FBI office had planned to take Jimmy John Vickers into custody that night. They had carefully thought through how they were going to bring him in. Because he had a prison record and did not want to go back inside, they knew he would try to run when he was being arrested. They would go in with plenty of firepower. Because Ridley had believed this arrest would crack the case against the hijackers, he had felt it was safe to ask the FBI office in Las Vegas for their help. He had kept everything close to the vest so far and had chosen not to involve anyone in the wider FBI organization except for his own small team and a few agents he knew he could trust absolutely. Ridley thought this would be one of the last steps in his long investigation. He knew the agent in charge in Las Vegas personally and had appealed to him to keep the Vickers arrest under wraps.

The plan had been for the Las Vegas team to make the arrest. Bobby O'Connor would take charge of transferring the prisoner immediately to Little Rock where Jimmy John Vickers would be questioned by Ridley Wilton. Ridley preferred that as few people as possible within the FBI know about the plan. Until they had a chance to bring in Billy Bob for questioning, Ridley wanted to be absolutely certain that Billy Bob Vickers didn't know his older brother was in custody. Wilton knew the two brothers didn't communicate with each other very often, so it might be weeks or even months before Billy Bob noticed he wasn't able to reach Jimmy John.

The team that intended to arrest Jimmy John arrived at the house. They'd made the decision not to knock and ask if they could come inside for a chat. They were going to break down the door and enter the house with guns drawn. Knowing Vickers' history, they'd expected him to resist arrest, and those designated to arrest him had obtained all the paperwork necessary for a surprise swat-team type entry. A stakeout unit and a drone had been watching the house. Three days earlier, Jimmy John had returned home in his car with two bags of groceries. He had not left the house since. It was a go. Vickers would be in the house, and he would be taken by surprise. It would be an easy pick up unless he happened to have his gun in his hand when they came through the door.

They burst in as planned, but Jimmy John wasn't there. At least, that's what they thought at first. One of the swat team members noticed the flies. Las Vegas was hot in May. Because the air conditioning had been on in the house, the smell had yet not become intolerable. But the blood on and around the body had attracted hundreds of flies. It was the unusual number of flies that let investigators know there was a corpse in the house. Jimmy John Vickers, the man who was going to spill the beans about where the money had come from for the hijacking operations, was dead in his bedroom. His throat had been cut. Jimmy John had been silenced. The FBI had been preempted. When he heard the news, Ridley Wilton was angry as hell and sick to his stomach. He'd thought he was finally going to be able to identify all the players and wrap up his case. It was not to be. Jimmy John Vickers' mouth had been forever closed.

Ridley demanded that the body be brought to Little Rock. This was not the usual procedure, but Ridley's colleague who headed the Las Vegas office knew how important this case was to him. The FBI boss in Las Vegas signed the paperwork and sent the body with Bobby O'Connor back to Little Rock that night. What a mess. What a disappointment. They'd been too late to learn anything more from Jimmy John, but Ridley refused to give up. He believed the dead still had stories to tell. He believed that Jimmy John Vickers had information for him, even though he was no longer breathing.

AGENT STEPHANIE ABRAMOWITZ HAD BEEN watching Billy Bob Vickers' stucco one-story home in Tucson. She was waiting for Billy Bob to leave the house so she could go inside and install cameras and plant listening devices. Without the ability to monitor his comings and goings around the clock, electronic surveillance was the next best thing.

As soon as Ridley Wilton knew that Jimmy John Vickers had been murdered, he was afraid that Billy Bob was probably also at risk. It might be too late to bring in Billy Bob. He might already be dead. Ridley called Stephanie and told her what had happened to Jimmy John. He hated to ask Stephanie go in and take Billy Bob into custody without back up. Under other circumstances, he never would have allowed her to go in alone. But this was an emergency. Stephanie was to tell Billy Bob that the FBI was afraid his life was in danger. Her mission was to bring Billy Bob in for questioning. She was to cuff him and take him to Tucson's FBI headquarters. Ridley told her to have her gun ready in case Billy Bob resisted. She was to take Billy Bob down if necessary. Ridley would arrange for Billy Bob to be brought to Little Rock. Ridley was willing to risk going outside his very close circle of confidents and ask the Tucson office for help because he did not want Billy Bob to be killed or to get away.

Stephanie entered Billy Bob's house with her gun ready, exactly as her boss had directed. She knocked on the front door, and there was no answer. The back door was unlocked, and she drew her gun and cleared each room as she searched the house.

Billy Bob was gone, and it looked as if he had been gone for quite some time. His clothes were gone, and his truck was gone. Stephanie could see where there had been a flat screen TV hanging on the wall, and it was gone. Billy Bob had taken his cell phone and his computer and everything else of value. There were a few cheap pieces of furniture left behind. The milk and the food in the refrigerator were spoiled and moldy, and the kitchen smelled. Billy Bob had not been in the house for many days. Stephanie had to conclude that Billy Bob had flown the coop before they'd even begun to watch him.

Ridley Wilton was furious with himself for having delayed bringing Billy Bob in for questioning. Now it was too late. He admitted his lack of personnel had meant their surveillance had been spotty. They'd mistakenly thought Billy Bob was staying put. He'd had a house he thought he owned. He had money. No one would ever know for sure why Billy Bob had split.

Had Billy Bob known he was in trouble and decided to leave town? Those who had known about Billy Bob's role in the hijacking scheme wondered if Jimmy John had warned his younger brother to get out while he could. Billy Bob could pretend to be another person for an extended period of time. He had many disguises. Billy Bob could create an entirely new persona and live that role without much effort. He was a person who had the ability to disappear.

Maybe whoever had murdered Jimmy John had already taken care of Billy Bob? Because the things that obviously mattered to Billy Bob had been taken from the house, Ridley Wilton believed he had left Tucson of his own volition. Ridley doubted they would ever know for sure what had happened to Billy Bob. The only thing Ridley and his team knew for sure was that Billy Bob Vickers had disappeared. He was gone, and none of them ever expected to find him.

To what extent had Billy Bob understood what was going on? Billy Bob appeared to be clueless, but he had actually carried out a very complicated con against the Imam and the other members of the Tucson mosque. The guy must have some talent to be able to accomplish that. Ridley wondered why Billy Bob hadn't tried to make it in Hollywood. Billy Bob was clearly a flake, but in Ridley's mind, so were many of the people who claimed that acting was their career and who made millions doing it.

RIDLEY NOW REALIZED THERE WERE quite a few serious players in on the hijacking. The layers of the onion were more numerous and went much deeper than he had imagined at the outset. Ridley knew that significant money had been spread around, but he had not realized that whoever had been behind the hijackings would send a clean-up squad to make sure nobody talked. Ridley was furious that they had missed the chance to grill Jimmy John and Billy Bob.

Arabella was heartsick that they had failed to arrest Jimmy John Vickers. She too had hoped he would be forced to tell them who was behind the attempted hijackings and who was funding the operation. She knew Ridley was beside himself, and she dreaded having to tell Mercedes that the end was no longer in sight.

After Ridley told her all about the arrest debacle, Arabella gave him a quick report on Mercedes. She said Mercedes was doing as well as could be expected. Arabella was happy to report that Baird House continued to be unknown to and unnoticed by anyone other than a few people. Mac had not been aware of anyone nosing around or showing any interest in the house or what was going on there.

Because of what had happened with Jimmy John, Ridley's level of alarm had risen. He worried about the people he was protecting. He was concerned about the real wannabe hijackers, both #1 and #2, who were sequestered. He was worried about his decoy Mercedes Carrington, and he was worried most of all about the real Mercedes Carrington. If whoever was behind all of this was intent on taking out the witnesses and the participants, the FBI would have to step up its game as well.

The hijackings initially had appeared to be somewhat amateurish, one-man-band type operations starring a not-very-smart band leader. But there was more to all of this than the martyrs. Ridley was also wondering what the unknown enemy was planning going forward. Their two attempted hijackings had not produced the desired results. No planes had been brought down. There had been no martyrs. Yet. But this organization's tentacles seemed to reach far and wide. Where would they strike next?

It seemed as if his own people were always a step behind. He was playing a triple game now...trying to keep what he was doing a secret from the larger FBI organization; trying to keep what he was doing away from the press and the public; and now attempting to keep his witnesses hidden from the bad guys who seemed to be intent on revenge and cleaning up their failed messes.

Ridley had been turning over in his mind why anyone would buy houses for the two brothers. Other than money laundering, the only thing he only thing he could figure was they had been given the houses so the people who'd hired them would always know where to find them. They wouldn't have to chase Billy Bob and Jimmy John all over the country to know where they were so they could kill them. It seemed like a lot of expense to go to just to keep track of a couple of kook-burger brothers. But until Ridley had a better explanation, that one was going to have to do.

Chapter 20

"You won't believe what happened here last night." Mason Haggarty was anxious to tell his young friend about the middle-of-the-night events that had transpired in the FBI hangar. Mason was not a government employee, but he'd been vetted because he worked around where the FBI jet was warehoused. He figured young Josh had also been vetted before he'd been offered the airport position.

Mason loved to chat and wanted to share his story. "This is the only hangar the FBI uses now that the Clintons never come here anymore. Until last night there was only ever one jet that stayed in this hangar. Since we haven't had more than the one jet in here for years, at least since I've been working here, the pilots got used to parking it in the middle of the space. Nobody ever complained, and it's much easier just to pull straight in and park the jet. It moves in and out more than anybody wants to admit, but even so, it doesn't move anywhere very often."

Josh was only half listening to Mason ramble on and on until he heard the story the old man was telling was about the hangar and the FBI jets. "So what happened? Did the jet make a flight last night?"

"No, the jet didn't make a flight, but it had to be moved. I got a call about ten o'clock that I had to come in. I'd had two beers with my dinner and was falling asleep on the couch. I'd dragged myself upstairs and was just about to get into the shower when my cell phone rang. I picked it up off the bathroom floor and saw it was my supervisor from the airport. I decided I'd better answer it. She told me to get my ass to the airport ASAP. She said another government jet was coming in from Las Vegas, and we had to make room for it in the FBI hangar. The jet that stays in Little Rock was parked in the center of the hangar, its usual spot for the past umpteen years. Chairs and couches and other kinds of furniture and equipment had kind of migrated away from the walls, towards the center of the hangar. The furniture had to be moved, too.

"The FBI pilots were coming in to move the jet, but I had to get in there first to move the furniture and the other stuff out of the way so they could move the jet over, all the way to one side. The second jet from Las Vegas was scheduled to arrive about midnight or a little later. I was going to have to clear all the stuff away on the other side of the hangar, too, to make room to accommodate that incoming jet. I don't move a lot of furniture and heavy equipment around anymore myself... because of my back. I had to call in the younger guys who do the heavy lifting. So, I'm standing in my bathroom buck naked making phone calls and telling my guys they've got to get to the airport to get the furniture and other junk moved around in the hangar to make room for the incoming jet."

Josh always tried to listen politely to what Mason had to say, but when he heard the second jet was coming in from Las Vegas and not from YHZ, he kind of tuned him out.

"Only one of my men could come in to help me, so it was going to be more work for him and for me and take longer. When I got there, the two FBI pilots were already there, and boy were they ever out of sorts. They were supposed to be off-duty, of course, not expecting to have to do anything, but there they were. It was more than a notion for them to maneuver that little jet over to one side of the hangar to make room for the incoming from LAS. We had to stack things on top of one another against the walls to make room. It was a real mess in there, and while we are in the middle of doing all that, here comes a hearse."

"We had the doors to the hangar closed, and here's this hearse right outside, honking and wanting to come in. Nobody had said anything to us about a hearse or a dead body or anything like that. If we let the hearse come into the hangar, there wasn't going to be enough room for the second jet to get in. So the hearse was going to have to wait outside until the jet arrived from Las Vegas. And I didn't think the hearse would have room to get into the hangar at the same time, with two jets parked in there anyway. A hearse is a long thing, you know. I talked to the man who was driving the hearse. He said he was an FBI agent. I didn't believe him, of course. Since when does an FBI agent drive a hearse? Anyway, turns out he really is an FBI agent. He showed me his badge, and he is not going be told what to do."

Josh was hooked on the story now and trying to keep from laughing at the pickle his friend Mason had found himself in. "So the FBI guy is driving the hearse, and he has shown you his credentials to prove he really is an agent."

"He did not want to sit outside the hangar. He said something about a top secret operation. He said if the hearse had to sit outside the hangar, he would be putting his operation at risk and blah blah blah. I explained to him why the hearse had to wait outside. He was very unhappy about that. But he seemed to understand what I was telling him. Then I had to tell him that I didn't think there would be room for the hearse to get into the hangar when both jets were inside. That was when he went nuclear. He screamed at me and told me there was a dead body on board the plane that was coming in. He said it absolutely could not be transferred from the plane to the hearse anywhere but inside the hangar. He really let me have it. He asked me if I thought the head of the FBI in Little Rock usually drove a hearse. He was so angry, but he seemed like the kind of guy who didn't usually get that angry. He seemed like a person who usually kept his cool and was very polite and didn't raise his voice. I realized he was under a tremendous amount of stress. I mean, the poor man was about to cry. I told him I would do my best to get the hearse and both planes into the hangar so he could transfer the body inside a secure space."

When Josh heard that the man driving the hearse had said he was the head of the FBI in Little Rock, he went on high alert. This was the guy who must have spirited Agnes MacGillicutty away from the Capital Hotel, maybe to YHZ.

"This fellow puts his face down on the steering wheel of the hearse. I thought for a minute he really was crying. He stayed that way for a few minutes. Then he raises his head up and speaks to me as calm and nice as you please. He's like a different person. He apologizes for screaming at me and says he would really appreciate it if I could squeeze the hearse into the hangar once the jet arrived from Las Vegas. He said it was a top priority transfer in an ongoing top secret operation. I told him I would do everything I could to help him out. He looked exhausted and like he was at the end of his rope. It had been a very long day for the man, and I could tell his long day hadn't gone at all well."

Josh was wondering if this story had anything to do with Agnes. Maybe he had been wrong about Halifax. Maybe they had taken her to Las Vegas to hide her. Maybe she had died. Maybe she was the body on the plane from Las Vegas.

"So the little jet from Las Vegas arrives, and it has a heck of a time getting into the hangar. I think the planes must have been a lot smaller if they really did build this hangar for two planes. These two jets barely fit. As soon as the plane had come to a stop, the hearse is trying to get into the hangar. But it can only get halfway into the building. So the guy who's driving backs the hearse up and pulls out of the hangar. He turns this giant black vehicle around and backs into the hangar, so at least the rear doors of the hearse are inside. I was afraid the FBI guy was going to get crazy again, but he kept himself together. Almost before the engine on the jet was quiet, two men unload a black body bag from the passenger compartment of the jet. Usually when we get a body, it's in a box and has made the trip in the baggage compartment. This poor dude is in a body bag, and he's ridden from Las Vegas with the passengers."

"So did they get the body transferred to the hearse?"

"It was the fastest and slickest magic trick you have ever seen. If you'd blinked you would have missed the whole thing. It didn't take two minutes for a young man and one of the pilots to carry the body bag off the plane and over to the hearse. They almost threw the body into the back of the hearse. The young guy who'd been on the plane, but was not the pilot, jumped into the front seat of the hearse with the driver. They were gone about two minutes after the jet arrived in the hangar. The pilot who had helped to unload the body went back to the plane to do whatever pilots do after a flight."

"I guess you didn't hear them say anything about what was going on, since they didn't have time to speak before they drove off."

"You're right, I didn't have time to hear those two FBI guys say anything about anything. I mean, the FBI people left in such a hurry. But I was real curious, and I eavesdropped on the two pilots while they were checking out stuff about the plane. I guess they have done all of those check lists hundreds of times and do them on automatic. They were puzzled and kind of ticked off about the flight they'd just made. They were doing a quick turn around and heading back to Las Vegas as soon as they could check things out and refuel the plane. They were not happy about having to fly back to Las Vegas in the middle of the night. They had been told they absolutely could never tell anybody anything about the flight to Little Rock and back. It would be erased from the flight logs. There was no dead body. None of it had ever happened."

Josh was in reporter mode now and had lots of questions. "Do you know if it was a man or a woman in the body bag?"

"I don't know for sure, but when they were rushing him off the plane and into the hearse, I think one of them referred to him as 'dude.' My guess is that it was a man in the body bag."

"Did they say anything about who he was or how he died?"

"Not really, but the pilots did say something about an arrest going down the toilet. I guess they'd had a swat team assembled to make an arrest, and they stormed into some guy's house only to find he was already dead."

"Was there anything else they said that gave you any idea about what the heck was going on?"

"Not really. They did say this was Ridley Wilton's 'baby' and nobody was allowed to talk about it or even admit that anything at all had happened in Las Vegas. They said it was a 'total black bag job' or a 'total black-out job.' Something like that. One of them said they were not even supposed to be talking with each other about it. That's all I heard. Next thing I knew the jet was on its way to refueling, and away it went.

"When I came in this morning, I was told to put everything back the way it had been when there was only one jet in the hangar. The jet that's always here was to be parked in the middle of the space as usual. I was told that there had never been another jet arrive from anywhere the night before. My supervisor even called in the man who had helped me move the furniture and told him the same thing. Nothing to see here. Nothing to see last night. Business as usual. No extra jet, no hearse, no nothing. It was curious how adamant my supervisor was about the whole thing. She almost seemed frightened when she was warning me not to talk about what had happened."

Chapter 21

Josh the journalist was on the scent again. He had a hunch the body that had arrived at the hangar in Little Rock the night before was connected in some way with the Agnes MacGillicutty story. He wondered if the lead he most needed to follow up on was in Las Vegas. Who had died there, and why was that person important to Ridley Wilton? Josh was certain there would be nothing in any newspaper about the death. For some reason, it was important to keep this death a secret. No one could know anything about whoever it was who'd been in the body bag.

Agent Ridley Wilton was the key. Josh decided he would have to follow Ridley if he was ever going to find out anything about Agnes MacGillicutty. There was no way the journalist was going to be able to hack into the FBI computer system. Following people in the real world had become a very outdated way to learn anything, but Josh was going to give it a try for a few days.

Rather than spend his time languishing in the underground garage of the building where the FBI had its offices, Josh decided to put a tracking device on the FBI agent's car. Josh left his airport job early, and he watched the FBI's parking garage for a couple of hours at the end of the working day. He was able to identify Ridley's white Chevy Tahoe when the agent unlocked it, got into the driver's seat, and drove it out of the parking garage. The next day Josh put a tracker on the vehicle and programmed his phone to watch where it went. If only he could put a tracker on the agent himself. Josh laughed as he imagined how he might accomplish that impossible feat. If Agent Wilton walked to any place of importance, Josh was going to miss it.

The first day Josh was watching, Wilton stayed in his office all day. The second day at about 11:30 in the morning, Wilton drove his SUV to the Capital Hotel in downtown Little Rock. Bingo. This said to Josh that the Capital Hotel was a place that was on the radar screen of the FBI. Josh had been sure the Capital Hotel was where Agnes MacGillicutty had been taken by the FBI the night of the foiled hijacking. He knew federal witnesses were taken there, and it was just a few minutes from the airport. Later that week, Wilton drove his car to the Capital Hotel again. This second trip really got Josh's attention.

On both trips to the hotel, Wilton stayed at least long enough to have lunch. Josh wondered if he was meeting a contact there, or if he just liked the food. The food was very good at the Capital Hotel, so it might turn out to be the food. It did seem like a long way to drive for a club sandwich, even if it was a really outstanding one. Josh found that Ridley Wilton usually drove to the hotel twice a week, on Tuesday and Friday. He also went at other times and not always for lunch. Josh wondered briefly if he had a girlfriend he was meeting there but decided Wilton wasn't the type for that.

Josh was waiting in the lobby of the Capital Hotel the following Tuesday at 11:45 when Ridley Wilton drove up to the front entrance and left his car with the hotel's valet. Josh wore a suit and was hiding behind a newspaper. Printed newspapers to hide behind were becoming harder and harder to find, just like pay phones. Josh was pretending to be a businessman waiting for a client. The FBI agent walked immediately to the rear of the lobby, turned left, and disappeared down a short hallway. The hallway didn't go anywhere. It was a dead end. Josh was curious.

He followed his quarry and discovered the FBI agent waiting by the phone in an alcove behind the registration desk. The phone appeared to be a pay phone, but it was not in a phone booth. It had to be one of the last few remaining pay phones in the city. It was curious to Josh that the head FBI agent in Little Rock would use an obscure pay phone in a hotel lobby to make phone calls. This was another red flag for the journalist.

Josh loitered as long as he could outside the alcove. His ears perked up when the pay phone rang and Ridley answered it at once. Josh couldn't hear what Wilton was saying, but clearly the FBI agent had been expecting the call and was waiting there in the alcove for the phone to ring. Josh returned to the lobby and put his newspaper up in front of his face. After a few minutes, Ridley Wilton came back through the lobby and went into the bar.

Josh returned to the telephone alcove and wrote down the number of the pay phone. He didn't yet know exactly how he was going to use the phone number, but he thought it might come in handy at some point. He realized why this particular pay phone was a desirable place to make and receive calls. It was in an obscure and quiet location, and it was protected in the sense that a phone booth outside a Stop 'n Shop was not.

It would not be easy to vandalize and destroy the phone that was located in an alcove behind the registration desk at the Capital Hotel. Somebody had even left a Little Rock phone book from 2007 beside the phone. Josh went into the bar and ordered his lunch, a club sandwich with fries and iced tea. If the FBI came here to eat, he was going to have what Ridley Wilton was having.

As soon as Wilton had finished eating, he took his claim ticket to the valet stand and drove away in his car. Josh, still eating his lunch in the bar, watched the man drive away on his phone app. He was going back to work. Josh debated about whether or not to try to follow Wilton to his home, but decided that would not gain him anything. If Wilton suspected somebody was following him, Josh could be putting himself in a bad spot. He opted to track Wilton on his phone rather than take more risks. It crossed Josh's mind to quit his job at the airport and get a job at the Capital Hotel.

It was illegal for somebody to bug another person's phone. Law enforcement agencies had to get a court order to put a listening device on someone's phone or in someone's house. But Josh was going to put an illegal listening device on the pay phone at the Capital Hotel. He suspected he could learn something useful by listening to Ridley Wilton's phone calls. There was a reason the man did not use his cell phone or his office phone for certain communications. Josh wanted to find out why the agent went to such an effort to conduct some of his business in secret, by using a pay phone in a hotel of all places. Did he suspect that someone was listening in on his office phone and his cell phone? Of course, everybody knew the NSA listened in on every phone in the country, but maybe Ridley knew that the No Such Agency had determined the pay phone at a hotel in Arkansas wasn't a high priority for picking up terrorist chatter.

Josh had bugged telephone landlines before to obtain information for a story, but it had been a while. Technology for spying on others had progressed rapidly, and Josh knew the "bugs" he already owned were dinosaurs. He needed new, updated equipment. Thank goodness he had a job. Between the spyware and the club sandwiches, he was spending more than he would have liked. The food at the Capital Hotel wasn't cheap, and the high tech surveillance equipment he needed to purchase wasn't cheap either.

Josh loved investigating and tracking down a story. He thought nothing about going outside the law to get what he wanted. He wasn't crazy about having a second job, but if he wanted to watch Ridley Wilton and listen to his phone calls, he was going to need a reason to frequent the Capital Hotel.

Josh had a college degree, and he looked pretty presentable, especially in his suit. He thought he could probably get a part-time position as a bellman at the hotel. He had a day job so the work he was after would have to be night and weekend work. Of course, Ridley came for lunch during the week, and that was when Josh was working at his day job. Josh thought he could rearrange his schedule at the airport to work a weekend day and have Tuesdays off. Nobody wanted to work on the weekends, so that change probably wouldn't be difficult to set up. Josh needed access to the Capital Hotel to have the opportunity to install his surveillance equipment and to have a reason for hanging out at the hotel to be able to monitor it.

Josh turned on the charm and got the position as a bellman. The hotel was glad to hire a part-time person because they didn't have to pay him any benefits like health insurance or contribute to a 401(k) retirement account. Josh made a point of becoming friendly with the valet who parked cars for the hotel guests. Josh let the valet know that he would be willing to take over for him when he needed a break. Josh explained to the valet that he loved cars and loved to see what kinds of cars different kinds of people drove. He chatted about cars with the valet whenever he had the chance. Josh was a convincing and accomplished talker; some might even say he was an accomplished bull shitter.

Josh had not given up trying to put a tracking device on Ridley Wilton. One of the fantasies he'd had about how to accomplish this involved putting something on Ridley's car keys or on the ring that held his keys. Because most men keep their car keys in their pockets, if Josh was able bring this off, it would almost be as if he had put a tracking device on Ridley himself.

After a couple of weeks, Josh made sure he was always hanging out close to the valet stand at about 11:45 on Tuesday mornings. He casually mentioned to the valet again that he was available to relieve him if he wanted to take a break. One Tuesday, the valet took him up on his offer. So, Josh was standing in as the hotel valet when Ridley Wilton drove up and left off his SUV. Josh took Ridley's keys and gave him his claim check. Josh was ready and wasted no time putting the tiny transmitter on Ridley's car key. He parked the car and put the keys in the valet's locked key storage along with the other half of Ridley's claim check. The tiny tracking device had a limited range and the battery had a limited life span. But Josh was elated that he'd been able to pull this off. He felt as if he was finally making progress.

Meanwhile he had put a bug on the pay phone. He quickly realized that Ridley didn't use the pay phone every time he came to the hotel for lunch. Sometimes the agent made calls from the pay phone and sometimes he received calls. Sometimes he didn't go near the pay phone and went straight to the bar for his lunch. If he used the pay phone, he usually spoke very briefly to whoever was on the other end of the line. Josh had no way of finding out where the calls were coming from when someone called in on the pay phone. But Josh had discovered that when one of Ridley's close group of special agents was out of town or was reluctant to speak with him personally in his office, anything important was communicated to their boss over the hotel phone.

Josh had figured out that Aunt Mathilda was probably Agnes MacGillicutty, or he thought he had figured that out. But he was confused because the agents who called also talked about someone who lived with Aunt Mathilda whose name was "Mac." Josh didn't know if Aunt Mathilda was Agnes MacGillicutty or if Mac was Agnes. These seemed to be two different people, and Josh had determined that both were women. He'd assumed, because one of these people was often referred to as Mac, that MacGillicutty was probably the old lady's real last name. He didn't have it all figured out yet. Most of all he wanted to know where the calls about Mac and Aunt Mathilda were coming from. Nobody ever mentioned the names of any places on the hotel phone calls.

Chapter 22

"We did exactly what we were supposed to do, so we expect to be paid. It is not our fault if the other people you hire are idiots and aren't able to do what you expect of them. The Vickers brothers did their jobs, and they did them well. Part of the deal we made with them was that we would buy a house for each of them. That was part of their payment, and we let them think they owned those houses. Billy Bob Vickers still thinks he owns his house. But of course, we bought them, and we are the ones who really own them. This is the way we have always done business. You knew that when you brought us into your complicated plot."

Anatoly Kuznetzov was adamant and angry. He didn't like doing business with these people. He didn't need their money. They always dangled a huge payoff out there—one he couldn't resist. He almost always fell for it and said yes to the job. Then they didn't want to pay up when something went wrong. It was not Anatoly's peoples' fault. They were carefully chosen and well-trained. If they made mistakes, they died. Anatoly was sick of fighting for what he had been promised.

"Then you wanted us to snuff Jimmy John, and we did that for you. No muss, no fuss. Now you don't want to pay us for that either? I don't care if buying those houses has caused problems or raised red flags or whatever you are implying has happened. Those are your problems, not ours. We do this all the time."

> **NEWS REPORT:** Delta Flight #329 from Boston headed for Los Angeles, crashed in California's Sierra Nevada Mountain Range at the edge of the Mojave Desert. The overnight "red-eye" flight departed Logan Airport at 11:00 p.m. on Saturday night and lost contact with air traffic controllers less than an hour before it was scheduled to land at LAX. No rescue crews have been able to reach the crash site. There are not expected to be any survivors. Drone surveillance has identified the exact location of the downed aircraft, but due to the weather, no helicopters have been able to land there. Because of the mountainous terrain, the wreckage is completely inaccessible to motor vehicles. Four crew members and fifty-two passengers were aboard the A321 when it went down. All are presumed dead. No alarms were sounded by the pilots. There was never any indication that the plane was in trouble until air traffic control realized they had lost all communication with Flight #329. The NTSB is on its way to the scene. Because there was no warning that the flight was about to crash, investigators are particularly anxious to retrieve the black boxes. The flight data recorder is actually orange and will help the NTSB determine what caused the plane to go down.

■ ■ ■ ■

"At least something went right for a change. Or should I say something went half-way right? It didn't happen the way we'd hoped it would, but at least there was a crash. It was a red-eye flight so not that many people were on board. Not many people died. More's the pity. I don't understand how could there not have been any May Days or alerts sent to Las Vegas or any of the California airports that they were being hijacked. The whole point of these crashes is to scare the crap out of the American people that the raghead terrorists are back and hijacking planes again. What good does it do us if a plane goes down, but nobody knows it was hijacked and intentionally crashed? If there really was no alert sent by the pilots that they were being hijacked, it's just a crash for no reason. We can put out a rumor that the plane crashed because of a hijacking, but it will be just that...a rumor without anything official to back up the speculation. Again, unless we can find some terrorist group to claim responsibility for bringing down this plane, we really have gained nothing. There will always be a few people who can be convinced this was another terrorist plot, but we need it to be a screaming headline with 24/7 coverage on the cable networks. We lost out completely with Jihadi #2, and we still have no idea where he is. There was never a peep on the news about his arrest, if he was arrested, or anything about him. He might as well never have bought that plane ticket. He might as well never have been born, as far as I'm concerned. This plane to Los Angeles went down, but there was not a word about its being a hijacking.

"Is it possible the authorities know there was a hijacking, but they decided to keep it quiet? You couldn't blame them for trying to bury that. They don't want the public to be too *frightened to fly. The airlines are just getting back on their feet after the COVID-19 pandemic of 2020. If I were running the FAA or Delta Airlines, I might decide not to mention the fact that this plane had crashed as the result of a hijacking. Maybe they think they can keep that a secret. Unless the government knows and isn't talking, we will never know for sure if anybody is aware that the plane was hijacked. We know it was, but how can we make that public and get people stirred up against the Muslims again if they don't know it was a deliberate crash?*

"The only one of the three crashes we planned that we got any mileage out of at all was one of the two that didn't happen. But that old woman and her cane became the story. She nearly made a laughing stock out of the hijacking attempt. A martyr for jihad was taken down by an old woman. That made him look like an incompetent fool...which he was. She's turned out to be the big spectacle, completely overshadowing the fact that the plane might have gone down.

"Now he is saying that if it's the last thing he does, he wants to find that 'miserable bitch' and take her out. She ruined that hijacking, and she made the whole attempt to crash the plane look like stooges on parade."

Chapter 23

*S**am Stevenson was professional when he spoke with Mercedes over the phone. He sounded older, not a whippersnapper,* and like he knew what he was talking about. Mercedes had called him to introduce herself and to begin a conversation about the house she was looking for. She had owned a great deal of real estate over the years, so she was well-versed in real estate terminology and knew what questions to ask.

She told Sam she was going to "make a killing" when her Arizona house sold. Mercedes also told Sam that she wanted to put whatever property she purchased into the Family Investments Limited Partnership that she'd set up years earlier. This was structured so that whenever she sold anything that was owned by the partnership, the proceeds from the sales of the properties went directly to her daughters. When she died, it would all go to her daughters. It was a good arrangement and avoided estate complications. Sam was familiar with all of this. Because he was used to working with the FBI and with

WITSEC, he also understood the need for confidentiality. It would be easy to work with Sam Stevenson. Mercedes felt lucky to have him as her agent.

Mercedes told him how much she loved the place where she was currently living and exactly what she loved about it. She told Sam why she wanted to buy her hideaway summer house in the United States, even though she knew it would be much more costly to buy an ocean front property in Maine than it would be to buy a similar home in Nova Scotia. She told Sam that if she found a fabulous house she could live in during all the months of the year when it was too hot to be in Arizona, she might want to sell her house in Lewes. She explained that the Lewes house was too large for her to continue living there alone.

If she wasn't able to find a house to buy in Maine that suited her, she told Sam she might decide to purchase a rental property. A high-end rental would be a good investment and provide income. After Mercedes had asked her questions and told Sam about all of her wishes, parameters, and limitations, she felt he understood her. He knew he was not dealing with a novice property buyer, and he knew exactly what she hoped to find in terms of an ocean-front writing retreat.

Sam listened patiently and answered all of her questions. Mercedes had the feeling he was anxious to tell her something and couldn't wait for his turn to talk.

"You have given me valuable information about what you are looking for in terms of a property in Maine. The fact that you love so many specific things about the place where you are currently living gives me an excellent set of criteria about the kind of house you hope to buy. I may even decide to come to Terence Bay and see the house for myself. You have made it sound like the perfect place to get away from the press and the world and write mystery novels."

"It has been perfect for me. I wish I could pick it up and drop it on a secluded island off the coast of Maine."

"This conversation we've had has been very enlightening, and I'm even more excited than I was before to tell you about a property that has just become available. It's not yet on the market. I happen to know about it because it has been the subject of a complicated court case that I've become involved in. The judge has, after two years, finally released the house to be sold."

"It sounds like it might be too complicated for me. I need to relocate at the end of the summer. The FBI doesn't really want me in this house longer than that. I'm not exactly sure why. I think they anticipate that something will happen by the end of the summer to change my status in some way. But tell me about the complicated house."

"The house itself is not complicated. The court case it was involved in was very complicated, but that's finished now. The complicated part has finally ended. The house in question is on a secluded island off the coast of Maine... just as you've requested. But you can drive there. In other words, it is not an island that's accessible only by boat. It is a very private island, and not everybody is allowed to drive there. Your handlers at the FBI will like the private and secluded part of the location. It is ideal for hiding away from everything."

"The location sounds perfect. But tell me something about the house and about the price. It's probably too steep for my budget."

"Actually, not everybody wants to live in a place that is as secluded as the island where this house is located. Not everybody is a writer or hiding out from the bad guys. Anyway, let me tell you about it. It is larger than the Nova Scotia house, but it has only one or two finished bedrooms, both on the first floor. I anticipate that you would use one of these bedrooms as an office or study, a room where you will do your writing.

The house has a second story, but the main bedroom is on the first floor." Sam knew Mercedes was handicapped, and any house she considered buying had to have the main bedroom and bathroom on the first floor.

"The original structure was built in 1880. It was built as a sheep barn, and it was superbly hand-crafted to withstand the sands, and the winds, of time. The sheep barn was part of a farm that was a family-run business. The farm was eventually abandoned, and the buildings were left to fall apart over the years. All the other buildings that were on the farm, including the farm house, have been torn down.

"Someone bought the farm in the late 1920s and cleared the property of all the derelict buildings. They got rid of everything else but kept this sheep barn. It was such a beautifully made building, they turned it into a summer cabin and fishing lodge. The cabin had no heat or inside plumbing at the time. There was an outhouse in the back yard and a pump beside the front door for water to cook with and wash with. It was a very primitive set up, but the owner, bless his heart, did put in gorgeous, wide-plank maple floors.

"In the 1950s, the farm was purchased by a woman who wanted a place to stay when she wasn't living on her sailboat. She needed a land base to store her furniture and clothes and household items, but she wanted to spend most of her time on the water. She made what was essentially still a barn with beautiful floors into a real house. She put in plumbing and a heating system. She installed a real kitchen and one full bath and one half bath. She added more windows and divided up the space into rooms with walls. She put in three fireplaces. The barn had previously been completely open on the inside—just one big open space. As one room, it was difficult to heat. The 1950's owner put in a second floor, but she didn't finish it off. It was used as an attic. She did quite a nice job of completing the first floor and put porches around the house. The first floor has ten foot ceilings. She never spent much time at the house, but it stayed in her family until the early 1980s.

"An older couple from New York City bought the farm from the woman's estate. These people didn't do much to change the house. They sold off everything but ten acres of the property to the state of Maine. All the rest of the island is owned by the state of Maine. Only ten acres stayed with the house. Most of that ten acres is still trees and fields. The house has a small yard. There are no huge grounds to take care of and no grass to mow. There's a plot for a garden. This is the Pine Tree State, so the yard has natural landscaping and is covered with pine shats. This is not suburbia.

"Enter the eccentric, retired botany professor who bought the house in 1995. He added a two-car garage and a huge solarium. He used the solarium as a greenhouse. It's a beautiful addition and looks like something from Victorian England. Supposedly he purchased a hugely expensive greenhouse kit and built the thing himself. And he did a first-class job of putting it together. You will love the all-glass greenhouse. He grew vegetables and flowers and herbs, but he was also into growing cannabis in his Victorian greenhouse. He realized he could augment his standard of living considerably by selling the cannabis in Bar Harbor and other places in the area. It wasn't long before he had quite a lucrative business going. Then he was busted and ended up in jail."

"This is all fascinating, but when are you going to tell me how big the house is. You dangled the fact in front of me that it was bigger than the house I'm staying in now, but you never said how much bigger."

"I wanted to reel you in with this story about the provenance of the property before I told you about the square footage. Adding on the greenhouse increased the size of the place considerably. The original sheep barn was square, fifty feet by fifty feet. Now it has a garage and a greenhouse added to it. But the way the rooms are arranged is very pleasing. The rooms are spacious, and I think you will like the layout."

"I can live with fifty by fifty, Sam. Is it in terrible condition? Didn't you say it had been vacant for the last two years?"

"Yes, it's been vacant for more than two years, but it is not in terrible condition. Let me tell you the rest of the story about the previous owners and what they did to the house. After the cannabis gardener went to jail, the house was sold to a professional athlete who intended to use it as a summer home. He completely redid the kitchen, the plumbing, and the electricals. He completely replaced the HVAC system and added air conditioning. He divided the second floor attic into rooms and added plumbing for bathrooms. He actually put in two bathrooms up there.

"He had finished all of the renovations and moved his furniture in just before 9/11. The athlete was not a gardener, so he'd put a beautiful swimming pool in the greenhouse. It's a very expensive pool. This may kill the deal for you. You would be surprised how many people want nothing to do with taking care of a house that comes with a swimming pool. Anyway, the guy's wife was a trader with Cantor Fitzgerald, and she died when the North Tower went down in New York City. Very sad, but then it was all ...." Sam paused for a moment, remembering. "The man was so distraught after losing his wife, he never wanted to live in the house. He'd paid all this money fixing it up and putting in the gorgeous pool, but he never spent a single day or night there. He rented the house to a family for two or three months during the subsequent summers. The same people came back every year for five years. Then they decided to buy their own place in Kennebunkport.

"I promise, there really is no curse on the property, but the last person to own the house disappeared. That's why I said it was complicated and why the house went to court. The previous owner was outrageously wealthy, and he was a classic recluse. He bought the place in 2016. It had essentially been vacant for quite a few years so at that point it needed a lot of work. The reclusive owner updated everything. He changed the rooms around a little bit and made a bigger main bedroom and bathroom on the first floor. He put solar panels on the roof of the garage. He put in new insulated windows. He was obsessed with fine finish carpentry work and moldings and fireplace mantles. He loved shelves and book cases. He had a carpenter working here full-time for two years. The owner, Gilbert Jones leased a place to live in Bar Harbor while he redid this house. He drove out every day, supposedly to oversee the work his carpenter was doing.

"The owner must have had thousands of books or some kind of massive collections of some kind. There are bookshelves everywhere. There are so many bookshelves, no normal person would ever buy this house. It was fixed up as such a custom place, and that will make it difficult to sell. Between the excessive amount of bookshelves and the greenhouse with the pool, there are very few buyers who would be willing to take on this house. The solar panels, or so the company that put them in claims, will heat the house in winter and cool the house in summer as well as heat the pool. If this in fact is true, energy costs should not be a deterrent. It's a beautiful place, but it is different."

"I can live with different. You've not told me anything so far that has put me off. What are you not telling me about the place, besides the price?"

"The second floor has been divided into bedrooms and bathrooms. The drywall is up, but the last owner never bothered to do anything about painting those upstairs rooms. The bedrooms and bathrooms are mostly finished, but the bathroom renovations on the second floor are incomplete. A few of the upstairs toilets are missing. One sink has no counter top. Little things that the previous owner never got around to taking care of. He just wasn't interested in doing anything much about the second floor. There's some furniture stored in one of the rooms up there now. You would probably just ignore those upstairs rooms or use them as storage.

"Another major drawback of the place is that you can't access the second floor from inside the main part of the house. There's no inside staircase. When the second story was just one big space, there was a pull-down staircase in the hall ceiling that was the only way to get up to the attic. When the garage was built, the professor put in a stairway to the second floor. But that stairway to the second floor is in the garage. A family with young children would probably not be comfortable living in a house like this.

"You can see that the house has a number of quirks that make it unusual. You might be able to work with these shortcomings. My understanding is that you want to redo the main bathroom and make a few other changes. You can get this house for a good price. I'm just saying. You will love the views, and the house itself is lovely. It has a gourmet kitchen. The ten-burner stove is already there, and it's never been used. You will have to buy a refrigerator. I promise you, it looks nothing like the sheep barn it was originally intended to be. So, what do you think?"

"I am quite overwhelmed with all this information. I will need to think about it and I want to see many, many pictures of the rooms. A video walkthrough is a must. But, I have to tell you Sam, nothing that you have said about this house so far has turned me away. It is larger than I'd hoped it would be, but it sounds like it has a suitable floorplan. The excitement in your voice has me excited. This is the first place I've heard about that is remotely close to what I've been looking for. Now, are you going to tell me about what happened to the previous owner and what the court case was all about?"

"There is nothing to tell. That's the problem. The previous owner, who said his name was Gilbert Jones, just disappeared one day. For two years, he had driven out to the house every day—religiously. He'd never missed one day coming here to participate in the renovations and hassle the carpenter. He was paying the carpenter, Donny Germaine, really big bucks, so I guess he'd decided that putting up with the owner's constant presence and annoying oversight was worth it. The owner relentlessly picked apart Donny's work, and that was part of the deal. The owner was a perfectionist. If something didn't suit him, he had the carpenter tear it out and do it over again. And I guess he had the funds to afford to do that."

"So the owner disappeared?"

"One day he just didn't show up at the house. Donny was surprised, and at first he assumed the guy was sick or something. After he didn't show up for the third day, he tried to call his cell phone. No answer. Then Donny went to the house in Bar Harbor that the owner had been renting. No one was there. The owner's SUV was parked in the garage, but Gilbert Jones was nowhere to be found. He had vanished."

"Did the police become involved? Did they search for him or for a body? What about his family?"

"The police searched everywhere. The absence of any family whatsoever was the strangest part of the whole thing. The man was a ghost. Nobody knew anything about him. Nobody knew where he'd come from. He obviously had a ton of money. He always paid the carpenter in cash, but he did have a credit card. The credit card bill arrived at his rental house every month. He had a checking account that he used to pay his bills. But he had no driver's license or passport, at least that anybody could find. He had never filed any income taxes under the name of Gilbert Jones, the name he used to purchase the house on the island. He'd paid cash for the house, so there was no mortgage. He paid the property taxes and the utilities on the island house. He paid his rent and the monthly utility bills for the house he was leasing. Money was no object, so when he turned out to be the man who never was, everyone assumed he'd been some kind of drug lord or mafia guy or criminal who was escaping from a former life."

"What about something like witness protection?"

"That's how I got involved. The local law enforcement people were out of their depth. They called in the FBI. The FBI could not find out anything about the guy either. They swore he was not in any kind of state or federal protection program and were just as mystified as everybody else. Donny Germaine finished up everything he'd been paid to do and went on to another job. The county sheriff closed up the house."

"It still belonged to the man who had disappeared, Gilbert Jones, but nobody had a clue about what to do with the house. When Jones's lease ran out on the house where he was living in Bar Harbor, the owners of the rental house had his things moved into the house on Flower Island. There wasn't much...his clothes, a few pieces of furniture. I'm suspecting he had a storage unit or units someplace. If he was going to fill up all those bookcases with books or pottery or some kind of a collection, he had to have a storage unit full of his stuff. The police and the FBI looked for a storage unit, but they could never find it. If he had a collection or a huge library, nobody has any idea where it is.

"If the owner was dead, the sheriff felt his body would eventually turn up. It never did. After a year, no one was paying the electric bill or the heating bill or the taxes. If the court waited seven years to declare the man officially dead, this beautiful house was going to deteriorate and become a ruin. The sheriff and the FBI went to court to try to resolve something. The laws in every state are different about what to do with abandoned property.

"I'd worked with the FBI in the past, and they called me in to put a valuation on the house. Because it is such a unique property, it was almost impossible to come up with a realistic price. The right buyer might be willing to spend millions for the place. Somebody else wouldn't take it if you gave it to them. I spent quite a bit of time in the judge's chambers with a bunch of lawyers trying to figure out what to do. The judge wanted to know if I thought I could find a buyer for the house. I said I thought I could. I didn't know you yet, but I figured there was some eccentric recluse out there somewhere who might want a summer place in Maine.

"The judge finally ruled a couple of days ago that the owner of the property was presumed dead and that the house was to be put on the market and sold. The proceeds from the sale, after all the court costs and attorneys' fees are paid and after the utility bills and property taxes and other expenses are paid, will go to the state fund that purchased the rest of the land years ago as a wildlife refuge. All parties agreed to abide by the judge's decision, but of course no one was there to represent the mystery man who actually owned the property. As I've said, it was very complicated. I'd never participated in anything like this before. I don't think the judge had either."

"What if the owner turns up or what if his heirs turn up and decide to go after the proceeds from selling the property or want to live there?"

"That's why the whole thing was tied up in a legal mess for so long. The owner's legal rights to the property, his ownership rights, have been vacated by the court. Gilbert Jones, or whoever he really is, can't have his property back, even if he shows up now and wants it back. Of course, everyone believes he's dead. And nobody could find any heirs. The court followed all the legal procedures and looked very hard for some family members. There aren't any. I don't think, considering the amount of time and money he'd put into the house, that Jones would have walked away from it unless he was deceased. He abandoned the place, and after all the legal maneuvering and official notifications in the newspapers were taken care of, the property now belongs to the state's wildlife refuge fund. At least when the property is sold, the proceeds will go to them."

"That is quite some story. In fact, you have told me at least two amazing stories about this house. The place has had a number of owners, most of whom spent a great deal of money and effort to update and improve the house. But hardly any of the people who have owned the house and spent money on it have lived there for any period of time. And I am intrigued by the story about the most recent owner who disappeared into thin air. That is very strange. Are you sure there isn't a curse on the property?" Mercedes laughed but she was only partly joking. "I don't believe in curses, but I do worry that the man might show up and want his house back. Things could get ugly."

"Trust me; that is not going to happen. The guy is dead. He's never going to show up to claim his property. But you're right, not every buyer would be willing to sign on for all that uncertainty and a potential law suit and court battle, however small the possibility, over its ownership."

"I think I would love the place, but I don't know if I can get into something this snarly at this point in my life. And I wouldn't want to leave my daughters a situation that is fraught with legal complications."

"Those are all the reasons why this place is such a bargain. The house and the island and the views are worth much more than $1,500,000, but considering the multiple encumbrances involved, I think it's a fair price.

"Send me all the photos. I want a lot of pictures of the exterior, porches, and lots of photographs of the views. I want a video walk-through of all the rooms. I also want photo close-ups of the millwork, the bookcases and mantles, and all of that. I will make my decision after I have seen the photos and the video."

"Of course, I realize the $1.5 million doesn't come close to equaling the amount you will be making from selling the Scottsdale place. I have a suggestion about another contiguous property that you could include in the contract. It borders on the Flower Island property and would give you even more security and protection—if you decide to buy on Flower Island.

"I like the name of the island. Is it on the map?"

"Several of the previous owners have wanted to change the name, but it's been known as Flower Island for over two hundred years. In the spring and summer, the fields are filled with wildflowers. It is quite lovely, although I understand you have allergies. So it may not seem that lovely to you. And it is not on the map. That is one of the great things about it. Not every one of these tiny islands off the coast of Maine made it onto the maps. There are just too many of them, and they are too small. You will have extra anonymity because your island doesn't exist."

Chapter 24

Mercedes decided to buy the house on Flower Island, and she was going to buy it sight unseen. She had looked at hundreds of photographs of the house and its surroundings, and she had seen multiple videos. She had done several Zoom calls with Sam Stevenson. She felt as if she had actually been in the house. She knew the floor plan and had already begun mentally placing her furniture in the rooms. She had asked all the questions that needed to be asked. She had fallen in love with the house and with the location. It had spectacular views of the Atlantic Ocean, which is what she'd been looking for. It was a larger place than the much-loved Baird House, but the open and functional floor plan was such that she could live with more space.

Part of the extra square footage included a heated swimming pool in the solarium, and for Mercedes, this was a plus. She would have to hire a pool company to take care of it for her, but she was happy to do that. She would be able to swim every day, and she would be able to heat her pool to a comfortable temperature. Swimming helped to keep her arthritis at bay and kept her moving. One of the reasons she had hated giving up her big house in Arizona was because she would no longer have her own back yard pool to use for exercise. She'd almost talked herself into using the heated pool in the building where her new condo was located, but the homeowners association didn't heat that pool for people who had arthritis and wanted to swim at a therapeutic 94 degrees.

Things needed to be done to the house in Maine to make it comfortable for Mercedes. The large bathroom next to the first floor bedroom needed some changes to make it more handicap accessible. The previous owner had left a few things unfinished, and Mercedes would take care of those. Mercedes wanted to put her personal touches on the interiors. All of this could be arranged remotely via Zoom. She began to be excited about her new house. She hadn't had to build it, and it didn't really need much work. She would be able to make it her own.

She had designed and done many home renovations in her life, and this would be a fun and easy one. She had designed and built her Arizona house, many years ago, long distance. She had seen the property and bought it. She had carefully drawn the floorplans using a design program on her computer. With a fax machine and her landline phone, she had successfully built that house in Scottsdale from the ground up while she was living 3,000 miles away. It had tried her patience at times, but she had been meticulous and on top of the process every step of the way. The result, when she had finally seen the finished house eleven months later, looked exactly as she had expected it would. This would be easy compared to building the house in Scottsdale.

Mercedes asked her real estate guy Sam if he would be willing to be her boots on the ground and help her with the renovations. He agreed to do this and was able to convince

Donny Germaine, the carpenter who had worked on the house for Gilbert Jones, to put the finishing touches on things for Mercedes. Sam also intervened with the judge who had made the decision in the abandoned property case. The judge gave permission for Mercedes to begin renovations on the house before she actually settled on it. This was unusual, to allow a prospective owner to do work on a house before she or he owned it. Sam had assured the court that everything Mercedes planned to do to the house would enhance its value.

Mercedes was delighted that Donny Germaine was willing to work for her. She had been concerned that he might not want to return to the house after his former employer had disappeared so mysteriously. Gilbert Jones had been a difficult taskmaster, and Mercedes would have understood if Donny Germaine had never wanted to cross the threshold of the house again. But he seemed eager to come back and work on the project for her. Mercedes knew Donny did beautiful carpentry work, and she knew exactly what she needed to have him do. She began making lists and drawings for her carpenter, for Sam, and for herself. Making lists was something Mercedes was good at and liked to do. Making lists about the cottage renovations gave her a great deal of pleasure.

The settlement on the Arizona house would take place at the end of June. The carpenter would begin working on the house in Maine at the end of May, and he said he would have plenty of time to complete everything Mercedes wanted done in three months. The house would be ready before September. Sam had agreed to be her intermediary and handle all the details. In addition to the real estate paperwork, he would take care of the financial dealings and the money transfers. Mercedes focused on the design and renovation issues. It was going to work out. She realized that once she'd made the decision to buy the Flower Island property and began to fix up the house in her mind and on paper, most of her melancholy lifted. She decided it had been the uncertainty about her future that had been a major factor in her anxiety and depression. Mac noticed how much more cheerful she was and commented that maybe it was because the days were warmer and the sun shone more frequently as Nova Scotia moved well into late spring.

Mercedes was still very attached to Baird House, but she had known all along that eventually she would have to leave it. It didn't belong to her. Nova Scotia was in a foreign country. She had loved her time in Canada, but she wanted to return to the United States. She never experienced any buyer's remorse for having bought a home on an island in Maine without first seeing it in person.

The owners of the rental house where Gilbert Jones had lived had moved a few pieces of his furniture to the Flower Island cottage. Sam told Mercedes that there were a few antiques stored in one of the second floor rooms. The professional athlete who had rented the house for several years had left his furniture behind. The mattresses and upholstered couches and chairs had been given away, but a few of the pieces from that era had been worth saving. They were also stored on the second floor. Sam said some of that furniture didn't look too bad and might be worth keeping.

Mercedes' daughter who lived in Delaware was going to have the furniture and books that Mercedes wanted from the Lewes house sent to Maine. After her husband died, Mercedes had continued to sleep in the king size bed she and Ford had shared in their Lewes home. She decided it was time to move on and resurrect the four poster antique double bed with the canopy that she had slept in as a child while growing up in Ohio. The canopy bed was currently occupying a guest room in Lewes, but it would be her own bed again at the house in Maine.

Mercedes would be able to use her father's office desk, which she had kept all these years, as her writing desk on Flower Island. It was huge, nearly the same size as the table she'd used for writing at Baird House. There was plenty of room for the desk in the room Mercedes would use as her office and writing room in Maine. The desk would need to be refinished or painted. She had two beautiful matching chests of drawers she wanted to use in her new bedroom. It was a large room and could easily accommodate both Chippendale chests. Some of the furniture she planned to use needed to be reupholstered. A couple of other pieces needed slipcovers.

Mercedes was having fun. She always had fun writing, and now she was having a wonderful time as she mentally and virtually furnished her new house. She was thrilled to be working on a project. She would make the cottage very handicap friendly. She would finish the bedrooms and the bathrooms on the second floor. She would paint them, and then she would forget about them. They would be ready if her family was ever allowed to come and visit her.

Most of all, Mercedes wanted Mac to come with her. She'd learned that in fact Mac was a United States citizen, not Canadian, as Mercedes had thought at first. All that talk about Canadian bacon and Canadian maple syrup had just been talk. Mac had been hired by the FBI to babysit their special witnesses and keep the safe house in Nova Scotia up and running. Mac had confided in Mercedes that the Mafia types the FBI sometimes brought to the house for her to take care of were scary and difficult to get along with. She didn't like having to babysit them. The men were messy and dropped their clothes on the floor everywhere. Some of them even smoked cigars. They had to go out on the porch to smoke, but they smelled like cigar smoke all the time. Mac hated that. She wanted to return to the United States.

Mercedes was crazy about Mac. Mac made all of her favorite foods and had introduced Mercedes to some of her own wonderful culinary creations. She wanted Mac to come with her to Maine and take care of her house on Flower Island. There was a caretaker's cottage near the causeway that went to the island. Mercedes thought Mac would love the house. Mercedes would fix it up to suit Mac. Mercedes had decided to purchase this additional property that guarded the causeway and the entrance to Flower Island. She didn't know what the FBI was paying Mac, but Mercedes thought she could match it. The rest of her life might turn out to be pretty good, even with somebody trying to kill her, if she could convince Mac to accompany her to the new house.

Ridley Wilton was delighted when he heard that Mercedes had decided to buy a house in Maine. The Nova Scotia safe house had worked well so far, and he trusted it would work until Mercedes moved to Flower Island. He'd never left a witness in one place for as long as he'd left Mercedes at Baird House. He usually left them for a few days or weeks at most. Then they were turned over to the U.S. Marshals and entered WITSEC or they testified in court and did not have to hide anymore. Some thought they could manage to hide themselves on their own, but they usually couldn't. Some just got fed up with having their lives disrupted and went on their merry way. Mercedes was different. She was not a Russian mafia thug trying to get out of working for Vladimir Putin. She was not a U.S. gangster testifying against a crime boss. Mercedes was special and required special treatment. Thank goodness he'd had Baird House with its handicap accessibility. He didn't know what he would have done with Mercedes if he hadn't had that house available and Mac to take care of her.

He knew Mac wanted to return to the United States, and he knew she had lost patience watching over the "wise guys." Putting up with them for long periods of time always led to burn out. Mac was a treasure, and he knew he was going to lose her. He'd had a feeling Mercedes might try to hire her away from the FBI. That was all right with Ridley. The two women were wonderfully compatible, and Mercedes was going to need somebody to help her at the place in Maine.

The choice of Flower Island was ideal for security purposes. Ridley knew Mercedes was a reclusive type. Most writers were. She had been very compliant about agreeing not to be out and about, not to go shopping or to restaurants, and not to get together with friends for lunch. Being in a foreign country where she knew no one had kept her from being able to socialize. Her disabilities helped keep her housebound, but he knew she missed her family. In the past, she'd always tried to spend birthdays and holidays with them if she could. Since arriving in Nova Scotia, she'd had sessions with her children and grandchildren on Zoom, but one of these days she was going to request an in-person visit. Ridley would have Agent Barnes arrange that for the summer.

After they moved Mercedes to Maine in September, the trail would go cold again. Ridley was counting on it. He worried that someone might be watching members of her family and follow them to the family reunion he knew Mercedes was hoping for and planning. He had to constantly remind himself that no one knew who Mercedes really was. She was not on the radar screen of the FBI in Washington, D.C., and she was not on anybody else's radar screen as far as he knew. Because no one ought to know who she was, no one should be watching any members of her family.

Ridley Wilton had struggled with the story Mercedes was going to tell her friends and neighbors and household help about why she was not going to spend her summers in Lewes this year as she always had in the past. He had talked it over with her, and they had decided a story about a writer's summer workshop on the coast of Oregon was a better lie than a story about a broken hip. Mercedes didn't want to upset the people who cared about her. They would worry about a woman in her late seventies who had fallen and broken a hip. They would applaud and be excited about an invitation to be a guest lecturer at the summer mystery writers' program in Depoe Bay.

They would understand why the workshop was an opportunity Mercedes couldn't turn down. They would be happy she'd decided to do something fun and interesting that had to do with her passion, writing fiction. Mercedes would tell her friends in Lewes she was busy in Oregon, but she would, from time to time, email them about the wonderful place she was spending the summer. Because Mercedes wrote fiction, she could easily create a writing workshop for herself and tell her friends, her relatives, and her housekeeper all about it. One problem solved.

When Ridley Wilton finally got possession of Jimmy John Vickers' body, he'd had a private autopsy done. Even though everyone knew what had killed Jimmy John, Ridley wanted to make it official. Then he'd made the somewhat questionable decision to have him cremated. He knew Vickers' only remaining family was Billy Bob, but nobody could find him to tell him or ask him anything. As far as anybody knew,

Jimmy John had also disappeared, and nobody ws able to say anything about what had happened to him.

Ridley's techs were combing through the video footage of people who'd visited Jimmy John's house. Jimmy John had been the contact person, the financial negotiator, and the one who had set up the mosque charade. He had been the planner, the brains behind that operation. They'd tried to follow his truck to see where he had gone and what people he'd met with in the weeks and months before Billy Bob began to pretend to be the blind Islamic worshiper. It was tedious work, but Wilton had nothing else to go on. His hopes for finding the trail of money and motivation for the hijackings had died when Jimmy John Vickers' throat had been cut.

Wilton knew someone had hired the Vickers brothers to infiltrate the mosque and convince the Imam to recruit the martyrs. He thought he knew what had happened inside the mosque with the Imam and the selection and preparation of the failed hijackers. But he was stumped about who had hired Jimmy John. The chronic protester with a completely disorganized lifestyle had not thought this up on his own. He had no motive. He was a paid troublemaker. He worked for money. He had no core system of values that drove his participation in any of the things he did. As far as Agent Wilton could determine, when trying to decipher what Jimmy John Vickers had done and why, it seemed to be all about the money and maybe also about the thrills.

Everything from Jimmy John's house had been boxed up and sent to Little Rock. Even what was in the wastebaskets had been collected and shipped to Ridley Wilton's office. The head FBI agent in Las Vegas was glad to have somebody take the body and the boxes of belongings off his hands. Because officially there had been no death and no body anyway, there had been no crime scene to investigate, only a cover-up that no one could ever talk about.

There had been hardly any furniture in Jimmy John's house. Most of it was cheap stuff, but Jimmy John had spent some serious money on his leather couch, his king-size bed, and his 90-inch flat-screen television set. Ridley hadn't wanted any of the furniture, so it was donated to secondhand stores. Ridley had wanted all the clothes, medications, papers, and memorabilia. It was probably a waste of time to go through it all, but Ridley was desperate to find who had bankrolled the Vickers. Of course, the story was that nothing had happened there. Nothing to see at Jimmy John Vickers' house in Las Vegas, and now it was empty.

Chapter 25

Agent Arabella Barnes had volunteered to go through the boxes that had been sent from Las Vegas. She knew her boss didn't have the patience to look through all that stuff, and the boxes would sit in the corner of Ridley Wilton's office for months. Arabella wasn't sure she had the patience to go through the boxes either. She doubted it was worth the time it would take her to sort through each piece of clothing and each piece of paper. But she was going to do it anyway. She always wore gloves when she examined evidence, and because this potpourri of belongings was anything but pristine, she was going to wear gloves and protective gear when she examined it, just in case.

Whoever had packed the boxes had not done a neat job of it. Things had been thrown together willy nilly, no doubt to get it all out of Jimmy John's house as quickly as possible. Clothes were mixed in with trash, and a half-used tube of toothpaste without the cap had been thrown in with a bunch of unpaid utility bills. Arabella knew how Jimmy John had died.

There was no question about his cause of death. None of his possessions were ever going to make an appearance in a court of law. What she was looking for was a lead to the person or persons who had paid Jimmy John to set up the mosque scam with his brother.

She didn't think the people who had killed Jimmy John had taken the time to search for anything. Because they hadn't even taken his cell phone, she doubted they had taken anything at all from the house. The cell phone had been in Jimmy John's shirt pocket when his body arrived in Little Rock. The phone had been the first thing they'd checked to try to find something of importance. They'd found nothing but numerous calls for pizza delivery and other food deliveries, quite a few calls to have beer and half gallons of Jim Bean delivered from a nearby package store, and a few calls to an escort service. The phone was a bust.

Arabella decided she would spend the first two hours of every morning going through Jimmy John's belongings. She knew she couldn't spend an entire day on the task and maintain her sanity. His clothes were expensive, but Jimmy John didn't wash them. It seemed as if he just went out and bought new clothes when his clothes got dirty. There was a stench in the room where Arabella was unpacking the boxes. She hated to touch even one piece of the filthy clothes that were smelly and stained. But she held her nose and meticulously went through all the pockets. It was in the hip pocket of a stiff pair of dirty blue jeans that she struck gold.

She'd gone through all the papers first and found nothing. Then she'd gone through the bags of trash. She'd put off going through the clothes because it made her stomach turn to handle any of them. She had pretty much finished going through all the boxes when she found the torn currency band in the pocket of the grimy jeans. The stamp on the band was in

Russian. Arabella didn't speak Russian but she knew enough to recognize that the Cyrillic letters stamped on the currency band were Russian. She took a picture of the lettering with her cell phone and carefully placed the currency band in an evidence bag.

The presence of the currency strap in the blue jeans was evidence, to Arabella, that Jimmy John had been paid in cash by someone who had given him a stack of money, banded for some odd reason by the Russians. The stack of money had to have been American money, probably hundred dollar bills. Jimmy John would have insisted on payment in dollars. But why would there have been a Russian band around the American currency? Whose stash was Jimmy John being paid from?

Arabella was ecstatic that she had found something. She hadn't expected to find anything at all and was just being thorough when she'd volunteered to go through the boxes of Jimmy John's belongings. She almost ran to Ridley Wilton's office, and her hand was shaking when she put the currency band down on his desk. When Ridley saw what she had brought him and when he saw the look on her face, he turned on his noise machine, in case he had missed anything in his daily search for bugs in his office.

Arabella couldn't wait to talk about her find. "There's no chain of custody for this, but I think it points us in the right direction in terms of figuring out who hired our guy and who paid him. I found this in the hip pocket of one of his disgusting pairs of jeans. I am betting that he was paid with stacks of bills. He must have torn this one off a fresh bunch and stuck the band in his back pocket. Why else would he have a currency band in his pocket? If the band had been blank or marked in English, it wouldn't mean anything. The fact that it is stamped in Russian is a big clue, in my opinion."

Ridley's eyes lit up. He reached out and picked up the transparent evidence bag that held the currency band. He turned it over and over in his hands. "I don't think there's a snowball's chance...that there would be a finger print on this, but I'm going to run it through the lab anyway. You never know." He grinned at Arabella. "Bravo! This says to me exactly what it says to you. This is where Jimmy John got his payment for the job he did. I know you took a picture of this with your cell phone. The first thing I'm going to do is find out what it says, the translation from Russian. If it says what I think it says, these packs of currency were bundles of one-hundred dollar bills...with a hundred bills in each. We need to find out what the Russians were doing banding our money."

Ridley was on a roll. "I want you to send the photo to my guy at Treasury, Simon Dunnaway. I'll text you his email. There was some kind of a flap in the early 1990s about a missing currency plate for the one-hundred dollar bill. They tried to keep it all under wraps, as you can imagine. This probably has nothing to do with any of that, but I want to know why stacks of United States money are apparently being handed out by the Russians."

He continued on another track. "I will bet you anything, if we could find out who owns New Vistas Properties, LLC, which we will never be able to do, we would discover that it's a Russian company. There won't be any Russians on its phony board or on any of the paperwork, but they are behind this. I know it. They've bought the Vickers brothers their houses, and they paid Jimmy John from some Russian stash of American bills. Billy Bob was probably also paid with these stacks of bills."

Arabella had already decided that Jimmy John was being paid by the Russians. "The next question is, why in the world would the Russians want to fund Islamic terrorists to bring down American airliners? We know the Russians aren't our friends, but this doesn't make any more sense than blaming the plot on the Vickers brothers."

"Nobody found any cash in the house, did they? I mean, he had to have kept his money somewhere. I'm sure he would not have deposited it in a bank."

"I found a few small-denomination bills and lots of loose change in the boxes I went through. But I didn't find any hundreds or packs of hundreds. What do you suppose he did with it? Buried it in his back yard?"

"Actually, that's not a bad guess as to where he might have hidden it. I'm going to see if this currency band has any soil residue on it. If he buried the stacks of bills in his back yard, there might be some dirt on the currency band. It could be worth our while to take apart his back yard to try to find the money."

"I'll bet that house will be on the market within a few weeks, if not a few days. It may already be on the market. Or, if it is part of some kind of a money laundering scheme, who knows what might be going on with the house? We will never get access to dig in the yard."

RIDLEY WILTON CALLED ARABELLA INTO his office. She could tell he had news for her. He was energized and smiling. He turned on his noise machine and couldn't wait until she sat down. "The translation on the currency band says: **10,000 USD**. As you probably know, all paper money is banded in stacks of one hundred bills. This is pretty standard, as a stack of 100 bills is easy to handle. This band was around a stack of one hundred one-hundred dollar bills. You do the math. That's ten thousand dollars. I would love to know how many of these bundles the Russians gave to Jimmy John Vickers."

Arabella had concluded from the beginning that the currency band had originally held ten thousand dollars' worth of American Benjamins. What she didn't know was why the Russians had the money. She'd decided in her own mind that every country must keep foreign currencies from other countries on hand as part of their treasury reserves. If that were the case with the Vickers' money, the fact that some of Russia's official currency reserves had made its way to the Vickers brothers, implied that the Russian government was in on this scheme. The implications for that fact were not good at all. It could be an international incident in the making.

Ridley had much more to tell. "But that is just the beginning of the story. The results came back from the fingerprint analysis. There are too many fingerprints all over the currency band to be of any use. The only good print the lab was able to get off the paper was one for Jimmy John Vickers. Of course, we already know he's had his grubby hands all over this money. No other prints were usable. I'd figured that. The real news is that there was soil residue on the band. Either he dropped his bundle of money in the dirt, or he had his stash buried in the ground. More tests are being done to see if they can identify where the soil residue came from. There wasn't much of it, and the techs didn't hold out much hope that more information about the soil would be forthcoming. But they are giving it a shot. One odd thing was that there also was tomato sauce on the currency band."

"I can solve that mystery for you. Jimmy John ate a lot of pizza. And I mean a lot. Like for every meal...even for breakfast. Tomato sauce and grease were all over his clothes. His phone had a ton of calls on it for pizza delivery. That's why there was tomato sauce on the currency band. It was on everything he touched."

Ridley knew that Jimmy John had ordered his pizzas with sausage, hamburger, pepperoni, and extra cheese. Greasy!

Ridley had more to tell about the money. "Day before yesterday, I called my friend Simon Dunnaway who works for the U.S. Department of the Treasury, at the BPE, the Bureau of Printing and Engraving in Ft. Worth. He received the photograph you sent and was very interested in the currency band. He was so interested in it that he flew to Little Rock yesterday morning. It's just an hour flight. He insisted on seeing the currency band. We had lunch together yesterday, and he had a fascinating story to tell me. Because I'm FBI, I guess he felt he could confide some details about that currency plate that went missing several decades ago. The fact that the plate disappeared is public information now, but the real story surrounding its disappearance is not. I'm sure it isn't the only currency engraving plate that's ever vanished. It's just the only one the public ever heard about. The Bureau of Printing and Engraving doesn't want to talk about missing plates or stolen plates and other bad things that have happened there. What agency does want to talk about things like that? But this particular missing plate has a Russian story connected with it, and that's what caught my friend's interest. His story also got my attention."

Arabella was now completely into the story, too. Ridley continued. "A currency plate that prints the face, the front side, of one hundred dollar bills went missing from the Bureau of Printing and Engraving, the BPE, in Washington, D.C. in the early 1990s. In mid-1990 to be exact. United States currency is printed at BPE facilities only in D.C. and in Ft. Worth, Texas. No place else. Nobody wanted to admit this plate might have been stolen. The plate could print the face design for 32 one hundred dollar bills at a time. All U.S. currency is printed on sheets of 32 bills. The plate which prints the bills weighs twelve pounds. The face design is the important side for any bill. Who looks closely at the back to see if it is the real thing? Who even knows what the back of any of the bills is supposed to look like? When you go into a store and they mark the larger bills with that special crayon to see if it's counterfeit, they only mark the front."

"So the official story inside the Treasury Department and the story put out to other agencies that knew about the missing plate was that it had inadvertently been destroyed with some other plates that were being melted down because they had flaws in them. Or the missing plate might have been mixed in with other plates that were scheduled to be destroyed. Metal plates wear out over time and have to be replaced with new ones. The ones with flaws and the old ones that are worn out are melted down to get rid of them. The truth is that BPE never actually accounted for the missing plate. They never knew what really happened to it." Ridley was glad he hadn't been involved in that SNAFU. "Embarrassing!"

"That might have been the end of the story, but a larger than normal amount of U.S. one-hundred dollar bills began to show up in the former USSR. The disintegration of the USSR happened to roughly coincide with the disappearance of the plate from BPE. Somebody had years to print plenty of phony one-hundred dollar bills. Our Treasury Department was all over this, trying to find out where all the Benjamins were coming from. The bills were not counterfeit. They were only partly counterfeit. The fronts of the bills had been printed with legitimate U.S. Treasury plates. They were printed on the official cotton and linen U.S. currency paper and with the officially correct ink. That stuff is relatively easy to get hold of.

"It was the numbers on the bills that were off. The serial numbers on these bills were duplicates of serial numbers on other one-hundred dollar bills that were already in circulation. Each paper bill that is printed is supposed to have a unique number printed on it. The bills that were coming out of Russia were perfect on the face in every way except for the duplicate serial numbers.

"The Soviet Union was in complete chaos during this period, and the USSR finally fell on December 26, 1991. When Boris Yeltsin took over, he was our new best friend for a while. He allowed our people from Treasury to go over to Russia and investigate the currency problem. Long story short, we found the printing press where the stolen plate had been used to print the partly-counterfeit one-hundred dollar bills. We shut down the printing press that was turning out the bills, but we never found the stolen plate. The bill-printing operation came to a halt. No more bad Ben Franklins with duplicate serial numbers were being printed.

"Between the time the plates were stolen in 1990 and the printing press was discovered and finally shut down in Russia a few years later, many bills had, of course, already been printed. Nobody knows exactly how many were printed, and nobody has ever been able to find what out happened to the money. Almost all of these bills disappeared.

"This part of the story can never be made public, of course. BPE will never admit that the plate was stolen. They'd already put out the story that it had been melted down by mistake, and they will stick with that story until the end. Of course, that was a lie. The last thing they'd want to admit was that the plate was stolen by the Russians and that the Russians printed a bunch of hundred dollar bills with it. They would never admit to any of that. Simon says that when they discovered the printing press in Russia, the place where the missing currency plate was being used, they found a few stacks of bills that had been left behind. What's interesting is that these bills were bundled with currency bands exactly like the torn one you found in Jimmy John's pants pocket."

Arabella had a hundred questions, but she let Ridley continue the story. "Treasury wants to take possession of the currency band when we are finished with it. The problem is that once they have it, the cat will be out of the bag. I don't know what to tell Simon. He was forthcoming and open and told me about the stolen plate and about how these bills came into existence. Now he wants the currency band. I told him he could have it after our investigation was completed, but that didn't sit very well with him. He wants it now. You see our problem?"

"Can you give it to him but make him promise not to tell anyone how he got it?"

"That's the whole issue. They want to find out where the bills came from, just like we do. They want to know how many of these bills were printed with the stolen plate and who has them. How many bundles of hundreds are still out there? They don't care much about a chronic bad boy protester and troublemaker who had his throat cut with a long knife. They want to find the Benjamins with the bogus serial numbers."

"How do they think they can find this out if we can't find it out?"

"They say they know the names of some of the Russians who were involved with the printing press back in the early 1990s. My friend says he thinks the BPE might be able to find out who stole the plate and sold it to the USSR. I don't understand why all of a sudden they think they can find who stole the plate. They've had thirty years to track down whoever stole it from the BPE, and they haven't done it. They want to arrest somebody for this crime, and they think our little torn currency band is evidence. I personally think that's ridiculous."

Agent Barnes agreed with her boss. "This seems like pretty old news to me. Why waste the time trying to track down who stole the plate? The person who stole it thirty years ago might even be dead by now."

Ridley Wilton was speculating, but he was pretty sure he was right. "I think it's a matter of pride with the Department of the Treasury. They don't know how the plate was stolen from the BPE building, and they don't know how it ended up in the USSR. I told Dunnaway we still needed the currency band for our case, but I would think about giving it to him sooner. I don't feel confident telling him how we happened to have this clue. I can't allow him to tell the entire Treasury Department about Vickers. The more people I tell about the Vickers brothers and all the rest of it, the less control we have over our investigation."

Chapter 26

Agent Ridley Wilton and Agent Arabella Barnes had put off the in-person meeting with Mercedes Carrington long enough. Arabella had made one trip to see her, but for the most part, they'd left her for Mac to take care of. That had worked well for several months. One reason Wilton had avoided visiting Nova Scotia was because it was so difficult for him to get to Halifax without a private plane. He didn't have time to drive long distances, but he was going to have to do some driving this time. Mercedes was that important.

He did not want to do anything to give away her whereabouts. They had been successful so far, hiding her from everybody, and nobody wanted that to be compromised. Ridley had taken a big risk when he'd flown her from Little Rock to Nova Scotia on the FBI jet. It had been an emergency, and he'd hired his own pilots and scrubbed the flight logs. He didn't feel as if he could use the FBI jet again to get himself to Nova Scotia. He so far had trusted his instincts and stayed completely away from Nova Scotia while he had a valuable witness living here.

It was almost impossible to find a commercial airline flight from anywhere in the United States that flew direct to Halifax. There were inevitably one or two stops along the way, and all the flights seemed to take forever. For his vacation, Ridley was going to fly to Detroit to spend a few days with his son and daughter-in-law who lived in Ann Arbor, Michigan. Ridley planned to rent a car from there and drive to Canada. The drive from Detroit to Toronto took a little over four hours. The flight from Toronto to Halifax was just over two hours. Ridley would use one of his alternative identities when he rented a car, when he drove across the Canadian border to Toronto, and when he flew to Halifax. He would rent another car to drive from Halifax to Baird House.

It would be a quick trip to Terence Bay. Ridley wanted to have a chance to spend some time with Mac. He would arrive at Baird House the day before Mercedes returned from her family vacation. He felt he needed to update Mercedes on their progress and let her know what he thought was going to happen to her in the next few months. He wished he had better news to give her.

Josh found he enjoyed his job as a bellman at the Capital Hotel. He'd made friends with the staff, and he enjoyed interacting with the guests. Josh was an extrovert, and he liked people. He loved chasing a story but he could be sidetracked, too. Nothing much had happened on the Agnes MacGillicutty case since the unnamed body had been flown in from Las Vegas. Josh checked his bug on the hotel's pay phone every few days, but he'd not learned much of anything new. Ridley Wilton had stayed pretty much on his schedule of work and home and lunch at the hotel. Nothing unusual had popped up on the tracker Josh had placed on the agent's car key.

Then one day, Ridley Wilton came to the Capital for lunch with somebody. In all the weeks and months Josh had been watching him, he'd always eaten in the bar alone. Here he was with a friend. They knew each other, and the other guy also looked like a government type. Josh was anxious to eavesdrop on their conversation, but he was in his bellman's uniform. He couldn't sit down at the next table and eat a sandwich as if he were a customer. He did have a listening device he'd paid big money for but never used. Today was the day.

He pretended he had a message for the people who were sitting at the table next to Ridley and his friend. He went up to the table and asked the people who were sitting there if they were the Tedescoes. He knew they weren't, but he said he thought they were staying at the hotel. He had an urgent phone message for the Tedescoes. When the people at the table said they weren't who Jason was looking for, he apologized, stepped back, and put his hand underneath the table where Ridley and the other man were eating.

He had one chance to get this right, one chance to put the listening device under the top of the table. If it fell on the floor instead of sticking to the underside of the table, he would be busted. He was successful in that the bug stuck to the table, but the reception wasn't good. He could only understand a word here and there of the intense conversation.

For the money had had invested in this listening device, he was angry that the reception was so poor. He decided he was going to take it back and get a different one. Josh listened to the conversation on his phone from the lobby. They were talking about a missing plate of some kind. They were talking about Russians and hundred dollar bills. Boris Yeltsin? Ridley Wilton had something the other guy wanted, but Ridley didn't want to give it to him until he had solved his case. He said the other guy couldn't have this thing that was in a little plastic bag, whatever it was. They were talking about packages of money, bundles of ten thousand dollars each. Josh could not figure out what this had to do with Agnes MacGillicutty. Had Wilton dropped the investigation that involved the old woman?

Ridley Wilton made a deal with Simon Dunnaway, his friend at the Ft. Worth BPE. The soil residue on the currency band was not sufficient for the lab to be able to determine where the dirt had come from. Ridley decided he would give the one clue he had to Treasury. Simon Dunnaway had agreed to tell only what Ridley wanted him to say in terms of where the currency band had come from. As far as any law enforcement people knew, this was the first time any of the hundred dollar bills that had been printed in Russia had turned up in the United States. In return for the currency band, Simon agreed to tell Ridley everything he knew about the people involved in the printing of the money in the USSR in the early 1990s. He would give Wilton all the names.

Several of the people who had participated in the printing of the one-hundred dollar bills in the former USSR had subsequently come to the United States. The shut-down of the currency printing press had been confusing and chaotic like everything else that was happening at that time in the former Communist country. Most of the names that were associated with the currency operation and its shut-down were now knee-deep in the Russian mafia.

Stacks of one hundred dollar bills that were almost the real thing could go a long way towards funding both legal and illegal

Russian enterprises. Collateral in the form of cash, deposited in banks abroad, could stake real estate purchases and arms shipments anywhere in the world. Banks in the United States might catch the fact that the back sides of the hundred dollar bills were not quite kosher, but the faces of these bills would pass scrutiny with flying colors at foreign banks. The faces of these bills were the real thing, except for the serial numbers. In a foreign country, serial numbers might be overlooked for a while, but duplicate serial numbers would eventually reveal the counterfeit bills.

Ridley was interested in the names of the Russians who had come to the United States and were currently doing business here. He still could not understand why the Russian mob would want to hire martyrs to bring down American airliners. That kind of activity was not at all in their wheelhouse. The only thing he could figure out was that the Russian mobsters were middle men. Someone had paid them to hire people and pay them for their dirty work. This arrangement worked for the Russians, too, if they were paying the people they hired in "dirty" money, or with half-counterfeit hundreds. The Russians would have insisted that they be paid in clean U.S. money or with clean bank transfers. The Russians were being well-paid to be middlemen and were laundering their dirty money at the same time.

Most Russian mafia in the United States, or Bratva, wanted to lay low and just rake in the money. They don't want to draw attention to themselves or to any of their activities. They use corporations with American-sounding names to launder and hide their money. Once in a while a dead body turned up, and it was obvious the killing was a hit by the Russian mob. But most of the time when the Russians take somebody out, they dispose of the body in such a way that law enforcement never finds a victim.

The whole plane hijacking scenario did not make any sense at all to Ridley, and he knew he still had more digging to do. The Russians had paid the Vickers, but Ridley was certain the Russians were not behind the planning of the operation. They had provided some of the people and had paid them, but this was somebody else's plan. It had to be someone with vast resources who was able to afford an operation this elaborate. Or could it be a nation state behind the curtain? Ridley, at this point, had no idea who that could possibly be or what the motive behind it was.

Chapter 27

Mercedes Zoomed often with Sam Stevenson and with her newly hired carpenter Donny Germaine. Donny was easy to talk to and seemed to understand exactly what Mercedes wanted done to the house. He liked her ideas, and he wanted to please her. Several times he commented that her concept for the house was so much better than what the previous owner had wanted. Without wasting money or making huge changes, she had come up with ways to remedy some of the excesses the disappearing homeowner had built into the house. Mercedes hated to waste money.

The lengthy center hall in the cottage had yards and yards of floor-to-ceiling bookshelves that lined both walls. Mercedes knew she owned way too many books and way too many dishes, but even she would not have been able to fill all the shelves. And who wants all of that stuff on display in the front hall anyway? It made the hallway look cluttered to have so many shelves, even when they were empty. It would be a nightmare to keep the dust off all of that open shelving. Mercedes designed doors that would put the bookshelves behind what looked like wooden wall panels. She'd had a similar configuration of hidden storage in the front hall of her Arizona house. The wooden wall panels hid the shelving. The wall panels were designed with wonderful moldings and decorative trim. They did not look like cupboards or doors. You could hang art work on the individual panels, just as you would hang art work on a wall. The panels would swing open with the touch of a finger. Donny had never seen anything quite like this before, and he was intrigued and delighted to try something new. He was an excellent craftsman, and Mercedes knew he would do a great job on the panels that hid the miles of storage shelves. A painter Donny had chosen was already at work finishing up everything else.

The handicap-friendly bathroom was waiting on some backordered tile and fixtures to bring it up to Mercedes' specifications. Donny was working on putting up railings around the pool area to make it easier for Mercedes to get in and out of the pool and in and out of the solarium. Finishing off the second floor bedrooms and bathrooms wouldn't take any time at all. The previous owners of the house had not made these upstairs rooms a priority, and this had always bugged Donny Germaine who liked to finish a job the right way. All the work would be completed by the first week of September.

Mercedes was planning a vacation with her family on Prince Edward Island. She had rented an entire bed and breakfast for the last two weeks in August, and all three of her daughters, one son-in-law, and five grandchildren would be there. Mercedes had never been to PEI, but Mac knew all the best places to eat and all the fun things to do. Even though it was early July, Mercedes was already making dinner reservations. She wanted the family reunion to be a special one. She planned to tell her family all about what she had done to bring down the terrorist on the airplane and all about her time at Baird House in Nova Scotia.

Meanwhile Mercedes was determined to enjoy her last few weeks in Nova Scotia. Mac finally convinced her that she could go outside and face the warm weather and the sunshine. They timed their forays to the ocean front and to the borders of the bird sanctuary so they didn't see any people. Mac rearranged her hours so she could take Mercedes for rides in the wheelchair during the middle of the day.

At first Mercedes suffered from agoraphobia and was reluctant to go outside. She said it was too cold. Mac bundled her up in coats and put throws over her legs. Mercedes complained that she didn't want to get sun on her face. Mac brought out the perfect sun hat to protect Mercedes' fair skin. Mercedes said she didn't think the wheelchair would be able to roll on the paths near the ocean. Mac proved her wrong on that score, too. The wheelchair was able to make great progress on the walkways near the beach.

Eventually Mercedes began to look forward to her outings. She slept better at night after she'd spent time outside in the sun and wind. She saw the ocean from several new points of view and was inspired by the tranquility of the bird sanctuary and the deserted beaches. The activity in this town was at the docks. Terence Bay was a fishing village, and Baird House had its own private beach. The house was positioned on a spit of land such that no one ever came there to walk their dogs or go for a swim. The water was really too cold to think about going in any farther than one's ankles. Mercedes looked forward to her excursions outside, away from the house. She found she loved Nova Scotia even more than she had before, when she'd been looking at it from the windows of the sun room. She was going to hate to leave.

Mercedes had finally worked up the courage to ask Mac to go with her when she moved to Flower Island in Maine. Mac spent hours pouring over photos of the location and the floor plan of the caretaker's cottage. She'd finally said yes. She had decided it was time for her to go back to the United States. She too loved Nova Scotia, but she was a U.S. citizen and had lived in Canada as an ex-pat long enough. Mac and Mercedes had formed a bond, and Mac was tired of taking care of the stream of witnesses the FBI had brought to Baird House. Mac submitted her resignation to the FBI. Ridley Wilton briefly tried to talk her out of resigning, but he knew he was fighting a losing battle. He was actually delighted that Mac was going to Maine to take care of Mercedes. He knew Mac was at the end of her tether with the mafia witnesses, and he was glad she had found a happy place to land back home in the USA.

Mac knew exactly what she wanted done to her cottage in Maine. She loved the size and style of the place. It had recently been updated to get it in shape to be rented out as a summer home, so there was not a lot to be done to bring it up to Mac's standards. She wanted all new kitchen appliances, but she loved the existing kitchen cabinets. She wanted all the rooms painted, and she wanted a few changes to the main bathroom. The porches needed some repairs and some painting. These were easy fixes, and Donny Germaine would be able to take care of everything. Mercedes was delighted to be able to make the house just the way Mac wanted it, and Mac was excited about her move to Maine.

Mac would stay on at Baird House until early September. After Mercedes' trip to PEI with her family, Mac would help her finish packing up her things for the move to Maine. Mac's cottage was also scheduled to be completed by early September.

The family reunion was a big success. The most difficult part of the vacation had been getting everybody to Prince Edward Island. One daughter had decided to drive. The others flew, but there were no direct flights to anywhere on PEI from anywhere in the USA. Once everybody arrived, however, they loved the bed and breakfast. They had the entire place to themselves, and the woman who ran the hostelry took good care of them and made their stay memorable. She made her specialties for breakfast, and Mercedes' family, always a fan of excellent food, loved her baked goods and her omelets. The owner of the B&B made box lunches for them when they requested them. They ate tons of oysters, raw and roasted and fixed in an infinite variety of ways. They saw all the sights there were to see on PEI.

Chapter 28

Josh worked hard all summer at both of his jobs. No one had flown the FBI jet anywhere close to Nova Scotia. There had been a few trips to Washington D.C. and back and a few other trips that left in the morning and returned to Little Rock the same day. Josh was losing his enthusiasm for the Agnes MacGillicutty story. Nothing was happening. Ridley Wilton came to the Capital Hotel for lunch almost every Tuesday, but he rarely received or made any phone calls on the pay phone. Just when Josh was about to give up on the story, one of the FBI agent's phone calls he had recorded from the hotel's pay phone made a reference to Ridley's trip to Michigan in August. It was Ridley's vacation, and he was flying to visit his son who lived in Ann Arbor.

In late August, Ridley flew from Little Rock to Detroit. He didn't make any attempt to hide the fact that he was flying to Detroit, so Josh figured he really was just on vacation. The only thing that peaked Josh's interest about the trip was that Detroit was in Michigan and Michigan was close to Canada.

Of course Detroit was nowhere close to Halifax. It took more than twenty-two hours to drive from Detroit to Halifax.

Josh had never taken any vacation from either of his jobs. He was ambivalent about trying to follow Ridley Wilton on his vacation to Detroit. He finally decided that he would give his pursuit of Agnes MacGillicutty one last shot and follow the FBI agent wherever he went during his time away from Little Rock. Detroit would not have been Josh's choice as a vacation destination, but Michigan was supposed to have some nice places, places other than Detroit. Josh gave his bosses at the airport and at the Capital Hotel a story about a death in the family, and he took several days off from both of his jobs. He was a responsible employee who had never missed a day of work, so no one complained when he asked for the time off to attend a funeral.

Josh flew to Detroit and rented a white Neon, the least expensive car rental he could find. Josh knew that his tracker had a range of less than one hundred miles, but once he was in Detroit, Ridley Wilton's keys led him to a brick ranch house in Ann Arbor. Josh had his computer with him, and his inexpensive motel had WiFi available for an extra fee. Josh found that Ridley was staying with his son and daughter-in-law who lived in Ann Arbor. Both taught at the University of Michigan. Josh watched and waited. He was about to give up on his vigil watching the brick rancher, when Ridley had his son drive him to the airport. Josh assumed Ridley was returning to Little Rock. This would be the end of his surveillance of Special Agent Ridley Wilton. Josh would move on...to someplace else, wherever that might be.

Josh followed Ridley to the airport and was surprised when the FBI agent's son dropped him off at a car rental lot rather than at the departure gates level. This was an unexpected curve that Josh had not anticipated. He kept his eyes on his phone app that tracked Ridley's keys as Ridley's rental car headed east out of Detroit into Canada. Josh watched as Ridley drove across the border into Ontario and drove in the direction of Toronto on Rt. 401.

Josh quickly drove back to his motel, checked out, and loaded his duffle bag into the Neon. He kept his eyes on Ridley's route and followed the car as it drove east. Maybe the FBI had stashed Agnes MacGillicutty in Toronto? A person could certainly be kept out of sight in a busy and cosmopolitan place like Toronto. It was more than a four-hour drive from Detroit to Toronto. Josh was about an hour behind Ridley Wilton's car. He pushed the Neon to try to catch up with Ridley but didn't want to get pulled over for speeding. Josh felt as if he was spending a lot of time and money chasing after Agnes MacGillicutty, and he wasn't any longer certain that it was worth it.

As he tracked Agent Wilton to Toronto's Pearson Airport, Josh was nervous about where Ridley was headed from there. Was he going to get on a plane and fly someplace? Was he going to drive to a condo or a safe house located in or around Toronto to meet with Agnes MacGillicutty? Josh pushed the Neon harder and closely watched his phone app that was following Ridley Wilton.

When Wilton drove his rental car to the short-term parking garage, Josh knew the man he was following was probably going to take a flight out of the Toronto airport. Josh was far enough behind Wilton that he was afraid Wilton would get on a flight before he could get to the airport to discover where he was going. Josh was also nervous about the power source in the tracking device that was attached to Wilton's key. It had been on there for several weeks, and Josh wasn't sure how long it would be until the battery ran down. Josh just hoped the tracker would continue to send its signal until he was able to find out where Wilton was headed. Josh searched on his phone for flights leaving Toronto in the next two hours. There were dozens of departing flights, and there was one to YHZ, to Halifax. Josh was betting that Ridley Wilton was headed there.

Josh pulled the Neon into the short-term parking garage and found a spot. The rates to park here were going to bankrupt him, but he had decided to put forth this one last effort to find the woman everyone had been seeking for months. If this trip was a bust, he was going to give up looking for the illusive white-haired hero. Josh raced into the terminal. The flight to Halifax was leaving in twenty minutes, and he didn't even know for sure if Ridley Wilton would be on that flight. Josh had to take a chance.

He went to the ticket counter and purchased his ticket. It was last minute, so he had to pay a premium price. He tried to hurry through the security lines, but that never works. Fortunately, he had remembered to bring his passport with him. The security people realized he was running late and didn't spend too much time scrutinizing his identification. He ran to the gate from which the plane for Halifax was scheduled to leave. He did not see Ridley Wilton anywhere in the line of passengers that were in the process of boarding. But Wilton might have already boarded. Maybe he had enough frequent flyer miles that he'd been able to board with first class. In any case, Josh was going to YHZ. When he finally stepped onto the plane, sure enough, he saw the man he'd been following, sitting in the last row of first class. He was jubilant that he had guessed correctly. Josh turned his head away in case Wilton saw him and remembered his face from the Capital Hotel.

Josh had long suspected that Agnew MacGillicutty was secreted away somewhere near Halifax. He was so close now. He couldn't lose track of his prey. He was newly energized and motivated. His enthusiasm for being a journalist came rushing back. He was ready to find Agnes. His diligence and persistence had finally paid off. He could almost taste the success and fame that would be his if he was able to break this news story.

As soon as the plane arrived in Halifax, Josh used his phone to reserve a rental car. It would be another Neon, gray this time. He didn't know what car rental company Ridley Wilton was using, but he didn't think the Halifax airport was so large that he would lose sight of him, even if his tracker gave out. Josh was vigilant and was able to pick up his rental car and follow Ridley when he drove off the airport grounds. Josh's phone app was still following Ridley Wilton's keys. The journalist would know precisely where Ridley was going and exactly when he stopped. He hoped he would finally know where to find Agnes MacGillicutty when Ridley got out of his car.

Chapter 30

Josh followed Ridley to Baird House. It had started to rain, but he parked his car a considerable distance away and walked to the house where he knew Ridley Wilton was, or at least where he knew Ridley Wilton's keys were. He had a brief look around the property where he was certain Agnes MacGillicutty, aka Aunt Matilda, must be hiding. Everything had finally come together for Josh. He would love to interview Agnes, but he didn't think that would be necessary. He just needed to get a photograph of her. His own story of tracking her down over the weeks and months since the aborted hijacking would be enough of a story to get him some kind of prize. At the very least he would be famous for having found the mysterious and brave woman everyone had been wondering about and looking for.

Josh and Ridley had been traveling all day, and the sun was going to go down within the hour. Rain was coming down now with a vengeance. Josh didn't really have a good plan for getting inside the house to take his photos, but he would play it by the seat of his pants. He usually did that, and it almost always worked for him. He crept around the house and looked in the windows. He'd forgotten a raincoat, and he was soaking wet.

Ridley Wilton had arrived at Baird House, as planned, the day before Mercedes was scheduled to return from her family trip to PEI. He wanted a chance to debrief and visit with Mac. She had worked with him for many years. Even though he was happy that she was planning to return to the United States and was going to be working for Mercedes, he was going to miss her. Mac made dinner for the two of them, and they talked and took care of business while they ate.

Josh was starving as well as wet through to the skin. He had not eaten all day and was jealous of the delicious-looking home-cooked meal he watched the man and the woman enjoy together at the table inside the house. The storm had intensified and there was loud thunder and lightning. As he looked through the window, Josh couldn't hear what these two were saying to each other, but he assumed that Mac was Aunt Mathilda and Agnes MacGillicutty, the woman who had taken down a hijacker with her cane. He didn't see the cane and was surprised to discover how agile Mac was when she got up from the dining table and walked to the kitchen. There was no wheelchair in sight. But who else could this older woman be? She was staying here at this house and was having a heart-to-heart conversation with the FBI agent. She had to be the elusive hero of Flight #66.

Ridley helped Mac carry the dishes into the kitchen and appeared to be telling her goodnight. He opened a door off the front hall and walked up the stairs. He was going to bed, Josh guessed, and his bedroom was on the second floor. This would be Josh's chance to get Agnes alone. He might even be able to convince her to talk to him. He took out his lock picking kit and got to work on the back door. It wasn't long before he was able to let himself into the kitchen. Mac was finishing the dishes and almost fainted when she looked up and saw Josh standing in the doorway watching her. His clothes and long hair were dripping wet, and he looked quite frightening.

"I know you are Agnes MacGillicutty. Don't try to deny it. I am not going to hurt you. I just want a statement from you about your decision to take down the hijacker."

Mac had never seen the cell phone footage of Agnes MacGillicutty that Josh had recorded in the parking garage of the FBI headquarters building, but Mercedes had told her all about it and about Agnes MacGillicutty and the Verrazzano-Narrows Bridge. Mac and Mercedes had laughed about the encounter quite a few times. Mac realized that this long-haired, wild-eyed young man in wet, rumpled clothes mistakenly believed she was Mercedes, aka Agnes MacGillicutty. How had he found Baird House? Mac didn't know who he was but hoped he was just a journalist and not someone sent to harm Mercedes. He did not appear to have a knife or a gun. He was dripping water all over her nice clean kitchen floor. She began shouting for Ridley.

Josh stepped forward and put his hand over her mouth. He didn't want to have to confront the FBI agent; he just wanted to have a statement from Agnes. "Don't shout for Agent Wilton. I just want to talk to you. I am not here to harm you."

Mac didn't trust him and turned around and kneed him hard in the groin. He fell to the floor in agony. By this time Ridley Wilton had come running down the stairs and was in the kitchen. "What's going on? Who is this guy?"

"He says he's looking for Agnes MacGillicutty. Because he mentioned Agnes, my best guess is that he's a journalist after a big story, but you never know. How in the world did he ever find this place? He must have followed you here. I can't believe that all of our precautions to keep this place a secret have been for nothing. This cannot have happened."

Ridley was dumbfounded. He also could not believe that anyone had been able to find the very secret, very safe Baird House. This place was his greatest hideaway, and now a journalist, or worse, had discovered it. He looked at the young man who was groaning on the floor. He thought he had seen his face somewhere before, but he couldn't remember where he'd seen him.

"I am going to arrest this guy and stash him where daylight will never find him. If he is a journalist, he will tell the world and anybody else who will listen, everything about Baird House and about our very special guest. We absolutely cannot allow that to happen. If he is not a journalist and is one of the conspirators in this mess, that's even worse. I'm going to take his cell phone away from him now, but I don't have any handcuffs with me. Believe it or not, I'm on vacation and didn't think I was going to need to arrest and hold a criminal while I was here."

"I've got plastic ties. I always keep a pair in my purse. I'll get them for you." Mac left the room to retrieve the handcuffs.

Josh had heard what these two had said to each other, and he knew he had to get out of the house right away. If he didn't escape, he would be finished. The FBI didn't need a reason to throw the book at anyone. He was trespassing, but that was really his only crime. That and breaking into the house with his set of lock picks were his only crimes. And what about the bugs on the hotel phone and the tracking devices on the FBI agent's keys and on his car? Maybe he was in more trouble than he knew.

Josh jumped up and ran. He made a break for the front door. Ridley Wilton was on his tail and knocked him down.

The man on the floor was up again in an instant. They were throwing fists at each other. Josh was trying to get away, and Ridley was trying to subdue and hold the intruder. They were going at it when Mac returned with the plastic ties. Ridley was almost able to keep Josh down on the ground to cuff him, but the desperate younger man gave a last burst of effort and freed himself. Mac had her gun out of her purse and was ready to shoot.

"Don't shoot him. I have to be able to question him about who he really is and how he found Baird House. I have to know if he is working with anybody else."

"Okay. I'll shoot him in the leg."

"Don't do that either. If he has to go to the hospital because he's been shot, that's a whole big thing I don't want us to have to deal with." Mac held her fire.

Because she had hesitated and hadn't shot him, Josh managed to escape out the front door into the dark and stormy night. He slipped and fell on the wet walkway. Ridley was right behind him. There were no street lights in the neighborhood, and there was little ambient light to show Josh where he was. The wind was howling, and the water was coming down from the sky in torrents. Neither man could see a thing through the sheets of rain, but Ridley knew this property well. Josh did not.

There was a stone wall between the Baird House grounds and the bird sanctuary. Baird House was higher up on a promontory. The bird sanctuary grounds were quite a bit lower. Josh easily climbed the wall on the Baird House side, but he didn't know the drop on the other side of the wall was over a steep cliff. He threw himself over the wall, hoping to get away... in order to be able to avoid arrest and to write his story. His body went over the cliff. He fell. He tumbled down, down, down. He hit his head on the rocks that were at the foot of the cliff. When he landed, his leg twisted with terrible pain. He knew he'd been beaten. He was bleeding and lapsed into unconsciousness. The rain continued to pour down on the unconscious journalist, and the lightening cracked all around the bird sanctuary.

Ridley Wilton was angry with himself and with the kid who had been able to track him all the way to Terence Bay. Wilton knew he would have to keep the trespassing journalist or the agent of the bad guys, whichever this jerk turned out to be, under wraps. And now the guy was injured. The idiot had gone over the wall, fallen into the bird sanctuary, and was probably badly hurt. It was a long way down on the other side. Ridley was going to have to try to save the man's life and attend to his injuries. He didn't need this complication. He walked around the wall and carefully climbed down the muddy and slippery embankment to examine the unknown person and determine how seriously hurt he was. Ridley had left the house without a coat and was shivering. The rain in Nova Scotia was cold, even in the summer.

The situation was complicated. The FBI didn't have jurisdiction outside of the United States, unless a host country specifically requested their assistance. The Canadian government had no idea and didn't care why Josh was investigating in Nova Scotia. They had no idea FBI Special Agent Ridley Wilton was in town. Agent Wilton was in Canada on vacation. He was not on official business and was not allowed to be. The Canadian government knew that the FBI maintained safe houses in Canada and kept their special witnesses in these safe houses. This was unofficially all right. Capturing a criminal who had committed crimes in the United States and who was injured and in need of emergency treatment was not all right.

The criminal would have to be guarded during his stay in a medical facility, and who was going to provide the twenty-four hour guards to do that? Ridley had to come up with something other than calling 911. His trespasser was bleeding from the head. One of his legs was twisted at an unnatural angle. His pulse was thready. The guy who had fallen over the wall needed medical assistance ASAP. Ridley had to get him out of Canada and back to the United States where he could be in control.

Ridley remembered a doctor he'd called a few years earlier when one of the witnesses he'd stashed in Nova Scotia had become ill. The doctor was a U.S. citizen and a former member of the military. He lived in Canada to be close to his children and grandchildren. He'd been old when Ridley had called him several years ago, and the doctor might not still be alive. The doctor knew about keeping secrets, and the greatest thing about this doctor was that he also knew how to fly a helicopter and had one of his own. At least, he used to have a helicopter. If the physician was still alive and flying, he would be the perfect person to get this injured journalist/terrorist out of the country.

Ridley was dead tired, cold, and soaked to the skin. He'd traveled from Detroit, Michigan to Nova Scotia today. He had been on his way to bed when this unknown perp had burst into Baird House and Mac had screamed for help. Ridley didn't have the energy to deal with this latest emergency. Maybe it really was time for him to think about retiring. As soon as he'd figured out the mess that surrounded these hijackings that hadn't happened, he would seriously consider turning in his badge.

Mac got on his phone and was able to reach Dr. Ernest Julian. The doctor lived in Halifax, and he sounded over the phone like he still had all of his marbles. Ridley knew the physician had to be in his eighties, maybe in his nineties. Could he still fly his helicopter? Did he still have his helicopter?

The answer to both those questions was yes. Ridley decided to confide in Julian. He really had no choice at this point. Without revealing anything about why the injured man had been at Baird House or saying anything at all about Mercedes Carrington, Ridley told Julian he had a battered fugitive on his hands. He explained to the doctor that he couldn't call the Canadian authorities or engage the Canadian medical system to treat this person.

Julian was still sharp and understood why the FBI had to keep the guy under the radar. He asked Ridley a few questions about the man's injuries and told him to cover the patient with blankets to keep him from going into shock. He told Ridley to try to stop any bleeding. Ridley listened and said he would do his best to keep the man alive until Dr. Julian arrived. Julian knew the bird sanctuary and said he would arrive within the hour. Ridley had known it would be that long before the doctor could reach him, but it still seemed like a very long time before help arrived on the scene.

Ridley sent a text to Mac at the house, asking for blankets, a first aid kit, a poncho, and some kind of tarp to cover the injured person who was now lying unconscious in a pile of rocks and mud. He didn't think the first aid kit would be much help with anything, but it was all he had. Mac drove her VW bug to the bird sanctuary and was worried she'd get stuck in the mud. She didn't often drive the old car off-road and into soaking wet ground.

She offered to sit with the man so Ridley could go back to the house and get some rest. Ridley refused to leave this man he'd failed to cuff and failed to keep from injuring himself. Mac, bless her heart, had brought the plastic ties for his hands, the blankets, the poncho, the tarp, and a thermos of coffee. The first thing they did was cuff the journalist's hands. Mac helped Ridley cover the troublemaker with the blankets and the tarp and tried to make him comfortable. His pulse was still not strong, but he was not bleeding out. It appeared as if the kid would still be alive when Dr. Julian arrived. Mac and Ridley sat in Mac's car, out of the rain, and waited for the old doctor who still made house calls.

Dr. Julian drove his ancient Range Rover as close to the patient's location as he could get. Dressed for the weather in a warm raincoat, the old man was bent over with age, but he was able to carry his medical bag to where the patient lay on the cold, wet rocks. The doctor carefully lowered himself beside the injured man and began to examine him. "I'm going to have to splint this broken leg. It may be his hip that's broken or the femur or maybe both. I don't think the head injury is critical, but he is still unconscious after more than an hour. That's of concern. He really threw himself over that wall, didn't he? He's not that old. In his twenties or thirties, I'd say. Do you know what his name is or where he comes from?" Ernest Julian chatted as he worked on splinting the leg and evaluating the other injuries.

"I know you want me to fly him out of here on my helicopter. I will do that for you, but you will have to pay for it. I don't fly at night anymore, and I certainly don't fly anywhere in weather like this. So this guy will have to wait until the storm is over and the sun comes up before I can fly him out of Canada. Where are we going with the young man? He doesn't really look like a terrorist. He looks more like a scrubby teenager."

"I know Burlington, Vermont is a long flight from here, but that is where I'd like for you to fly him. I have people who can take care of him in Burlington. There's a medical facility that can do surgery on him if necessary, and they can keep him off the radar and safely in restraints until he has recovered. I need to have him alive so I can question him. I'm assuming he's going to have a fairly long recovery." Ridley was almost too tired to speak, but he wanted to assure Dr. Julian that the bills would be paid. "And I am happy to pay all of the expenses for his transportation and for this house call. I am in your debt."

"Okay. That's all settled. You look worse than this guy looks. How are we going to get him to my truck? I have someone on standby at the airfield who can transfer him from the truck and put him directly into the helo. I will stay with him there until the wind and rain have slacked off and it's light enough for me to be comfortable taking off for Burlington. Where am I going in Burlington? I assume I am not going to the airport but to some other place."

"I will make all the arrangements and text you everything you need to know about where to take this guy. I don't know his name. He doesn't have any ID on him, but I am assuming he has left his car parked somewhere near here. I will find the car, and I will find out who he is." Ridley thanked the doctor again.

The doctor had brought along a rolled-up canvas and wood stretcher, the kind sometimes seen on the battlefield. They loaded their nameless offender onto the stretcher. Mac was strong and a huge help moving him to Dr. Julian's SUV. It wasn't easy. The rain was still coming down. They slid in the mud, and it was impossibly awkward to lift the young man off the ground, even with the primitive stretcher. They were trying to be careful and not injure their patient any more than he'd already been hurt. At last they had him laid out on the back seat of the Range Rover.

Ridley and the doctor went over the plans and the communications that would be forthcoming. Ridley and Mac waved goodbye to the good man who had come out in a storm in the middle of the night to take care of a criminal. Ridley made several phone calls and exchanged several texts with his special covert military contacts in Burlington, Vermont. He hoped he hadn't messed anything up and had given the right information to the right people. He was so tired and so cold, he didn't trust himself to do it all.

Finally, the young man was out of Ridley's sight and on his way to the medical care he needed. Ridley rode back to the house with Mac in her VW. Besides being wet and cold to the bone, he was covered with blood and dirt and badly in need of a shower. He pushed hard to make himself take that shower before he fell into the bed in the one furnished bedroom on the second floor of Baird House. Mercedes would be arriving in the late afternoon. Ridley hadn't seen her since she'd been in Little Rock. He wanted to be somewhat rested when he talked to her the next day.

Chapter 29

Ridley and Mac had decided they were not going to say anything to Mercedes about the man who had broken into Baird House the night before. She had enough to deal with. She had just said goodbye to her family and did not know when she would be able to see them again. She was leaving Baird House and Nova Scotia. This place had been her adopted home and refuge for the last six months. With Mac's help, Mercedes had already packed up most of her belongings in preparation for the move to Maine. Mercedes had been busy with some last-minute changes and a few delays involved with the renovation of her Maine house. She had just completed another mystery novel and had sent it to her editor. She'd had a lot to think about. She did not need to know that her safe place had been compromised or anything about the fellow who had come to Terence Bay trying to find her. Thank goodness she had not been at Baird House. Thank goodness the stalker had thought Mac was Agnes MacGillicutty.

When Ridley woke up in the middle of the afternoon, he still did not feel rested. The storm had passed, and the sun was shining. He was relieved when he received a text confirming that the person who had broken into Baird House had arrived in Burlington and was still alive. He would call to get the details and give instructions later in the day. Ernest Julian, M.D. had returned to Halifax and had sent him a bill via text. Ridley grabbed some coffee and a quick bite of the breakfast Mac had left for him. His first priority of the day was to find the stalker's car. Wilton suspected it was parked not too far away from Baird House. Hopefully, a search of the car would answer some of the questions that were driving Ridley Wilton crazy.

A fifteen minute walk around the neighborhood yielded the gray Neon rental that Ridley was certain belonged to the stalker. The car had been left unlocked, probably in anticipation of a quick getaway. The man's wallet was tucked under the driver's seat. The name on the driver's license, Joshua Ferris Dawson, didn't ring any bells with Wilton, but at least he now knew the man's name. Joshua was thirty-one years old.

Ridley searched the glove compartment and found a badge on a lanyard from the Capital Hotel in Little Rock. When he looked at the photograph on the laminated ID, he remembered he had seen the young stalker at the hotel. He knew that Joshua Dawson worked as a bellman there and was sometimes the person who was the valet for Ridley's car. Ridley realized that the young man had been watching him for months. Ridley had never suspected that anyone was keeping track of his movements, let alone that one of the bellmen or the valet at the Capital Hotel had him under surveillance.

Ridley thought about the many times he had handed his car keys to the valet parking attendant. He took his key ring out of his pocket and looked over his keys one at a time. He saw the tracking device. He knew immediately what it was. He was furious with himself for not having noticed it before. He scolded himself for not being more careful, for not paying more attention to what was going on around him. His failure to be aware that he was being tracked and stalked was one more vote in favor of his making the decision to retire.

He searched the rest of the rental car and put Joshua's electronics, wallet, and all of his other belongings in the young man's duffle bag. Ridley already had Joshua's cell phone. He would have his technicians scrub the phone and the computer. They would know soon enough whether Dawson was a journalist or a terrorist.

Dawson had been delivered to the special medical facility in Burlington, Vermont in late morning. He'd had imaging studies done, and it had been determined that he had broken his right femur and his right ankle. He had immediately gone into surgery to have these injuries repaired by an orthopedist. His head injuries were superficial. There had been a lot of bleeding and quite a few cuts and scrapes. He had probably suffered a slight concussion, but there was no brain damage or brain swelling. Dawson's lower body had absorbed the impact of his fall. He had literally landed on his feet...on his right side. The fact that he had not regained consciousness since the fall was of concern to the neurologist who was following his case.

The doctors at the covert military medical facility in Vermont understood that their patient was under arrest and was to be guarded and kept secluded. As soon as he was conscious and able to speak, Ridley Wilton would go to Burlington to question Dawson. The FBI agent hoped he might be looking at something of a break once he was able to interview Joshua Dawson. At least he would be able to find out how Dawson had found Baird House.

Dawson's doctors would be able to talk with him about his medical condition, but otherwise Dawson would exist in an information vacuum. Ridley had left strict instructions that no one, other than his prisoner's doctors, were to ask the young man any questions or answer any questions Joshua might ask them. The FBI agent did not want Dawson to know where he was hospitalized or who was holding him. This is the way terrorists were handled, and until proven otherwise, Dawson had to be treated as a terrorist involved in the hijacking plot.

After he'd met with Mercedes Carrington and she was on her way to Maine, Wilton would fly to Montreal and drive a rental car across the U.S. border to Burlington, Vermont. All of this would be under the radar and using one of his alternate identities. He had already arranged for his rental car that was parked in the Toronto airport's short term parking garage to be picked up and returned to the car agency. Ridley Wilton was no longer on vacation. He was back on the case.

Of course, once Ridley Wilton had the man's name, he immediately knew everything about Joshua Ferris Dawson. He knew that Joshua Dawson was a journalist and had most recently been employed at the Little Rock airport in the maintenance department. Ridley also knew that Joshua had a part-time job as a bellman at the Capital Hotel in downtown Little Rock. Wilton knew that Dawson had taken the Agnes MacGillicutty video on his cell phone in the FBI's underground parking garage. The FBI agent knew Dawson's grade point average from high school and the name of his teacher from the second grade. Wilton wanted Dawson isolated, scared, vulnerable, and ready to spill his guts when he arrived in Burlington to begin questioning him.

Meanwhile, Wilton's top priority was to make sure that Mercedes Carrington left Nova Scotia and arrived at her new house on Flower Island off the coast of Maine. No one was ever to know that Mercedes had lived at Baird House or where she was going when she left Terence Bay. She had never been there or anywhere at all, and she would disappear again. Mercedes would be arriving at Baird House by car that afternoon. Her itinerary at the beginning of her vacation had taken her on the ferry between Nova Scotia and Prince Edward Island. Her driver would be using the Confederation Bridge, the longest bridge in Canada, to return her to Baird House.

The original plan had been for Mercedes to spend her last night at Baird House and have a good rest after her drive back to Nova Scotia from PEI. Mercedes and Mac would pack up the few remaining things Mercedes still had at Baird House, and they would be on their way to Flower Island by car the next day. The drive would take longer if there was congestion at the U.S. border. Because Ridley Wilton was so paranoid about allowing Mercedes to be seen in public, the idea of flying her to Maine on a commercial airliner had never been considered. Ridley also felt it was too complicated and too risky to contemplate using a U.S. government jet to fly Mercedes back to the USA.

Because of the Joshua Dawson situation, Ridley had completely changed Mercedes' travel plans. He had rented a motorhome for Mercedes and Mac to use to travel from Nova Scotia to Maine. Mac knew how to drive the motorhome, and it had a wheelchair lift so it would be easy for Mercedes to get into and out of.

The only sketchy part of the plan was that Mercedes was going to have to lie down in a secret compartment under the built-in bed of the motor home while Mac drove the vehicle across the border from Canada into the United States. Mercedes had never officially been in Canada so there could not be any record of her crossing back into the USA from Canada. She was going to have to be smuggled back into her own country. Mercedes did not yet know that she was going to have to hide in a secret compartment. It would not be easy for her to get into the compartment or to get out of it, but Mac had assured Ridley that she would be able to make it possible for Mercedes to hide successfully.

Mercedes was tired from her trip when she arrived at Baird House, but she was delighted to see Agent Ridley Wilton. Mac had made cold lobster with homemade mayonnaise, orzo salad with tomatoes and feta cheese, and fresh asparagus. The three of them sat down to have dinner together. Mac brought dessert to the table, a deep dish blueberry cobbler. She served generous portions with scoops of vanilla ice cream on top of each.

Ridley didn't like the idea that Mercedes would be spending the night at Baird House that night. He would have preferred that the two women set out immediately after they'd eaten to drive to Maine. But Mac didn't like to drive after dark, and she was too tired after the Dawson fiasco to begin a long drive at night. She needed a good night's sleep, and so did Mercedes. They would leave the next morning after breakfast.

During dinner, Mercedes talked and talked about the family trip she'd had with her children and grandchildren. Everyone had enjoyed Prince Edward Island. "You two are awfully quiet. Agent Wilton, you have enormous bags and dark circles under your eyes, and Mac, you are much too chipper. You are smiling too much. Something isn't right. What's going on? What happened while I was away?" Mercedes was too perceptive to be put off with a superficial explanation. Ridley Wilton finally ended up giving her an edited version about the appearance of Joshua Dawson and his fall into the bird sanctuary.

This was Mercedes' last night at Baird House. She was sad to be leaving. This place had been a haven for her. She had written a new mystery book here. She had found Mac here. Baird House had provided a safe and comfortable place for her to hide. But Mercedes was excited about the move to her new place on Flower Island. She had never been there in person. When she arrived to move in and live there, it would be the very first time she had set foot on her property or in her house. Mercedes and Mac packed a few last items that were going to Maine, and everyone went to bed.

The trip in the motorhome was uneventful except when Mercedes had to hide under the bed when Mac drove across the border into the United States. Before they reached the border crossing point, Mac stopped the motorhome and helped Mercedes lie down in the secret compartment. Mercedes thought getting into a secret compartment was incredibly ridiculous and voiced her annoyance with Ridley Wilton for forcing her to do it. She had to lie down and stay in the space, which was very claustrophobic, for about fifteen minutes. Fortunately the border crossing between Canada and the USA that Mac and Mercedes were using was in the middle of nowhere and not a particularly busy one.

Mercedes had to be very quiet and very still if the border guards decided to come on board and thoroughly search the motorhome. They would be looking for drugs or arms, and sometimes they did search motorhomes. Larger vehicles could carry big payloads of illegal contraband. Mac was not a suspicious-looking person. She was able to chat with the border guards and talk her way through the process and into the United States without any fuss. The border guards were not looking for old ladies, and they merely glanced at Mac's U.S. passport and waved her through. They never considered searching the motorhome.

A few miles down the road, Mac pulled the motorhome over to the side of the road and helped Mercedes climb out of the secret hiding space. Getting out was more difficult than getting in. Finally, they were on the road again. Mercedes was still put out about having to hide, but a glass of iced tea with mint perked her up. She was soon herself again.

The drive was more than eight hours, and Mac had decided to split the trip into two days. There was no rush, now that Mercedes was out of Baird House. They could take their time, and the scenery was beautiful. Mac had prepared food and brought it with them. They stopped briefly so that Mac could make sandwiches for lunch. They stopped again for the night. Mac reheated the creamy seafood chowder and the cheese muffins she had made the day before. She brought a half gallon of chocolate gelato out of the motor home's tiny freezer. Mac didn't want to get too tired and wanted to take her time and enjoy the trip. They had a good night's sleep. The two women were both on their way to new homes and to new lives.

Chapter 31

They arrived at the entrance to Flower Island late in the afternoon. It was that magical time of day, the hour when daylight was just about to give in to the beginnings of a sunset. The first part of September is still summer, so the flowers on the island were at their peak. Wildflowers had always filled these fields with a riot of color, and after some years of neglect, the formal landscaping in the cottage garden had overflowed into the meadow. Previously cultivated delphinium, asters, larkspur, hibiscus, and Russian sage now ran untamed among the sunflowers and Shasta daisies and other volunteers. It was a fully packed compendium of hues, and the view from the dirt road above the bridge to the island was otherworldly. Both Mac and Mercedes were awestruck. Mac stopped the motorhome so they could take it in...this first look at their new homes, both surrounded by nature's own magnificent display.

Mercedes had tears in her eyes. "Do you think I have died and this is heaven?" She really did wonder.

"I think God has given you a wonderful gift to enjoy for the later years of your life. And the later years of my life, too. Wow! I was not expecting anything like this."

The cottage where Mercedes would live could not be seen from the rustic wooden bridge that connected the mainland with Flower Island. She could only see the fields of flowers against the background of pine trees. "I am almost afraid to see the house. I don't want to break the spell. No matter how wonderful the house turns out to be, it will have to be a let-down."

But it wasn't. They drove across the narrow causeway and continued on the dirt road until it turned the corner. A magnificent view of the Atlantic Ocean greeted them, and there was Flower Island Cottage, serene and welcoming, quietly comfortable in its perfect setting. Mercedes caught her breath. She had seen hundreds of photographs of the cottage with its weathered, gray shingles, the porches and solarium, and the views of the ocean. But, all those photos had not done justice to the real place in its real locale. The air was just the right amount of hazy, and Mercedes could hear the waves breaking on her very own beach. Sam Stevenson had hired a landscaping company to plant masses of bright red geraniums in the long wooden planters that lined the porch that faced the sea. By late summer, the exuberant blossoms had overflowed their containers and presented a magnificent display.

"We will unpack the motorhome tomorrow. Let's just enjoy the view and take a tour of the house." Mac was being generous. Mercedes knew Mac had to be incredibly anxious to get inside her own new house and begin to get to know it. It was a new house to Mac anyway. Mac helped Mercedes get into the cottage. All the specified ramps and railings had been installed, exactly as Mercedes had indicated they should be. Everything in the house looked just as Mercedes had hoped it would.

After they'd been through the house, they sat outside for a while on the covered porch that faced the ocean. Mac disappeared, then reappeared with glasses of iced tea. They absorbed it all without saying a word. Mercedes dozed off after her long road trip. Mac woke her with a tray of lobster salad, shrimp salad, sliced ham, and some ripe tomatoes she'd conjured up from somewhere. They ate together in silence. Mercedes realized she had been more than a little bit anxious about seeing her new home in person. She was suddenly exhausted. Although it was not yet dark, Mac helped her unpack her nightgowns. Mercedes took a shower in her handicap-friendly bathroom. She fell asleep in the poster bed that had been hers when she was a child.

THE NEXT MORNING, MERCEDES SLEPT late. Mac finally brought a tray of coffee, toast, and fruit to her bedroom. "Why don't you stay in bed today? You look worn out. Moving is the most stressful thing there is, and transitions are always difficult. You have been through a lot. Don't underestimate any of it. I will unpack the boxes, and you can tell me where you want to put everything. My little house is perfect, by the way. Donny did a great job with it. I am thrilled with the house, with this location, and with my new job. We won't tackle too much today. Honestly, all the furniture is pretty much where you told Sam to put it. There are some boxes to unpack, but most of the moving in is already done." Mac was walking around the bedroom, opening the shutters that covered the windows. When she looked over at the bed, Mercedes had already fallen back asleep.

That afternoon, Mercedes was more rested and ready to tackle some of the boxes. It suddenly occurred to her that she needed a car. Sam Stevenson had mentioned that the previous owner's car was stored in the garage. It had been sitting there for more than two years. Sam had said he was going to have the car checked out, soup to nuts and head to toe, by the dealership in Bangor and also have the car detailed. All traces of the previous owner would be removed. The car had only 12,000 miles on it. In spite of its being abandoned after Gilbert Jones had disappeared, Sam said it was a beautiful car and was in great condition. One of the keys to the car was missing, but the other key had been found on a hook inside the back door of the house the previous owner had leased in Bar Harbor.

Mac came back from the garage with a report. "It's a white Range Rover, and it's a beauty. It started without a problem. Sam must have had a new battery put in it."

"Sam didn't say anything about its being a Range Rover. Do you think I'll be able to get in and out of it? It's not a standard transmission or anything like that, is it?" Mercedes wondered if the Range Rover really belonged to her and made a mental note to ask Sam Stevenson about the ownership of the car. Her contract on the house had said something about including all the contents of the house, but Mercedes didn't know if that included the car that had been sitting in the garage.

"It's more like a crossover than a real truck-type SUV. You won't have any problem getting in and out of it. My VW Bug is going to look pretty small next to it." Mac's vintage car that she loved was red. It was currently on a moving van with most of the furniture and household goods she was bringing from her house in Nova Scotia. The moving van was scheduled to arrive the next day. They would be settled in no time.

Mac unpacked Mercedes' boxes from Arizona, Delaware, and Nova Scotia. She put Mercedes' clothes away in the walk-in closet. She arranged books on the copious shelves.

Mac organized the gear in the kitchen to her own satisfaction. She would be doing most of the cooking at Flower Island Cottage. She learned how to use the fancy new washer and dryer. Mac and Mercedes together learned how to program the heater and the pump for the swimming pool. Mercedes had her first swim in the pool. It was glorious. They spent time on the porch overlooking the September waves that ebbed and flowed on the sandy beach east of the house.

Mercedes' father's desk had arrived. She'd had it cleaned up and had the top refinished. The top was a warm chestnut color. The rest of the desk had been too beaten up to refinish, and she'd had it painted navy blue. Mercedes was thrilled with the way it looked. The company that had refurbished the desk had custom cut a sheet of thick glass to protect the newly restored chestnut top. Mercedes was delighted to have this family heirloom as her writing table. She made sure it was positioned in just the right spot in her study to have the best view of the Atlantic Ocean. There was a fireplace in the room, and the evenings were almost cool enough in northern Maine to light a fire at the end of the day. Mercedes knew she would be able to write in this wonderful room. Her creativity was already at work on a new plot.

The two weeks on PEI had been wonderful for Mercedes. She had loved reconnecting with her grandchildren who were growing up much too fast. She had enjoyed every minute of the family vacation, but the constant stimulation of people talking and laughing and moving about was exhausting for someone who had been essentially living in isolation for many months. She had absorbed every word and shared every outing with her kids and grandkids. But now she was ready for some down time. As an introvert, she needed time alone to recharge her batteries. As she had grown older, she'd found she needed more time to regroup after intense social interactions. Her new cottage by the sea would be the perfect place and would provide her with the solitude she was seeking.

Mac was the ideal housekeeper. She knew when Mercedes needed her and when she needed to be alone. Mercedes was thrilled that Mac liked her own new home. Even though Mac had essentially retired from working for the FBI, she still insisted on observing their security protocols. The FBI had intercepted Mercedes' mail in Delaware and arranged for it to be sent to a post office box in Nova Scotia. The envelope that contained the mail was addressed to Mac, and the post office box was in Mac's name. Mac had picked up the mail at the post office box every day. Now Mercedes' mail would be sent in a large plain envelope to a mailbox at The UPS Store in a nearby strip mall. Again, Mac would pick up the mail and bring it to Mercedes. Mac did their grocery shopping mostly in Bangor. She felt it was important to drive the extra miles farther away from Flower Island to gain the anonymity. Mac would eventually become known to the local people who lived in the vicinity of Flower Island, but she was keeping a low profile for the time being. Maybe the situation with Mercedes would be resolved and the bad guys would be taken into custody. One could hope. When that happened, they could both go out and enjoy the lobster pounds and the art galleries and the many other things northern Maine had to offer. For now, Mercedes was staying put on the island.

Sam Stevenson and Donny Germaine knew Mercedes' real name. Sam had known her name from the beginning, and he'd also known why she was in hiding. No one had wanted to bring Donny into the small group that knew who Mercedes really was, but it had been unavoidable. However, Donny knew nothing about Mercedes' past or anything about her being the woman who, months earlier, had stopped a hijacking from taking place. Donny did not know she was in hiding from anything. He knew Mercedes Carrington only as an eccentric and kindly recluse who wrote books under pen names that were not her own. He liked Mercedes from the numerous interactions they'd had over Zoom calls as they'd ironed out the details of the house renovation. No matter how demanding Mercedes might be, she could not hold a candle to the mean, obsessive, and controlling man who had been his previous employer. Mercedes was a breath of fresh air compared to Gilbert Jones.

Mercedes wondered frequently about Gilbert Jones. His name had always sounded to her like a fake name, and she was sure he'd been living in Maine as someone he really was not. Mercedes wondered what had happened to the man. How had he been able to completely disappear, and why had he left this wonderful place behind? He had to be dead. Mercedes was quite curious about what in the world Gilbert Jones had hoped to put on the yards and yards of shelves he'd had Donny build for him.

Gilbert Jones remained an enigma to Mercedes. He was a mystery, and she loved a mystery. She hoped that one day she would be able to unravel this one. She didn't believe that Gilbert Jones was ever coming back to Flower Island, but she was going to do a little digging of her own into where Gilbert had been and who Gilbert had been before he had bought the cottage. She suspected he was a former criminal of some kind who was attempting to escape his previous life. She assumed he had adopted a fake name and chosen to live in a very isolated spot because he was trying to hide from his enemies and save his life. He obviously had oodles of money. Only someone with oodles of money buys a Range Rover.

Mercedes kept the keys to the car in the drawer of her bedside table. Mac preferred to drive her own red VW bug to do the grocery shopping and other errands that needed to be taken care of. Mac drove the Range Rover one day a week to keep the battery from going dead. She knew it was a good idea to drive any vehicle on a regular basis to keep things working the way they should work.

Mercedes had not paid much attention to the keys at first, but as she thought more and more about the former owner of her cottage, she paid more attention to the keys. She'd noted the first time she'd had them in her hands that there were a couple of extra keys on the key ring, along with the keys to the Range Rover. She had thought these two extra keys looked like they were for ordinary locks, and she'd pretty much forgotten about them. She was sure the authorities had examined everything they could put their hands on when they'd been trying to figure out what in the world had happened to Gilbert Jones. She was certain they had examined the key ring. She would make a point to ask Sam Stevenson about that.

One afternoon, Mercedes decided she would try out her Range Rover to see how difficult it really would be for her to get in and out of it. She didn't plan to drive the car, just practice getting in and out a few times while it sat in the garage. She'd had Donny put in a ramp from the back entrance of the kitchen to the floor of the garage. There wasn't too much difference between the heights of the floor of the cottage and the floor of the garage, so the ramp was not very steep or very long. Mercedes easily made it down the ramp to the door of the Range Rover. Getting in was easy, and she could tell that getting out would be easy, too.

Now, if she was just allowed to go someplace, she would be all set. She could drive up and down the road between the cottage and the bridge to the mainland, but that would only take about five minutes round trip. She really wanted to drive off the island and go in search of the best lobster rolls in her neighborhood. Every place that made them, from the shacks beside the road to the fancy white tablecloth restaurants, put a little bit of a different spin on their lobster rolls, and Mercedes loved them all. It was an outing she would look forward to. On an impulse, Mercedes started the car and backed out of the garage. She drove down the dirt road and turned around and drove back to the cottage. It had been a quick trip, but the car was very easy to handle. She was thrilled. This was her car!

She started to put the key ring back into her pocket and was just about to get out of the Range Rover when she fumbled the keys and dropped them. They'd fallen down between the driver's bucket seat and the center console. Darn it! She was afraid she would have to call Mac to retrieve the keys for her, but first she would try to find them on her own. She stuck her hand down underneath the driver's seat and searched for where she thought the keys must have landed. Her hand grabbed hold of a squarish plastic something that had been stuffed back there. Or maybe what she'd grabbed hold of was part of the seat's mechanism. If it wasn't actually attached to the car's seat, it was wedged in very, very tight. Mercedes was curious and kept tugging at the box. It finally came loose from where it had been stuck.

When she brought it out, she realized it was a portable GPS device. It looked like a really expensive and fancy one. It was the kind that years ago you would plug into a cigarette lighter receptacle to provide power. These days, and with more modern cars, there were plugs in the console to charge cell phones and other electronic devices. This GPS had its cord attached. Mercedes was puzzled to find the device under the seat. She knew it was the kind of GPS that kept a record of where your car had been and when it had been there. All GPS devices did that these days.

This fancy Range Rover also had a GPS built in to the dashboard. Most newer cars came with the GPS built in. Why would someone, who already had a GPS built into their car, also have a portable GPS that had to be plugged into a receptacle? Putting these portable devices on the dashboard was cumbersome. Mercedes had had one years earlier and knew they were always in the way.

The mystery writer in Mercedes immediately answered the question she'd asked herself about why the previous owner of the Range Rover had needed the portable GPS when he already had a built-in system in his car. All built-in GPS devices were programmed to keep a location history of where the car had traveled. A person might need to use a GPS device to be able to find their way to someplace, but maybe they didn't want anybody to know about all the places where they'd driven. It would not be difficult to disable the built-in GPS that came with the car. If one used a portable GPS, one could use it and take it out of the car. One could even throw it away, if one didn't want anybody to know where one's car had been.

Mercedes knew she had to start the car to know if the built-in GPS had been disabled. She still had to find the keys. After a few more minutes of groping under the car seat, she found them. She started the car, and sure enough, the built-in GPS had been disabled. There would be no record of where this Range Rover had been driven. Mercedes was intrigued and couldn't help but wonder why the owner of the portable GPS had not wanted anyone to be able to trace his car's comings and goings. She assumed that Gilbert Jones was the owner of the portable GPS since he was the owner of the Range Rover.

She was afraid if she plugged in the portable GPS and tried to fiddle with it to figure out its travel history, she might drain the car's battery. The travel history in the portable GPS might have been erased anyway after all the time that had passed. It had been years. There might be nothing to find, even if she could access the relevant software. Mercedes decided her Range Rover needed to be driven a little bit more anyway. She backed out of her garage for the second time that day and drove across the wooden bridge to the mainland. She turned around near Mac's little house and drove back onto Flower Island. She stopped outside the garage and kept the car running as she tried to discover where this GPS and this car had traveled. Where had Gilbert Jones been going that he didn't want anybody to know about? He'd gone to considerable trouble to keep his car's travels a secret.

She also had to assume that the GPS had been looked at by the authorities when they were investigating Gilbert Jones and trying to find out where he had gone. Mercedes assumed they'd thoroughly searched this portable GPS, if indeed they had followed every possible lead to try to learn about the man's life and disappearance. They said they had pursued everything that they could find about Gilbert Jones, but maybe they hadn't. Maybe they had never found the portable GPS, wedged tightly under the driver's seat of the Range Rover. Mercedes had almost left it alone under there. Because it was so far back and so securely fitted into the space, she had thought at first it was part of the mechanism that moved the driver's seat backwards and forwards. She'd had to exert some effort to get the GPS out from under the seat.

She seemed to remember something Sam Stevenson had said to her about the car. She thought he'd told her in passing that Donny Germaine had driven the car from Gilbert's rental house in Bar Harbor to the garage of the cottage on Flower Island. Maybe no one had ever discovered the GPS that had been tucked back underneath the driver's seat of the Range Rover... until now, until she had found it. The authorities might have checked the built-in GPS to try to find out where Jones had been driving his car, but nobody would have been looking for a second GPS stuffed underneath the seat. Had she found a new clue in this mystery?

Chapter 32

As soon as they had closed Baird House, Agent Wilton flew to Montreal, picked up a rental car, and drove across the border to Burlington, Vermont to interview Joshua Dawson. He already knew the kid was just a journalist looking for a story and was not connected in any way with the complicated and layered groups that had used Middle Eastern hijackers to try to bring down airplanes. This was a relief in a way. Only the free-lance journalist, working alone, had been able to find where Mercedes had been hiding. And he didn't even know for sure that he had found her safe house. He had not actually found Mercedes, the woman he still thought of as Agnes MacGillicutty. Dawson had not really found her, and none of the really bad guys had been able to find her either.

Agent Wilton already knew that talking to Joshua and picking his brain for everything he knew was not going to get him any closer to identifying the mastermind behind the planning of the hijacking crimes and solving his case. Ridley was beginning to wonder if maybe this was one of those cases that would never be solved. He knew he would not stop trying to figure it out, if only for Mercedes' sake. She wanted to return to her previous life. Even though she was now safely ensconced on Flower Island, he realized she wanted and needed her freedom.

Joshua Dawson had regained consciousness but was still under the influence of pain-killing drugs. He'd had very serious surgery on his right hip and femur. The first operation had lasted five hours, and had also included a difficult reconstruction of his broken ankle. Joshua would require several more surgeries before he would be able to walk. Then he would have to have months of physical therapy to be able to walk at all normally. He would probably always walk with a limp. Hopefully, he would only temporarily have to use a wheelchair or a walker. He might always have to use a cane. There was a certain irony in that.

Ridley Wilton knew this kid was not a terrorist, but Joshua had brought all of this terrible trouble on himself. He had become obsessed with his story and had carried his pursuit of a headline to extremes. And he had broken the law. Agent Wilton had tasked Arabella with the job of checking out the Capital Hotel. She'd found the listening devices on the pay phone and in the telephone cubicle. She'd found the tracker on Ridley's Chevy Tahoe. Dawson had broken into Baird House. Joshua Dawson had stalked an FBI Special Agent over many months and had used electronic tracking to help him do it. He had followed Ridley Wilton to Nova Scotia. Considering his crimes, Joshua could be sentenced to jail for a very long time.

Agent Wilton almost felt sorry for the kid. He'd not murdered anybody or really hurt anybody except himself. He was probably going to be partially disabled for the rest of his life because he'd done some stupid things. Maybe the consequences of his injuries were punishment enough for this young man who didn't seem to be a hardened criminal, just an ambitious journalist with terrible judgment. The information Ridley Wilton had about Dawson indicated that he'd done fairly well in school and had graduated from college. His work history was good at both the Little Rock airport and at the Capital Hotel. He could write an interesting news article. He wasn't all bad.

Ridley made sure Josh was isolated and had given instructions that no one was to let him know where he was hospitalized or anything about the status of his arrest. He was being kept manacled to his hospital bed. The FBI agent knew this was overkill, that Dawson was not a terrorist. He wanted to frighten the journalist so he would confess everything, if indeed he had anything to confess.

Agent Wilton had asked the doctor to hold off on Joshua's pain medication so that Dawson would be awake and alert when Wilton arrived to question him. "So, you finally found me. And what good did that do you, Mr. Joshua Dawson?"

Joshua stared at Agent Ridley Wilton with wide eyes. He was clearly in some pain and very frightened. "Where am I, and why are you keeping me here?"

"It's my understanding that you had a bad fall and that you are lucky to have been given excellent medical care. I am told you may be able to walk again one day."

Dawson's face was pale, and he was obviously agitated and depressed. "I will tell you everything you want to know. But first, I need to get out of here and return my rental car that's parked in the short-term parking garage at the Toronto airport. It is costing me a fortune to keep my car there. I don't even know what day it is or where I am. Why are you keeping me in the dark? Am I at Guantanamo in Cuba? I am not a terrorist. I don't know what I have to do to convince you of that, but I really am just a journalist. I was just doing my job."

Joshua Dawson was not feeling any regret for what he had done. His first concern had been how much the parking for his rental car was costing him. Did he not realize he was under arrest? Why did he think he was handcuffed to his bed? If Joshua had shown even a little bit of remorse, Agent Wilton would have been more sympathetic to him. This kid was angry and actually insulted that he was being held. He really didn't think he'd done anything wrong. His attitude infuriated Ridley Wilton. He might have been willing to cut the kid some slack, if he'd been the least bit sorry for what he'd done. But the little twerp felt he was "just doing his job" and was entitled to destroy lives in the process.

"Do you have anything you want to say to me? I know about the trackers on my car key and on my car. I know about the listening devices at the Capital Hotel. Is there anything else I ought to know?" Dawson seemed surprised that the FBI agent had discovered his secrets.

"I just want to get out of here. I demand a lawyer. I know I am within my rights to have a lawyer represent me."

"Do you think you are actually being held within the jurisdiction of the U.S. justice system? Do you really think you have any rights in this situation?"

"I will sue you. You don't have any right to hold me here."

Agent Ridley Wilton knew there was nothing of importance that Joshua Dawson could tell him. He was going to allow the arrogant youngster to simmer and sweat for the time being. Wilton gave Dawson a hard and accusatory look. He looked the young man directly in the eyes and said, "Grow up!" Wilton turned around and walked out of the room without another word.

Dawson screamed after him. "You can't do this to me. I want a lawyer. I know my rights."

Agent Ridley Wilton drove to the airport in Burlington, Vermont and made arrangements to fly back to Little Rock. He had work to do. He had a case to crack.

❀

WHILE HE'D BEEN OUT OF his office, trying to be on a vacation, Ridley had received a communication from his friend at the Bureau of Printing and Engraving. Simon Dunnaway had sent the list of Russians who had been involved with the printing of the partly counterfeit U.S. one-hundred dollar bills in the 1990's. Many of these Russians were dead. Most of the rest were old. But money can outlast the human condition, and the FBI agent was happy to have the names. This was the only remaining clue he had left to pursue to try to find out who was behind the plot to hijack the airliners.

■ ■ ■ ■

"We watched him and followed him, but maybe we should have been following the FBI agent, Wilton, instead. Dawson was following the FBI guy and flew to Detroit. We assumed Agent Wilton was on vacation, visiting his son in Ann Arbor. Then out of the blue, Wilton took off for Canada. He rented a car and drove to Toronto. Dawson was right behind him. We don't know how Dawson knew where Wilton was heading. It almost seemed as if he had a tracker on the guy. Embedded in his arm maybe? Ha! Ha! We are the ones who should have thought of that. Anyway, he seemed to know where Wilton was going and followed him all over Eastern Canada.

"We almost lost him at the airport in Toronto. He had to run to buy his ticket and get on the plane. Both Wilton and

Dawson flew to Halifax and rented cars. We had to hustle to get our drone in the air over Halifax to watch where Dawson was going. There was a terrible storm that night in the Halifax area, with pouring rain and thunder and lightning. The wind was horrendous. It must have been the tail end of the north eastern storm that hit the East Coast. The visibility was really poor, and we lost sight of Dawson a few times. But we didn't lose him for good. Dawson didn't seem to need to keep Wilton's car in view, and he knew exactly where Wilton was going all the time. Wilton drove to a house on the water in Terence Bay, Nova Scotia. That's a really small fishing village outside Halifax. When Dawson arrived there, it was dark, and it was raining hard. He prowled around the house and looked in all the windows. The rain was fierce, and Dawson was getting soaked checking out the house.

"*The car Agent Wilton had rented at the airport was parked in front of the house, so we assumed he was inside. Dawson had some lock picks, and he broke into the back door of the house. Because he was inside the house, at that point, we lost our view of what was happening. We could tell from thermal imaging that there were three people in the house. One was Dawson, and we assume one of the other two was Agent Wilton. The third one was a woman, but she wasn't the woman we wanted her to be. We had hoped maybe Agent Wilton had gone to the house in Terence Bay to meet with our avenging granny, the woman whose name nobody knows for sure. It turns out the woman at the house was someone else, someone much younger than the woman we are looking for. We know she is younger because we saw the woman later when she got out of her car.*

"*Next thing you know, Dawson comes running out the front door. Actually it was about five minutes from the time he'd let himself into the house through the back door. Agent*

Wilton was chasing after him—out the door and through the yard. With all the rain, it was impossible for our drone to see everything. It would have been very difficult for either Dawson or Wilton to see anything either. There aren't any street lights out there, and none of the outside lights on the house were turned on. There was a chase on foot, and all of a sudden Dawson disappears over a wall. Wilton didn't go over the wall after him. Wilton went around the wall and climbed down another way to get to Dawson.

"That's when we tried to get a closer look at what was going on and lost the drone. Dawson fell into an area that was full of trees. Turns out, it was a bird sanctuary, so you might expect there would be a lot of trees there. The guy who was manipulating the drone couldn't see what was happening on the ground. He tried to get in closer with the drone. It looked like Dawson had gone over the wall and fallen down twenty or twenty-five feet on the other side. Dawson wasn't moving. He was just lying there. Like I said, Wilton went around the long way and climbed down a hill to get to Dawson. Visibility just kept getting worse and worse. Wilton reached the spot on the other side of the wall where Dawson had fallen and was laying there unconscious...maybe dead. After a few minutes, a woman drove a car close to where Dawson had fallen and where Wilton was. The woman got out of the car, so that's how we were able to see what she looked like. We got a pretty good view of her when she opened the car door and the car light went on. She was not using a cane and seemed very agile and spry, athletic even. She was much younger than the woman who used her cane to take down our hijacking martyr. Just as the woman got to the place where Dawson was on the ground, our drone crashed. Too many trees and too much rain. Even with the night-vision cameras that are installed on our drone, there is no substitute for getting close. When we tried to get close, we lost the whole thing. We think the drone might have been struck by lightning.

"It was a hell of a storm. I'm surprised we got any pictures from the drone at all. We didn't get much. The FBI agent might have just been visiting his aunt or his cousin or a girlfriend in Terence Bay. We saw no signs of the elderly woman that everybody, including Joshua Dawson, has been searching for. We'd been tracking Dawson using his phone, and after the drone went down, the phone completely disappeared, too. By the next day, Dawson's computer had also gone dead. We couldn't get another drone in the air for more than twenty-four hours. By the time we got a drone back up, the house by the water in Terence Bay was empty. The shutters were closed, and no one was there. By then the rain had stopped, and we could see everything perfectly. But there was nothing to see.

"We don't know anything after that. Dawson might be dead. The fall might have killed him. We just don't know what happened. By that time, there was no one at the house and no one anywhere around in the bird sanctuary or anyplace else. They were all gone. So now we have lost track of everybody except the FBI guy. And we always knew where he was anyway."

Chapter 33

Mercedes' husband, Ford, had loved gadgets, especially gadgets that had to do with cars. He'd had a GPS for his car before anybody else he knew had ever heard of a GPS. He'd fiddled with these gadgets, and inevitably Mercedes became curious and then intrigued. He'd taught her how to fiddle with the gadgets, too. Mercedes thought she knew how to figure out the portable GPS she'd found in the Range Rover. She knew how to access the location history and would be able to interpret it—if there was anything on it to interpret. It was possible to clear the history on the GPS and erase everything that had been recorded. If Gilbert Jones had not wanted anyone to know where he'd driven and if he had been smart, after he'd made a trip to one of his secret places, he would have erased the history on the GPS when he got out of his car. Mercedes was counting on the fact that he hadn't been that smart or that conscientious.

Gilbert Jones had been sloppy. He had not erased the GPS. Mercedes felt a surge of excitement. She worked with the portable GPS, and she checked the locations where Jones had driven against the Google Maps app on her cell phone. Voila! Gilbert Jones had traveled many times to a location in Bangor. It was a business called Downeast Easy Self-Storage. All along, just as Mercedes had suspected, Jones had a storage unit. She was certain the authorities had wanted to find this place, hoping it might reveal something about the mysterious Mr. Jones. But they had never found the portable GPS, so they had probably never known there was a self-storage unit. Mercedes could hardly keep her anticipation under control. She couldn't wait to tell Mac what she had discovered.

MERCEDES HAD PROMISED THE FBI she would not leave Flower Island, but this was too good a find to hold her to her promise. Even Mac was willing to ignore the rules to pursue this latest information. They both realized that the storage unit, which had once belonged to Gilbert Jones, might have been cleared out years earlier. If he had not paid his rent on the storage unit for several years in advance, the contents of the unit would be long gone. Both women were familiar with the television show *Storage Wars* and realized that all of Gilbert Jones' precious secrets may have been auctioned off a long time ago. Even though they knew this, they were eager to investigate Downeast Easy Self-Storage. Downeast advertised that it offered twenty-four hour access to its units.

Mac and Mercedes did not know how many storage units Gilbert Jones had rented. Even if he had paid the rent years in advance, they had no idea which unit or units might be his. They didn't know what name Gilbert Jones had used to rent his storage units. They doubted he had used the name Gilbert Jones. Mercedes thought she had the keys to the locks for the storage units. The mystery of the extra keys on the Range Rover's spare key ring would be solved if those keys went to Gilbert Jones's locks. There were many ifs and unknowns to be wrestled with, but the two women were determined to do their best to find out what unit or units belonged to Gilbert Jones. They had a plan.

Access to the storage units in all storage facilities is usually controlled by a wide gate that can be opened only if one knows the combination. Both women had used storage facilities from time to time in the past and knew how this worked. They would go into the office, which did not require knowing the combination or going into the gated area where the storage units were. They would rent a small unit of their own. Once they had rented a unit, they would be given the combination to the entrance gate.

This first visit was designed to be a reconnaissance run, a preliminary trip to scope out the situation and get to know the people who kept watch over Downeast's computers. Both Mac and Mercedes were personable and chatty and smart. They thought they would be able to make friends with the manager at Downeast and maybe glean the needed information from that person. They would take Mac's VW. They were saving the white Range Rover for a later date when they would pretend to be Gilbert Jones arriving to check out his unit. The Range Rover would have been a very noticeable vehicle whenever it arrived at Downeast Easy Self-Storage. Although most of the people who had worked at the facility, when Jones had come there years earlier to check on his stuff, were probably long gone, you never knew who might still be around and remember the expensive car.

They'd struggled to fit the wheelchair into the back seat of the VW. It was an essential prop for the performance they intended to put on for the manager of Downeast. They were posing as a woman and her elderly aunt. The story was that they were cleaning out the elderly aunt's house because she was planning to go into assisted living. They needed a storage unit to hold the furniture and boxes of things Aunt Alice could not yet bear to part with but could not fit into her new accommodations. The people who operated Downeast heard some version of this story every day. The pair of older women would be believable.

Mac again wrestled with the wheelchair to get it out of the tiny car. This part of the drama was very real, and it attracted the attention of the woman in the office. Mac had parked in a handicap spot and secured the handicap hanging tag on the rearview mirror. The woman in the office came to the door and watched the two as Mac put forth a tremendous effort to get Mercedes into the wheelchair. Both women were wearing wigs—wigs that Ridley Wilton had insisted they keep on hand just in case. Finally, Mac wheeled Mercedes into the office of the storage facility. She explained why they were there.

"Aunt Alice insisted on coming inside to check you out. She doesn't want to get rid of her stuff even though she doesn't have room for it where she is going. I tried to talk her out of coming with me, but she always wants to participate in everything. I tried to convince her to stay in the car, but she doesn't trust me to handle things. So here we are." An expression of exasperation on her face, Mac rolled her eyes at the facilities manager. The manager had witnessed scenes like this before.

"We aren't sure how big a unit we're going to need." Mac continued to take the lead in the negotiations. "I have a list of everything we want to put in storage, so maybe you can help me with this?"

The manager handed Mac a brochure that outlined how much space was required for storing the contents of households of different sizes. "Let me see that." Mercedes reached out to take the brochure. The manager, with a weak smile, gave a second brochure to Mercedes. The manager, who had introduced herself as Darlene, realized that this rental was going to take some time. She would not be able to get back to her romance novel again before lunch.

They poured over the brochure. "How long do people usually rent the units for? Months? Years?"

"We usually bill on a monthly basis, and we like to have a credit card on file to be able to do that. But some people prefer to pay in advance. We have quite a few clients who pay for a year in advance, for example."

"Does anybody ever pay in advance for five years?" Mac was curious. Darlene would be thrilled to make a sale that resulted in five years' worth of rent on a unit, paid in advance. She summoned some additional charm to attempt to make a sale to this pair.

"I heard that once we had a guy who paid rent for ten years in advance on two units." Darlene was willing to share the gossip about their best customer. It had happened before she'd begun working at Downeast.

"Wow! Why would anybody do that? Two units? That's a lot of money to put out all at once." Mac was gleeful. This was the information she had been fishing for. She was astounded that it had been this easy.

"Yeah, wow! Supposedly it was thousands of dollars, and he paid for it in cash. Can you believe it? Who carries around thousands of dollars in cash? I guess he never comes around anymore either. It's a mystery, but we already have our money."

"Those must have been big units. I mean, if he needed two of them. Where are the big units? I don't think we need a really big one, but maybe we do."

"All the 15 by 30s are way in the back. People leave cars and boats in those." Darlene was chatty now.

Mac had taken one of the maps of the facility. It showed the number and location of every unit, and she easily found the larger units. "You don't have many of those really big units. Are any of them free right now?"

"We have ten of them, and only one is currently empty. A guy just moved his boat out of that one. It hasn't been cleaned yet, but it should be ready in a couple of days."

Mac looked at Mercedes and Mercedes looked at Mac. They had planned an elaborate scenario in which Mercedes would fall out of her wheelchair in a back hallway on her way to the bathroom. She would pretend to be hurt. She would keep Darlene occupied taking care of her while Mac was in the main room pretending to call 911. In fact, Mac would be in the main room of the storage facility, searching through the computer for the units Gilbert Jones had rented. It was not a great plan, and it might have led nowhere. Gilbert Jones could have used a different alias to rent his storage units. Even if he had used the name of Gilbert Jones, Mac might not have had time to find his units on the computer. It would have been very dicey. It might have worked, and it might not have worked.

Now that they knew there were only ten of the largest size units and if Darlene had inadvertently given them the information they needed to know about Gilbert Jones, they would not have to put on their show with Mercedes falling out of the wheelchair. They were both relieved they didn't have to use the performance they had planned. They could save it for another day.

They would rent their unit and be given the combination for the gate. The only reason they were going to actually pay to rent a unit was to get the gate combination. They could come back at night and gain access to the units. They could try the keys on the key ring to see if they opened the locks on any of the ten largest storage units.

"We'd like to see some of the empty units to get an idea how big they are. It's hard to tell just looking at dimensions on the brochure. We'd like to see the largest unit and go from there. I don't think Aunt Alice has enough stuff to require her to rent the largest size unit, but we will have a better idea after we take a look."

Mercedes was incredibly thankful she hadn't had to fall out of the wheelchair onto the floor and try to get up. Someone might have had to call 911 for real to get her back into the wheelchair. Mac pushed Mercedes in the wheelchair. The three women made their way to the back of the facility, behind all the other rows of storage units. The ten largest units were lined up together. They were obscured behind smaller units which were closer to the entrance gate and closer to the office. Anyone trying to open the locks on these largest units would be completely out of view of the office and the gate. This might work.

Chapter 34

They made a decision about the size of the storage unit they would need. Mercedes insisted that she was tired and wanted to go to the car. Mac and Darlene struggled to get Mercedes into the passenger seat of the small VW and wrestled with the wheelchair to stow it in the back seat. Mac went into the office to complete the paperwork for the storage unit they did not need. But she came back to the car with the coveted combination to the entrance gate. They would be back tonight to try the keys on the key ring.

Both women were tired and napped during the afternoon. Mac made pork chops and applesauce for dinner. They loved seafood, but every once in a while they wanted to eat meat. Tonight was the night. Mercedes would rest after dinner, and Mac would wake her at midnight. They would wear their wigs, and this time they would drive the Range Rover. They were hoping to get into Gilbert Jones's storage units, so they were going to drive Gilbert Jones's car. The wigs were intended to fool any security guard who might accost them at the storage facility. They didn't think Downeast employed a security guard at night, but just in case.

They drove to Bangor again. Getting through the gate at Downeast was no problem. The place was deserted. Darlene was nowhere to be found, and there was no security guard. They drove directly to the ten largest storage units. Mercedes had trouble with little keys and opening locks, so she left dealing with those fine motor movements to Mac. When they'd reached the fifth unit in the row, the key went in and the lock came open. It had not been easy getting to this point, but they were delighted and excited to see what was inside. Mac positioned the Range Rover so that Mercedes would be able to see into the unit. She raised the door. They had brought a big flashlight so they could see inside. Mac shined the light on the contents of the storage unit. Both women gasped. They were speechless. They had not been expecting anything in particular, but whatever they might have imagined was in Gilbert Jones's storage unit, it was not this.

After several moments of complete silence, Mercedes spoke up. "Have you ever been to The Hermitage in St. Petersburg, Peter the Great's Winter Palace? I was there almost thirty years ago. That's what this looks like to me." Mercedes had nothing else in her experience to compare this to, except for the treasures of the Czars. There were paintings and gold and furniture and rugs and dishes and objets d'art. The unit was packed.

"I've never been there, but I have seen pictures. You are right. This is treasure beyond belief. Let me see if I can open the next unit." Mac removed the lock and raised the door of Gilbert Jones's second unit. It was more of the same. The gold was blinding when Mac turned the flashlight on the interior. She stepped into the second unit and picked up a candelabra that was sitting on the floor by the front of the opening. Mac was certain it was solid gold. She opened the door of the VW and put the candelabra on Mercedes' lap.

"We need to take some proof with us that there is treasure in this place. I am going to take several photos of the contents, but we need one piece of the gold to prove we are not making it all up. I have no idea right now what we are going to do about this situation. After I take some pictures, I am going to put both these doors down and put the locks back on. We are going to get out of here ASAP. Then we will figure out what we are going to do next." Mac took her photographs. She secured the units and double checked to be sure the doors were all the way down and the locks were in place.

They had been on the grounds of the storage unit for about fifteen minutes. Mac turned her flashlight on the units opposite the ones they'd just opened. She knew what to look for, but she didn't see any cameras pointed at the large units that could have recorded what their search had just revealed. If anybody ever discovered what was inside the two units that Gilbert Jones had rented and filled with his hoard, they would stop at nothing to break down the doors and help themselves to riches beyond their wildest imaginings.

They were silent for the first few miles of the return journey to Flower Island. Both women were overwhelmed by what they had discovered. Mercedes was the first to speak. "I knew he must have collections of some kind because of all those shelves he had Donny build. What normal person needs that many shelves? But I never dreamed he had the contents of a Czar's palace to display. He could never have anybody into his house to show them any of this stuff. Did he want to put it all on display just for himself? We know he was a wealthy man. The contents of these storage units could be the source of his wealth. He could sell off something when he needed more money. He paid cash when he bought the cottage. He paid Donny in cash for his work, and I know that wasn't cheap."

"No wonder he was hiding out on a remote island and living under an assumed name. If he stole all of that, there must be a great many people who are looking for him. That candelabra alone would pay the bills for a year. The furniture and the paintings look Russian to me. He must be Russian mafia." Mac had been with the FBI for many years, and she could easily understand why Gilbert Jones had tried to hide himself, either from those who'd owned the treasures he had stolen or from those who wanted a part of his loot.

"Of course we have to call Ridley about this. I don't want to touch any of it or be associated with any of it. Anyone who has stolen a huge amount of valuable stuff like this will always be a target. No wonder the guy disappeared without a trace. But whoever made him disappear never found his treasure. That must have been a huge disappointment to somebody. They are probably still looking." Mercedes wanted to wash her hands of the storage units and their contents. Even just knowing about what the storage units contained troubled her.

Mac was nervous, too. "I will call him tonight, as soon as we get back to Flower Island. He won't be able to grasp the enormity of this find. No one could. I am glad I took some photos. But even with the photos… he will only really get the point when he sees with his own eyes what's in those units." Mac hoped Ridley would immediately grasp how dangerous and how urgent this find was for Mercedes and for herself.

"Sam Stevenson said Gilbert Jones's English was perfect. Nobody had any idea he was a foreigner, but he must have been. He had everybody fooled." Mercedes was trying to recall everything Sam had said to her about Gilbert Jones. He hadn't told her much, because nobody had known anything much. The man had been mysterious, and then he had vanished. There were no clues of any kind.

Both women were completely exhausted when they arrived back at Flower Island. It was four o'clock in the morning in Maine. They had driven to Bangor and back twice in less than twenty-four hours. It had been a big day, especially for the sedentary writer, Mercedes Carrington, who didn't really go much of anyplace any more. Mac insisted they call Ridley Wilton right away, even though it was three in the morning Little Rock time. "I can only tell him to go to a pay phone and call me back. He won't talk on his own cell phone about anything that's the least bit confidential. I can barely get him to talk about the weather on his cell phone. This could take some time. I know you are even more worn out than I am, but I need you with me to tell him your part of the story. You are the one who used the GPS to figure out how to find the storage unit. I want you to explain all of that to Ridley. I am going to insist that he come up here today. I hope he will understand how serious this is. Why don't you lie down and get some rest. I'll wake you up when Ridley is on the phone and is ready to talk to you."

Mercedes wanted to take a shower, wash her hair, and climb into her own bed for a long and uninterrupted sleep, but she lay down on the couch in her study, ready to talk to Agent Wilton when he called back on a secure line. The wig had made her head itch, and she was drained and more than a little bit frightened by what they had discovered today. She drifted off as soon as her head reached the pillow on the couch.

Mac was shaking her. Ridley Wilton wanted to speak with Mercedes. It was six in the morning. "I've told him everything. He just wants to know about how you found the GPS and located the storage unit in the first place. And he wants to know what you think the story is behind the treasure."

Mercedes told Ridley Wilton everything about how she'd found the portable GPS under the seat of the Range Rover and everything else that had happened after that. "How do you think Gilbert Jones got his treasure to Maine? If he stole it from someplace in Russia, how did he get it to the U.S.?" This was Ridley Wilton's first question for Mercedes.

"Shipping container. Look for a Russian guy who sent a big shipping container from Russia to the U.S. in the years before Jones showed up in Maine. You might be able to find out the guy's real name that way. I'm sure his name isn't really Gilbert Jones." Mercedes answered a few more questions, and confirmed the astonishing value that both she and Mac had put on the discovery. It was quite priceless, and they were both sure it amounted to many, many hundreds of millions of dollars. Were these Russian national treasures? Ukrainian? Mercedes was happy to leave trying to find the answers to these questions in the hands of the professionals. She had thought the previous owner of the house was gone forever, but it seemed she had sought him out through the GPS. Now he and his incredible treasure would haunt her waking moments and her dreams.

Agent Wilton would fly into in Bangor that evening. Mac would meet him at the airport, and they would go directly to Downeast. The FBI agent did not want Mercedes to leave Flower Island or to be anywhere close to Gilbert Jones's storage units. She was to continue to lay low. Wilton diplomatically didn't mention anything about the two unauthorized trips Mercedes and Mac had already made to Downeast. The FBI would handle things going forward. This was a tremendous relief to Mercedes. She knew it would be almost impossible to keep such a find secret for very long. She knew Agent Wilton wanted to distance her involvement with the treasure and keep her far away from whatever happened with the storage units in the future. He was worried that her part in the discovery would eventually come out, but he was going to do everything he could to keep her completely isolated from the dramatic find in Bangor.

Mercedes was quite independent and did not usually want any assistance with her daily life's activities. This morning, she was so fatigued, she asked Mac to help her take a shower and wash her hair. She fell into bed not long after eight o'clock in the morning. She would sleep all day. She felt old, and she was very tired. Mac promised to leave something for her dinner in the refrigerator. Mercedes wasn't thinking about food right now. All she could think about at the moment was sleep.

Chapter 35

The last thing Agent Ridley Wilton wanted to hear about was the news he'd just received from Mac about what she and Mercedes had found in a storage unit in Bangor, Maine. He was disgusted with his lack of progress in the hijacking case, and he was disgusted with the injured journalist he had on his hands. He did not know what to do about either one of these dilemmas. He did not need another random crime on his plate.

The storage units that belonged to the missing wealthy man who had previously owned Mercedes' house were not really his problem. This dilemma was legally within the jurisdiction of Maine law enforcement, and they ought to handle it. But Ridley put a tremendous amount of trust in Mac's judgment. When she called for his help, he knew it was something extraordinary. He had to at least listen to what she had to say.

After Mac had explained what she and Mercedes had seen with their own eyes and after she had sent the photos she'd taken of the contents of the storage units, he knew he had to become involved. He arranged to fly to Bangor and meet with Mac. They would open the storage units at Downeast after dark, and Ridley would decide what to do next.

He'd agreed to take on this challenge, that was outside of his geographic purview and outside of his area of expertise, because he wanted, above all things, to protect Mercedes Carrington and keep her from being tied in any way to Gilbert Jones's affairs. He had to keep this discovery out of the news. He had to take care of this unusual and vexing difficulty without anyone becoming aware of what he was doing. Anything and everything about the Gilbert Jones treasure would have to remain off everybody's radar screen. How would that even be possible? He was too old for this. He was definitely going to retire as soon as he'd wrapped up these cases. He wondered if that day would ever come.

When he saw the two storage units with his own eyes, Agent Wilton was also dumbstruck. The photographs had given him an idea of the magnitude of the cache, but touching the gold and seeing the extraordinary mass of valuables in person took the situation to an entirely different level. The FBI agent was fascinated with the items he found in Gilbert Jones's units. Wilton had visited The Hermitage decades earlier and agreed with Mac and Mercedes that the treasure was Russian. What complicated kettle of diplomatic fish had he just jumped into? He did know he had just found himself in a mess of unknown ramifications.

Ridley had bought a burner phone to use while he was in Bangor because he didn't want anybody to know he was there. And, he didn't want anybody to know he had ever been there. He called Arabella on the prepaid phone and told her to fly to Bangor the next day and to use one of her alternate identities. He didn't want to say anything over the phone that might get anyone into trouble. Arabella asked, using code names, if Mac and Mercedes were all right and was relieved when Ridley told her that both women were fine. Arabella said she would text the details of her arrival at the Bangor airport.

Ridley's first priority was to move Gilbert Jones's treasure trove. He had to transfer it to a more secure location than Downeast Easy Self-Storage. It was only a matter of time until the increased activity around the storage units attracted someone's attention. Before that happened, the FBI agent had to make arrangements for it all to be relocated. He knew he was pushing the limits of his authority because he had made the decision, once again, not to tell the powers that be in Washington, D.C. anything about what was happening in Bangor. He could be in trouble if his superiors found he had failed to inform them about something as momentous as a lost Russian treasure worth many millions of dollars. At this point, he didn't care. He refused to tell anyone outside of his few very trusted agents anything about it.

Ridley struggled with his decision about where to move the Russian artifacts. It would all have to be catalogued and valued. It would probably have to be returned to somebody somewhere, although at this point Ridley had no idea who or where that might be. It would take weeks, if not months, to inventory the massive number of items. It would be a nightmare to try to value these things. It might not even be possible to put a value on many of the antique and unique pieces. Who in the world would he ever find to do the valuations?

He knew he could not leave the contents of the storage units anywhere in Maine. That was too close to where Mercedes was now living and hiding. He did not want to draw any attention to or have anyone show any interest at all in anything having to do with Maine. The artifacts would have to leave Maine, and the farther away, the better. He did not want to move it all to Little Rock. He did not want this ridiculously valuable mess that close to his own backyard. Washington, D.C. or anywhere close to there was also out for all the obvious reasons.

He needed a warehouse to store the stuff, and the warehouse would have to be secured. Ridley had already made the decision to turn the inventory, sorting, and valuation chore over to Arabella. He trusted her completely, and she was the only agent he knew who had the smarts to do the job. She would not particularly like the assignment, but she would take it on without complaint. She liked more action than making lists of Russian icons would provide, but she would do a careful and thorough inventory for Ridley.

Arabella, too, was overwhelmed when she saw the collection for the first time. They went at night again and used a flashlight. She was, like everybody else had been, speechless when she first laid eyes on the contents of the storage units. But her mind was already at work planning what had to be done. She was making mental lists of what she would need to move this massive volume of relics out of the storage units and out of Maine. She wondered how Gilbert Jones had ever managed to move it all into the units at Downeast and if he had done it alone.

Arabella was good at this kind of thing. She was particularly adept at making quick assessments. After clawing her way with difficulty through both of the storage units, she began to form an idea about how to move the treasure. She had good spatial judgment and trusted her ability to estimate the right size truck they would have to lease to transport the contents. She would need boxes and tape and packing materials. She would need inexpensive blankets to protect paintings and furniture. So many of the items had been thrown into the units loose. Priceless art objects lay in jumbled piles on the floor. Arabella thought she saw something that looked like a Faberge egg. It had been carelessly wrapped in what appeared to be some hand-embroidered antique altar cloths. If Gilbert Jones were Russian, she would have expected him to treat these artifacts with more respect. Some things were already in boxes, but the masses of individual random items would have to be carefully packed for transit. She knew it would take her at least a week to prepare this extraordinary hodge podge to be moved.

"I'm going to need your help. None of the pieces is very heavy, but quite a few are awkward. You and I can move the furniture and the rugs into a truck. Most of the packed boxes are not that heavy. The paintings ought to be crated, but cheap blankets are going to have to suffice for this rush job. Most of the work here is packing up the artifacts and books and dishes that are lying on the floor and stacked on the furniture. I know the priority is to get the stuff out of here and out of the state as soon as possible. The inventories will have to wait until the collection is secured." Arabella was in charge now, and Ridley was taking orders from her. She texted him a list of what she needed—the size of the truck he was to rent and how many dozen cardboard packing boxes he needed to buy.

Ridley had picked her up at the airport in a rented van. Before they left Downeast that first night, they carefully filled the van with as many of the loose items as they could pack into it. They locked the units and left. Ridley had rented a house in the countryside outside Bangor where he and Arabella could stay while they unloaded the storage unit. It was a one-story rancher and was not in particularly good condition. But it had an attached two-car garage that would be perfect for boxing up the items they had in the van. Arabella would begin her packing project later that day after she'd had some sleep.

Although he had frequently referred to Mercedes in code as Aunt Mathilde, in fact neither Mac nor Mercedes was Ridley Wilton's real aunt. But he did have a real aunt who lived in New Jersey. She was a retired college professor and had no children. She'd always had a soft spot in her heart for Ridley. He thought she was almost ninety years old, but nobody knew exactly how old she was. She wasn't telling. She lived alone on a small farm in the New Jersey pine barrens, and she spent more than six months of every year at her house on Long Beach Island, New Jersey. She had a cottage in Beach Haven. Her house in the New Jersey pine barrens would be empty until after Thanksgiving. Aunt Dorothy always celebrated Thanksgiving with a big turkey dinner at the beach. She invited all of her neighbors and cooked everything herself. Every year, she closed her house on Long Beach Island and returned to her farm in time for Christmas. Her house and barn in the pine barrens would be the perfect temporary home for Gilbert Jones's collection of artifacts.

Aunt Dorothy was delighted to allow Ridley to use her farm. She wanted to know if he was going to use it for something secret and dangerous. Ridley assured her that indeed her farm would be used in an operation that was unequaled in his thirty-year-long FBI career. Aunt Dorothy had a sense of adventure, and she was thrilled to know something exciting would be going on at her farmhouse, even if she was not there and would miss all the fun.

Ridley knew where the key to Aunt Dorothy's house was hidden. Arabella would have Dorothy's house and barn to herself as she did the inventory. Ridley would look at the barn to determine if everything could be stored there permanently or at least until its ultimate fate was determined. Arabella thought using a farmhouse and a barn rather than a warehouse was a brilliant idea. She could sleep and eat there and would be right on site to keep an eye on the treasure.

Aunt Dorothy's New Jersey barn was attached to her house in a style similar to the way houses in New England are attached to their barns. Because of snowy winters in the Northeast, this well-known house design made it possible to get to the barn to feed the animals without having to go outside in the cold. One could reach one's barn through a series of connected and unheated additions to the house. Going through the cold pantry, the root cellar, the mud room, the ice house, and other rooms necessary to maintaining a farm was the way many New England farmers got to their animals during the winter. Aunt Dorothy had no animals, and her barn was empty. New Jersey did not have as much snow as Vermont had, but they did have a lot of rain. Arabella would have access to the barn without ever having to go outside. She would hide her car in the barn, and no one would ever know there was anyone staying at Aunt Dorothy's farm. She could walk from the house to the barn without going outside. No one would ever see her.

It was decided. A destination had been chosen. Arabella packed the artifacts in boxes at the rental house garage while Ridley transported loads from the Bangor storage unit in the van. They worked all night every night for five nights. They slept during the day. Ridley was constantly afraid someone would notice his nightly forays into Downeast. Mac prepared meals for them and drove her delicious food to the rental house outside of Bangor every other day.

Finally, they were ready. Ridley had rented the largest truck he could find, and Ridley, Mac, and Arabella spent five hours at the rental units moving furniture, paintings, rugs, and boxes into the truck. It was backbreaking work, and Mac was too old to do this anymore. She drove the truck and gave directions to the other two. Arabella and Ridley finally collapsed on the bench seat of the rented truck while Mac scoured the now-empty units to be sure they'd left nothing behind. Even one piece of gold or the tiniest priceless Russian cross dropped in a corner would have raised too many awkward questions.

Mac drove the truck and the two exhausted movers back to the rental house. They would risk leaving the truck parked outside for the night. They were all too tired to continue loading the truck with the boxes Arabella had packed and stored in the garage. After a good day's sleep, Arabella and Ridley would load the remaining boxes into the truck and clean out the rental house. Arabella would be on her way to New Jersey. She would be able to park the rented truck inside Aunt Dorothy's barn and unload it at her leisure. Ridley would be on call to help with the larger pieces she could not move by herself.

Once the truck was unloaded and they had returned it to U-Haul, any and all ties between the storage units at Downeast in Bangor, Maine and Gilbert Jones's treasure would have been severed. It had been a tremendously difficult job, but they had accomplished it. All of their tracks would soon be erased. No one would know.

Chapter 36

FBI Agent Ridley Wilton now had three problems, and he didn't know what to do about any of them. The journalist, Joshua Dawson, would not be going anywhere any time soon. He needed more surgery, and then he would require months of physical therapy. Ridley decided he wouldn't think about that problem for a while. There was nothing he could do about Dawson until he was back on his feet.

Arabella was taking care of the inventory of Gilbert Jones's treasures. She was in the process of photographing everything, and she was doing a great deal of research about Russian icons, furniture, and art work on the internet. The U-Haul truck had been returned to New Hampshire. Nothing had ever been moved into the storage unit Mac and Mercedes had rented using assumed names and wearing wigs. The inexpensive lock on the door remained untouched. Downeast Easy Self-Storage had just made a quick one hundred fifty dollars on storage space that was never used.

Instead of renting a car, Arabella had convinced Ridley to buy an inexpensive, second-hand van. The registration was transferred to a name Ridley sometimes used, but Arabella paid the seller extra to be able to keep the Pennsylvania license plates. They would still be legal for eight more months. Arabella developed a connection over the internet with an expert in Russian artifacts who was based in New York City.

Periodically Arabella drove to New York with a few pieces of furniture or art work in the van and consulted with her expert. He had no idea Arabella was an FBI agent, but he was very curious about where she had found so many unusual pieces. She told him that her grandmother, who had lived the early part of her life in Russia, had recently died and left her home and its contents to her. Arabella told the man her grandmother had been a bit of a hoarder and that nobody'd had any idea the elderly woman owned such a houseful of treasures. Arabella confided in her New York expert that she'd never realized her grandmother had brought so many valuable things with her when she'd left Russia.

Arabella could see that the expert was drooling to get his hands on some of the pieces she brought to him to be valued, but Arabella was cagey about what she intended to do with her inheritance. She was always careful to take a different and circuitous route when she left New York City, in case the expert decided he wanted to follow her and find out where the amazing mystery house full of Russian valuables was located.

Ridley knew that when Arabella had finished her inventory of the cache of Russian artifacts, he would know exactly what he had on his hands. He would probably still not know where any of it had come from, and he was certain he would not know what in the world he was going to do about disposing of it.

His primary focus, he told himself, should be on solving the mystery of who was behind the attempted hijackings. But he had exhausted all of his leads, except for the list of Russian names his friend at BPE in Ft. Worth had given him. The list was from the 1990s, and Ridley already knew that many of the people on the list had died or disappeared. Those who were still alive were mostly older members of the Russian Mafia.

After some time-consuming research, Ridley Wilton found that only two men on the list, Anatoly Kuznetzov and Gregory Balakin, were currently living in the United States. He had no idea how to find them. Even if he was able to find two men with these names, there was no guarantee that they were the same men who had been handling U.S. counterfeit money in the 1990s. Mafia people had many names. Criminals had many aliases. Ridley had to assume the men who had been making the partially counterfeit one-hundred dollar bills were not currently using the same names they had used several decades earlier in another country two continents away.

The two names, which came from his list of people who might or might not have some connection to his case, were not promising leads. He really needed CIA help to locate the Russians. He thought the CIA made some attempts to keep tabs on the Russian Mafia types who were currently living in the U.S., but he was reluctant to share his case with the intelligence agency.

Ridley's spirits lifted, and he thought he might have a break, when he received a call from his counterpart in Las Vegas. "Ridley, we have a situation here that might have some bearing on a case you were involved in a few months ago. We have a dead Russian on our hands, and he has some kind of a connection to Jimmy John Vickers. I know how anxious you were to grill Vickers and how disappointed you were when he was found murdered. We think the dead Russian's name is Anatoly Kuznetzov. When we began investigating him, we found some camera footage that showed him meeting with Vickers a few times. We kind of stumbled onto this Russian's body out in the desert. Do you want to hear about this or have you moved on with your case?"

"You're darn right I want to hear what you have to say. I want to know every detail about this Russian, Mr. Kuznetzov. I have not moved on at all with my case. What you have to tell me might be what I need to get somewhere. The murder of Jimmy John Vickers was a real blow. I was sure he was going to tell all to try to avoid going back to prison." Ridley was ecstatic to hear the name Anatoly Kuznetzov and hoped against hope that this was the same man whose name was on the list Simon Dunnaway had given him. Wilton wanted to hear every last detail about how the Las Vegas FBI had found Jimmy John Vickers' Russian connection.

The Las Vegas chief continued his story. "A rancher was driving out into the desert to tend to one of his injured horses in the middle of the night. He lets his horses run on the range and has a GPS tracking device attached to each one. It's really kind of a neat set up. He had noticed that one of his horses hadn't moved for a couple of days. That's not their usual behavior, and the rancher knew something was wrong. He drove out to find the horse, and sure enough the horse was down. He went back to his barn and hooked up his horse trailer. He headed out to the desert again to pick up the horse and take it to the vet.

"When he was on his way to pick up the injured horse, he happened on two guys digging a hole out in the middle of nowhere. It seems they intended to bury the Russian. The rancher had a gun, and the guys only had a couple of shovels and a dead body. The rancher knew they were up to no good, being out on the range at that hour of the night. They were on his property, so he had them for trespassing at the very least. He didn't like the look of things, and when he investigated what they were doing, he found a dead body in the body bag in the hole. He tied up the two grave diggers and put them in his horse trailer. He documented the whole thing taking photos with his phone. He dragged the body bag into the horse trailer. Then he proceeded to pick up his injured horse out on the range. He took the horse to the vet as planned. Then he dropped off the body and the two men with the shovels at our office. He was waiting outside the FBI building when I arrived at work yesterday morning."

"That's quite some story. But how did you make the connection with Vickers?"

"The two wouldn't tell us anything when we questioned them. They still won't say a word. We think maybe they don't speak any English. Whatever has them tongue-tied, they aren't talking. So we don't know what language they speak. We had no idea who the dead guy was. The diggers wouldn't tell us. Maybe they didn't know. We found a long knife in the old beater they'd driven out into the desert. There was plenty of blood in the vehicle, on the knife, and on the two guys who aren't speaking. We are sure one or both of them killed the Russian. We're charging them with pre-meditated murder." The FBI chief from Las Vegas was thinking he had all his evidence lined up for a conviction in this crime.

"We ran the dead guy through facial recognition, and we got a hit. The man is Anatoly Kuznetzov. So we looked at some other video footage we had of Kuznetzov. We wanted to find out who his associates were and who he was doing business with. That was when we came across Jimmy John. He met with Anatoly three times, one time for more than an hour. I can show you all the video if you want to see it."

The FBI agent in Las Vegas knew his colleague Ridley Wilton was hooked.

"I want to see it all. If we need a lip reader, find one. I will put it on my budget. I'd love to know what Kuznetzov and Vickers said to each other. I'll be on the next plane to Vegas. Can I talk to the two grave diggers?" Ridley grabbed on to this lifeline. Maybe he could save his case after all.

"You can talk to them, but I doubt they will tell you anything."

"Do you know who they are? Do they have records?"

"That's the odd part. We have their fingerprints on file, but what we have in the computer linked to those fingerprints are not these same two guys. Somebody has been into our records and put different faces and different rap sheets with these fingerprints. As you can imagine, this has caused another big brouhaha, and we've got a whole investigation going on to try to find out who messed with the computer files. That is on top of our trying to figure out why these two were burying the Russian in the desert. Come on out. I'd welcome some help with this one." The Las Vegas FBI agent sighed. There was always something that went haywire, even when he had a slam dunk case.

"Could the two grave diggers also be Russian? Have you done their DNA?"

"Those results should be back tomorrow by the time you get here. We should know more about their nationalities at least. That doesn't mean they will talk to us."

Ridley Wilton hoped he finally had something. He spent a restless night, going over and over in his mind all the possible connections there could be between the dead Russian and the Vickers brothers and his complicated, dead-end case. He remembered that he'd had a case years ago where someone had broken into his filing cabinet and substituted different faces and paperwork in the files with the fingerprints they'd found at a crime scene. They'd never found out who had changed the files in the filing cabinet, and they'd never found the people who belonged to the fingerprints. Now someone was doing the same thing electronically, substituting the faces and backgrounds of the offenders. He hoped the Las Vegas office would have better luck straightening things out than he'd had. He could scarcely wait until morning arrived and he was on the plane.

▪ ▪ ▪ ▪

"We had to get rid of the Russian. He was beginning to be a problem. He made a stink about getting his money, and he was determined to keep on with his money laundering schemes. He was attracting too much attention from law enforcement. They were curious about the houses he'd bought for the Vickers brothers and about New Vistas Properties, LLC. He'd become too much of a liability. Then he threatened to go to the FBI and tell them who he's been doing business with. He wanted even more money not to do that. It was turning into an extortion situation, and we couldn't continue to put up with it.

"I told them to make it look like a heart attack and to leave him at his house. That's easy to do these days, and the autopsy, if anybody bothered to do one, would show he had died of natural causes. But those two idiot Ukrainians had to slit his throat. Then they decided they had to bury him in the desert. So we are in a bad spot now that they've been caught digging the Russian's grave and have been arrested. We got into the computer files right away and put different names and photographs and rap sheets with their fingerprints. But that won't fool the FBI for long. These two don't speak much English, but if they get a Ukrainian translator in there and

start to threaten them, we could have trouble. They're both dumb as posts. They're assassins and grave diggers. They didn't follow orders, and look where it got them. As soon as they are put in with the general prison population, we will have them taken out. It's just a problem between now and when that happens."

⁌ ⁌ ⁌ ⁌

"We still don't have anything on where she is. We know the journalist went to Halifax, but then we lost him completely. He had a terrible fall and injured himself badly. We're sure about that. So, he may be dead. His phone is gone. He is gone. So who knows what's going on with him?"

"I think we need to give up trying to find the old woman. It just isn't worth the resources we're going to have to devote to tracking her down. She may already be dead. I think she is. I think that's why we can't find her, whoever she is or was. If she were still alive, somebody would have trotted her out in front of the press by now and made a big 'to do' over her taking down the hijacker and saving the plane. That's what they always do, and this is really quite unusual, with her being so old and disabled and all of that. It would make great television. You can tell him I think we ought to drop trying to find her. I know he gets all hung up on these revenge projects, but he ought to just let this one go. It isn't worth it. She's old anyway. She isn't going to live forever, even if she is still alive. And I don't think she is."

Chapter 37

Agent Ridley Wilton spent three days in Las Vegas, trying to get the two gravediggers to reveal who had paid them to kill Anatoly Kuznetzov and bury him in the desert. The duo turned out to be a Ukrainian and a Russian, according to their DNA. Actually both of them were part Ukrainian and part Russian. A Russian translator and a Ukrainian translator were brought in, but the two still refused to say a word. Even when they were informed that they were being charged with first degree murder, they never offered to give their names.

Ridley had insisted on hiring a lip reader to watch the videos of Jimmy John Vickers' meetings with Kuznetzov. The lip reader had been able to see Jimmy John's lips in the videos. But Anatoly had been facing away from the camera so she had not been able to follow much of what he had said. Unfortunately, the meeting had been mostly about the Russian giving directions to Jimmy John Vickers and telling him what to do. Jimmy John shook his head a lot in agreement. He told the Russian repeatedly that he understood what he was supposed to do. The only really important evidence gleaned from the videos was that it definitely showed Anatoly Kuznetzov handing off a bag of money to Jimmy John Vickers.

Jimmy John had opened the bag and checked the contents—all in view of the camera. The video had shown banded packs of one-hundred dollar bills inside. Jimmy John had lifted one packet of bills out of the bag and looked at it more closely. Kuznetzov had been furious with Jimmy John when he'd insisted on checking the contents of the bag. It wasn't necessary to hire a lip reader to see that the Russian was yelling at Jimmy John and telling him to put the bills back and close the bag of money.

This was proof of the payoff. This was the proof that the Russian had paid the Vickers brothers for the Mosque charade. The question now was, who had ordered the hit on the Russian? Somebody was eliminating anyone and everyone who'd had anything at all to do with the operation. Anyone in the chain of participants and witnesses, who might have been convinced to squeal about who had hired them, was dead or gone. Ridley was frustrated with his inability to learn anything from the grave diggers, but the circumstances surrounding Kuznetzov's murder had yielded some valuable information, even if no one had been able to get his killers to talk.

From the beginning, the attempted hijackings had not made sense to Ridley Wilton. He had always felt as if he were missing something, something important. His investigation had constantly been at least one step behind whoever had orchestrated the elaborate plot. Whenever Wilton thought he had a key witness within his grasp, the witness was murdered. These witnesses had often been murderers who had taken part in the crimes. Ridley Wilton had not been able to interview a single one before he had been conveniently silenced.

Ridley Wilton slept fitfully on the return flight from Las Vegas to Little Rock. When he arrived in Arkansas, he had finally put his case together. After all these many months, he thought he knew who was behind the grand plan to bring down the two planes. He did not understand the motive behind the crimes, but he had a pretty good idea who was responsible. He also knew, if he was correct about who had planned and financed this many-layered scheme, he would not be able to bring the ultimate culprit, the mastermind planner, to justice. Ridley had gathered the last few pieces of his puzzle during the trip to Las Vegas. If Ridley was on target and had solved this case, if he had indeed figured out who was behind it all, he knew without any doubt that he was never going to be able to arrest anyone else for plotting the hijackings.

A series of crimes and murders had been committed, but no branch of law enforcement was ever going to be able to punish anyone for these transgressions. Those responsible were either already dead or had disappeared. Or they were untouchable. If Ridley was ever able to find him, he might be able to bring charges against Billy Bob Vickers. If Vickers was still alive, he was kind of the last man standing. But it hardly seemed worth it. Billy Bob was a very tiny fish in this huge sea of bogey men. Billy Bob had no idea about the wider conspiracy that was beyond his own small role. Billy Bob might be on the run, or he might be conveniently dead and resting in an unmarked grave in the desert.

Given the complexity of the plot as well as the huge amount of financial resources that had been necessary to attempt such a series of events, Ridley knew there were only a handful of people who would have had any hope of undertaking this diabolical scheme and being successful. Because of Ridley's experience, he was familiar with the way those on the list of the possible backers of the plan worked through their malicious ways. He was now certain he knew who was behind it all. Ridley had been bringing criminals to justice for decades, and he was able to recognize the signature that this untouchable perpetrator had left on his crimes.

Ridley decided to call and talk things over with Arabella. She was his best agent, and she might have some insight into the motive behind this complicated crime. Or, she might have a different point of view or disagree entirely with Ridley about who was behind the hijacking plot.

※

Ridley told Arabella everything he'd learned in Las Vegas. He told her what he had concluded about who was behind the hijacking plots. He didn't mention any names. She agreed completely with his reasoning and was likewise discouraged that no one would ever have to answer in a court of law for the multiple crimes they had so intricately choreographed.

"The hijackings were so random and really out of place. It's almost as if they were a distraction. So many other things are going on in the world right now." Arabella had also been puzzled by the hijacking attempts that had come out of the blue. When she made this statement about the hijackings being a distraction, Ridley had the epiphany he'd been hoping for. The motive for the complicated conspiracy made sense to him for the first time. At last, he thought he understood what had happened. He could finally close his case, but there was little satisfaction in it.

※

Arabella had completed the inventory of Gilbert Jones's cache of Russian artifacts. She had concluded, with the help of several consultants, that the treasures had come from a Russian Orthodox Church in Estonia. Because of the large number of religious icons in the collection, Arabella had decided that a church had been the original home of these objects. The sets of dishes, the gold, the furnishings, the art objects, and the paintings argued for a more domestic origin. The Russian style of the items convinced her that all of the artifacts were from the geographic area of the Baltic States.

Some of the more fragile and breakable pieces had been wrapped in newspapers published in Tallinn, Estonia. The newspapers were dated 1940, and there was a significant amount of dirt mixed in with the things that had been wrapped in newspaper. Arabella had no proof of the provenance of any of it, but she speculated that in 1940, when the Soviet Union had invaded and occupied Estonia, someone had rescued the gold and valuables from an Orthodox Church in Tallinn and buried them in a field on their farm or in their back yard or garden.

The Soviet Union was an atheistic state. Orthodox priests might have anticipated that the Soviets would strip their church of its gold and icons and other valuable pieces and take them back to enhance the coffers in Moscow. To preserve their heritage and their assets, the priests, or even the congregants, might have decided it would be better to secretly bury their relics than to allow the Soviets to steal them. Another explanation, of course, might be that the objects had originally come from someplace in Russia. Estonia shared an extensive border with Russia. But, the 1940 Tallinn newspapers were all the proof that Arabella needed that Estonia had been the home of this collection.

Arabella could easily imagine that someone knew all along where the treasure had been buried. The valuables could have languished under the soil for decades. Even the paintings, if they had been carefully preserved in waterproof wrappings, might have survived since 1940. Arabella, however, suspected that the paintings and the furniture, had probably been secreted in someone's attic.

Arabella shared both her discoveries and her speculations with her boss. They still had no idea about what to do with the treasure. They both felt strongly that it should be returned to Estonia, and if possible, returned to the church where it had originally been. But to relocate the massive treasure from this country and send it back to Estonia was entirely out of their orbit. They had done all they could to track its ownership. They did not believe that Gilbert Jones had ever been the rightful owner.

How Gilbert Jones, or whatever his real name was, had come to have possession of the treasure would probably always remain a mystery. Was the man Russian? Estonian? How had he known where the Orthodox treasures were hidden? Had he dug them out of the ground himself? Had he stolen them? It was hard to imagine he had stumbled on these things by accident.

Tallinn was on the seacoast. It would not have been impossible to fill a shipping container with the fabulous find and transport the shipping container from the city on the Baltic Sea, across the ocean to the United States. Arabella was curious, but she was reconciled to the fact that she would never know about all the steps in the journey these valuables had taken from the time they had left the Orthodox Church in Tallinn, Estonia until they had found their way to Downeast Easy Self-Storage in Bangor, Maine.

Ridley's Aunt Dorothy had lived a long time. Many of her friends, acquaintances, and colleagues had died, but she had always realized the importance of making younger friends. One of her younger friends on Long Beach Island was a man from Latvia who was in his 60s. He had once been an Orthodox priest but years ago had given up religion for high tech. For the last thirty years he had designed web pages, and he'd made a small fortune since he had moved to the United States in the early 1990s. Ridley had met the man at Thanksgiving dinner one year when he'd spent the holiday with his Aunt Dorothy at her cottage in Beach Haven, New Jersey. Ridley wondered if the man was still hanging out in Beach Haven and if his aunt was still in touch with the former priest.

Dorothy was delighted to hear from Ridley. She asked if her barn and house were still standing, and he laughed when he told her that her barn especially had never been better. He knew his aunt would have loved to see her barn filled with millions of dollars' worth of Estonian gold and religious artifacts. Ridley asked his aunt about her Latvian friend. His Latvian name had been Andris Jansone, but he had changed it to the Americanized Andy Jamison. Andy had retired and was living full time in Beach Haven. His house was three doors down from Aunt Dorothy's. Dorothy wanted to know why Ridley was all of a sudden interested in her friend Andy.

"I am hoping he might be able to help me with a problem. I have some religious artifacts that were discovered, kind of tangentially, as part of a case I've been working on. I suspect these artifacts originally came from the Baltic States, Estonia in particular. I would like to talk to Andy about what to do with them. They ought to be returned to the Orthodox Church where they originally came from, if it's still standing. The least I can do is return them to their country of origin. It's complicated, Aunt Dorothy."

"It seems to me that everything you get yourself involved in is complicated, Ridley. I will be happy to give you Andy's contact information. But we are only a short drive away from my farm in the pine barrens. It's less than an hour. I am assuming these religious artifacts are in my barn. Do you want Andy to see them, or are you trying to keep all of this a big secret?"

"I think he needs to see what is in your barn. I think it would be all right if you and Andy came and had a look at the treasure. You will be shocked. Everyone is stunned when they first view the enormity of this collection. But I must insist that you and Andy keep all of this strictly confidential. No one except the two of you can ever know anything about any of it. It is so overwhelming you will want to talk about it and tell everyone you know about what you have seen. But you absolutely cannot do that. You must swear to keep this secret."

"Oh, Ridley, of course we know how to keep a secret. You are such a stick in the mud with your security and your confidentiality."

BUT EVEN AUNT DOROTHY, WHO had seen it all in her almost ninety years on earth, was shocked when she saw what was being concealed in her barn. Andy Jamison's eyes grew wide, and he let out a soft, long whistle. "I see what you mean, Ridley. This is unbelievable. What in the world? Where did all this come from? Oh, I know you can't tell me any of that, but please tell me what in the world you are going to do with all of it."

"That's why I wanted you to come here and view it for yourselves. I am asking for your help, Andy. I want to return the treasure to Estonia. I know you are Latvian, but all of this is going to go back to Estonia. As a former priest, I am sure you can understand why this needs to go back to the church from which it was taken." Andy of course knew that Ridley was an agent with the FBI. Arabella had asked that she be allowed to be present to answer questions, but she did not want to be introduced by name to either Aunt Dorothy or to Andy Jamison. She preferred to keep her name and status unknown.

"My father tells a story about when the Soviets came to Latvia in 1940. Everyone took their silver and their jewelry, their gold, and anything else of value, and buried it in their gardens and in their farm fields. They knew the Russians would steal everything we had if we didn't hide it from them. We left our valuables buried. Then the Nazis came. We left our valuables buried. Then the Russians came again. We left our valuables buried. Only after the Soviet Union fell apart in the 1990s did some people even think of digging up their entombed family wealth. Sometimes it was the grandchildren or great-grandchildren of the people who had buried it who brought it back from the earth." Andy was remembering the years of turmoil that war and occupation had inflicted on the Baltic States.

Ridley wanted Andy's attention in the present day. "What do you think we ought to do about all of this? It is worth an incredible amount of money, and many people would love to get their hands on it and keep it for their own. I trust you because I know you are already a wealthy man and do not seek more riches."

"I have to say that if I were a collector, which I am not, I might be sorely tempted to take some of these things for myself. I wonder about the person who brought this to the USA from Europe. I wonder if he was interested in the wealth this collection could obviously provide for him or if he was a collector and wanted to display these things to be able to look at them."

Ridley was never going to mention Mercedes Carrington or Maine when he spoke about the Gilbert Jones treasure, but he answered Andy's quandary. "I happen to know that he wanted to look at his collection every day of his life. I also think he sold off pieces of it to buy a house and a car, to renovate the house he'd purchased, and to pay his bills. I have to wonder if someone he did business with, someone he'd sold one or more of the pieces to in order to raise some cash, decided they wanted in on the largesse and killed him, hoping to find where he kept his goodies. The man who once had all of this in his possession disappeared one day without a trace. After he had been gone for several years, the court declared him dead."

Andy had been listening, but he had also been thinking. Ridley could almost see the man's brain cells spinning as he deliberated what to do about this dilemma. "Do you have expenses as a result of rescuing this treasure hoard? You must. If you have already decided to return it to Estonia, I am assuming you're not going to ask the FBI accountants to reimburse you for what you've spent to deal with all of this."

"I made the decision to take care of this part of the case completely apart from the rest of what I do for the FBI. Bureaucracies are cumbersome and leaky. I did not want to compromise this unexpected discovery by getting it mixed up with the FBI bureaucracy." Ridley Wilton knew he was on shaky ground here and hoped Andy Jamison would not pursue this line of questioning.

Andy seemed to get this, and he understood that the discovery and the return of the treasure did not and would not involve Ridley's day job. Andy moved on. "I have a couple of ideas. I still have a few friends and connections in Latvia. I gather that, going forward, you would prefer to wash your hands entirely of any involvement with this matter. You would like to walk away and have everyone forget you ever laid eyes on these artifacts."

Ridley looked long and hard at Andy. "You have hit the nail on the head. I want to completely forget the entire thing, and I never want to have to account for knowing anything about any of this."

"Do you trust me to take over from here? Do you trust me to make the best decisions I can make for you?"

"I do trust you. I want to be certain this goes back to Estonia. That is the only demand I have for what happens to any of it."

"Why don't you and Arabella go home to Arkansas as soon as possible and leave the disposal of this collection to Dorothy and myself. I will tell you as much as you want to know about what we're doing, but you must leave it to me."

At that moment, Arabella realized what a huge burden had just been lifted from her shoulders. Her FBI career was important to her, and she had worried, more than she would admit even to herself, about what this "off the books" project might do to her relationship with the FBI. She gave Ridley a look and saw that he was also delighted to delegate the entire problem to Andy Jamison.

Arabella had purchased a laptop expressly for the purpose of keeping track of the Gilbert Jones inventory. She turned the laptop over to Andy, along with all the relevant paperwork and photographs. She gave him an email address where he could contact her with questions about the collection. She went to her bedroom in Dorothy's house and packed up her clothes and personal items. There were two cardboard boxes taped up in the bedroom. Arabella took the boxes and her duffle bags to Ridley's car. They were leaving the van with Andy and Dorothy. Arabella shook hands with Andy and thanked Dorothy for allowing them to use her house and barn.

Ridley and Arabella drove to the Newark Airport and were on the plane for Little Rock later that evening. They were worn out, but the stress that had been hanging over their heads was gone. They had successfully managed to dispose of millions of dollars' worth of stuff. They hoped they would never lay eyes on any of it again.

Chapter 38

*R*idley Wilton updated Mac and Mercedes about the Gilbert Jones treasure. They were also more than a little bit relieved that someone else had taken on the challenge, and when they'd heard all the facts, they applauded the plan to return everything to Estonia. The drama of dealing with all those priceless artifacts had been stressful for them, too. Mercedes wanted to get back to her writing. The discovery at Downeast had definitely been a distraction, but it might also have provided the beginnings of a new mystery novel plot.

Before Mercedes could settle into a quiet life, Ridley knew he needed to visit Flower Island and have a serious talk with her. She was nervous about what he was going to say, but he told her not to worry. He was going to make a proposal to her about how she could get her life back. He had a plan. He wanted to discuss it with her and get her approval to go ahead.

Ridley Wilton was certain he knew who was behind the hijacking attempts, and he realized he was never going to be able to bring that person to justice for the multiple associated crimes. He had the Iranian and the Yemeni, and they would be dealt with accordingly. They would be tried in a court reserved for terrorists. They would be found guilty, and they would be punished. At least he had those two, but he realized that they were very small potatoes in the larger scheme of things. He would never be able to do anything about the mastermind who had conceived of this operation and put it into play.

Ridley would never be able to prove it, but he now believed with all of his being that the hijackers' crimes had been envisioned as a distraction. He was aware of the political philosophy of the person he knew in his heart was behind the planning of the hijackings. The billionaire was a tremendous advocate and cheerleader for Communist China. Communist China had just suffered a huge black eye because of their handling of the COVID-19 pandemic disaster. China was distrusted and despised by most of the countries of the world. Too many people had died because the clique in Beijing had told so many lies.

In spite of the loud apologists who argued for a contrary opinion, everybody with any common sense knew that the pandemic had been China's fault. Even if they had not engineered the virus, which the entire world knew they had, they had tried to cover up what was happening. Millions had died because China had denied there was a problem and had delayed informing the human race about how deadly the virus really was. Everybody on earth knew this, even if the Chinese Communists pretended otherwise.

The mastermind behind the hijackings had wanted to distract the eyes of the world from the terrible things that Communist China had done. He wanted to make Muslims the monsters again. He especially wanted to get Americans riled up with memories of 9/11. It was difficult for Ridley to admit this, even to himself. Who could be so cold blooded and so evil as to want to bring down airliners full of people in order to distract the American public from blaming the Chinese for the pandemic? It was crazy.

As difficult as it was to accept, Ridley was completely convinced that it was true. Money could buy anything. Money could distract. Money could successfully hide evil beneath a cloak of philanthropy and political activism. This billionaire would never be made to account for anything. He was too well-insulated. He'd been funding violent causes for decades. Ridley would have to find a way to rid his conscience and his consciousness of the man.

Because he would never be able to bring the real criminal in all of this to answer for his misdeeds, Ridley had to find another way to allow Mercedes to come out of hiding without putting her in danger. After thinking about the problem for months, he had determined that the only way to do this was for the woman who had brought down the hijacker on American Airlines Flight #66 to die. Only in death would the elderly hero with the cane be truly safe.

Very few people knew the real name of the woman whose bravery had saved lives on that fateful day. Ridley Wilton had jealously guarded Mercedes Carrington's identity. He had kept another woman, a decoy, hidden, and he had told his superiors at FBI headquarters the actress he'd hired was the hero. No one had found Ridley's substitute hero, and no one had found the real Mercedes Carrington. The time had come for the brave elderly woman to pass away. It would be very sad. There would be speeches and flags and ceremonies and all the rest of it to commemorate this septuagenarian and her selfless and majestic deed.

Ridley Wilton had initially chosen the name Edwina Carroll and substituted it in place of Mercedes' name on the passenger list for Flight #66. Edwina Carroll was a real person who had lived in Ardmore, Pennsylvania, but she had not been anywhere close to the spectacle that had taken place in the skies over Little Rock, Arkansas in early March. In real life, Edwina had been a wealthy woman who had never married and never had any children. Ridley had selected her name and her background because she had no family who might have questioned the fact that she was said to have been a passenger on the plane from Phoenix to Philadelphia. Edwina had also been something of a recluse.

A few years earlier, Edwina's housekeeper had alerted her doctor that Edwina needed more care than the housekeeper was able to provide. Edwina's dementia had advanced quickly, and the housekeeper realized she needed to be in a care facility. The doctor had agreed, and Edwina had been transferred to a nursing home outside Newtown Square, Pennsylvania. Her house and furnishings were sold. Edwina lived comfortably for quite a few months in the luxurious memory care unit, and she had died peacefully in her sleep. There had been a brief death notice in the local paper, but because there was no family, no one had written an extensive obituary. Almost all of Edwina's friends had predeceased her.

Edwina had already passed away when American Airlines Flight #66 was threatened with a hijacking. Ridley Wilton had selected Edwina's name and biography to stand in and cover for the real hero, Mercedes Carrington. Ridley was now going to propose to Mercedes that Edwina Carroll be given full credit for saving Flight #66. Edwina Carroll would die quietly in her sleep, again, this time as a national hero. The FBI would announce her death to the world and praise the woman for her courage and quick thinking on board the airplane she had saved. Ridley would have his actress sit for photographs. The actress would be well-disguised, and photos would be given out to the press to accompany the story of Edwina Carroll's demise.

The hero of Flight #66 would no longer be a mystery. Her story would be told. Her photograph would be on all the television news stations. She would receive a hero's funeral and a hero's burial. Hardly anyone would know that the coffin that was lowered into the ground with great fanfare was empty.

If Edwina Carroll was given credit for taking down the hijacker and if the public and the press and the secret mastermind behind it all believed the story, Mercedes Carrington could come out of hiding. Only her family and a few people in law enforcement would know the truth. Mercedes could return to her former life, but she would never be able to receive the recognition and praise she deserved for being the actual hero of Flight #66. She would remain herself, safe and sound. Ridley was taking a chance that Mercedes Carrington would welcome this resolution of her situation with open arms.

Ridley explained to Mercedes his views about the very big fish he believed had planned the hijackings, and he gave her his opinion about the likely motivation behind the operation. He never mentioned any names but discussed in great detail and with great regret why no one would ever be called to account for orchestrating these crimes. Only the little fish would pay the price.

Ridley and Mercedes discussed all the ramifications of giving someone else credit for Mercedes' heroic act. She could never talk about what she had done. She would take the secret to her grave. What her family decided to do about the truth after Mercedes died would be up to them. Mercedes agreed immediately to Ridley's proposed plan. She thought it was brilliant and didn't give a hoot whether or not she ever received any recognition for her part in foiling the Iranian hijacker.

Ridley Wilton told Mercedes he had decided he was going to retire from the FBI when her case had been resolved. He told her he intended to move to Nova Scotia and live in Baird

House. He explained that he owned the house. He'd had it renovated for his mother who was Canadian. She had been disabled, and that was why the house had been handicap friendly and ideal for Mercedes. Sadly, Ridley's mother had died before the renovations were completed. She had never had the chance to live there, and Ridley had used it as a safe house for FBI witnesses. Ridley loved to fish, and he stayed at Baird House when he went on fishing vacations in and around Terence Bay. He'd enjoyed knowing that Mercedes had been happy at Baird House, and he wanted her to know that someone would continue to love it and live there.

With Mercedes' blessing, Ridley and Arabella proceeded to resurrect the illusive Edwina Carrol and then allowed her to die a hero's death. Ridley wanted to see if the Edwina Carroll story would pass muster with the press and public and with the powers that be in the FBI. He asked Mercedes to allow some more time to elapse before she came out of hiding completely. If the world bought the Edwina Carroll narrative, it would finally be safe for Mercedes Carrington and Mac to go to the lobster pounds in Southwest Harbor, Maine. Mercedes could begin her quest for the perfect lobster roll.

Ridley wanted to speak personally with Mercedes' children and grandchildren and explain why Edwina Carrol was to be given credit for Mercedes' act of bravery. He would impress on the family why it was necessary to perpetuate the deception. He would answer their inevitable questions. He wished he'd been able to bring to justice the entire array of bad guys who had been involved in the conspiracy, but that was not possible. This was the best he was going to be able to do. He was looking forward to his retirement.

Ridley Wilton was old school. For most of his life, he had played strictly by the rules. He'd had a successful career in the military, and he had advanced in his career with the

FBI. He had brought many criminals to justice. He believed that a person who committed a crime should be punished for that crime. But the country he loved so dearly had been changing around him over the years.

The institution he had spent his life working for and had championed and been proud of had also changed. It had grown and become large and unwieldy. He had begun to feel he no longer had a place in the organization for which he had given his all. Because it had become so politicized, he no longer felt he belonged at the FBI. There were so many leaks from headquarters, he no longer trusted that anything would remain confidential. He was philosophical about it and decided that every generation of agents probably felt this way as they aged out of the mainstream.

It was time to leave. In recent years, because of the changes at the FBI, Ridley had stepped outside the strict standards he had set for himself. He told himself that he had done these things to compensate for the cracks he saw at the head office in Washington, D.C. He was desolate when he realized he could not continue to do his job any more. It was past time for him to retire. The old rules no longer applied. Some people indeed were above the law. Ridley could not live with that.

When he had been a brand new special agent, he'd worked on a case that had never been completely resolved. Everyone who had worked that case knew exactly who had hired the killers who had actually committed the crimes. Ridley's superior explained to the very unhappy and very frustrated young idealistic newbie that because of the "important man's connections," he was essentially untouchable. The man behind the curtain was so rich, so well-connected with the powerful in Washington, D.C., and so influential with the intelligence community and with law enforcement agencies, he could not be charged.

At the time, Ridley did not understand this. His boss explained that because of their wealth and connections, the very rich and very powerful can insulate themselves from the ugly things they want done. They hire people to do the things they don't want to do for themselves. They hire people to clean their houses and take care of their yards and swimming pools. They hire people to drive them around in their limousines. The very rich can also hire people to kill those who get in their way. The very rich are able to pay for the many layers that insulate them from any connection with their crimes. The shooters go to prison or to the gas chamber, but these hapless thugs may have no idea who had ultimately wanted the crime committed or who had paid to have it taken care of.

Billionaires had been few and far between thirty years ago. Now, it seemed to Ridley, they were everywhere. Athletes, pop stars, and especially high tech adolescents were billionaires, and they were always in your face and always on the news. And they had power, lots of power. Some were good guys and gave back to their communities with grace. Others used their positions, power, and riches to further their own personal agendas. This is their right in a free society.

Even some of those who had been the greatest philanthropists and had seemed to take the high road for most of their lives were later revealed to have actually taken a very low, even a disgusting road. A few of the richest were known child molesters, even rapists. Some of the richest were known to pay for the assassinations of those they didn't like. Many knew that some of these ultra-rich would never have to take responsibility in any way for the grandiose plots they had paid to have executed.

Ridley's values were old fashioned. He did not believe it was right for anyone who had committed a crime to get away with it, no matter how much wealth or how much power they had. He did not believe the darlings of the press and public should be immune from punishment for their wrongdoing. In Ridley's eyes, even those who had held the highest office in the land and their families and their foundations should be made to take responsibility for their actions. These beliefs made Ridley completely out of step with the current leadership at the FBI and with law enforcement's general trends in bringing criminals to justice. If you had enough power or enough money, you would probably never have to answer for your crimes, no matter how egregious those crimes might be. If you donated enough money to the correct humanitarian and political causes, you became untouchable.

Ridley could no longer stomach allowing the rich and famous to escape prosecution. He had a good pension coming. He had done his job well and with integrity. He had been successful. He grieved for what had happened to the institutions he had worked so hard to uphold. He realized the world had changed, and he was an old man. It was impossible for him to accept that the old school rules were no longer in effect. He wondered if his grandfather had felt this way about the world when he got old.

The discovery of the Gilbert Jones riches had impacted Ridley. Viewing the vast wealth on display in two storage units had shaken him with the realization that due process could never compete with the kind of money that was running and ruining his country today. Seeing numbers on a balance sheet or in a report conveyed information about wealth. Being a billionaire was nothing to be sneezed at. It sounded impressive, and it was impressive. But seeing for himself what hundreds of millions of dollars looked like in real goods had shocked and sobered Agent Ridley Wilton. He knew that the rule of law would continue to lose out to big money. There would be more and more untouchables.

Chapter 39

Mercedes and Mac finally had their evening at the lobster pound in Southwest Harbor. Mac got in line and ordered for the two of them. Mercedes found a chair at the end of a picnic table that she could manage to get into and out of. They would feast on clams, corn, potatoes, lobsters, and melted butter. They were going all out today. It was a celebration. Mac was Mercedes' employee, but they had become friends in the months they'd spent together. Mac was of a younger generation, but they shared many interests and looked at the world in much the same way. Mac was old school, too. She eschewed vegan cheese.

Mercedes was jubilant that she was able to have dinner in a restaurant after all this time. She loved Flower Island and was happy spending most of her time there. It was the perfect spot for writing, and writers are often reclusive by nature. But knowing she could go anywhere she wanted to go for lunch and could order a lobster roll, was a kind of freedom she had taken for granted most of her life. She would never take it for granted again.

Mercedes and Mac had each ordered two lobsters. Lots of people who came to the lobster pound ordered two lobsters. They were enjoying every bite. "You know, I was half-way expecting we might find Gilbert Jones's body in one of those storage units. I have to admit I was a little bit disappointed that he wasn't there." Mercedes was confessing what she had imagined and perhaps what she had hoped. "I will always wonder what happened to the man. His treasure has been found and returned to its rightful owners...I think. But he is still a mystery, and what happened to him will probably never be known."

"Considering what we found in Bangor, don't you think he was killed because of the treasure? He might have been done away with by someone who had helped him steal it and transport it to the United States. Maybe his helpers didn't think he had paid them enough. People had to know about this treasure. It would not have been a small thing for him to pack it all up and get it into a shipping container to move it across the Atlantic Ocean. Other people had to know."

"If he was a member of the Russian Mafia, which I have always suspected he was, they might have killed him for any number of reasons. The person who killed him might not have known anything at all about the treasure. I can write a book about it and make up any kind of ending. I can make him anybody I want him to be, and I can kill him off any way I choose. I will probably do that, but I would really love to know what happened to him in real life. That will always bug me." Mercedes would not lose sleep over the fate of Gilbert Jones, but she would think about it from time to time.

"I would like to know what his real name is. We know it isn't Gilbert Jones. It is probably Ivan Ivanovich or something like that. You know who would have loved to get their hands on the Estonian artifacts...the current ruler in Russia. He's already the richest man in the world, but he would love to be able to steal something from the Baltic States. He really wants to steal the Baltic States themselves. He believes they belong to Russia. What a ridiculous man he is." Mac did not like or approve of the current Russian ruler.

"If he had murdered Gilbert Jones, or Ivan Ivanovich, don't you think he would have done it with poison, in his tea or in his food? Polonium is one of his weapons of choice. How do you think he would have completely done away with the body? Chipper shredder?" Both women cringed at the thought.

They took their time driving back to Flower Island. The sun was going down, and they decided to sit and watch the water from the ocean-side porch of Mercedes' cottage. Donny Germaine had installed six long built-in wooden planters around the edges of this part of the porch. The planters were lined with tin and had holes for drainage. They had been beautifully crafted of weathered wood and were perfectly positioned for geraniums. Earlier that summer, Sam Stevenson had arranged for a landscaping company to fill the porch planters with a profusion of bright red geraniums. He wanted a splash of color to greet Mercedes when she came to her new Flower Island home in early September. The red blossoms were the perfect addition to the view Mercedes had of the sea. At the end of September, the geraniums were still going strong. They filled the planters to overflowing. Mac liked to garden, and she had weeded and watered the geraniums and kept them deadheaded.

"I love these planters that Donny built. He must have built them years ago for Gilbert Jones. The wood has weathered to such a beautiful shade of gray. I had him build several to put around my own porch. I've been keeping my eye on your geraniums and making sure they had water. It rains enough here, but sometimes we have a run of dry days without any rain. I've always wondered why Donny made this one planter so much shallower than the others. When I dig in this one, I am always running into the metal liner. You can see that the geraniums in this shallow one don't do as well as those in the deeper planters."

Mercedes heard what Mac was saying about the planters. Because of her pollen allergies, she had never been much of a gardener. Anomalies, however, piqued her interest. "Donny is coming tomorrow to put up some additional railings around the pool and in the hallway at the back of the house. I love the secret door that goes from the solarium into the rear of the center hall, but I am afraid I will fall going that way when my feet are wet. When he's here, I will question him about the shallow planter. I'll ask him if he can make it deeper like the others. It won't do this year's geraniums any good, but it will make next year's better."

Mac left to go back to her own house. Mercedes kept looking at the planter that wasn't like the rest of them. Her curiosity got the better of her. With a great deal of difficulty, she lifted the two metal liners out of the shallow planter. Each of the metal liners was about three feet long, so they were not easy for Mercedes' arthritic fingers to lift and manipulate. The geraniums were planted in the metal liners, and she set both of them aside. She found an enclosed wooden box underneath where the metal liners had been. The box looked as if it had been tightly constructed. It looked like it was pretty permanent. It was not going to be an easy thing to have Donny make the planter deeper, and he would probably argue against rebuilding it. Mercedes would insist that he redo it. They would have healthy red geraniums in all six of the planters next summer. Mercedes was suddenly tired. Before she could go to bed, she needed a shower to wash off the lobster, the butter, and the dirt from messing with the planters.

The next morning, Mac came to make Mercedes' breakfast as she always did. She noticed through the bedroom window that Mercedes had lifted the geraniums out of the shallow planter. She laughed to herself and wondered when *The Mystery of the Wilting Geraniums* would be written.

Sure enough, as soon as she was dressed, Mercedes was back out on the porch, inspecting the box she'd found under the planter's metal liners. She had a hammer and began to hack away at the box. Mac came to her rescue with a crow bar. It was the better tool for taking apart the box. Mac could have lived with the shallow planter, but Mercedes was determined to rectify this botanical aberration. The box had been sealed up tight, tighter than planter construction on a porch would require. Now Mac's curiosity was aroused.

Just then Donny Germaine appeared on the porch. The two women had been so intent on their deconstruction project they had not heard his truck pull into the driveway. Donny looked as if he had seen a ghost, as he stood there and watched the women tear apart the box he had so carefully built and sealed up years ago.

"Why did you have to go and start tearing things up?" Donny was resigned, but he also looked frightened.

Mac was watching Donny's face. Mercedes answered. "This one planter was shallower than the others. The geranium roots couldn't go as deep in this planter, and these plants didn't thrive like the others did."

Mac was still watching Donny's face. Mercedes pulled away the piece of salt-treated wood that was the top of the box structure that had been built at the bottom of the planter. Mercedes screamed. Mac looked down. Sure enough, there was Gilbert Jones, inside a plastic bag and laid out in the coffin-like planter box. At least Mac and Mercedes thought it was Gilbert Jones inside the plastic bag. Years of being outside and taking a beating from the elements, as well as the inevitable decomposition, had made him unrecognizable. Mac looked at Donny. He had turned around and was heading for his truck and who knows where from there.

"Wait, Donny. Come back. I am going to call 911, and the police will be coming here. We know you did this, and we want to know why. We know you, and we like you. You are a good person. We want to know what happened. There must have been a reason for you to have done this. We want to hear your side of the story." Mac was pleading with Donny to defend himself.

Donny germaine stopped escaping towards his truck and came back to the porch. He hung his head. They could barely hear what he was saying and had to ask him to speak up. "Gilbert Jones was always a little nutty. When it came to carpentry work, he was more than just a little nutty. I hated working for him, but he paid me so much money, I couldn't turn him down. I could earn more working for Jones than I could working for anybody else. He paid me three times my hourly rate. I was his. Even when he berated my work and made me tear out shelves and moldings and trim that I knew were perfect, I kept on working for him. He was a mental case. He was just bloomin' nuts!" Donny was giving them his story, just as he would later tell it to the local sheriff. Mac and Mercedes were captivated.

"One day he came at me with a hammer. I'd done some work that didn't suit him, and he attacked me. He pounded me over and over again with the hammer. He'd never attacked me physically before, and I decided I wasn't going to let him kill me." Donny Germaine pulled up his shirt and showed them the scars from the wounds he said had been inflicted by Gilbert Jones pounding him with a hammer. "We were in the hallway. I had my table saw set up there. He was so enraged, I was sure he was going to kill me. If he'd gone after my head with the hammer, I would not be here now. He was a mad man. He had completely lost his marbles. I fought back. I pushed him away from me, and he fell back against the table saw. He struck his head when he went down. His eyes rolled back, and I knew he was dead. I didn't know what to do. I panicked." Donny Germaine put his head down in his hands. He was remembering and reliving the horrible scene that had taken Gilbert Jones's life.

"I had all these wounds on my chest, and I knew I couldn't go to the hospital to have them taken care of. I was sure I had several broken ribs. I decided to get rid of the body. No one could ever know. I built the planters. Each of them is six feet long, long enough to hold a body. One is shallower than the others. That's because I built Gilbert Jones's coffin underneath the metal liners for the flowers in that one. It was a hasty decision to put him on the porch and build the planters. I should have buried him in a better place. I didn't know the geraniums wouldn't grow as well in a shallow planter. I wasn't thinking about that. I just had to hide him."

Donny continued. "I am glad this is over now. It was an accident, but I didn't think anybody would believe me. He was so rich. The rich can do no wrong. He would never be prosecuted for attacking me. I had to fight back. I knew I couldn't afford a fancy lawyer to get me off, even for self-defense."

The sheriff arrived as Donny was telling his story to Mac and Mercedes. The sheriff took Donny away in handcuffs. It was a small community. The sheriff was devastated. He had known Donny Germaine all of his life. He was astonished and saddened to have to take him into custody. When the sheriff arrived, he insisted that Mac and Mercedes go back inside the house. This was a crime scene. He told them he was doing them a favor by not making them leave the property altogether.

Mac and Mercedes went back inside the house as they'd been told to do, but they wanted to watch what was happening on the porch. They were able to see most of what went on by looking out the window of Mercedes' writing room. The crime scene people from Bangor arrived to photograph the planters and the porch and the body. They took apart the planter box. The attendants from the Medical Examiner's office carried the remains on a gurney to the waiting morgue van. It was hours before they had completed their measurements and their sampling and all the rest of it.

Both women were in shock. Although she had written about murders and dead bodies for decades, Mercedes had actually seen very few in real life. Although Mac had worked for the FBI much of her life, she likewise had seen few dead bodies, especially ones that had been decomposing for years in a plastic bag. The women were told not to discuss with each other anything about what they had discovered in the planter box until after their official statements had been taken.

They were interviewed separately. It was way past lunch time. Once Mac had given her statement, she made sandwiches and lemonade for the crime scene people, the sheriff, Mercedes, and herself. Mac and Mercedes sat in front of the study window as they ate. They didn't want to miss a thing.

"I believe Donny's story. Donny's not a murderer. I don't think he would hurt anyone unless he thought his life was threatened." Mercedes trusted that Donny had told the truth.

"I believe him, too, but the fact that he covered it up and hid the body works against him. If he'd been honest from the beginning and called the sheriff, he would have had a much better case. I totally understand why he didn't call law enforcement, but he lied to everybody when he was questioned. He had to have been the one who drove Gilbert Jones's car back to Bar Harbor and parked it in the garage of his rental house. Donny went to great lengths to cover up what he had done. It's not the crime that gets you. It's the cover-up. I'm going to talk to Ridley about this, but I don't think we need to say a word to the sheriff about what we found in Bangor. That will just confuse and complicate things. Ridley has already dealt with all of that. I think we should leave it alone."

"I agree completely. No one needs to know about any of it. None of that has anything to do with Donny's situation. He never knew the treasure existed. Bringing in the storage units will only be a distraction. Let's not mention anything about it." When Mac told Ridley what was going on with Donny and Gilbert Jones's body, Ridley approved of their decision not to mention the storage units. They were all in agreement. Their lips were sealed.

When the corpse of Gilbert Jones was tested for his DNA, it turned out he was mostly Slavic, Russian with a few percentage points of Viking in the mix. No one was surprised with this result. Could Gilbert Jones had been at least partly Estonian? The missing set of car keys for the Range Rover was found in the pocket of Gilbert Jones' disintegrating trousers. Mercedes would now have two sets of keys. In addition to the keys for the car, there were two extra keys on the newly-discovered key ring. These were the extra keys that went to the locks that had kept the now-dead man's secret treasures safe. That treasure had been returned to its rightful owners. The locks from the storage units had been thrown away. The keys on the key ring would no longer open anything at all.

Chapter 40

Ridley Wilton had gone outside his jurisdiction in quite a number of ways when he had dealt with Joshua Dawson, the journalist. Wilton was leaving the FBI in three weeks, and he wanted the situation with the journalist to be resolved before he left. Joshua was still being cared for at a medical facility known to very few. He had been treated as a prisoner and had not been allowed to watch the news or even know where he was being held. He was incommunicado. Ridley Wilton did not know what to do about the young man who had stalked him and then had fallen and been so badly injured. He had pushed Dawson's situation to the back of his mind, but he could no longer ignore the problem.

Ridley flew to Burlington, Vermont. Joshua Dawson was using a walker and was making an effort with his physical therapy. He was going to have one more surgery in a few weeks, but for the most part, medical science had done all it could to fix Dawson after his foolish pursuit of Agnes

MacGillicutty. Ridley hoped that after their encounter today, he would be able to decide Dawson's fate.

Dawson had been moved to a prison cell at the Burlington facility. Ridley Wilton brought a chair into the cell and sat down. Dawson was asleep on his cot, and he was startled to find Ridley Wilton sitting beside him when he woke up.

"I've come here today to have a serious talk with you." Ridley had been planning this speech for a long time. He wanted to reach this young man who had broken the law but was not a terrorist. "I know you are not a hardened criminal. But you have repeatedly broken the law with bugging the phones and putting tracking devices on my car and on my keys. Tracking and stalking an FBI agent is a serious criminal offense. I could throw the book at you and keep you in prison for years."

"I was just doing my job. The laws I broke were not that important. You have kept me here without due process. I know my rights."

"I know your rights, too. As I have said, I could put you in prison, without the usual due process, for years. I don't want to do that. But you are going to have to change your attitude. You are going to have to lose your arrogance and realize that you were in the wrong. Journalists get away with too much. They break the law with impunity. They disrupt people's lives and cause a great deal of pain with their intrusive ways. You broke into my house using your lock picks. That's breaking and entering. You are going to have to come to terms with the things you have done and acknowledge that they are wrong. If you are not able to do that, you will go to prison, and you will end up being a career criminal. You are right on the edge now. You can go either way. The choice is up to you. I can leave you here. I can transfer you to a high-security facility for terrorists. Or, I can transfer you to a minimum-security half-way house situation where in time you will be able to re-enter society and live a normal life. The choice is up to you. You have threatened to sue me. If you try to do that, you will be staying in prison for a long, long time. You have to grow up and learn to take responsibility for your actions. Behavior has consequences. Your generation doesn't seem to believe that, but it is the truth."

Ridley Wilton looked at Joshua Dawson for a long time. In spite of being disabled by his fall, and in spite of the weeks he had spent in a prison-like facility, he was still the arrogant young man he had been when he'd confronted Ridley at Baird House. Ridley didn't think this guy could change his attitude, and he was ready to cross him off as a lost cause. Just as Ridley was leaving the cell, Joshua Dawson called him back.

"What do I have to do to redeem myself in your eyes? I don't want to spend the rest of my life in a terrorist prison. I don't think my crimes deserve that. I am smart enough to realize I broke the law. I just don't think my crimes are that serious. If I promise not to sue you, will you let me out?"

Ridley Wilton didn't know if redemption was a possibility in this case. He did not know if Joshua Dawson could be rehabilitated. It was a fifty/fifty toss up in his mind. He'd wanted this settled before he left the FBI. Ridley fully realized he may have overreacted because this law breaker had stalked him, and Ridley had not known it was happening. He had bugged the phones that Ridley used. He had put a tracking device on Ridley's car keys and on his car. He had followed Ridley relentlessly for months. He had broken into Ridley's house. Ridley took the crimes personally. He felt violated. He couldn't help it.

"If you get out of prison, will you get a job? Will you go back to journalism? Will you go back to your job at the airport? Will you go back to your job at the Capital Hotel?

What will you do? What about your family? What do you think they believe has happened to you? Do you care about how much distress you may have caused them? You need to think about all of these things before you are ready to go anywhere."

Ridley left Joshua Dawson's prison cell, still undecided about the young man's ultimate fate. He hated to turn Dawson's case over to Arabella, but maybe that was the best thing to do. She might have a more objective view of things and might be able to make a fairer determination of Dawson's ultimate punishment.

Agent Arabella Barnes had been promoted and was now the head agent at the FBI's Little Rock office. Ridley Wilton had leaned on everybody to make this happen. He knew she was the smartest agent he had, and she knew the Little Rock office inside and out. He knew she was the best person for the job, and he had been determined that she would get it. The big wigs in D.C. had favors to grant and wanted to give the position to one of their cronies. It was all politics all the time in D.C. But in the end, Ridley had enough clout, and he had prevailed. Arabella was now the top agent in Arkansas.

DONNY GERMAINE WAS NOT INFECTED with the hubris that had taken over Joshua Dawson's personality. Donny Germane had killed a man. It had not been intentional, but Donny admitted he had pushed Gilbert Jones during the fight which had caused the man to fall into the table saw and hit his head. Donny was sorry. Mercedes hired a smart criminal lawyer for him, and the lawyer had worked hard to arrive at a plea bargain in Donny's case. Donny presented the scars on his body as evidence that he had been attacked and beaten by

Gilbert Jones. The court had believed his story and believed he was sorry about what had happened.

The cover-up was the sticking point. Donny pled guilty to involuntary manslaughter and would be on probation for two years. He would be required to do a significant number of hours of community service work. Donny tore out the offending planter that had once served as a coffin. He rebuilt an entirely new planter on Mercedes' porch. There was no longer any need to hide a body, so all the planters were now deep ones. Geraniums would bloom in profusion the following summer in all six identical planter boxes.

Mercedes received a package in the mail from Arabella Barnes. It was a box of carefully packed exquisite blue and white plates. Mercedes knew these plates had come from the Estonian collection. Arabella had enclosed a note.

Dear Mercedes,

You could have kept the entire treasure for yourself. No one would ever have known. I know you love blue and white. None of the rest of the treasure will ever grace the shelves at Flower Island Cottage, but I wanted you to have these plates. They are not so costly that you or I need to feel guilty about not turning them over with the rest of the artifacts. Enjoy the plates and think of me when you see them on your shelves.

Best regards,

Arabella Barnes

In november, mercedes and mac would drive to Arizona in a rented motorhome. Mac would drive. The two women would have fun. They would enjoy their travels and see the sights. Mac would help Mercedes move in and get settled at her new Camelback Creek condominium in Scottsdale. Mercedes couldn't wait to see her friend Rose Lutzy again. Mac would fly to California to spend some time with family. She would return to Scottsdale in time to drive Mercedes back to the East Coast for the summer.

Mercedes was working on another mystery novel. The plot of the new book centered around a Russian treasure found in a rented self-storage unit and a body found hidden in a planter on the porch of a cottage in Maine. Hmm. Sometimes truth is stranger than fiction.

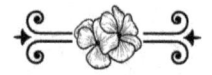

Epilogue

Ridley spent the Thanksgiving holidays with his Aunt Dorothy on Long Beach Island. Andy Jamison joined them several times for drinks and dinner. He'd been especially jolly at the big Thanksgiving feast. Ridley was celebrating his retirement from a life-long career at the FBI. He was ready to do some fishing and maybe start a part-time business. Andy asked Ridley to sign over the title of the van Arabella had used to transport the treasures. Andy's eyes had twinkled when he'd asked for Ridley's signature. When Ridley said his goodbyes to his aunt and to Andy at the end of the week, Andy had said to him "Be sure to keep an eye out for your snail mail." It was a curious remark, especially coming from someone who was all about the internet. Snail mail was so old school.

Sure enough, a few days before Christmas, an envelope without a return address arrived at Baird House. Ridley knew it was from Andy. Inside was a bank statement and all the paperwork for a new bank account that had been opened in Ridley's name. The balance in the bank account showed $200,000 dollars. There had to be some mistake. There was an additional piece of paper in the envelope. On it was an itemized list of everything Ridley had spent to deal with the Gilbert Jones treasure. Ridley had, of course, never billed the FBI for any of these expenses. But how in the world had Andy been able to find every single thing Ridley had paid for out of his own pocket? It just wasn't possible, even for an internet whiz kid. But here it was in all of its glory. Here was the list of everything Ridley had paid for—the rental truck, the packing boxes and packing tape, the used van he'd bought for Arabella, the cost of the rental house in Bangor, everything. He'd used a false name and credit card to rent that crummy rancher outside Bangor. Nobody knew about that name and that credit card. All of the reimbursements added together didn't come close to equaling the $200,000 that had been deposited in his new bank account.

Then he saw the note. The Estonian People's Fund had gifted him a finder's fee for discovering and returning certain long-lost artifacts to the people of Estonia. Ridley didn't want this money. He could accept the reimbursement, but he did not think he deserved any finder's fee for what he had done. He had to admit that it was tempting to have the money. He could use it to pay for the renovations he wanted to do on the second floor of Baird House. He was curious about whether Arabella or Mac or Mercedes had also received any part of the finder's fees.

Ridley made some phone calls and found that everyone who had participated in the Estonian Treasure Caper, as he had come to think of it in his own mind, had been reimbursed for the money they had put into the project. Even the one-hundred fifty dollars Mercedes had paid to rent the unit at Downeast, the unit she had never used, had been reimbursed. Everyone had also been gifted money as part of the finder's fees, and each had a new and hefty bank account. All were stumped by how anyone had been able to find even the smallest amount they had spent. They had even been reimbursed for their gas mileage, driving to and from Flower Island to Downeast Easy Self-Storage in Bangor, Maine.

Ridley knew his Latvian friend had been behind the reimbursements and the payments of the finder's fees. He would have to think about how he was going to deal with the finder's fee money. Should he return it? If he decided to return it, to whom would he send a check?

The next day, Ridley received a Christmas card from Andy Jamison. Andy had written a note on the back of the card. He told Ridley that he and Aunt Dorothy were planning a cruise of the Baltic Sea in the spring. The cruise would visit Lithuania, Latvia, and Estonia, among other places. Ridley was invited, along with Andy and Dorothy, to attend the grand opening of a new wing of the art museum in Tallinn. The wing was being added to the museum to house an exciting new exhibit of artifacts from pre-World War II Estonia. The collection had originally come from a church which had been destroyed by fire during the first Soviet occupation in 1940. The recently discovered large and valuable treasure had been donated to the museum by the Estonian People's Fund. The grand opening of the new wing would be in May. Andy added in his note that they would also be visiting his own family home outside of Riga.

Ridley looked again inside the envelope in which Andy's Christmas card had been sent. He found a printout of an electronic reservation for a luxury suite on a first-class cruise line for a Baltic cruise the following spring. Ridley laughed. He would call Mac and Arabella. He thought the two of them and Mercedes, if she thought she could do it, would also like to take part in the cruise and the grand opening at the museum in Tallinn. Sometimes things worked out for the best, even when you were an old school guy in a world that had passed you by.

LATER THAT WINTER, RIDLEY RECEIVED an anonymous newspaper clipping in the mail about a death that had taken place in Latvia. The article had been published in a British newspaper. A reclusive billionaire, who held U.S. citizenship and resided in the United States, had been found dead in his hotel suite in Riga. The man was a well-known philanthropist. He had given a great deal of money to a wide range of political causes. He'd had a history of heart disease, but his death was suspicious. The night of his death, the eighty-five-year-old billionaire had attended a dinner to honor the children and grandchildren of World War II Latvian resistance leaders. Ridley read the article over and over again. He had never mentioned the man's name aloud to anyone. Ridley alone knew the name. How in the world could anyone else have known?

Acknowledgments

Heartfelt thanks to my readers and editors. I couldn't have done this without you. Thank you to Jamie at Open Heart Designs who developed this beautiful cover and who does everything else to turn my manuscript into a book. Thank you to my photographer Andrea Burns who always makes me look good. Thank you to all the friends and fans who have encouraged me to continue writing.

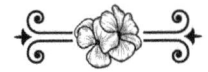

About the Author

CAROLINA DANFORD WRIGHT *is a grandmother. She uses a blue and white cane. She has lived in many places and traveled far and wide. Carolina has had several fulfilling careers and began writing mysteries when she was seventy. She believes that behavior has consequences and that it is critical to fight for truth and justice. The women of the Granny Avengers series echo Carolina's crusade to help right the wrongs of the world.*

Coming Soon

MARFA LIGHTS OUT